THE IRON SERVICE

THE CAPITAL ADVENTURES
BOOK 7

ALLEN IVERS

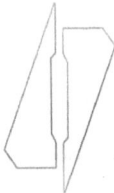

Illustration © Tom Edwards
TomEdwardsDesign.com

For my wife, Lyn
For my friend and armorer, Evan

And this one goes out to my sister, Jessica, and all of the other sisters out there.

MAP & CHRONOLOGY

The Solar Imperium, also called the Gnostic Empire by the more faithful citizenry, stretches over a fifth of the Milky Way Galaxy. This map features the primary locations featured in the series thus far.

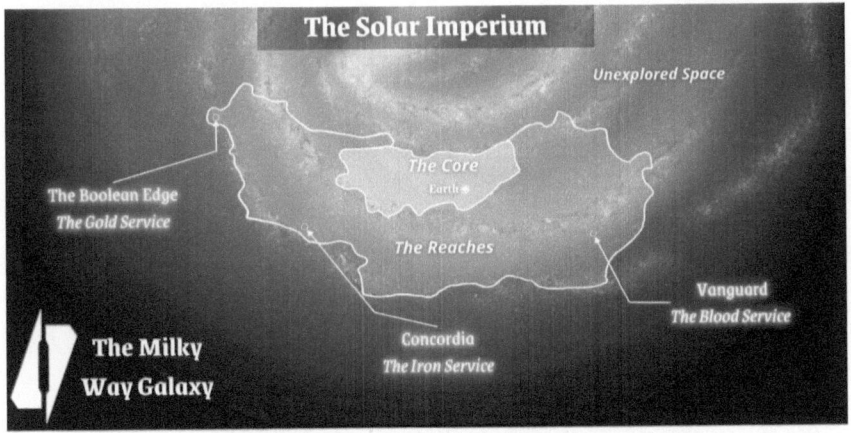

| Map of Solar Imperium controlled space, 2241 CE

The events of the Capital Adventures occur entirely within these borders. Events from one book may be mentioned in another, or characters may cross over from one trilogy to another. Think of it as a shared universe, with the individual stories having unique tones and flair, while building an overarching plot.

You may enjoy each trilogy independent of the others—and I've meticulously built them so that your enjoyment is not contingent on having read the others! But if you want the full experience of the Capital Adventures, I do encourage you to pick up the other books to get a full sense of the Imperium's reach. The official reading order would be to read the trilogies starting with The Blood Service, then The Gold Service, and finishing out with the upcoming Iron Service.

If you're like me, however, and you were looking to read the novels in chronological order, the events of all nine books are as follows:

1) The Gold Service
2) The Blood Service
3) The Iron Service

4) Ranks of the Blood Service
5) Cost of the Gold Service
6) Swords of the Iron Service (Coming soon)

7) Command of the Blood Service
8) Shards of the Iron Service (Coming soon)
9) Powers of the Gold Service

With even More to Come...

FOREWORD

This is the first book in *The Iron Service* trilogy.

This book contains the following content matter:

- *Graphic Violence & Traumatic Injuries*
  - *Gunshot wounds, stabbings and impalement, bone breaking and neck snapping*
  - *The human body at high speed behaves a lot like water.*
  - *Bodies in various states of chemically-assisted decomposition*
- *Frequent Foul Language*
  - *Though not as excessive as I have been in the past*
- *Aquaphobia Warning*
  - *Mild Sequence of Torture & Interrogation*
- *Acrophobia Warning - Fear of Heights*
  - *They're not called Orbital Strike Command for the acronym.*

We're here to have a good time with characters we love. If any of this material distresses you, it's okay to grab another book instead.

Hope you enjoy!

CONTENTS

"Youth is easily deceived—
  because it is quick to hope."

ARISTOTLE

PART ONE
PROTOCOL

CHAPTER
ONE

SOMEWHERE IN THE BOOLEAN EDGE...

———

CONFLICT ZONES always sounded like a euphemism to her. It was a comfortable way to phrase something that was profoundly uncomfortable. Like how every base and every ship she was ever stationed on was 'in theater' or how every time she tripped over her tongue, she was guilty of 'conduct unbecoming.'

Lieutenant Adrianna Riley nestled herself behind a flashing neon sign—

Sorry, she 'utilized environmental factors to provide adequate concealment from opposing forces.' That was what would go down in her report for some brown-nosing major half a galaxy away. Then he would offer up some armchair advice on how she could've improved her performance.

So long as everyone got home and the target got shacked, Adrianna had no complaints. Efficiency markers, percentile analysis—that was the sole domain of board rooms and white gloved hands. Her unit was routing out pirates from small mining towns built into the side of asteroids, not chalking points on an obstacle course.

The way she saw it, success in the real world was of the pass-fail variety.

The Boolean Pulsar winked overhead, searing the night sky of this industrial rock with ghostly grays and ashen whites. The cold star served its part-time duty, reminding them all how small they really were in the scheme of things. That star had burned since before human writing, lighting this system with overwhelming tidal waves of cosmic radiation. And it would continue to do so long after she and her team were all buried.

This rock was only one of hundreds in the Boolean Edge, a quadrant of space once a safe haven for more than a dozen disparate pirate clans. Each and every one had grabbed the proverbial torch and pitchfork to stand against their Consul, their Empire, Earth, and all the other stuff that made life bearable. They much preferred their little corner full of abusive labor practices, human trafficking, and pharma that came with a warning label.

Now the Empire might have once been content to let them have their whimsical rabbit hole, but the pirates had pursued an Imperial Fleet carrier and every soul aboard into that pulsating monster that trailed over her head. And because of that, Adrianna was now squatting in her glowing pillbox, elbows in an oil slick and hair matted to her forehead.

If the pirates and scum out in this end of the 'verse had the wherewithal to let that lost ship just be 'missing' instead of 'willfully destroyed by our superior firepower', Adrianna might be somewhere that actually mattered. But no! Some great pooh-bah of the criminal underworld had to pick 'civil war' out of the box options. So here she was, lying in a pool of filth.

Making a difference, she told herself.

It had been a fair fight—the way a bear has a fair fight with a rabbit. Like a sculptor trims clay, the Navy had culled the rebellious down to the bone in a short three months.

And today, with a bit more patience, Adrianna's unit was about to excise another.

Two hundred plus asteroids orbited the pulsar, and more than half had small mining towns bolted to them. Gravity generators, environment domes to contain an atmosphere, and a few other key imports made frontier living not all that bad. There was even a rural charm to it, living rough. Made a person get their hands dirty.

Most everything in this small shanty town was handmade or recycled from something else, including the neon sign Adrianna was perched under. She'd picked the sign with purpose and malicious intent. Some might say the glowing pink actually drew attention, but it was also hard to look directly at it. And the intermittent flash would cover any minor movements she made, like how thunder hid gunshots. Three other signs nearby advertised Kevalky whiskey and other hallucinogenic retail compounds. Exposed rebar stuck in the air near her from some unfinished—or future planned—construction.

All together it was a right mess of visual noise. If they spotted her up here, they deserved a gold medal.

It was maybe twenty feet down from her little hidey hole to the dry cracked pavement where an intersection of some footpaths met with an auto crossway. All of it was tucked behind residential buildings, so the team would have to take care with shot placement. Civil war or not, there were innocent people out here whose only political affiliation was tomorrow's meal. Callum and Yurek might not have seen it that way—they expected patriots to stand up to injustice—but if the locals weren't shooting at her, Adrianna didn't see the need for an uneven trade.

After ten years of pirate rule and three months of open conflict, there were bullet holes in every wall. Scorch marks scattered about like violent graffiti and the pathways transformed by shaped charges. If the neighbors were going to resist, they'd have done it by now. These people just wanted the shooting to stop long enough to get their breakfast.

Adrianna had tried to stick her hand through one of the bullet holes once—ended up pushing her fist through the weakened drywall right into somebody's living room. It was all very awkward.

"Callum, you in position?" Adrianna asked.

"Almost, sister," said the gruff behemoth. "Finally found a suitable spot."

Adrianna squinted, letting her augmented display kick in over her eyes. No bright color or bulky equipment needed. Just a flicker of yellow light across her iris, like a cat's eye in the dark. She could see every corner of the plaza, measure out the dimensions, gauge the various materials for likelihood of over-penetration. Instant tactical assessment.

And she could pick out the three other sets of identity tags strewn around the space.

Her CO, Captain Graccus Ontarim, was proper close to the action. Ground level, pressed against a building wall. He'd found a corner so dark that even Adrianna wouldn't have spotted him without that tag flashing for her heads-up display. His skin was so cold that her infrared vision confused him for brickwork.

His augments knew how to hide the little gray man from more than just light. His shock of black hair and simple features made him interchangeable from any other man in uniform, by careful design. The captain from Naval Counter-Intelligence was unremarkable and dry, but there was a dark intensity behind his eyes.

Conversely, Lieutenant Commander Callum Remus was a hard man to forget. He was across the plaza from Adrianna, suspended underneath a balcony like some kind of mutant gargoyle, his arms spread wide against the structure to get a good grip. The man flexed his back to hold himself in place, pressing so hard she could see the muscles peeking out from under his arms. His biceps had biceps and not a single piece of him was without violent purpose. And what's more, he made it look simple, just hanging there by pressure alone, ten feet up in the air.

Deceptively good hiding spot. Nobody ever looked up.

"Area clear?" Callum asked through the peer-to-peer radio link.

A single tight-beam laser could transmit quiet whispers to the rest team without risk of interception, so long as they had line of sight.

Adrianna scanned the walls again, seeing sound waves of scuffling inside a building on the far side of the plaza. Whispers, old shoes creaking on wood, the faint hint of salt on the air. "I got bodies on the northwest corner."

"Yeah, it's a mother and her two kids. Shifty and uneasy," Graccus noted. "They're scared and alone."

"Want me to simplify things?" asked Lieutenant Yurek from a block away, sitting behind a sniper scope.

"Negative," Graccus said. "They're unarmed and sitting still. Let 'em be."

Far down the lane, with a beautiful view from the rooftops, Lieutenant Maxim Yurek had secured himself a nest. Belly down on a sheet of tin, he was no doubt fiddling with the optical equipment on his rifle. Syncing up his implants with the rifle's bore was no quick thing, as he busily calculated the mathematics unique to their area: windage, moisture, uneven points of gravity. Adrianna didn't envy the sniper for all his homework.

Graccus' active camouflage and Yurek's hyper-optics sounded maddeningly useful, sure, but neither were as fit for close quarters as she or Callum were. Adrianna always said she was the 'strike' part of Orbital Strike Command.

Overwatch, assault, heavy and bait. Throw in the variable of a civilian pop and an overwhelming opposing force, and they were sitting in a textbook. Who knew? Maybe they'd be written about someday, some scholarly captain looking to modify the theory, get his name stapled on a stratagem.

The Riley Maneuver. Sounded so pretentious.

The team were all set up, lying in wait for their prey to stumble into the snare. How many late nights had Adrianna sat in the frigid morning mud at Holkstad Academy waiting for some junior instructor to come passing by her spider-hole? She had been fifteen years old, hungry and pissed off, counting the hours till daylight or her next meal.

Waiting was a part of the service.

How many hours till she was back in the sky and off this rock? All she could think of was a nice stack of steaming buttermilk pancakes. Pad of butter on top, not yet soaked through. Picturesque steam wafting up.

"Three vehicles," Yurek interrupted her hungry daydreaming. "Two from the north and a third from southeast, pinching in."

Callum already knew, but he had to ask. "Pirate colors?"

"Yellowjackets all," Yurek confirmed. "What's the play, Cap'n? High speed, low drag?"

Her radio crackled with interference from the pulsar that rippled overhead, but her friends were too close for that to be of much trouble. "Hold your fire, Yurek," Graccus ordered. "We spook this guy, we may not see him again."

Op was a simple one. High-value target was going to show his face. They were going to snatch him up, but only if they could lure the sucker out into the open and dispatch his security detail.

Graccus peeled himself out of a shadow, causing Adrianna's heart to skip a beat. She could see his ident; she knew he had been back there, somewhere in that silky black. Heavily augmented as she was, her five senses got a boost from some of the best technology available —but those five senses still obeyed natural instincts. And seeing someone phase shift out of a shadow was something the human mind did not agree with. It played to every sense that there were monsters in the dark.

And the Captain walked freely among them.

Graccus always looked like a bird to her and he certainly liked to preen like one. The slender man shrugged on a ratty jacket with shoulder pads and a torn hem, edges scuffing against the ground. He took a moment to fix his collar, getting the position just right.

"You look like a jackass," Callum sniped over the radio.

"Hey now," Yurek said with a dry humor, "let's keep it professional."

Graccus looked down at his get-up. Thick cotton pants tucked into sturdy boots, a high-collared pale work shirt and the requisite Duster long coat. "I didn't pick their uniform."

"And you look like a jackass in their uniform," Callum repeated.

Two cruisers came gliding into the plaza right in front of Graccus, mag-motor grinding to a stop, lowering the vehicles to scrape against the stone. And parking like absolute assholes, all cock-eyed and diagonal. The third hover-car came idling in behind, bathing Graccus in headlights and cutting off any escape.

Graccus gingerly lifted his hands, showing the occupants that he was unarmed.

They must've been satisfied because the gullwing doors on the cruisers all popped open. Goons of every shape and stripe popped out, presenting gnarled and rusting firearms. More concerning, the cars popped turrets out of their respective roofs.

"Fleshy boys most, some prosthetics. Two mechs in civilian dress," Callum reported. "Ten triggers by my count. And that big one's got a bracket gun slung."

Adrianna glanced at the big meathead at the front of the wedge approaching Graccus, and he did indeed have a blocky thing made of welded copper wire. Nothing more than a battery with a grip and a trigger. One squeeze and it would dump a blast of energy with enough power to slag anything ten yards in front of the muzzle.

The drop off was pretty significant though. At eleven yards, it would warm up lunch.

Meathead squared up on Graccus, jutting out his chin. "Were you followed?"

Graccus looked over his shoulder at the car behind him. "By *you*, maybe."

"Answer the question."

"If I was followed," Graccus growled, "I'd be very impressed by the guy who did it."

"Kiss-ass," Callum grunted over the radio.

Graccus couldn't answer back, instead forcing a smile for Meat-head. The goon sneered at him, showing a bit of...what would have been teeth, but the front four were all replaced with a single bar of composite amalgam. It made it look like he had one big mutant tooth.

That drew a reflexive grimace from Graccus, but Adrianna knew better than to think Graccus was actually disgusted. Her entire unit was Aug-Four class Orbital or above. Once you've seen a man's ribcage 'splash', nothing was grim or gross anymore. Graccus just knew how to play the part.

"I was told," Graccus forced out past a fake gag, "that Thibodeau would be joining us?"

"You're dealing with me today," the goon said, glancing back at the assembly of firepower he'd brought with him. They were all scanning rooftops and listening for Imperial air power. The turrets panned the corners while the goons moved across the plaza, light on their feet and weapons tight to shoulders.

Being on the losing side of a war made folks a mite twitchy.

"I don't deal with the help," Graccus said. "So we can sit and wait for Teebo, or I'll be on my way."

"Thibodeau's got more important fish to fry."

"I hope he does," Graccus pressed, "because that fish is the only ration your men'll be eating this week." Graccus turned to leave, causing the tail car's shooters to raise their weapons.

It may have been twenty feet down and thirty feet out, but Adrianna could see Graccus' heart rate spike, his body temperature rising as the network of augmentations throughout his body primed hot. If they shot at him, he could get out of the way. Graccus was fast even by Orbital standards. But enough triggers could fill every pocket of air with steel, and then all Graccus would be capable of was breathing through a hole in his chest.

And that bracket gun was worrisome. There was a morbid joke amongst the young cadets at Holkstad: you can dodge a rock, a knife, a punch. Enough science can help you dodge a bullet—but no one can dodge sunlight.

"You talk very large," Meathead snarled at Graccus, "for a man so small."

"That, in and of itself, should be interesting information, shouldn't it?" Graccus said.

Narrow eyes and a threatening encroaching step. "Or maybe you're lying. We don't care for liars."

"Calm yourself, comrade." A rotund walrus of a man came clacking his way forward, a bushy mustache across his face. He was dressed in pirate business casual: slacks, simple tunic with overly complex cuffs, and a tapered jacket wrapping about his broad shoulders. He moved with the airs of a man who demanded gravity but had none; he had no power he hadn't bought.

"That's our boy," Yurek caroled like the choir boy he was.

"Just tell me when, boss," Adrianna said, as she raised her carbine into line with his fat head.

"Cut the chatter. I'm getting strange radio traffic off him," Callum said. "Riley, can you lock it down?"

Adrianna squinted, studying the electromagnetic aura around the pirate leader. Sure enough, he was broadcasting something off his person. "Affirm, big guy. Sig is so hot, he's practically glowing. He's got an active link to something nearby."

A transponder in case of emergencies? No, thirteen-centimeter bandwidth, and low power. Which meant short-range radio device. He was working with something hundred meters or less, something in the neighborhood. Yurek was further away than whatever he was talking to.

Her eyes glanced over at the few mechs in attendance. And bingo, there were active receivers. He was driving the mechs by remote. Which meant fine detail response, more than just slug-throwing automatons.

Two big bodyguards made of armor plating. Not exactly something that could be gunned down. But Orbital had their ways. "Icarus Four-One. Uploading target spec for line spike."

She designated the targets with her eyes and uploaded the intel. "*Erinyes* Actual. Targets received, lieutenant. Commandant is acquiring their signals now."

Good, that was one advantage peeled away. But until the AI in orbit could lock in, Graccus would be stuck downrange with the mechs—and that still left a more-than-sufficient complement of fleshy goons.

Thibodeau walked up to Meathead, laying a soothing hand on the man's shoulder. Taking over the conversation. "I trust you understand the precautions, *ser*? Trustworthy traders don't come to the Boolean Edge anymore."

"Trustworthy you can always find," Graccus said. "It's honesty that may be a touch more scarce than usual."

"You'll understand of course...that an Orbital officer, such as yourself, will fetch a mighty fee." Graccus tensed and Thibodeau let loose a laugh more akin to a cat's purr. "Yes. Orbital Strike Command. The vaunted 'Oskies.' You think I don't know everything about everyone that I meet? Boy, I gauged your value from satellite."

"Oh no," Adrianna said, completely stone-faced. "Quick, act surprised."

And Graccus was a master performer. He held his stoic expression, but blinked a few too many times at this revelation, betraying uncertainty and wariness. He had to play out all of those microexpressions that people interpreted without thinking. Repetition, blinking, muscles tightening and skin wrinkling—everything had a message attached to it.

"Please do not resist," Thibodeau urged. "I'm sure you're worth more...intact."

"I think you're going to be troubled," Graccus cautioned. "My commanders won't pay for my return."

"Oh?"

"No, Orbital doesn't negotiate. And they won't let you harvest me either. You're just going to piss 'em off."

Thibodeau growled, looking to his men. "Then perhaps we just kill you."

Batteries hummed, chambers clacked shut, and the turrets cranked around to lock onto Graccus.

"Cap'n," Adrianna started, a nervous song on her lips, "Captain, call the play."

She could feel Callum tense up down the lane, ready to leap into the fray. And Yurek charged the capacitors in his railgun. But they were disciplined soldiers. They'd wait for Graccus to give the order.

Unannounced, unwelcome, unwarranted—a door flung open on the far side of the plaza.

A boy, no older than ten, jumped the small set of stairs to the floor. He was all thin limbs, gangly like twisted wire, a jumbled mess of awkward growing pains. He gripped a shaft of rebar in both hands like a spear. Shouting, challenging. But was he taunting Graccus or the gangsters?

Protecting his home from the scary men. It didn't matter who. He was trying to be a hero.

Slaved to one another, the three turrets moved as one but fired independently. Adrianna heard the magnets discharge. Tucked down one barrel there were six consecutive rows of batteries, each grabbing a hold of a magnetic slug. Each in turn pulled that slug forward to the next, propelling it further and further down the twenty-inch barrel. By the time it hit the muzzle, it was moving so fast and with such pressure that the friction burst the air into violet plasma fire.

Adrianna had standing orders: stay put, stay quiet, stay hidden. Don't spook the target. After seven years in Service, there was a reason she was still a lieutenant.

She knew what those guns could and would do to that little boy's fragile frame.

An Orbital Officer sees the world differently: light moves at its own fixed speed and the human brain can interpret and respond only so fast. Electricity snaps through the nervous system, interpreted by the brain and then fed to the muscles. Squishy evolutionary meat limited the speed of that response.

But those traits could be...optimized. The speed of an Oskie was the speed of their decisions.

She saw the door open, the kid run out. And before the kid's feet had even hit ground, she had made hers.

Adrianna leapt from her hole, a single forceful leap powered by silksteel and servos. Her frame silhouetted under the glittering pulsar like a crooked nightmare beast.

She was in a mad dash to beat a bullet to its target.

Mid-air, she saw the pressure wave ripple outward as the shell exited the muzzle, faster—far faster—than she could move. It was making up lost ground, a sonic boom warping the air behind it as it lanced out for the boy.

That child, that stupid brave boy...felt her hand first. Just in time to yank him out of the way of hypersonic death.

What the boy felt in the blink of an eye, Adrianna saw play out moment by moment. She saw the musculature of his body react, the snap of his shoulder dislocating from the hard impulse. And the bullet searing past the boy's ear, tongues of flame reaching out to singe his cheek and catch in his hair. Half a kilo of ferrite slammed into the concrete wall, ripping through the building and sending up a cloud of materials that were certainly unhealthy to breathe.

An anti-material slug for an unarmored civilian? She was certain that the gangsters hadn't maliciously planned that, but why was that the first response to a generic intrusion?! They could've defused this moment with a bag of candy.

She didn't dare slow down too suddenly or the boy's physiology would absorb the G-forces in an instant and crush him into raspberry jam between her fingers. She needed to get him to safety before slowing down: no turns, no sudden stops, nothing that could impart sudden graphic death.

Her implants were already cooking hot under her skin, fine

orange streaks outlining the surgical scars on her wrists and neck. Her chest tensed and burned like someone had set a scalding iron to her collar. But she didn't dare slow down.

Only way out was through six inches of solid concrete buildings or...well, past the goons and their cars. Two cars to the right and one to the left. She knew where the odds makers were.

Adrianna darted at the single car and its computerized turret. The computer tracked her movement better than any human eye could, snapping hard on its guide rails to follow her and pelt off three more shots.

While the occupants of the plaza were still reacting to the sonic wave of the first shot, she was vaulting over the side of the gangster car, slamming down one hand into the hood so hard she shaped the steel to her palm, with the kid clutched under her other arm.

As she went by, she could hear the oiled rotor of the turret scream against itself as it tried to keep up with her. Its barrel tracked square on her head. She could see down inside along the grungy rifling, the flecks of copper jacketing that had peeled and clung to the poorly maintained barrel.

But that turret stopped hard as she dragged her foot right across the base of the turret, snapping something critical inside. It might not have been all that theatrical, but she'd cut a necessary component. The turret jostled with the hit—and froze.

She tore down the alley with the boy in her arms, shoes burning on the pavement, squealing rubber as she vanished around the corner to safety.

"Riley!" The scolding surname was all Callum could get out.

Before Meathead threw an arm up around Thibodeau, drawing him back to the cars and bellowing the call to war. "Ambush!"

Thibodeau flicked his wrist, deploying a small holographic display and tapping out a handful of commands into the glowing amber keys. The turrets snapped around, targeting Graccus. Goons both fleshy and mechanized converged on him.

And all the captain did was raise an inquisitive eyebrow. He glanced back in Adrianna's direction, pointedly. "What are you waiting for, boys?"

"You wouldn't be the first Oskie we killed!" Thibodeau hissed the threat.

And Graccus' face went dark, all compassion vacating his expression. "If only I remembered how many pirates I'd killed."

And the group of posturing badasses got to witness the etching of a three-inch hole carved through one of the turrets, a shower of sparks as the metal slug slammed through the chamber housing and sheared the barrel clean off. The shot exited and deflected downward into the second car. A splatter on the windshield's interior, something vital and distinctly human. Both turrets suddenly hung limp.

"Let's get messy!" Yurek shouted as he racked another round into battery.

Turrets down for the count. That left nine goons—plus Teebo—everyone's got guns and itchy fingers. Outnumbered a little less than two-to-one.

Sounded like a healthy day at the office to her.

Adrianna shouldered her carbine and glanced down at the kid. He had gone pale, eyes wide and hair blown out into a wispy mess. "Stay put," Adrianna said, pointing at the ground—a single yellow line traced up the back of her hand and the sweat and oils on her skin had already started to steam with the exertion. Unblinking, terror shaking right down to his bones, the kid didn't dare take his eyes off the meta-human before him.

But Adrianna didn't wait for any yes or no. She had work to do.

Without the kid, she could move freely. She flashed around the corner, tapping off three shots at the nearest three goons. Her finger worked the trigger with perfect timing, listening to the cyclic rate of her rifle to perfectly match its mechanical limits. It sounded more like one long shot than three individual ones. And the third man was dead before the first had hit the floor.

Now down to six goons.

The two mechs shed their cowls, thick black fabric slipping to the ground to cover the fallen dead. The mechs weren't proper automa-tons—these were remote-controlled units made for miners or indus-trial work too dangerous for humans. Of course, if they could remotely work on mining equipment, they could work triggers too. And with Thibodeau issuing commands at light-speed, the machines were at least as potent as any soldier.

And far more resilient.

The soulless machines pivoted on their waists to face Adrianna, firing their crusty guns with cold efficiency. Her own return fire wasn't much use against their hardened steel frames. So she fell back behind the alley wall, watching as their individual shots pecked away at her precious brickwork cover. "*Erinyes*, want to handle these sparkies for me?"

"Stand by, lieutenant," came that smoky voice of the warrant officer in orbit, barely even tense.

If the mechs were being piloted by remote, then there was a transmitter/receiver for each platform. Scanning for an open port, brute-forcing any control key, and uploading a simple hack could be done by a shipboard Naval AI in less than a second. Nothing on-board a mech platform that small could hope to compete against the hardware behind a Naval frigate.

The little blinky lights on each mech flickered and the machines slumped forward, power cut. One even dropped its gun roughly to the cracked concrete floor.

Thibodeau shook his wrist in the air, waving at the mechs, desperate to reawaken them. But no joy. Whatever control he had over his mechanical bodyguards had been severed.

Four goons.

All this chaos and Graccus hadn't even moved yet, hands held out wide as the gunfire swirled around him.

Two of the remaining goons sprayed from the hip, hoping to shred Graccus under a volume of fire. Adrianna didn't envy them; sparring with Graccus was like trying to tackle a cloud.

She saw the captain corkscrew in the air, finding the space

between the shots that no normal human could even see, let alone get to. His longcoat twirled, the bullets shredding the fabric and turning it into a ragged cape.

Toe-tapping one foot to the ground, Graccus found the forward thrust he needed to lunge in-between the gangsters.

He snagged one searing hot barrel in his hand, the steel tube still spitting flashes of fire from its muzzle. And before the shooter could react and let go of the trigger, Graccus yanked the gun to bear onto his friend—at that range, without proper armor, it was a bit like throwing rocks at a red-colored pond.

The gangster mewled like a sick cat at the morbid sight, letting go of his weapon and falling to his knees in despair. Looking down on him, Graccus simply snapped the gun over his knee. He'd broken the man's sense of reality and his heart. No need to do more damage than he already had.

Meathead forced Thibodeau down behind him, hiding him from the sniper as he tucked his bracket gun into his hip. Aimed right at Graccus.

Graccus pushed out a breath, focusing on the end of that barrel. Listening for the charge, the trigger, tracking the waver of the muzzle. Where would he go with it, and when? If Graccus guessed wrong...

And as Meathead squeezed the trigger, Graccus picked a direction, darting right. The blast missed him, scoring a three-foot chunk of hot yellow slag out of the ground.

That was his one shot to do this right. Before Meathead could chamber a fresh battery, Graccus snap kicked the end of the gun, kicking it up into Meathead's face with a wet thunk. The man fell back, hands cupped to his face and blood seeping between his fingers.

And before he could do another thing, Callum struck Meathead from the side hard enough that half a dozen bones broke on the spot and a splash of blood slapped across Graccus' face.

The captain wiped the fluids from his face, listening to the ugly crunching noises on the ground. He extended a hand, pulling Callum up from the pile of stew meat that had once been an adult human.

The blood was caked thick, oozing off both their fists, binding the two men together as each waited for the other to let go first. Their eyes locked on each other, nostrils flaring, lips parted with some great weight—

They heard the gunshot and both flickered out of the way, separated by the violence. The last two goons standing both panic-fired at the Oskies, no aim or strategy. Graccus and Callum calmly side-stepped the rounds that were relevant and ignored the rest.

To the horror of the simple human men, the Oskies both stood there, eyeing each of their attackers. The glowing orange implants issued hot steam into the air and their hot skin warping the air around them with a silky mirage.

Orbital Strike Command: they were ghosts. Ethereal. Unreal.

And in that hesitation, a dinner plate sized hole punched out of one of goons' chests, misting whatever had been inside. Adrianna heard the satisfied Yurek hum a pleasant tune through the radio at that positive result.

Seeing his friend practically explode, the last remaining shooter just dropped his gun and shoved both hands in the air. "*Fra tow zu ytrit!*" he cursed in Colonial creole.

Adrianna hadn't picked up much of the language in the last six months, but she knew expletives when she heard them. They always had a lovely kineticism to them in almost any language.

The surrendering gangster received a bullet to the head for his trouble. Thibodeau's shaking hand clutched the smoking gun. "*Montah zu T'aie!*" he whimpered at the Imperials.

Adrianna knew that one. It was a battle cry. 'Wealth to the Victors.'

Graccus sauntered over to Thibodeau, crouching down low. He looked at the gun, right down the barrel, and then back at Thibodeau with a blank expression. "Do you want to see how that ends?"

Thibodeau glanced at the gun, at the battlefield of strewn body parts, dead gangsters, and silent machines. His elite unit was dismantled like a simple exercise.

And he dropped the gun.

"That's a good lad," Graccus said, reaching out to tussle the man's hair. Thibodeau winced at the interaction, but he didn't make any other moves. Callum loomed over him, clenched fists and a curl to his lip.

The innocent kid poked his head around the corner, looking up at Adrianna. Trembling, grabbing at the wall with bony fingers, like he was afraid to let go and drift away.

She nodded to him with a crooked smile. "All quiet now, kid. Song of silence."

No response. The kid shifted, inching away from her. Eyes wide, mouth agape. She reached out for him, open palm. But the motion was too much. "*Diamau!*" he shouted, scampering away into the night.

Diamau. He knew what she was: a demon.

"Nice work, Riley," Yurek coughed over the radio. "Real people skills."

Graccus didn't use the radio. He just shouted her name. "Riley! Get out here!"

<hr />

And that was how the last battle of the Boolean Civil War came to a close. A wee little skirmish in a dark little alley with about a dozen people, over in less than a minute. And started by a lack of impulse control.

No medals. No notice. Dropping the curtain on an entire rebellion and flicking out the lights. That's what Orbital Strike Command did best.

CHAPTER
TWO

THE BRIG on the *Erinyes* wasn't an elaborate thing. It was a singular cell, no more than a repurposed storage closet, but they had to take all the shelving out after Adrianna refused to stay confined in her quarters during her first infraction of the trip. With the minor matter of disobeying orders in the Boolean, this would be her fifth stay in the Hotel Broom Closet.

Of course, after five separate stays, they had made some battle-field upgrades to the jail cell: there was a guard post and a control console, proper plumbing, and even a cot. They'd redone the whole thing special for her.

No idea what the charge was going to be this time. Could be a slap on the wrist, maybe some public service.

But with no warning or even a gruff explanation, the guard of her cell presented his palm to his control console for a biometric scan. The bars clacked, the locks released, and the door swung open, releasing Adrianna from her time out. The sergeant had her personal effects waiting in a small bag: her sidearm, the small brass officer's orchid for her jacket collar, and her wrist-mounted Entiglas computer.

But he had more for her than a handful of confiscated items. "Captain says grab some grub and then report to the Jump Deck."

"The Jump Deck?"

"That's the call."

"Good ol' Alpha Charlie," she muttered, shaking her head. No good deed without a requisite Imperial Navy ass-chewing. And Graccus knew how to read the riot act with a special flare. At least they must have decided against other forms of discipline. A public dress down was probably a kindness. "He say anything else?"

"Don't step on your air hose on the way over there."

"Eh, sounds like him," she said, clipping her pistol to the magnetic retention clasp on her hip. "What do they got cooking in the mess?"

The guard shook his head. "I'm in the middle of a double, ma'am. I haven't eaten for ten hours."

"You shouldn't do that. How else you going to grow into a real boy without a proper three square?" She clapped him on the shoulder as she popped into motion. "Want me to bring you something?"

"No, ma'am, I'll manage."

She waved a hand at him as she walked off down the hall, a skip to her step.

Every time she was told to sit still for an extended period, her augments got grumpy. Muscles would tighten, then spasm. Occasional spikes of pain. Let it build and snap-snap, she'd have a charley horse.

Adrianna was still learning her way around the *Erinyes*. She consulted the minimap that popped up behind her eyelid. Getting directions like that without even looking down at her Entiglas felt like a cheat code. She didn't look lost with her head buried in a map and brow scrunched. Rather, more like a tourist, head tilted back in wonderment.

It was something of a unique ship, the *Erinyes*, first in its class.

Fast, light, and low profile—perfect for clandestine operations. In its six-month deployment, it had gone everywhere Imperials weren't supposed to be and nobody even knew they were around. They'd seen every side of the Boolean conflict, and they had been the ones to close the door on it. Unofficially, of course. That honor probably went more publicly to Rear Admiral Hugh and the big guns on the *Persephone*.

After shaking out both legs and rolling her shoulders off a nearby doorframe, Adrianna drifted on through the barracks: home of the twenty-four bootstrappin', gun-totin' badass Naval Regulars that the *Erinyes* funneled from hotspot to hotspot. Little more than support infantry for the elite Oskies, but they were a fun bunch of lunatics.

Nothing fanciful. They just needed to pack twenty-four people into a small space. That made for what amounted to a broad hallway with lockers and triple stacked bunks on either side. Most of them were empty, with their ship duties taking them elsewhere—places like watching the brig and its super soldier occupant.

She stomped her way through the Regulars' home-away-from-home like a timpani drum announcing its presence. This drew some whistles and hollers from the few off-duty Regulars she passed, those tucked away in their coffin-sleepers or shirking on their brown jumpsuits.

She waved to her adoring fans as she went. "That's enough outta you, 11-Bang-Bang. As you were."

"They were never going to hold you! LT Oskie!" One Regular crowed. That call-and-response got a few others to bark that playful nickname with their full chest, like hollering monkeys in the jungle.

"I'll bring the flash, you bring the thunder!" She shouted back over her shoulder.

"Bang bang, ma'am! Huah!" Heard. Understood. Acknowledged. Of course, it could just be thick skulls grunting happy noises because enunciation was hard. Either way, it made her smile.

Immediately after the berth and past a short airlocked causeway was the Galley. Rank-and-file Navy woke up hungry after all, and food was first on their minds at the top of a shift. It wasn't a large room but it occupied most of the *Erinyes'* narrow structural profile. Three long tables with bench seating folded up from the floor, allowing the entire room to be cleared in ten seconds flat. They did it during battle conditions, Jump prep, or extreme maneuvers. She'd seen meals ruined as the tables sucked down into the floor with barely any warning.

The Replicator built into the nearside wall was the newest model at the cheapest cost—a delicate military balance. A line of deck officers in Naval gray and Regulars in brown had already formed, and they were awaiting whatever programmed slop the machine was printing out.

She smelled it before she heard the thick slap hit the first platter. The smell of bacon and gravy immediately sent a shot through Adrianna's reptile hindbrain and set a tingling behind her ears.

Salt. Fats. A bit of black pepper. The soft crunch of fresh biscuits.

"Clean yourself up, little sister." The gruff voice of Callum cut through her haze as the big guy shouldered up to her, dropping a hot towel in her hand. "Proper hygiene saves you, me, and the latrine."

Callum looked like a mountain had grown a face and a sour attitude, a slab of granite with sentience and homicidal tendencies. She had been called his 'little sister' for the entire deployment, despite being over six feet and two hundred pounds of military tech herself; she was still 'little' next to him.

"We got a latrine up in this bucket?" she asked with a smirk. "Here I've been shitting out the window the whole time."

"Nobody said you were smart." Callum cracked an unnerving half-smile. The goliath had collected a platter of food that resembled a mound of salty, oily dirt. It made Adrianna's stomach ache. He noticed, looking her up and down. "You haven't eaten since before the hop, have you?"

"I have not. I look that bad?"

He squinted, his implants scanning her vitals in half a second. "Your muscles are currently in atrophy."

"So melodramatic," Adrianna scoffed, though she should ensure the brass had something to chew on before reporting for her public abuse. It'd be a shame if they had to wring her out to find anything of value.

Adrianna slid past Callum and the big guy just shook his head, wandering off to the far side—notably alone. She spied Graccus and Yurek at their own special little corner, watching that exchange from afar. When a young soldier's senses were heightened as much as an Oskie's were, listening to a bored warrant officer gnaw on slop was close to actual torture. The clicks, smacks, and moist splats of the human mouth were only the beginning compared to hearing teeth tear and smash. So while the deck crew and grunts rotated in their little cliques, the Oskies usually sat alone.

Adrianna liked the noise. Noise was good. Laughter, joviality, chatter. It meant no one was bleeding.

She meandered over to Yurek and Graccus's table, striking a parade rest. It was a good little corner where all other sound was muted and far away. "You wanted to see me, sir?" she asked.

"Food first, lieutenant," Graccus said, pointing to the Replicator and the line of grunts. "What I have can wait ten minutes."

Her eyes narrowed. There was a touch of sadness in the veteran's eye.

Graccus was the senior officer on the *Erinyes*, Master and Commander of Local Allied Forces. Regulations gave him broad authority in battlefield matters, and shipboard concerns had a way of falling under that same fiefdom.

So if it had to wait ten minutes, it would wait ten minutes. Her disciplinary action could wait ten years if Graccus willed it so.

May as well get some grub then.

Adrianna felt the stares from both superior officers as she marched to the back of the line. They couldn't be that mad about her saving a kid's life, could they? That alley was always going to turn into a shoot-out. Pirates like Thibodeau and his ilk didn't make a habit of going peacefully into the night.

Ten minutes. No use splitting hairs or burning brain cells about it. They'd tell her what she needed to hear in ten minutes.

The Replicator was a complex tool. All she knew was that it could print out recipes programmed into its system, taking carbon stock stores and assembling the molecule compounds in the appropriate order to make everything from simple bread to heavy proteins and sugars. Energy costly, but raw carbon didn't spoil, making for a naval logistics dream.

She pulled out three servings, building a potato mountain, multiple biscuits, and sopped the whole platter with gravy.

Adrianna wormed her way over to the nearest open seat at the end of the table. She settled in, swiping a hand back to pin her jet-black hair. And in one smooth motion, she brought both hands up and forward to clasp into a prayer position.

Someone to her left coughed up their food and she could feel the entire table fall into formation with her. And so began the formal muttering under their collective breath: "Bless our burdens, for they weigh on our shoulders. Bless our feet, for our Road is long. And bless this food that we may forget our hunger."

Most mumbled just enough to be audible. It didn't bother her, though. For many, Faith in the Pilgrim was an abstract concept: a practical explanation for the naturally occurring Jump Points that connected human civilization. But Orbital took their Faith a bit more seriously than the general population. Side effect of flirting with their own mortality so much.

Grabbing an oversized spoon and keeping time with a schoolyard hymn in her head, she shoveled into her face with an adopted rhythm. If she finished eating before her third repeat, she'd have just enough time to get to the Jump Deck on time for her scheduled abuse.

"You look just like a pig in its sty," said someone with a deliciously smoky voice.

Those cool and rich words always drew Adrianna's smile from hiding. "And just as happy, chief," Adrianna grunted back.

The speaker sat down across from her, all elegance and smooth motions. The Naval gray uniform seemed tailored to her slight frame —or she was born for it. Her long hair, dyed a rich emerald green, hung straight down to the middle of her back with a single lock straying in front of her left ear and framing her sharp jawline.

Chief Warrant Officer Vivian Bannister seemed to make every move like she'd planned it ten minutes before. All smooth motions and strong foundations without a single augment. Adrianna graduated at Aug-Four from Holkstad and could leg lift a good-sized truck —but Vivian made her look clumsy and oafish.

Despite Vivian's fae-like qualities and the commentary on Adrianna's messy plate, the Chief Warrant Officer's platter didn't look much better. That's what gravy and grits will do, Adrianna supposed. This was not a meal for the neat and tidy.

"I see they let you out for good behavior," Vivian commented, stirring the gravy into her potatoes with an idleness that bordered on poetry.

Adrianna smiled. "I tried bribery, but I don't have anything anybody wants."

"Was that intended to be self-reflection? Or self-flagellation?"

Before Adrianna could respond, someone swung their leg over the bench to sit next to them. "Those are not mutually exclusive," they said with a cheery lilt.

Vivian squinted playfully at Officer Richard Voight as he settled in next to her. He had his biscuit jammed in his mouth to make more room for mess on his plate, scruffy blonde hair falling in ringlets out from under his cap, and a round face with rosy jovial cheeks.

He looked like a dog that had found a very good stick, wagging his proverbial tail in pride.

"Officer! If you're here, then who's flying the ship?" Vivian asked.

"Nobody. No jockey, no stick," Voight said, dry and straight-faced. "We're all going to die."

"Any way we could hurry that up?" Adrianna quipped. "I've got about five minutes before I face the music. I'm ready for some end of the world debauchery."

"What did you have in mind?" Voight asked. "We talking stupid amounts of good food and drink? Or like Coliseum games: two men enter, one man leaves?"

"I'm game for whatever," Adrianna said, just a blanket endorsement of the Vees and their unique brand of banal insanity.

"Could break out the white robes. Sacrifice one of the bang-bangs to a god," Vivian suggested.

"Which god?" Adrianna asked.

"I'll make one up."

"Good god needs a good name," Adrianna said.

"Or no name at all," Vivian corrected. "Spoken of only in hushed whispers in quiet chambers."

Adrianna laughed, a light bubble of joy up from her belly. These two always had a way of breaking her tension when fresh from lock-up.

Voight hunched over, turning to his food and studying the three identical biscuits on Adrianna's platter. "You ever think about it?"

"You *have* to be more specific," Vivian pressed.

"Every single person at this table is eating the same biscuit. Not the same recipe, but a recreation of the exact same biscuit."

"Viv, can you get me a Philip's head?" Adrianna asked with a grin. "The jockey's got a screw loose."

Vivian twirled her fork in the potatoes like she had a witch's cauldron. "All I have is a soldering iron and a dream, darling."

Voight scoffed at the both of them. "You know that every single time we Jump, the Commandant AI is breaking us down, shoving us through an impossibly small gravity well, and recreating us on the other side. Not really all that different from these biscuits?"

"Steamy and delicious?" Adrianna asked, throwing up a hand to get a high five from Vivian.

"All of our personalities, memories, feelings: they're just chemical markers. All that can be rebuilt. So—have we died thirty some odd times and we just don't remember it?"

"Voight, my man, whatever stims they give you to fly this ship nonstop...you're holding out on me," Adrianna said, shoving the second biscuit in her mouth.

"You've never thought about this?" Voight prodded her.

"You've thought about this multiple times?"

He nodded. "Keeps me up at night."

"You need to experience more life-threatening events," Adrianna muttered, more dismissive than she intended.

"What a weird thing to say to a person," Voight retorted with no delay and a half-smile. At least he didn't take it too personally.

Across the galley, Graccus stood up from his seat, giving Yurek a polite nod as he took his platter over to the kitchen side. He had barely made it there when Callum squared up behind him. "You wanted to see me, sir?"

Graccus set down his platter with an exasperated sigh. "Why does everyone want to get bad news right on top of breakfast?"

He knew he couldn't hide what he was saying, at least not from the other Oskies, so he always adopted a tone when he did. The Vees didn't hear the conversation, but Adrianna couldn't help it.

Bad news? Adrianna perked up at that. She had reported to get smacked. There was bad news?

Callum's neck twitched like he was going to glance back at the rest of the room but held firm. "You called me, sir."

"My cabin," Graccus said, depositing his tray into the slot. The two slunk out of the galley like a pair of panthers wandering into the back enclosure.

Adrianna caught Yurek's eye and the two exchanged a series of rapid-fire facial expressions. She leaned at the door the two commanders left out of, and he just shrugged back. She squinted at him. *Like Hell he didn't know what was going on.*

But he shook his head. He just caught his two dads fighting over the top of his breakfast. He knew when to keep his head down.

Adrianna waited till she was sure the two superhuman commanders were out of super earshot, before leaning forward. "Okay, help me out. I thought they broke up."

"I have no earthly idea what you mean," Vivian said with six months of shipboard gossip pent up behind that statement.

Adrianna jerked her thumb at the door. "That's what they used to say. As an excuse. The 'my cabin' line."

Voight smirked, adopting an almost mocking tone. "Lieutenant, shipboard fraternization rules are painfully clear."

"And I was the last one to figure them out!" Adrianna hissed like she was conceding the point and desperate to move on. "But I thought they'd ended it."

Vivian finally broke her masquerade, leaning forward to match the conspiratorial tone. "Last I'd heard, it was over. And not pleasantly. Don't fret. I sincerely doubt *that* was a romantic rendezvous."

Adrianna chewed on that, looking towards the door. Then what Graccus had said about bad news wasn't code for something. It meant they had dredged her out of the brig because of bad news.

She couldn't help but wonder what.

She finished the last of her meal, sopping up the gravy with her third and final biscuit, before depositing her dirty tray into the kitchen slot for sanitization. From there, she followed her orders and left for the Jump Deck. The Vees would be taking their own posts there shortly, but Riley would likely be there and gone before they finished their own meals.

Bad news? What kind of bad news could Graccus have? Had the mission developed a quirky extra edge to it? Or was she going to get some brand-new discipline, some heinous assignment or new transfer?

She didn't want to transfer! She liked it here on the *Erinyes* with Vivian and Voight, Graccus and Callum. This was a good assignment, doing good work. It had taken a long time to get a billet as primo as this. An Oskie would dream of this placement. And one with her spotty record? Graccus had to request her personally or she'd never have been plucked from the pile.

This was home. They did good work with good people. If she could just go from planet to planet, do this dance until whenever... yeah, the war was over, but why did *this* have to end?

The Jump Deck was at the very heart of the ship, the nerve center, deep behind steel plating and armor where it was most protected. No windows, just holographic displays and command consoles. It was a circular room with three seats encircling a commander's station and its monolithic plinth of a projector. Made the captain the center of a tiny universe. Any function of the other three seats could be reviewed or controlled from there.

Voight's navigator seat sat empty. He'd be at the balanced true 'center mass' of the ship so that any G-force effect on him was minimized. The last person anybody needed blacking out was the jockey.

Turret operators were the psychopaths, out on the end of the proverbial crane arm, taking pot shots and soaking brain damage.

But Voight's console was active with an amber image of the Boolean Edge's many asteroids flickering with every passing wave from the pulsar. Adrianna could make out at least a dozen other signatures of Naval ships, all making their way back to the Jump Point. Headed for home, for dry dock.

The second seat on the deck was Vivian's Commo & Systems chair, left empty while the ship passively reviewed all nearby traffic. The last was the Power & Engineering officer, Mikhail Sizemore, who looked up from his work as she entered.

Sizemore was a quiet man of old farm stock, thoughtful and reserved, though he never enjoyed looking her in the eye. She could understand why. He liked machines more than people—the kind of lad who just wanted to go tinker in the barn until sunset. That, and the yellow iris typical of Oskies wasn't the most inviting look to begin with. It made a normally difficult interaction for him even more unnerving.

"Captain called me out of the boot," Adrianna explained. "Reporting for duty?"

"Haven't seen him up here for a few hours," Sizemore said, his breathy voice thick with a Colonial accent. He looked to the ceiling, expectant. "Commandant?"

The ship's sophisticated Naval intelligence flickered the lights in confirmation before its booming bass voice responded. "Yes, Officer Sizemore?"

"Any lingering directives for Lieutenant Riley?"

"No directives," the Commandant said, "but there is a message received from Sol marked for her attention."

"Hit me," Adrianna ordered, bouncing nervously on the balls of her feet.

Her heads up display flickered and Sizemore looked away—as her eyes undoubtedly did something freaky. The eyes were windows to the soul, so went the old saying, and Orbital implants could project all kinds of mission-critical data right into the backside of their cornea. From the outside, that had to be right strange to look at.

Adrianna had seen it for the first time when she was twelve years old back at the Academy, when her instructors were reviewing lesson plans. It looked like their brains were shorting out.

The Commandant loaded her message up and she sifted through it by just thinking. A simple text message beamed through the many Jump points out past Edgewater and Backwater Stations, all the way to the Boolean Edge. Didn't even bother to make it a video.

Which made the message brutally brief:

Marcus Riley, Colonel
Master and Commander Local Allied Forces,
Colony HR-2056.
Status update:

KIA.

Her brother. Just nineteen. And that was as old as he'd ever get.

THREE YEARS AGO...

SHE REMEMBERED BEING TERRIFIED, hungry, and half-deaf. Running an obstacle course while a man in a wide-brimmed hat screamed obscenities at you was one thing, but doing so while thirty caliber solid copper slugs snapped past your ear? It was a potent combination that released just about every stored chemical in the body.

And she had gotten a terrible seat. There was a colonel with a very shiny head in front of her. Did he buff that thing before going out in public? Get out a rag and a little spit, give it that extra bit of reflection just to torment the people he'd encounter throughout a day? It was much too glossy to be naturally occurring.

Adrianna sat almost a hundred feet in the air with the glittering colonel and about two hundred other civilians and military officials safely behind a thick panel of two-inch glass. Speakers on either side of them carefully curated which sounds to play from the course below so as not to bewilder and overwhelm the viewing public.

An average of 16.4 cadets were killed in this exercise every year, all observed by the Empire's rich and powerful.

Far below Adrianna's observation deck, a hundred cadets from Holkstad Academy were being put through their final paces. They wore gray fitted jumpsuits with thin blue ropes stitched on their left shoulder. They wore frayed flat caps and torn uniforms. Some boys had their early merit badges pinned to their chest.

Adrianna shook her head at that choice. There may be a couple dozen important heads looking down at them now, but this was the wrong day to bring out the show and tell.

Among the Holkstad cadets was her brother, the short and sinewy Marcus Riley. Her optical implant found the young man with ease: chin pointed high and chest puffed out. He didn't exactly blend in with the rest of the cadets. Older than most of his class but a full six inches shorter than either of his neighbors—that did nothing to dim the hungry glow of his brown eyes.

They had granted Adrianna special leave to appear for his test. She herself had graduated not four years before and it seemed that they hadn't updated a single syllable of the test since. But it was rather strange to be seated in an elevated pillbox while listening to a fresh-faced corn-fed officer in possibly the bluest shoes on Earth condescend to the gathered civilians in the box.

The man didn't spare a single glance for those Naval in attendance. His speech was for the Ministry and Dunsweir officials, that they may notice him and cherry-pick him for some research or press division in the Home Office.

Adrianna's attention was focused on the ground where the drill instructor was leading the cadets in some opening calisthenics. She had graduated and received four separate surgeries to complete her augmentations. These cadets didn't have any of that yet, so getting the muscles warmed up was very important.

Marcus was sweating hard, pushing breath with puffed cheeks

and unblinking focus. Ever since they were little, they'd wanted to be soldiers, be elite—be Oskie. Be better than flesh and blood.

Adrianna had been the first. And here was Marcus's chance to do the same. Maybe his last chance.

"This is a live-fire exercise," the aww shucks lieutenant began, "to determine if the cadets below you can achieve the goals that Orbital Strike Command asks of its members. Surgical augmentation will give them the body that can complete the task; we need to know if they have the will for it."

Adrianna allowed herself a little snicker—and the graceful, bony hand of Admiral Winnifred Grace fell on her shoulder. She didn't have to speak loudly. "Keep it together, Lieutenant."

"You think the brown nose is going to explain how guns work next?"

"Keep. It. Together."

Graduation itself was a misnomer, anyway. There was an entire year of training to follow as they recovered from 'graduation.' But those cadets would now be considered full and proper Oskies. Those selected from the crop today would join members from other classes in a series of surgeries to enhance and advance their bodies. It was a perilous set of procedures, as silksteel casings and computer chips were adhered to the nervous system and bones, motors and micro-threading to the muscles, and coolant pumps to their cardiovascular system.

Sometimes the body just rejected the implants.

Lieutenant Kiss Ass pulled up a holographic image from his Enti-glas, giving it a quick spin so his captive audience could see every angle. "We'll be deploying the GA-57 Magnetic Accelerator Autonomous Weapons System—or G-MAWS—for today's exercise. Naval Regulars call this machine 'the Screecher.' And I mention this because you should be ready for what you're about to hear."

Only contractors and civilians called it G-MAWS. The Screecher was an advertising term for the suits over in Procurement.

36

Everyone else called it either 'the turret' or the far less affectionate 'Grandma.'

Adrianna remembered her qualifier well enough. Squad-based movement, securing a location and demolition of a target while being dogged by an actual live angry turret system that could see your body heat and fire twelve hundred rounds a minute. It spat molten copper twin barrels with a cyclic rate that made it feel like a beam weapon.

The angry Grandma was loud and violent.

There was a hundred yards of open field for the cadets to make their way across, littered with bunkers, hillocks, and craters. They'd then have to prime a small explosive and detonate the control panel—shutting down the turret. The test boiled down to solving a problem they couldn't reach with limited resources; it was a common condition for seasoned Oskies. Today was the first day they would face those kinds of odds.

They did not design the obstacle course to test bodily ability—but willpower. Not everybody would be cut out for it.

Adrianna watched the GA-57 Grandma creak its way out of its armored housing, deploying its twin barrels forward. A technician was running a pre-check on the weapon before the test began.

The door to the room opened and a small formal retinue entered. Wing-tip shoes and well-tailored suits—and followed by a face that she knew well.

Spymaster Philippe dei Mogglin didn't try to make an impression on people, but he knew it was impossible not to. His giant frame was more than twice the average man with a wide jaw and booming voice. Philippe couldn't avoid attracting attention, but he tried to understate his presence. It was so easy to underestimate him then.

"The, uh..." The lieutenant coughed, struggling to get back on script. But a simple nod from Philippe was enough encouragement. He pulled a holographic image of the turret up for view, exploding out its various parts like he was shilling for investors. "The cadets will be... required to evade this weapon system. The firing chamber on this weapon reaches vacuum pressures in excess of two hundred kilopascals —roughly two entire earth's atmospheres of pressure. That's tough on a piece of metal not meant for the bottom of the ocean. A gasket system allows air to freely pass into the firing chamber, ensuring maximum muzzle velocity and accuracy, but that high-speed air causes a nerve-shattering whistle." Here came the advertising copy. "When the Colonial Dusters hear this thing go off, they know they've stepped in it."

Polite and political chuckles of approval rippled through the crowd. Adrianna rolled her eyes. She'd heard this turret crack off before. She didn't want to be downrange to catch it, and she had been on more than a few professional occasions. It was as much a weapon of terror as one of death.

She made note that Philippe wasn't laughing along with the rest of the nobility.

The drill instructor below shouted at a nearby cadet with a blue rope stitched to their shoulder. "You want to be elite, ROC?" ROC—Recruit Officer Candidate, also the platoon leader.

"Yes sir, I do, sir!"

"You think you're special, ROC?"

"Yes sir, I am, sir!"

"You got quality?! You got fire?! *Show me* you are elite!"

The ROC gave a sharp wolf-whistle and the cadets all dropped their calisthenics and sprinted for the starting line of the course, reforming into ranks there. The drill sergeant stepped off to one side, joining a row of assessors and judges. Made sense—this was as much his exam as theirs.

"Our Service is to the People!" The instructor called, pointing at the box of onlookers.

And Adrianna mumbled along. "For they are the Kings."

"Our Service is to the Crown!"

"For he is the Sword!"

"Our Service is to Each Other!"

"For we are the Shield!"

There was no warning. But being it was Marcus' third time—he knew it was coming and had spread the word. A good half of the cadets were already falling into a prone position as soon as the chant was over.

Some of the rookies weren't so fast on their feet.

The very first test the Academy wanted to confirm was on the little hairs on the back of your neck. Could you sense danger without seeing it? They were here to test not strength or agility, but decision making under fire.

And gunfire rarely announced itself.

The GA-57 cut loose on the exposed column of cadets. There was a simple hum as the magnets charged—and then the scream came, the barrels chugging back and forth. The first cadet to be hit was the blue-roped ROC. He hadn't moved from his spot. And he exploded like red ribbons and dry confetti.

Marcus was already leading a small team forward, shouting over the shrill whine of the turret.

A ricochet skipped up to the pillbox, striking one side and sending spiderwebs creeping along the glass. Which was exactly why the onlookers were in a hardened bunker. The light snap sound made the civilians ooh and aah, and the veterans tensed up in their seats.

Adrianna felt her implants kick alive in response and the whole fight slowed down before her. She saw each whistling blast from the turret, the gouts of flaming gases escaping from the barrel. She saw the dirt tossed in the air, hanging like picturesque snow fall, the high-speed rounds chewing dirt and man alike.

She didn't remember this part of her own test. It was more like sense memory. Chaos, screaming, running, and an explosion that finally ended it. It all happened so fast and so brutally. Now, with the assistance of a vantage point and surgical implants, she had a very clear view of the events and she could watch it play out beat for beat.

The cadets had broken into three teams and pushed in a classic trident move. One squad would move, drawing the turrets' attention. They'd shelter in place while the other squads moved up, utilizing the turret's narrow field of focus against it.

Marcus' team had made it halfway across the field, demo charge in hand, but some cadets were lagging behind, suppressed by the gun turret, unable to move.

Crying. Screaming. One of them was dead, laying in their class-mate's laps, blood gushing over legs and hands.

She couldn't hear the worst of it, but she could lipread him calling for his mother.

How Marcus heard their screams over the banshee of the turret, she'd never know. But Marcus did, and he perked up, looking back across the field at the cadets taking shelter.

This was a golden opportunity. The turret was preoccupied with easy prey. Push, get the bomb in place. He could save them by neutralizing the threat. If they die, they die, but the mission gets done!

Adrianna would have sworn in front of a full court that Marcus looked right at her, up to the bunker and right at her. There was no way he'd be able to make out her face over that distance, not without implants like hers. But the longer he stared, the more his resolve grew.

"No! What are you doing?" Adrianna cursed under her breath. Admiral Grace laid a hand on her shoulder, trying to quiet her niece.

But they all had something to gasp at soon after. Marcus turned to his team, issuing some orders. There was dispute, confusion, but he barked at them and they continued on. Without him.

Because Marcus ran backward towards the trapped cadets.

Philippe sat forward in his seat, eyes narrowed. What was this little brat doing?

The turret took notice as well, screaming off a new set of rounds at Marcus as he slid into position with the lost cadets. He got them low, got them talking.

And the turret grew disinterested. A group of cadets lunged from cover, hoping to use Marcus's theatrics as cover. The turret snapped over, putting thirty caliber slugs through center mass. The kids dropped into the dirt, writhing and twisting.

And Adrianna heard Philippe scoff.

The turret had engaged a new column and Marcus dragged his frightened cadets to the safety of a larger bunker. He got them settled, squared, and then leapt forward back to his team, dodging super-heated copper slugs the whole way.

Boots on steel. She heard it like it was louder than the gunfire, the wrong pitch and timbre. Right now? Someone was walking, here in the bunker.

The civilians hadn't noticed him get up. But Adrianna tracked the disgruntled Philippe already halfway out the door. Even his entourage was confused, looking at each other with shrugs.

The old Spymaster didn't get to see Marcus's team successfully detonate their charge and end the test. Orders followed had won the day and Marcus had saved a few lives while he was at it. Seemed like a good and successful test. Some civilians popped champagne, hugged and cried. Their little boys and girls were going to become Oskies. Even those that fell did so in service to the Empire and the Pilgrim. Any tears being spent were tinged with a kind of bitter patriotism.

But not Adrianna. She looked back at her uncharacteristically quiet aunt. The admiral's lips drew tight and her eyes were full of dread.

"I give it an hour before we're called to his office," the admiral said. "Bring your dress uniform, would you?"

"For the Spymaster?" Adrianna asked.

Admiral Grace looked down, picking at the dirt under her finger-nails. "I need you to look strong for your brother now. 'Cause he's about to be discharged."

***

Ministry offices always smelled like citrus, all sharp acid tingling her nose. It was the cleaner that was used to wipe down every surface like it would grow treason if left unchecked. The featureless halls stretched to infinity in both directions with a band of dark wood at waist-height.

A minister's office had the same look as the Consul's from outside. Inside, of course, would be an entirely different matter. She'd seen big and small, heavily ornamented and ostentatious, and those that were pure function, exposed hardware and steel components. She'd even seen one done up as a small apartment, as the owner only went to his actual home about once a week.

Adrianna sat outside the Spymaster's office, her cap folded up in her hands. Marcus stood opposite her, hands flat against his sides, and halfway to animalistic panic. The mud and blood still darkened his fingernails.

"Why'd you do it, Marcus?" she asked him. Not a judgment, and he knew her well enough to not take it as one.

He huffed, his lip twitching. Not a smile. Not even recognition, really. "Couldn't just watch, Anna. Would you?"

Would she? Would she have even had the wherewithal to look back?

They wouldn't punish him for saving somebody's life—would they?

Marcus just stared at the minister's door, likely trying to picture what was going on inside. Adrianna didn't have to guess. Spymaster Philippe and Admiral Grace were whisper-fighting inside.

They could try to keep their voices down, keep it private from the officers in the hallway, but Adrianna's implants made true privacy impossible. The Empire had spent a pretty penny turning her into an intelligence-gathering and rebel-smashing super soldier; she could practically hear their thoughts. They were busily debating whether they should give Marcus the same treatment.

Well...debate might have been a charitable word for it.

"For a logistics officer, admiral, you're not reading enough into the mathematics of it. To save two people, he killed three and risked a helluva lot more than that. Ignored his orders, the parameters of the exercise—"

"Seventeen died on the course last year alone. That field is no stranger to blood."

"That's a spectacularly narrow-minded view. Holkstad doesn't train them to die on that patch of dirt just because some teenager decides he knows better than his orders—"

"Of course you do. This field, the next field. You know a whole lot of Oskies sipping gin and tonic on the porch of their mountain cabin? They die in theater doing the Empire's will. Every single one and those kids know it! It's what they signed up for."

Adrianna thumbed the Orchid insignia on the brow of her cap: a single silver flower. The symbol of the Dunsweir family and of a united Gnostic Empire. A young Marcus had a made a hat of tin and scraps of fabric. He had stapled a drawing of the patriotic image to his shirt.

They'd fought rebels and monsters and spies and dragons. More than a few dragons. Slay the evil, save the world. Medals, commendations from kings and queens. He had a pet lizard man at one point.

So many nostalgic homespun legends—two children squaring off with a galaxy filled with evil. And they did it together. He'd worked so hard to follow her into the Service. And here he now stood, sweating clean through his tunic.

"You train these young people to be adaptable in the field, Phillipe. If that unsettles you, maybe you should adjust their curriculum."

"We train them to follow orders." Philippe was getting exasperated with how long this conversation was continuing. "Moral flexibility is a *hazard* of our profession. It's not a feature, admiral. The orders are gospel."

"And they shall be called to write their own verse."

Philippe sneered at that, lips smacking. "We don't decide what's right in Orbital Strike, admiral. That's the Consul, the Dunsweir, and the Pilgrim. *We* make it a point to not be the center of attention."

"Careful, Philippe. That sounded almost parallel to sedition."

Those words from the admiral sent a fresh shock through Adrianna's blood. What was Aunt Winny thinking?!

But Philippe didn't rise to the bait. "Just the facts as I see them, admiral. I see spotlights and high fashion and weekly broadcasted speeches; I don't assume that person is trying to lay low."

"Got a beef with Caldwell I don't about?"

Philippe's desk creaked as he leaned forward. "Do you really think Marcus Riley saves those cadets if no one was watching? Play the moment back, admiral. He looked at the *audience* before he did what he did. He wants to play hero, but only when we're watching. If there hadn't been two hundred people in the grandstands, he'd have taken that objective like any other day. But he had to play to the crowd. He's not a soldier, he's a diva, and I don't need any of those."

Adrianna shriveled at that, resetting her cap on her head and sitting up straight.

Marcus saw that. "What? Anna? What're they saying?"

She didn't answer him. All Marcus ever wanted was to make the world safer. And now? He may not even get to serve.

"Philippe, he's been held back twice already. He cleared the target. What more do you want from him?"

"Cleared it at *unnecessary* cost," Philippe hissed. "Human cost. Orbital is not a humanitarian service. We strike hard and fast. We save lives by deleting threats. He wants to be a soldier in Orbital Strike, he needs to be capable of making that distinction! His team was not the objective. Now stop trying to convince me you're right and get around to your sales pitch, admiral."

Admiral Winnifred Grace took a deep breath, anchoring herself. "You want additional resources in the field to combat emerging threats in the Reaches?"

"Yes," Philippe growled.

"Supply & Logistics is prepared to agree with your proposal at next week's briefing on Boolean counter-terrorism."

"In exchange for what?"

"Duty and love to the Flag and the People?"

"In exchange for *what*, admiral? Say the words."

"Give Marcus Riley his commission to the Oskies and you'll have my full support."

Philippe snorted at that flagrant quid pro quo, but he didn't say no. "Because he's your nephew?"

"Because the Duke of Favors can spare me one for a change."

Adrianna heard Philippe settle into his chair, the leather creaking with his weight. "He may not survive the surgeries. And I cannot promise him a prestigious posting."

Admiral Grace nodded, accepting that requirement. "What he does with the Orchid is going to be entirely his own doing. I just want a good officer given a fair chance."

"Yes, because this conversation has the unmistakable air of 'fairness.'" Philippe's thick fingers clunked away on a holographic display, the heavy sounds of haptic feedback clipping the air. He must like the kinetic feel of it pushing back on him. "I'll make arrangements for him."

Admiral Grace stood up, sweeping her cap back on her head. "Thank you, minister."

As Admiral Grace turned to leave, Philippe called to her exposed back. "This whole conversation—"

"Never happened?" the Admiral asked.

"Has been *recorded*, admiral. Marcus Riley better be everything you think he can be."

The Admiral didn't give Philippe another sound bite. She just smiled and turned for the door. The latch clicked, the security system released, and she stepped out into the hall.

Adrianna stood up—which only sent a shiver down Marcus' spine. He stood high like he was reaching for the roof with the crown of his head.

The door swung open and Admiral Grace looked at the two young officers. A flash of warmth, and then momentary dread. What had she just done? Was it worth it?

And then she smiled. But it wasn't a happy one. "Your parents would be proud." And with a great shame, Admiral Grace lowered her head and stomped down the eternal hallway, leaving Adrianna and Marcus standing in parade rest.

Adrianna looked toward the office as the door slid closed. Her eyes caught the Spymaster's over his steepled fingers. He was considering the meeting, the deal—and young Adrianna too. But the door clicked shut, blocking the Duke of Favors from her view.

She exhaled. Her brother wanted to be an Oskie. And he would be one now.

CHAPTER
FOUR

PRESENT DAY

SHE ENJOYED SITTING by the reactor. The sounds of the ship faded away behind its distant thrum, a small star cooking away underneath a silksteel shell at her back. Almost one hundred percent efficiency meant the only radiation it gave off was a pleasant warmth that baked against her back and warmed her bones.

And probably edited her genome with loosely contained gamma.

But right now, she felt cold. She held Marcus' flat cap between her fingers, the one he'd made as a boy with a cheap stencil of Imperial glory stapled to the brim and his kid name for her scrawled underneath: Anna. There hadn't been room for the first half of her name.

Nobody else called her Anna. Not her parents, her aunt or uncles. Her instructors just called her Riley.

Only Marcus called her Anna...

Little Marcus. He could've joined the Navy, been a Regular

soldier like any other; maybe join the Engineering Corps to build some bridges or serve the Diplomatic Corps building narratives; sidestep over to the Academie Pacem and become a Cleric of Justice. He'd always loved those cop dramas growing up. The world was full of bad guys and the select few good that stood against them.

There had been so many ways to serve.

Instead, he went to Holkstad like his big sister. He became Orbital. He even earned a command of his very own. A little frontiersman.

He was a ranked chess player; he wrote bad poetry about this one girl in his graduating class; he snorted when he laughed.

And in thirteen simple words...he was dead. No pictures, no explanation. Just gone.

Her chest throbbed, a line of sweat carving its way down her collarbone. She could see the faint waft of steam climbing off the back of her hand as the sweat burned off. It made wonderful little patterns that pulled upward toward the ceiling.

She kept time with the thud of her heartbeat as she drew shapes in the air. like a conductor of some ghostly orchestra. One, two, three...

Nineteen years old. Now she'd have to remember him for longer than she had known him.

She heard Sizemore's clunky boots clomping down the hallway, but it was a good moment before she heard the soft and controlled footfalls of the captain following in tow. The ship's engineer pointed Graccus toward the reactor where she sat. And the captain nodded his thanks. "Can you give us the room, Officer?"

More than happy to, the engineer took two steps back and cranked the door shut.

Graccus let his head crane backward, taking in the vaulted dome overhead that would contain any accident with the smaller sphere in the center. He traced his way down to the knobby shell of the reactor itself in the center of the room and its asymmetric attachments. Two great conduits reached down to the eggshell of doom, siphoning off the fusion power the frigate needed to run everything. A catwalk wrapped around the core, letting the technicians access whatever they needed to.

Finally, Graccus let his eyes settle on Adrianna, slumped beside the reactor with one leg pulled tight to her chest. He didn't force a smile or twist into a frown, no tension to his lip or wrinkle to his brow. But his voice had a cautionary softness: "I wanted to talk to you before you read that."

And what was he going to say? Was he going to break the news in twenty words instead of thirteen? Maybe take fifty, really smooth it over?

"Everything alright with Callum?" she asked.

"I'll get him anchored," Graccus assured her. "Right now, I'm taking care of you."

"I'm fine, sir."

"You're overheating."

"I said I'm fine."

Graccus bludgeoned with the obvious. "Lieutenant, that wasn't a question. You're steaming while sitting on the damn *floor*."

It wasn't terrible advice. The machines in her body were cooking hot and she wasn't even doing anything. Chemical triggers and subconscious panic told everything to run at full bore. Doctors called it the sabertooth response.

But evolution had dictated a very precise window for sustainable life. Living with a persistent fever had very lasting effects. Anxiety made her blood vessels contract.

She needed a cold shower. Now. May even help with the rising panic.

But she couldn't make herself get up. Her scalp burned, a pulsing wave of frustration every time she pictured Marcus's face. She couldn't make herself move or even put her hand to the steel grating she sat on. She just swayed it back and forth in the air, watching the steam.

Maybe calm was somewhere in those clouds.

ALLEN IVERS

Graccus sighed, gearing up to do this the hard way. "Your brother was where he wasn't supposed to be. That's the truth."

"He was *supposed* to be with us in the Boolean," Adrianna groused. "He was Orbital; he got the orders just like we all did. But he chose to hold his post."

"Yeah, he *chose*," Graccus pointed out. "Violating like eight articles of his Oath. He stayed put, defended his colony. Only 'thank you' he was going to get? A demerit, demotion, a firing squad? He was very much on his own in a place he chose to be."

Chose it. Like it was his fault. But Adrianna just bit her lip, keeping her anger locked away.

"He drafted up a Capital militia, Riley. That's the truth of it."

Adrianna perked up at that, raising her head. "Capitals?"

Graccus nodded. "That's right. He took convicts–those serving life sentences in labor camps–and he gave them guns to fight his enemies. What happened next was inevitable."

"How do you know all this?" Adrianna asked. There was a second question implied: wasn't this classified? If Adrianna was supposed to know, surely it would have been in that memo. And here the captain was, spilling all the redacted tea all over the floor.

"I know everything." Because he liked to cultivate a persona of omniscience.

"So...the Capitals rebelled?" she asked.

"Well, no, the *colony* rebelled," Graccus emphasized. "See, Riley, I'm going to break this rose-colored glass for you right now: no matter how you remember him, Marcus Riley turned out to be neither a fair nor gentle leader. He commanded respect from a position of power, flexing it whenever he could, and when that power started to erode, he just pressed harder. Oskies are not any better than fleshy folk, no matter what Callum or Yurek might say. No amount of augmentation, training, or speed can make up for bad decision making. You just end up being stupid faster. See, with the Boolean Conflict turning to a close, your brother was shit out of luck. Reinforcements were on the way. All those soldiers that got whisked away from him? They were coming back. But he still *played* like they were out on the edge, anything to justify his fantasy. Colonel Marcus Riley didn't want to put the hero flag down. And so his people put it down for him."

She couldn't look up at him. She couldn't entertain this story.

But Graccus would not let her ignore it. He leaned over her, pressing the facts down into her like molds to clay. "He *wasn't* murdered, Riley. He got dead. Pound that into your skull right now before something else sets in."

Murdered. Someone had killed her brother and Graccus was in here acting like he'd been in some kind of accident. "That the official line, sir? Murder?"

Graccus sighed, exasperated with her takeaway. "Official line is an outstanding officer was murdered by Capital criminals in open revolt. Far as the Home Office is concerned, that's all that matters. How we behave is irrelevant; you don't get to kill Imperial officers when the mood strikes. Ministry has pretty strong opinions about that."

That had stank to high hell, so Graccus had gone sniffing around. And he found dirt. Whenever something looked squeaky clean, there was always dirt swept under a nearby rug.

But Graccus wasn't done. "I'm telling you this because they *won't*. And it's your brother. You deserve the truth. Not...not whatever they give you."

Now that was a loaded sentiment, but Adrianna didn't really care to be exploring it right now. She was angry. Fuming, boiling. And Graccus just came in to tell her that there was nowhere to go with that anger, nowhere that would make her feel better. She wanted to go find her brother's killer...only to find out that her brother was the aggressor.

Now what was she to do with all this sour in her gut? The tremors in her hand?

Adrianna sighed. "For what it's worth, I'm sorry about the stakeout. Won't happen again."

Graccus stared at her for a few seconds, blinking incredulously.

"You think I deep sixed your ass for saving a kid's life yesterday? Lieutenant, I've never been more proud of you in my life. That was damn fine work—stuff we don't see often in our vocation."

"A fair fight?"

"As opposed to what?"

"I don't know. They don't typically get to see us coming, for one."

The captain studied her for a moment. "Kindness, lieutenant. You showed kindness. Your instinct was to screw the mission, screw institutional priorities, and protect an innocent person. Not enough of us do that anymore."

Adrianna huffed, remembering the words of the Oskie creed. "Our Service is to the People..."

"For They are the Kings," Graccus finished, with punctuation from a pointed finger. "That's not a club password. You don't start every day with those words because the Ministry likes the melody. You're supposed to think about it every day."

She couldn't listen to another patronizing word out of his self-righteous mouth. "I screwed up, I get it. I busted our cover, I ignored your orders, and I leapt in chin first. Just like my brother. Going to end up jus' like him. Is that all, sir?"

He was hunched over, head tilted, and half her size...but Graccus darkened and his voice filled the room like he suddenly found where they'd stored the rest of his voice, somewhere deep in his chest. "You really going to take that tone with me, lieutenant?"

Oops. That might've been a bit out of pocket. "No, sir," she apologized.

"You're not your brother," Graccus corrected. "Marcus was a walking textbook. In three years, he made colonel and was commanding his own post, while you're seven years deep and still a butterbar." He flicked his finger against the simple yellow stripe and orchid on her collar. Marcus would've had a full three flowers adorning his. "That's not because he had a brown-nosing gene in him that somehow skipped you."

"This is a really strange pep talk, sir," Adrianna remarked.

"Marcus never doubted his ability for a second. Why do you?"

"Well, my parents were very particular," Adrianna quipped, dry and flat-faced.

Graccus' face soured. "He killed his own men, y'know. Governor of the colony too. Any Statesmen, Oskies that stood up to him. Anybody who disagreed. He *should've* been put down. And despite all that, the Navy is going to go over there, guns blazing."

Adrianna swallowed that statement, choosing instead to pick at the grime on the catwalk than meet her captain's gaze. She knew he made sense, real logical sense. But all she could think of was coming into orbit over the people that killed her brother, the celestial silhouette of an Eisenclad dreadnought spreading fear through the population. Regret, remorse, cries for mercy, hailing up to them like prayer.

And it would sound like songbirds to her ear. "There's a response scenario in play?" Adrianna asked.

Graccus popped up to his full height, sharp and snappy. "Why? You want in?"

"Damn right I do."

"Well, you're not going to get to."

Adrianna stood up, drawing herself up to her full height. "Captain, how did you think this conversation was going to end?"

"With the Ministry of Civil Defense Office of Personnel & Management," Graccus said. "A Schedule DD 256. It's already been submitted. You're joining the 1st Civilian Division, lieutenant."

Discharge. Adrianna's stomach fell into her shoes.

Orbitals died in Service, either on the operating table or on a battlefield. Dying in Service meant a guaranteed spot on the Sojourn, to walk with the Pilgrim through all of time and space. If she went back to being Citizen Riley...

The discharge certification might say 'honorable', but nobody at any end of the Empire saw it that way.

Graccus saw the wave of nausea hit her, and he didn't give a damn. "You're not going to be demoted this time, lieutenant. You're not going to be given a scrub duty. But you *are* going to be confined to the ship. And when we get back to dry dock...you're going home."

No. No! This *was* home. And he was just going to eject her like the rest of the garbage?!

She watched his back as he stalked to the door. "Sir, I don't understand," she called after him.

"Your memo wasn't the only memo we got, lieutenant. I got my own orders direct from Admiral Grace herself."

"My Aunt is Naval Logistics. She doesn't have jurisdiction over Orbital!"

"No," Graccus agreed, "but I owe her a favor—and I think she's right."

"She's right?" Adrianna blurted. Admiral Grace, with her chess boards and her tea ceremonies and hokey wisdom—

"*Yes!*" Graccus said, with the crooked eyebrow and infuriating heft of something being obvious. "You're an excellent soldier, Riley, but you're impulsive, emotionally compromised, empathetic."

"Because I saved a kid?!"

That was one liberty too many. Graccus exploded at her. "I don't care about the kid, Riley! I don't care what Home Office thinks, what Admiral Grace thinks! And Philippe dei Mogglin doesn't know your name; he doesn't give a *damn*! But here's what I know: your family has given enough blood to the Empire and to the Pilgrim. If the great big tour guide in the sky wants you so bad, he'll just have to get you the old-fashioned way. By waiting his damn turn!"

If they went through with this, what would she even be? She'd never find Marcus's killer. She'd never see Vivian or Voight ever again. All because Aunt Winny got cold feet?! "I want to talk to Admiral Grace."

"You'll get to," Graccus promised, "just as soon as we make Gateway. She'll be waiting with half a dozen ministers ready to debrief you."

"This isn't right, captain!"

Graccus hung in the doorway like the simple statement caught his conscience flat footed. "It may not feel that way. But when you live to be sixty-eight, you'll have outlived me twice over. You might feel differently then."

"Sir—"

"Your Service is at an end, Riley."

Her skin burned. Her heart screamed. And her world got foggy. "He was *nineteen*..."

Graccus nodded, his eyes falling away to study the floor. "Too many of 'em are."

And he shut the door. On the conversation—and her career.

IT WAS a long and strange two weeks. Nobody said anything about it. Nobody even looked at her differently. Maybe they didn't know. She had no reason to believe that Graccus had told anyone, so she hadn't either. The Vees were as casual as ever. Even Sizemore was busy with his usual tasks, not a care in the world.

Graccus managed to be out of sight any time she came into the room. Probably not wanting to re-litigate the issue and after three days, she stopped trying to find him. The other Oskies, mainly Callum & Yurek: they may not have been told, but they knew. It was as if their whole demeanor shifted backward ten feet, observing her through frosted glass.

Like she was on display.

Space was big and empty, so even at high speeds, ships took periods of weeks before they got anywhere. And if anything was going to happen, it would be around two types of celestial objects: the first were planets, stations, shipyards, places with lots of people gathered.

The second was Jump Points.

She knew how long it was from the Backwater Jump Point back to the major network: sixteen days of open cruising. So on day fifteen, the announcement caught her off-guard. When it came, she was back with the Regulars in their thin berth, absorbing their usual sandpaper charisma. They didn't know or didn't care where she was going—only that she was with them.

"Place your bets! Place your bets! All manner of coin or credit is accepted, here at the House of Poor Decision Making!" Corporal Josef Gallantine was a gregarious fellow who looked like they had stretched him on a rack as a child. His once buzzed hair had grown out into bouncy brown curls. The gangly oaf was all giggles as he jogged up and down the barracks in oversized boots, collecting from his colleagues: money, valuables, promissory notes. Anything people had he would take for the pot.

Gallantine, being the oddsmaker, had Adrianna twenty to one. She was almost offended. Suppose he had to lure in his colleagues' money somehow.

Staff Sergeant Tatanka Mastiff stood by the door, the big leather-neck playing adult for a room full of idiotic children. The human brick, with his shaved head and brown pocked skin, watched the crowd with a bittersweet curl to his lip. He already had the first aid kit out and ready, surveying the room of children for any sterling example of stupid or reckless. Quiet lord of all he could see. He neither took part in the lunacy, nor did he put a stop to it.

All of this energy abuzz because somebody had gotten both bored and a little too big for his britches.

Private Stefan Holt had just come off medical reserve—had his left arm blown off at the elbow in the early days of the Boolean Conflict—and he had just redeployed to the *Erinyes* with his new metal replacement in time for the whole affair to be over. The private spoke soft but direct and he wore the slenderness of his youth well, not as disproportionate and flailing as Gallantine. Instead, Holt looked more innocent, soft—except for the gnarled scar that peeked out from under the steel of his augment.

Decked out with the very best of new shiny chrome, one of his peers had deigned to suggest that the new robo-private could best the reigning champion Adrianna in a straight arm curling contest. He had a steel arm; she was confident in her Aug-Four ranking.

Nobody in the room knew that Aug-Four meant, really. It just sounded impressive to their thick skulls. She had once tried to explain the four separate surgeries she'd undergone to receive her many varied augmentations, all of them subtle and hidden underneath her skin. But for some surgical scarring, she looked like any other very impressive-muscled woman. The grunts bet that metal would beat flesh.

It did. She was going to wipe the floor with this poor kid.

The private had stepped up to the challenge of his peers with confidence and spirit. He was the more exterior and visible machine than she was, after all, but Adrianna wasn't concerned. He was a few slots further down on the tech tree.

Holt twirled his arm, rotating it in the unnatural way only a machine could, with a flat stare, like he could intimidate her. And she matched that stare with an almost doe-like innocence.

Two privates worked to fill ammo cans for each competitor with as much dead weight as they could find: lead bricks, spare armor plates, spent batteries. They meticulously shook the cans every few seconds, trying to level off the contents to squeak in more debris. A corporal was busily weighing the different canisters to be sure they were equal, passing them back if they needed adjustment.

Someone gave Holt a good shoulder massage, loosening him up. The private leaned forward, bowing his head but never breaking eye contact. Adrianna watched as he fished a necklace out from under his collar.

She recognized the pattern: a flat circle, with a bar through the center, that split once and split again, until it had fanned all the way out to fill the opposing side of the amulet. It was the official emblem of the Pilgrim and the Dunsweir: many roads becoming one, one road becoming many.

It was his silent invitation, in good sport, to a pre-game prayer. She obliged him, nodding, and the room fell quiet.

"Bless our feet, for the road is long," the private intoned. "Bless our shoulders, for our burdens are heavy."

Adrianna knew the words like they'd been tattooed on her eyelids. The room mostly kept quiet, but a few muttered along with him.

Satisfied in the benediction, Holt squared up with Adrianna, spreading his legs to place his boots toe to toe with hers. He rolled up the sleeve on his utility tunic, exposing the barest hint of the gnarled stump his sleek augment had been fused to—the most elite of battle-scars. The sight drew a handful of spirited crows from the audience.

Adrianna did a spot measurement of her weight, tapping its handle with two fingers: sixty-two and a half pounds, give or take.

"Purses are now closed and we ask you to please take your seats! We are ready for the action to begin!" Gallantine's voice broke the silence. He held both arms in the air, the display of his Entiglas flashing a comical padlock symbol. "Okay, three-two-one: drop, shock, and rock!"

Adrianna lifted her box like it was empty and the look on Holt's face was an immediate tell: he knew exactly how much he had fucked up. Someone had suckered him into something he had no hope of surviving.

The metal and servos in his prosthetic would do just fine with the load, but his metal arm was still connected to an entirely fleshy body that had limits of its own. His bicep, shoulder, back—they were all blood and sinew. And those pieces did not have the strength his arm did.

Adrianna's body was modified through and through.

Of course, he would not beat an Oskie in a contest of strength. But he was also too pumped full of testosterone to acknowledge the better angels that he prayed to. And so, off they went, pumping iron and assessing life choices.

"How are you holding up, private?" Adrianna asked, her arm warming up with gossamer strands of yellow under her skin.

Holt was too gassed to answer, neck strained and veins popping as he tried to lift the can for the tenth time. The prosthetic was fine; it was his shoulder that was about to snap off.

That's when they were rudely interrupted by a surprise announcement over the PA. "All hands—stand by for Jump Prep. Stand by for Jump Prep."

The words hit Adrianna's ear, and she reached over to pluck the heavy ammo can out of Holt's grasp. Freed of his load, the poor, sweating infantryman curled around his arm and bleated like an injured sheep. And the whoops and hollers in the room that came forth, playful and empty accusations she had cheated, while others laughed at Holt's crumpled form. She was standing. He was not—game, set, match.

But Adrianna didn't stop to worry about him. She set the two steel boxes aside, eyes turned up to the ceiling.

Jump Prep? A day early? Physics didn't bend out of convenience, not even for Spymaster Philippe. Fifteen days instead of sixteen meant...they weren't going home just yet.

"Riley?" Mastiff asked a lot, using just her name.

"Nobody tells me nothin' anymore."

He raised a bushy eyebrow. "Nobody's talking? Or are you not asking?"

Point taken. She wiped the slight sheen off her forehead with a rag, casually tossing it to the spent private huffing and puffing on the floor. "Might want to get him cleaned up. I'll see what's going on."

Mastiff nodded, dragging Holt off for a quick infantry pick-me-up, while Adrianna pushed forward. She stomped up through the galley. The tables were all collapsed into the floor in preparation and a few deck officers were still clearing out—including Vivian.

"Bannister! What the hell?"

Vivian looked back at her. "You haven't heard?"

No, she hadn't, because who had cause to tell her anything? But Adrianna just shook her head.

"Priority Message," Vivian explained. "The *Erinyes* has one more stop."

"They say where?"

"Concordia."

"Oh man," Adrianna groaned. "They just got this ship! Now we're going to slalom through the Exeter Nebula?"

"Voight will take care of us," Vivian assured her.

Adrianna knew the planet, though she'd never been. It was friendly territory, no pirate antics—but more than a few natural hazards for careless space travelers. Statistically, they didn't lose any more ships than any other major hyperlane, but that didn't cut into the mysticism of the nebula and the ships that went missing inside it.

What possible reason could the Home Office have to force this kind of sidestep?

The Jump Deck itself was pretty well packed. Half the crew must have been up here. And Graccus Ontarim was at his command post, looming over the sapphire holographic display. One great arm of the Milky Way Galaxy swept away before him, further and further away from the safety of Sol, the far-flung ends of the Empire where colonists made their stand against the elements: the Galactic Reaches.

Vivian slipped off to take her post, leaving Adrianna alone. But she felt the warm and firm grab of sausage fingers pull her to one side.

"Commander Remus," Adrianna addressed him without looking at the obvious owner of that unique gorilla grip. "What's the news?"

Callum looked down at her, a gruff authority in his whisper: "You shouldn't even be on the Jump Deck, lieutenant."

Ah. So he knew the big secret, at least. Graccus had told *someone* about the situation. "You're still calling me 'lieutenant?'" she asked, testing that assumption.

His lip twitched in confirmation. "You're still a lieutenant till we get home."

"Not giving me a whole lotta reason to ever go home, then."

And that twitch turned into a warm smile. "Oskies home is in the sky."

Graccus didn't need to shout to take control of a room. His voice seemed to carry from every corner, like he knew just how to project against the back wall and let everyone hear the music. "If you're standing in this room, you've guessed correct. Commandant: tell 'em what they've won."

The booming voice of the Commandant made Graccus seem small. "Priority missive, direct from Minister Caldwell and the Defense Council. Order reads: retask operations to Concordia for Tier One target."

The murmur rippled through the room and Adrianna could hear the news being passed down the ship like a slow motion echo. The Regulars in the very back made a bit more noise than the rest of the crew.

But Graccus had more to say, pinching the hologram to zoom in on the craggy and gray planet: all sharp mountains connected by a giant bridge, platforms that early colonists had built the city upon. A fragmented moon was stuck in orbit. Whatever pieces of it that hadn't been dragged back into the moon, or fallen to the planet, were slowly coalescing into the barest planetary ring.

"This is Concordia," Graccus explained. "Population three hundred sixty-eight thousand twenty-nine. At least a thousand of which were plotting serious attacks on Imperial Power Relays. We had an asset in play to join up with the dissidents and provide intel for counteraction. Who wants to guess what happened to our agent?"

"He disappeared?" Callum asked.

"That would have been good news," Graccus said with a look of distaste. "Word is he's changed teams and took all of his wildly useful intel with him."

Adrianna drew a breath. With that kind of knowledge, five people could do the damage of hundreds.

Callum wasn't satisfied. "We're long overdue for drydock, sir. Gear, munitions, carbon stock: we're stretched thin."

"Make it work. Our intelligence says we don't have time to even stop for bathroom breaks."

"Our intelligence?" Yurek asked from his very edgy position leaning on the wall. "Did we have a whole other guy on the ground to watch the first guy?"

"We do like redundancy over in counterintelligence," Graccus said. Which drew a huff out of Callum, but Graccus ignored that. "This is actionable, not some a spy satellite. We already have boots on the ground. Codename: Janus. And Janus tells us that our asset has targets already picked and they are in motion. Our bad guy knows exactly where to hit to really make it hurt. Hence the urgency."

It was uplifting, comforting, bracing to hear Graccus give a briefing again. The quiet authority in his voice washed away concern and secured them all in simple executive functions: they just had to do what needed to be done, and all the complex stuff up high? That was someone else's problem.

"The portfolio was relayed back to C&C on Gateway and Terra Firma. All parties agree. Nobody else in the neighborhood can get there in time, so we've been reassigned for immediate action on the asset. Extraction for judgment is preferred, but if he gives us no other option, we have clearance to terminate with extreme prejudice." Graccus paused, letting the room internalize that information before moving. "We'll have specific mission briefs for all teams when we hit periapsis, but for the meantime, settle up for the Jump. And get your gear tooled for one more hop."

Dissatisfaction didn't stop Callum from following orders. The commander thumped his hand on the ceiling to punctuate the briefing and he made for the door, triggering the rest of the crew to follow out like he'd blown some kind of block in the plumbing.

Adrianna wormed her way through the crowd, catching up to the big bald head. "You ever been to Concordia?"

"Once," he said.

"When was that?"

"I was born there."

Adrianna wasn't going to take that dismissal. "Well, should I bring a camera, capture any magnificent vistas?"

That got Callum to stop in the hallway, turn and plant both hands into the ceiling with a loud thud. Man had some frustration built up, but he was keeping a lid on it.

Still, every other crew member that passed averted their eyes and kept walking. Not Adrianna. She stood right in front of him and stared into his steely gray eyes. "You're going to need every trigger you have."

"It's an upper city full of merchants," Callum said, "with all the hard labor miners living in the valley below. It's a Reaches colony. Seen one, you've seen 'em all."

"Now that's an exceptionally cynical viewpoint. I better check for myself!"

"Captain says you're skylocked," Callum grunted, with a small curl to his lip. "So you're skylocked, lieutenant."

Somebody coughed as they passed, a subtle reminder that they were not alone. Adrianna took the note, leaning in closer to whisper. "Worried I'm going to go flying rogue again?"

That almost brought a smile to his face, but he fought it back. "Captain's orders."

And the rebellious words were out of her mouth before she had finished the thought in her own head. "Not really, though."

Callum let his head drift to one side, inquisitive and maliciously curious. "Say that again."

Uh oh. That was trouble. Quick. He's waiting. Say something.

But what came out of her mouth was just a useless noise. "Hmm?"

"'Not really the captain's orders?'" He wasn't questioning her over some reckless insubordination—which it was. No, that statement was a revelation he wanted more of.

Well, the captain hadn't put her on restraint or marked the info as need-to-know. And Callum, being a superior officer and her direct superior at that, had asked her a direct question. Was she supposed to lie to him now? Regulations had something to say about that.

Of course, she *was* being discharged already, so what more could they do to her? Strip her name, rank, childhood dream *and* yell at her?

"Admiral Grace heard about my brother," Adrianna said, "and she decided to pull the ripcord on me. Guess she wants to make sure there's somebody left to pass on the gene pool."

Callum blinked, processing that revelation. "Admiral Grace? Not the captain?"

"Captain agreed. Cap'n pulled the plug. But 'twas my aunt that made the call. Like always."

And it was like the blood flowed up into his face, flush to his cheeks and a mild warmth to his brow. "Excuse me, lieutenant." And Callum marched back up the hallway toward the Jump Deck.

He passed Yurek, who himself came sliding up to her. He kept his distance, like he was afraid to get within range of a left hook, as he whispered down a pointed finger. "You're a fire starter. You hear me? You start fires."

"He asked the question!" Adrianna hissed under her breath. "I'm not a liar, Yurek."

"Yeah, we know." And with that, he buzzed off for the rear of the frigate. Whatever was about to happen on the Jump Deck was neither his circus nor his monkeys anyhow.

Adrianna lingered. She could hear the two commanders fighting right up until the Jump.

CHAPTER
SIX

MASTIFF WAS HALFWAY through his review by the time Adrianna made it down to the launch bay. The staff sergeant had his Regulars working through gear and materials. The leatherneck didn't even need to shout anymore, the old bulldog. He could motivate his infantry with a handful of words and a disgusted look.

Most sergeants were loud, abrasive, even violent. Mastiff was quiet. He marched up to Holt, holding the young private's gaze for a moment, like the staffie was trying to psychically light the man on fire. Slowly, Mastiff reached forward to pick Holt's chest rig, sliding two fingers between the straps. Too loose.

Holt got the message and cinched it down tighter.

"Feel like a man?" Mastiff asked.

And Holt's voice cracked. "No, staff sergeant."

"Feel like Regular Navy?"

"I feel like steam rolled shit, staff sergeant."

"That's good. Keep it that way."

The rest of the Regulars were checking battery packs on their Gauss rifles, adjusting sights with a bore-mounted laser, and adjusting the fit on their ceramic armor plates. Gallantine was even unloading and reloading all his magazines; something of a paranoid ritual after a failure to feed on his second hop.

Adrianna sallied up, giving Holt a casual nod. The private stiffened up, now intimately aware that she could fold him half in a very real sense. He might've known how strong she was conceptually, but now he had some more practical experience.

Young guns: they all thought themselves the hottest things on two legs, infantry in particular. That recent attitude adjustment may just keep him alive.

"Chalk four, huddle up!" Adrianna called out as she queued up the mission briefing on her Entiglas and in her heads-up display. In various states of dress and gear, the Regulars formed up around her, jaws slack and boots loose.

It was a briefing. She'd given dozens. But this one felt so strange. Because she wasn't sharing this time; she was telling. They would go and she would have to stay.

And if some didn't come back...

She coughed and forced the words out. "We...got ourselves a Tier One target on Concordia. Intel places him at the Caldera Market Uptown just as we hit orbit. We are smash and grab. Nothing fancy. Captain Ontarim, Lieutenant Commander Remus, Lieutenant Yurek, and Staff Sergeant Mastiff will command the four chalks on the ground."

Some murmurs. Mastiff himself blinked louder than any human in history, but he didn't say anything. Still made Adrianna's throat clench up for a moment.

"Shuttle drops off the Regulars to secure the building exterior, with Icarus Drop Pods bringing in the Orbital. Oskies will hit the structure, storm the interior, while Regulars repel any QRF in the area. *Erinyes* will provide observation and coordination from high orbit. Primary exfil is via shuttle craft from the drop site: where you came from is where you're going. Secondary extract, if needed, is set ten miles south-southwest from the drop zone, where the *Erinyes* will swoop in to provide close fire support in the event we all shit the bed."

Gallantine whispered to his neighbor. "So pack your diapers I guess."

She didn't disagree. "All goes well, mission time from boots down to jets up is no longer than twenty minutes. We're in, we're out."

"ROE?" Mastiff asked.

"We've spent the last six months getting shot at from all directions, children, but the Caldera Market's not a war zone. And Concordia's a civilian pop with an admittedly mixed history with Imperial Military. Do not fire unless fired upon. And check your background. You miss your shots, those rounds are going to keep going until they find something worth stopping for. Might just be a school, y'hear me?"

"I'll try to leave a good impression, ma'am," Gallantine quipped.

"Well, you'd have to eventually, Gallantine. Even your mother didn't seem to take much of a shine to ya." The corporal took that burn, tucking his chin into his chest with pursed lips, even as his neighbors gave him a slug to the shoulder.

"Hop begins at 0830. You're on standby till then. Go word: Constellation. Give 'em Hell." And with that, Adrianna pressed the hologram back into her wrist and turned for the door.

She had to get out of this room. Away from their judgment. Away from their knowing glances.

Why wasn't she going? They didn't object to Mastiff being in charge, but why wasn't the lieutenant coming?

Because of other people. Because of their needs. Because she couldn't be trusted, shouldn't be trusted. Or maybe because she *could* be trusted to do certain rule-breaking things. Pull the answer at random out of a hat and it would probably be at least halfway accurate.

"You're not coming with us." The stoic and gravelly voice of Sergeant Mastiff caught her like a fishhook into her side. He had followed her to the door, far enough to get away from easy hearing of the other grunts.

She hung in the doorway, almost free, but she couldn't leave that unanswered. "That's the order," Adrianna lamented.

The sergeant nodded, very much aware of the eight infantrymen behind him who were keenly watching the conversation, all of whom were trying to look busy counting each other's brain cells. He approached her and lowered his voice to a volume that could only be called conspiracy. "You going to follow those orders?"

She bit her lip to stop herself from laughing. "'Twas the plan."

"Well, we all know how plans go."

Sergeant Tatanka Mastiff was big, rough, and salty because as a child he'd swallowed a bag of road gravel and had grown a beard on the spot. Legend had it, he was ten years old when his first chin dust made its appearance.

He had to shave it for shipboard regulations, but Mastiff's hair had flecks of gray in it these days, and his brown eyes had little spots of amber-gold. Adrianna was a foot taller than the staffie, but Mastiff's charismatic gravity could stop a loaded train. And it was always with a soft voice.

He never, *never* raised that voice. Never had a reason to.

"You'll have Yurek, Callum, the captain," she said. "You'll be fine."

Mastiff softened, a hand going over his cracked and salty heart. "Lieutenant, I'm touched, but I've done fifty-seven hops before I ever had Orbital at my back. Doesn't mean we ain't going to miss you down there."

Her throat choked up on her, but she couldn't let him know that. "I'm going to miss you, too."

No matter how much of the universe she'd seen, she always managed to catch something new that took her breath away.

The clumps of gas, dust, and powder that made up the Exeter Nebula were the contents of a cosmic trash bag, but that didn't make them any less beautiful. A dozen different nearby stars lit up the cloud like a violet cloak. And the *Erinyes* was sailing right into it.

The vista was holo-projected around the interior of the Jump Deck, giving the crew an exterior view of the ship, despite the room itself being buried deep within the hull. But for a once-in-a-trip view like this, they practically summoned the crew for it.

Adrianna poked her head on to the Jump Deck like she was sneaking into the kitchen for a late-night snack. When Graccus didn't say anything, she took a few cautious steps inside to gaze at the beautiful view.

Startling, rich blues contrasted with golden yellows and deep reds. The ship was gliding through a technicolor wonder.

She settled up near Vivian's console, staring up at the view. Vivian glanced down from her seat with a smile. "Beautiful, isn't it?"

"It's gorgeous," Adrianna said, breathless.

The chief hummed a singsong agreement, looking back at the beauty. "Reminds me of nature's greatest rule: if it's not camouflage, it's a warning."

"Yeah," Voight called over from the helm as he worked his controls. "This gigantic cloud of dust eats six ships every year."

"Superstitious," Graccus snarked.

"Well read, captain," Voight countered. "We're playing chicken with statistics right now."

Didn't stop it from being captivating. Vivian's hand fell to Adrianna's shoulder, giving a light squeeze. Affection, her own reservations, and a bit of balance.

Voight wasn't wrong; there were dozens of ships over the years that went into the nebula and never came back out. Not enough to disrupt markets, but enough to inspire treasure hunters and scientists alike looking for the cause.

Adrianna had no idea what might cause the most advanced navigation systems in history to just lose entire starships in what amounted to a big dust cloud—but she also knew that next year's computers would be the most advanced navigation systems in history. Technology always got better.

"Old sailors used to draw great wyrms on their maps," Sizemore mused aloud. "Guideposts for those that followed to steer clear of these waters."

"'Here there be dragons,'" Voight said with the hush of mild agreement.

"You know that turned out to be rocks and whales and extreme dehydration, right?" Graccus said.

"I'm just sayin', we're in a stellar nursery, sir. Going to have freak twists of gravity, pockets of heat. Things that go in here have a non-zero chance of staying in here."

Sizemore huffed. "Makes you ponder: why'd the Pilgrim lay their Jump Point in the middle of this mess?"

"Makes you wonder if they had a choice in the matter," Graccus said. "Maybe they were following the dragon on the map."

Adrianna chuckled to herself at the idea of a big space dragon living in the nebula. She could picture worse places to live than among glittering blues and violets all around her like clouds of gemstones. In retrospect, it was probably *horribly* radioactive.

Vivian's console barked and the chief warrant officer tapped the message open. "I have Concordia on scope."

Adrianna heard Graccus let out a sigh. Hah! Even he had been nervous about the trek through the rainbow fog. "Land ho, sir," she said.

Graccus scowled back at her, bemused. He crooked two fingers, calling her over. Adrianna slunk to his side like she was in trouble, but Graccus' tone set that concern aside right quick. He tapped the side of his temple, indicating the text feed flowing across his eyeball.

"I've got our asset, Janus, on an encrypted chat, and the man simply cannot focus. It's like his brain has to track at least three things at once or his head explodes."

"Janus a local informant, or one of ours?"

Graccus bobbled from side to side. "Column A, column B. He's following our target into position and confirming the exact building right now—but the line is scrambled all to hell."

"Weird," she said. "Thought the profile said we weren't expected."

"We're not," Graccus said, acknowledging that mystery, "and ground traffic isn't all aflutter with our approach, so I don't know what to tell you. We're not detected; but the words, they are a-scrambled."

That was concerning. No expedited response, but they were jamming digital traffic? "You think he's burned?"

Graccus shook his head. "If I had compromised a source, I'd feed him bad intel, not fuck his transmission. This guy's got something to say and somebody doesn't want us to hear it."

"The Commandant can't crack it?" That sent a chill down her spine. Meant there was some serious computational power behind it. This wasn't dropped packets from a poor signal, some static mess that needed cleaning; no, this was an effort made that defeated top-of-the-line Imperial hardware. "Anything that we *can* make out?" she asked.

Graccus's implant flickered again as he scanned through the message. "The name 'Scylla' mean anything to you?"

Mythology, Greek, Homer's Odyssey—six-headed-beast driven mad that devoured all that came near it. Adrianna threw another glance at the nebula on the star chart. "Spooky."

"You like mythology?" Graccus asked.

Adrianna shrugged. "I like my Gilgamesh. Big battles, cities burned, forbidden love. Gilgamesh is so impressed by this champion Enkidu, that he falls in love with him on the spot."

"I read that back at Holkstad. Were they in love?"

She shrugged. "Kinda depends who you ask."

"And historians would say they were roommates," Graccus said, mocking. He lowered his voice, adopting that subaural tone for Oskies only. "Y'know, skylocked or not, you'll still be the ranking officer aboard. Regulations get both prickly and fuzzy in this area. Seeing as it's your last hop and I can do basically whatever I want, would you like the Conn today, or do you want Bannister to take it?"

And Adrianna's throat clenched shut. She almost wished it had been trouble.

Not long for the uniform and stuck on probation, the highest ranking member was still Adrianna at first lieutenant.

But Vivian should take it. Vivian knew what she was doing. Every time that Graccus and Adrianna had gone into the field, Vivian had been the officer-of-the-deck. She knew how to run this ship in a myriad of ugly circumstances.

It would mean a lot less worry for Adrianna. Adrianna was usually rifle in hand and feet wet in dangerous and exotic locales. Her ability to do harm was pretty localized. A squeeze of a trigger killed one, maybe two.

But the bridge of a Naval ship? Even a frigate? This was a weapon of mass destruction with 240-millimeter guns firing kinetic breakers with nuclear payload tips. On top of which, there was a crew of two dozen loyal technicians, operators, and crew looking for direction at any given second.

Too much responsibility. Too many things that could go wrong. She preferred the rifle.

Graccus saw the answer go across her face and he just nodded. "We'll keep it simple. Chief'll have the deck. You'll advise and liaise with us on the ground. No wild parties while I'm gone."

Adrianna sighed in relief. "Can't possibly, sir. You're taking the party with you."

He smiled, opening his mouth like he had something else to say, but he stopped himself, instead turning for the door. "Chief Bannister, you have the Conn. I'll see you when it's over."

Vivian acknowledged the order as he marched off down the hallway.

Adrianna felt the pull, the urge, the need to follow. This was a break from habit, routine. Her calf cramped up on her and she kicked it out in the air, trying to loosen up the muscle before it went full nerve pain on her.

But social nimrod Sizemore must've missed the entire conversation, blinking erratically as his head panned from the door to Adrianna and back. "Not you, lieutenant?"

Adrianna tongued her cheek. "I mean, you want the technical answer or the practical one?"

"She don't want it, she don't want it," Voight said. "Captain's prerogative, anyhow."

Vivian wasn't having that explanation. She hopped off her station, sliding forward with a hug, folding her soft hands across Adrianna's waist and pulling her in tight. The squeeze was a little too strong to be casual, too earnest to be friendly. It was the squeeze you gave someone at the docks.

It was a goodbye.

Getting it out of the way early, it seemed. Had she hoped that Adrianna would take the lead? Of course...it was one more reminder that Adrianna was leaving.

Adrianna tapped one hand onto Vivian's, gently peeling the chief away. "I just...don't think I'd be any good at what you do all day long."

"You trust your training, listen to crew reports, then go where your gut tells you," Vivian said softly. "There's nothing to it." She said that like she was offering to turn it over.

The thought made Adrianna's stomach gurgle. "Don't sell yourself short, chief. Nobody can do what you do."

"Due respect to the chief, whom I love and adore," Voight said, "but a good sixty percent of her job is reading."

"And?" Vivian posed the playful threat.

"And you are very good at it. I'm just sayin', if we're talking jobs nobody else can do, only one person in this room knows how to fly a hundred and eight tons of steel and attitude."

"You know how to balance a cold fusion reactor?" Sizemore asked.

"...Alright, point taken."

Vivian read the discomfort on Adrianna's face and offered a smile. "I'm always afraid I won't know what to do, but the Navy didn't spend fifty grand in training to leave me out on the ledge. And they spent quite a bit more on you." She emphasized that last bit with a delicate poke to the chest.

She was right, of course. They had spent closer to two and a half million on Adrianna's implants alone. She had known what to do in that Boolean alley, and in a dozen battlefields before that. She'd know what to do here, too. Right?

"I'm afraid of heights," Sizemore said awkwardly.

Adrianna almost jumped on that statement but stopped herself. At its most simple, interstellar travel was what happened when a piece of metal got very high going very fast, and Sizemore didn't need to think about it with that context.

Vivian saw the moment flash across Adrianna's face and she gave a subtle wink before turning back to her own station.

So what would Adrianna do with herself? She stretched out her hands, gave a flexible twist at the waist, before settling in at Graccus's spot at the projector. Twin rails on either side for support and an overhead rig could get the captain strapped in. She ran her fingers over the steel pipes, feeling for the divots where Graccus had bounced his hips into them during maneuvers.

What had he been doing just before he left? He had been on an encrypted chat with the informant. Wonder if there was anything else to be had there? Adrianna tapped a few lines on her Entiglas, finding the secure chat log was kept—conveniently—secured. But the subject line was visible.

In a blink, her eyes and the Commandant's minimal access were able to crack the brief text: Scylla and Charybdis. Twin leviathans of

Greek legend. The man really was leaning into this mythology theme. And he mentioned a 48-hour timeline until something called the Gateway.

Two days until evil monsters did a whatever thing. That seemed like the salient detail. Two days till vague apocalyptic event.

Still, it made Adrianna give a second look at that nebula and whatever dragons that might be hiding in there.

CHAPTER
SEVEN

CONSTELLATION T-MINUS 00:004

THE *ERINYES* TOOK their place right behind the crushed moon, hiding in its radar shadow from the colony below. It was a little high up to properly support operations, what with the six light-minute distance from the ground to their orbital altitude. But Graccus had been very specific for them to hide behind the moon.

So they dropped a repeater satellite within line of sight and took up their new residence.

Concordia's moon was nearly twice the size of Luna, even if the colony itself only spanned one mountain range. And it was a mountain range that could be seen from outer space—peaky bumps that made the otherwise gray marble look scuffed and scratched. Somewhere in those mountains, enormous platforms had been constructed so that humanity had something flat to build on.

From what little Adrianna knew about gravity and tidal forces, the moon they hid behind and its collection of lunar shrapnel...sorry, the naturally occurring environmental concealment...was eventually going to slip, fall, and collide with the planet below.

But some mathematician somewhere had decided it wasn't soon enough to give a damn. In the meantime, the intense weather on Concordia's peaks provided excellent clean power generation: wind farms, tidal generators, geothermal plants. This one planet could store enough power in one hour to run an Eisenclad dreadnought for a week.

And that resource couldn't be interfered with.

"All units, Constellation," Vivian said, broadcasting all over the ship. "Say again, Constellation."

"Icarus pods, you are locked for deployment," Voight announced. "Hope you packed a lunch because it's going to be a long ride. Catapult is all yours."

"Copy, 1-1," Graccus confirmed. "Orbital has the sling. Smooth sailing everybody."

Adrianna rolled out her neck, thinking about the cramped interior of the Icarus pods. They were big enough inside to host a single Warcom exosuit for an Orbital operator. 'Course, she had never been certed to operate a Warcom unit in theater. And the ship didn't come with one anyhow—power armor wasn't really the best fit for the work they did.

Sizemore looked up from his console, catching Vivian's eye. "We're at combat dark, chief. Engines cold, thermal sig is below the green line."

Adrianna looked back up at the officer-of-the-deck. The green-haired sculpture adjusted herself in her seat, getting settled for the day's work. "Shuttlecraft Echo Romeo Two Niner, you are cleared for departure."

"Two Niner, clear forward. Copy."

Adrianna chuckled to herself: 'shuttle.' Shuttles were small, shuttles were domestic, even pleasant. Shuttlecraft in this context was practically a euphemism. Romeo wasn't a shuttle, it was a tin can with twin-engine K-106 thrusters and half inch armor plating, the best and chunkiest cinderblock DeHaans Atmospheric had ever produced. And they were known for their flying potatoes.

The DH-65 Bravo, playfully called the Nimbus, could get an entire platoon down to a planet and then up again, all while being shot at. While that may technically fit the definition of a 'shuttle', being that it could descend and ascend unassisted, it still made Adrianna laugh thinking about it. This was a flying brick and its belly full of Naval Regulars affectionately called it 'the shuttle', like it was the morning A-Line off Gateway Station.

This one fell out of the sky at Mach 9.

Romeo would exit the tail of the *Erinyes* and begin its long, arcing path down to the planet below. The little dot emerged from the back of the hologram, tracking Romeo as it craned up and around the moon's debris. The cloud of bullshit would do a good job of hiding its thermal output.

They'd look just like any old meteor cruising into the atmosphere —until it was too late.

"Checkpoint Alpha," Graccus radioed in. "What's the ground chatter look like, 1-1?"

Vivian glanced down at Adrianna, giving her a start. That was for the lieutenant, to liaison to with ground. Adrianna quickly put a damper on her heart and pulled up the radio traffic on her display. "No change in the last hour. If they saw us come in, they're keeping it to themselves."

"Then how are we going to get a proper welcome?" Yurek laughed, and Adrianna could hear his cackle echo up through the drop pod's wall, all the way up on the Jump Deck.

"Can it, Yurek," was all Callum had to say to that.

"Icarus team, we are go for catapult in three, two..." Graccus silent counted the last. Adrianna heard the three separate clangs, her boots vibrating underfoot as the Icarus drop pods hurled out of the tubes on the ship's stern, launching the Orbital Drop commandos to the planet surface.

The pods had thrusters but minimal fuel; the eponymous electromagnetic 'catapult' instead launched them. Enormous weights slammed one way, and that motion provided the energy to hurl the pods out of the nose of the *Erinyes*.

They'd reach the target building sixty seconds behind the shuttle. Ready to add some shock to the awe.

And now they waited, listening. Adrianna tapped her foot. Listening.

But nothing. No words. No idle banter. Just grinding awful nothing.

Voight said what she was thinking. "It's the silence that gets me every time."

"I was always talking up a storm," Adrianna said, folding her arms across her chest. "Sometimes I even brought music into my pod."

"Music?" the jockey asked, full of doubt.

Sizemore jumped on it, leaning forward on his console. "What kind of music?"

"Symphonic metal," Adrianna said, tapping her ear where she had a couple terabytes stored away. "Anything with multiple movements, good energy, syncopation. Give an odd time signature and good rhythm."

"I imagine it's quite easy for music to bore you," Sizemore said.

Adrianna hadn't thought of it that way before, but the logic tracked. When you can hear things in slow motion, it better be complicated enough to keep attention. "You listen to anything while you work?" she asked.

"You hear anything playing right now?" Vivian asked, rather unamused by the line of conversation. Offended, even.

"Maybe we could. Help with all this misplaced tension. Instill some calm, some focus."

"And she thinks she's not cut out for command," Voight said with a laugh.

But nothing. So they all just sat in silence, the only sounds the chirping computers and humming air systems.

"What I'd give to lay some EMP coverage for the ground team," Adrianna guffed.

"Or some Locust Riot Control," Sizemore said. "A couple hundred drones would keep any QRF held back."

She'd seen the little bastards in theater and she didn't care for them. Little flying bots with knives that just flew into their targets, rending muscle and bone. As if that wasn't terrifying in its own right, they had a thirty percent friendly fire percentage, which some commanders deemed as unacceptably high. She had a commander in her first year that felt it to be a reasonable margin for his objective.

Her knee still hurt thinking about it.

The radio suddenly crackled. "Romeo Two Niner, taking ground fire."

"Copy Romeo," came the faint voice of Graccus, "adjust approach, 900, click and lock."

"Click and lock, 900. Confirm."

"Well, that's a choice," Adrianna muttered. The Oskies wanted to hit ground first, let the shuttle pacify ground attacks with repeated air strikes from nine hundred meters up. Once they were sure they could land safely, they'd get the Regulars boots on the ground.

More chatter. "QRF is in the field. Mobile—and organized. Count at least three groups on approach to the target building."

"Were they waiting for us?" Yurek asked.

"It won't matter," Callum said with a grim confidence.

"Get that perimeter secure, sergeant. Icarus, stand by for air brake and evasive. On my lead."

"Why didn't we see the QRF deploying?" Adrianna asked the room.

"Because they're tiny little people on a gloomy little planet and we're like a hundred and fifty *thousand* miles away," Voight said. "Our cameras are good, but they're not *that* good. I can see buildings, mobs—not individual faces."

Made sense. Adrianna was used to being a lot closer. She never really thought about how far away the *Erinyes* usually is from all the action—compared to where they were today.

Too far away to help.

Vivian glanced down at her display and saw something that displeased her. "Voight, why are we firing thrusters?"

"I'm not," he said, throwing his hands in the air as an illustration.

"Well, we're moving."

Voight's pause was more informative than his response. "...We can't be."

"Engines are cold, ma'am," Sizemore said. "He couldn't fire them if he wanted to. We should be geolocked into lunar orbit."

"Well, we're lunar *falling* at the moment."

Adrianna glanced down at her projection to see the small hologram of the *Erinyes*...leaning to one side. Towards the big, fragmented moon. She clapped her hands together and then drew them wide, hurling her projection to the walls and revealing what was outside the hull.

The wall panels flickered, revealing the majesty of what was outside: the fragmented moon, the planet's gray colors peaking through the guts, the glittering white star lighting the horizon ablaze with golden light, and the purple nebula cloud behind it.

Its horizon was shifting.

"Hate to be the indicator of the obvious," Adrianna said, "but if we're not moving, why is that moon getting closer?"

The jockey consulted his computer screens, swiping and swiping through a dozen different ones before finding what he wanted. His voice was strained. "Clearance to run hot, chief?"

"Granted," Vivian said. "Sizemore, give us thirty percent attitude thrusters, please. Nice and easy. Don't want to throw too big a footprint."

Sizemore went all business very quickly. "Thirty percent, attitude thrusters, mark." His tone made every hair on Adrianna's neck stand on end.

She heard the thrusters fire as Voight gave the commands. He grunted in frustration and cursed under his breath. Still no luck.

And that moon kept getting closer. Adrianna could make out definition in the many caverns and canyons that ran deep into the fractured planetoid.

"Voight, you wonderful sandy blonde? What's going on?" Adrianna asked, worried.

"Well, we've got seven meters per second of lateral acceleration and I don't know where it's coming from," Voight said. "Commandant, can you isolate the thruster that's pissing me off?"

"No thrusters are supplying this particular impulse, officer. We have no power to those sections."

All three crewmen looked at each other with a shared sense of mixed dread. Adrianna looked back and forth between the three. "We bust a seam somewhere, have some atmo leak that's pushing?"

"Commandant would flag that," Vivian said with a hushed tone, lips tucked like she was trying to contain her anxiety behind a solid seal. But then she popped: "I'm calling it. Sizemore, give me full power, full systems. Voight, we can't support ground if we're crashing into the moon. Get us away from this rock."

"Aye-aye, ma'am!"

Instinctively, Adrianna reached up for her straps, clipping the cords into her chest rig, and she soon heard the others do the same. Those cables would keep them safely anchored as Voight did whatever he had to do, and the Commandant could apply tension or rigidity to those cables as needed.

Vivian keyed the ship-wide PA: "Set Condition Two. Brace for aggressive maneuvers."

Somewhere behind them, crewmen and engineers grabbed on or strapped into whatever they could. This was going to be bumpy.

Adrianna watched as the stars wheeled overhead as Voight put the moon at their back and pushed as hard as the *Erinyes* could. She felt the spike of warm air wash over her as the reactor pushed, the engines flared...

But the laser altimeter kept reading lower and lower.

There was no explaining it: despite full throttle burn, the *Erinyes* was falling out of the sky.

Adrianna looked left and right, seeing the scraps of mineral and metal floating by them, former blocks of the moon bigger than some countries. And those incredible weights were suspended, floating at rest while the *Erinyes* just sank deeper, deeper...

How was this possible?! This ship had the chutzpah to break orbit from a gas giant and now it couldn't escape a broken moon? How?

Her training said only one thing: sabotage.

"Oh, Hell with this!" Voight said, dropping the nose of the *Erinyes* flat to the horizon.

"Voight?!" Vivian exclaimed.

The jockey had an answer ready for her, straining with his control. "We're going down. I don't plan on hitting that moon. It's a race to the edge, chief."

Vivian tapped open a comm channel. "Icarus 1-1, this is *Erinyes* 2-1 declaring emergency. We are losing altitude and commencing suborbital descent."

"Commandant, time to impact?" Adrianna asked.

"Impact with lunar surface in twenty seconds."

"Come on, baby, open up. Give me everything you got," Voight growled to the ship underneath him.

Adrianna could make out the edge of the broken planet dropping away ahead of them, but plenty of craggy shards between here and there, great stone fingers for them to dodge on their way to freedom.

"Lieutenant, I can't raise the captain!" Vivian said.

"Try again!"

"I'm not evening seeing their pods, lieutenant! I don't have Romeo. Nothing!"

Adrianna grabbed her own projector. Whatever force was pulling the ship down wasn't changing its trajectory. If lunar gravity had somehow done this, their own vector would adjust as

Voight tried to move laterally. Instead, that line stayed constant, ignoring the moon entirely. But there was *some minor* mathematical drift.

So Adrianna quickly sketched it on her console. The force was coming from Concordia, somewhere on the surface.

Not sabotage. Betrayal.

"We're hooked to Concordia!" Adrianna announced.

"Come again?" Vivian asked.

"We're being pulled down to Concordia, not the moon. The moon's just in the way!"

"That shouldn't be possible!" Sizemore exclaimed. "The power you'd need—"

"All hands!" Voight shouted, cutting him off. "Brace for impact!"

Adrianna looked up to see what got Voight so alarmed.

The moon...they were inside it, walls of rock rising up on either side of them. There was no stopping it. They were being dragged down through the broken moon's crust. The ship descended, dropping out of the sunlight and into darkness.

But Voight held his controls, tilting the ship sideways to slide through a narrow passage. Something scuffed the belly, jamming the ship hard upward.

Adrianna felt her harness cinch and tighten about her shoulders and chest, the Commandant exacting the right amount of pressure to keep her anchored and safe.

Sizemore was less lucky—the hit was hard enough to pop the bolts on his entire console, sending the computer block rolling forward and shooting Sizemore into the air like he'd been sitting on a cannon.

Adrianna watched him go up, seeing the expulsion of compressed gas in the wall that tossed him, the severed conduits spraying all over the floor. The ship's engineer had barely any time to notice he'd been hit, his eyes only just beginning to squint.

He was going headfirst into the ceiling. It would happen so fast, he would close his eyes, and never get to open them again.

Sharpened senses, superior strength, acute awareness. Everything in Adrianna kicked awake.

And Adrianna leapt off the floor, fighting her own harness's desire to keep her secure, as she lunged to intercept the ship's engineer. She tumbled upside down, planting both feet into the roof—just in time to catch Sizemore and his chair as one.

Her strained harness tugged her back to the ground, pulling both of them down to the safety of the deck. She twisted hard to get her feet underneath her, dropping to one knee and cradling Sizemore in her arms.

His eyes fluttered, the G-forces of both the launch and the catch nearly blacking him out. He coughed, looking around him. "Thank you," he muttered.

Adrianna gave the man a smile, detaching one harness clip from herself to slip it around Sizemore's broken one. "Commandant, what's the damage?"

"Air pressure dropping in the cargo bay," the AI said. "Emergency bulkheads in place and holding. Electrical fires in Charlie through Gamma server banks. Compression damage—"

Another strike sent the ship jarring and Adrianna reached down to ensure Sizemore didn't go flying again.

"Voight!" Vivian called out.

"We're almost through! Just a few more seconds."

A few more seconds, and then whatever was pulling them down would keep pulling. All the way through a planet's atmosphere and to whatever waited on the planet below. "Chief, any ping on the source of that tether?"

The chief blinked for a second, a half-smile flickering over her face. Adrianna couldn't sort out what her malfunction was. And she didn't have time to check.

The ship was listing low in the canyon, and there was a nice sharp rock jutting up. Flying at about Mach Forty...there was nothing Voight could do but shout, "Hold onto something!"

Adrianna bent over, covering Sizemore's head while Vivian

grabbed a hold of her harness—as the *Erinyes* blasted through the rock with its left engine nacelle.

The ship immediately tumbled into an ugly spin and Adrianna felt her blood slosh down into her shoes—and her veins tightened down to fight. Poor Sizemore wasn't as aftermarket as she was. The engineer immediately slumped as he lost consciousness.

The room plunged into darkness, the walls turning opaque again, as if a great hand had clenched around them and squeezed out all life. When the gravity generator went out, Adrianna felt the impulse of the spin pulling her and Sizemore to the wall of the room. She lifted her boots, kicking off the ground and landing them both safely on the wall.

Great, now they were in a funhouse version of their ship, everything topsy-turvy. Twin bands of running lights on the floor lit up, casting dim and long shadows.

The actual impulse on the ship may have been brief, but the ship was in an ugly flat spin and surrounded by rock and metal shrapnel. It was a good hundred thousand miles of dead stick before they'd hit atmosphere.

Adrianna unfurled enough to check Sizemore for any further injury. He was still blacked out from the Gs, but he'd be all right. His eyes were already fluttering, coming to.

So Adrianna stood up. "Commandant?" No answer. "Commandant!"

They'd lost power and it took the AI with it. She could hear fires burning below deck. Voight was coughing and Vivian was straining against her harness, the spin pulling her in a strange direction.

She could smell the acrid burning plastic and wires, the mild wind from a hull breach. The cold hiss of fire retardants spraying from tubes overhead.

When they hit atmo again, there'd be precious little anyone could do but go down with the ship.

Gasping, Vivian clambered down from her seat, looking for something to lean against. She stared at Adrianna. She'd seen Oskies perform parlor tricks, flicker around the ship at high speed, but it was an entirely different thing seeing an Oskie operate in a dangerous environment.

Vivian looked at her different. Hell, Vivian *looked* different. It was like the chief warrant officer no longer believed she was real.

Sizemore stood up beside Adrianna, hair frazzled and sniffing dust out of his nose. "Chief?"

Vivian stiffened, thinking, then looked at the demigod in the room. And so did Sizemore. And Voight. Everyone looked to her...

So Adrianna took a breath and exhaled. "Everyone to the escape pods."

CHAPTER
EIGHT

THE SHIP WAS EQUIPPED with twice as many escape pods as would be needed in any emergency, to accommodate for any POWs or other VIPs. More than half of the ship's crew were already planet-side on the mission. They should have had no issue finding a lifeboat.

Instead, they found fires burning, emergency lights flickering, bulkheads warped or cracked. Gratefully, someone had engineered the ship as something meant for zero-gravity: while individual rooms may have a layout, they built all the doors for ease of access from any orientation.

With the new 'floor' under her feet, the pods to be found would be through the floor or above her on the roof—though a few feet about her head was hardly out of a reach of an Oskie. While the rest of the crew struggled through the doorways, Adrianna was picking her way through the mess and assessing each pod. She found the four escape pods directly behind the Jump Deck to be damaged by the impact with the moon. None of them had a hermetic seal—they'd just freeze to death before making it to the ground.

One pod found its roof caved in. Bodies inside, evidence of struggle. Crewmen had tried to take it before it had suffered damage. Somebody had been pinched under a jagged bulkhead only to rip themselves free, leaving a smear of blood along the wall.

One body was left behind and it was clear why. They'd been killed almost instantly as a chunk of wall ripped out and speared through their chest, their face frozen in a moment of shock. Blood still seeped from the wound like some kind of crimson spring water.

"Riley?!" Vivian called from somewhere behind her.

No time to linger. People still alive needed her. Adrianna reached forward, yanking the dog tag from their neck. She had the worst feeling that it wouldn't be the last of the day.

And she kept moving aft. Every single pod she found was damaged, destroyed, or already launched. Voight, Vivian, and Sizemore stumbled after her, trying to keep pace with the Oskie as Adrianna bounced forward through the ship.

She cursed to herself over and over again. How was it possible that the ship's primary safety mechanism could be this badly compromised?! Of course, the ship was rated to take kinetic fire, not slam into moons.

"I don't know if I should bless your driving, jockey, or curse it!" Adrianna shouted over her shoulder.

"Hey, you're walkin' and talkin', aren't ya?" Voight said, somewhat groggy himself.

She led them through the galley. There had to be healthy pods in the front half of the ship. The impact had been on the port side aft, so the starboard stern had the best odds to find minimal damage.

She let the heat build in her veins and the glow take to her muscles as she dashed on ahead. They had very little time, and stumbling her colleagues around the ship would be a waste of it. She needed to confirm there was a place for them to go first. Her feet pounded the steel grating, darting on through the weapons deck.

And somebody had the same idea—when the call went out, they immediately took these pods. She could peer out the closed airlock hatch, a flash of white light appearing with every rotation of the tumbling ship

Every pod. Every single pod aboard. Gone or destroyed.

The crew made it into the room and all three came to the same ominous conclusion.

"So that's it then?" Sizemore asked.

"The Hell it is," Adrianna grunted, frustrated.

"Yeah," Voight said with a heavy exhale, "we'll freeze to death long before we crash."

Vivian smacked him. "Not helpful."

Voight laughed, full of gallows glee. He raised his head to meet Adrianna's gaze, sweat giving his brow a light glisten. He couldn't fully lock eyes with her, like he carried some shameful weight, but he forced a smile anyhow: a thanks.

No. No! Her own calculations said that they had half an hour of air left with the rate it was leaking. That would happen before the ship hit atmo and long before they froze. She had plenty of time to think. Could they stop the spin somehow?

What if she chose wrong? What if she chose something and that choice hurt them?

And if she delayed and did nothing? Some people learned best when they operate without a safety net, and there was nothing so motivating as operating in free fall. Imminent death, bullet on the way to your brain pan. No time to weigh your options, just make a choice!

Now think, goddammit! These people need you. A way down to the planet, the shuttle, the pods, the...the pods.

The Icarus Pods. They were rated for Orbital Strike Commandos. Would the fleshies even survive the landing? And Sizemore was afraid of heights.

But they wouldn't survive staying on this wreck.

She gave a nervous chuckle. "I have an option you're going to hate."

Loading the Icarus launch tube without machine assistance was cumbersome at best. The shell was a ton and a half all by itself, meant to carry an Oskie and full Warcom into theater at terminal velocity.

But it would hold four people.

After all stabilization and air brakes, it would also hit the ground at around thirty meters per second. Adrianna could leap out of that pod ready for combat, and often had to. The other three may burst their kidneys upon landing like somebody had dropped a boiled potato.

Didn't matter. She had ten whole minutes to consider how to keep them alive through a rough landing. One problem at a time.

The pod sat on guide rails that would slide it down the launch tube. Airlocked gates would swing open at the mathematically timed intervals to ensure no breach of ship integrity—nothing to do about that right now. They'd have to plow right through those doors.

Air was getting thin and she could hear it in everybody's breathing. Drawing deeper, chests rattling. The air pressure was dropping. Pascal's law said the fluids in the human body would very much like to become gas in low pressure environments; if they didn't get off this ship soon, they'd boil in their own skin, even Adrianna.

"How are we launching without the catapult?" Voight gasped as he tried to help Adrianna heave the pod into place. Every little share of effort took a chunk of weight she didn't have to lift, so she wasn't going to complain. But he was burning precious oxygen.

"Simple," Adrianna said. "We take the brake off and open the door."

"The angular momentum will hurl us free," Voight said with a thoughtful nod. "How are you going to remove the brake without power?"

"The old-fashioned way," Adrianna said, resting a socket wrench the size of her arm on her shoulder.

"Are you breaking my ship?" Sizemore asked, almost delirious as Vivian helped him into the pod.

Voight had a thin laugh at that. "Ship's already broke, buddy. Up ya get."

Once he was inside, Sizemore reached back to help Vivian and then Voight.

Which is when she heard the first pop. Then a more bass-filled pop-snap.

Adrianna looked back at the bulkhead behind her, yellow eyes scanning for the source of the sound. She could see the vibrations originating from a steam coil. With no way of dumping heat, it was getting hotter and hotter. Fracturing.

She ducked behind a support column before the explosion even hit, bolts shearing out of their posts and sailing through the air like bullets. One sank into the column, the red-hot dart biting through the pot steel like it was butter. They skipped and peppered the pod, scuffing and sparking. Ten seconds earlier and that buckshot would've shredded the crew.

But now fire was suddenly belching into the room like a dragon's maw was cupped to the doorway.

"Now or never!" Vivian shouted from within the pod.

First the doors, then the brake.

Adrianna dropped below the pod, leveling her wrench against the doors. These were electronic airlocks for deploying ground troops— no need for a manual override. But she knew how to make one.

She bashed at the doors with her wrench, carving out dents big enough for her boot heels. Bracing herself against the frame, she laid her feet into the foothold she'd made and pushed against the gears. There may not have been power, but hydraulics were a hard beast to fight.

Despite that, the door creaked under her force, moaned, and then popped free. She looked down into the airlock she'd opened—just one thin door between her and the vacuum of space, a cracked moon, and a colony that ate her entire away team.

Sweat sizzled on her skin and her muscles ached. No time to take a break. Not yet.

She took one big leap up to the front of the pod. She coiled that wrench up behind her, winding up, swinging for the fences.

Wrench hit steel and the brake snapped free. Nothing held the pod in place anymore. It immediately slid down the guide rails, down and past her.

And she saw Vivian's hand reaching out for her.

Silly goose. Adrianna was a full two hundred pounds, and the pod was moving at a good clip—she'd wrench that poor girl's shoulder out of its socket. But it was a sweet gesture, the reflex to reach out.

Instead, Adrianna snagged the pod's entry handles, tossing herself inside and yanking the hatch shut behind her.

The Icarus pod hit the edges of the first door, shearing a bit of unhappy metal. Just some sparks to add to the light show. Then they hit the second door with a bang, jerking everyone in the cabin, and slamming Vivian into Adrianna's side. The girl clung to her, squeezing hard, full of terror. Adrianna's skin had to be scalding hot but Vivian didn't seem to care.

Had they made it out safely?

Adrianna wasn't sure until she saw Voight's curls dance around his face. Weightless nothing. They were in free fall down to Concordia.

And Sizemore immediately had to swallow the vomit in the back of his throat. It wasn't the zero G—all Naval officers were intimately familiar. It was the given knowledge that these four people were now falling to ground in a device that didn't know the definition of 'soft landing.'

It was rather cramped inside the pod with the four of them in there, floating alongside one another practically shoulder to shoulder.

But they fit, and they were free of the falling ship. And they were breathing easier with the pod's own life support kicking in.

Adrianna squared herself at the center of the pod, planting her feet on the bottom and letting the magnetic floor grab onto the plates in her boots. A simple cable jack in from her wrist and she could see everything: the *Erinyes* tumbling out of orbit, the meteor shower in its wake, and Concordia below.

Nothing on radio channels, like a blanket had been cast over the entire planet.

Just a quick stop before dry dock, not a war zone. Easy in and out. Intelligence really screwed the pooch on this one.

"Direct interface," Voight said, impressed. "Just think it and make it happen?"

Adrianna smiled and gave the pod a little wiggle with the attitude thrusters, which promptly made Sizemore gag. "Please—don't do that again."

"Oh, you're going to *love* re-entry." Voight chuckled at him.

"And it's wise to assume they'll be shooting at us," Vivian said, and Sizemore made a noise that could only be described as a sick goat.

The Icarus was aptly named; it fell to the ground, a torpedo with a soldier inside. Orbital could survive the impacts and they were equipped to operate the pods in atmosphere, directing them with air brakes, canards, and thrusters to hit specific target sites as small as five meters. They could land the pods in a traffic intersection and be out and ready to wreak havoc before the dust had settled.

But the Regular Navy—these squishy deck crew? The landing would shatter their hip bones, squish all their organs, make 'em bleed from every hole. Assuming they didn't split open like spoiled meat.

Adrianna had to find a way to take the very sudden stop and make it less sudden for the fleshies. Maybe drive the pod into a building, something softer that would break and absorb some of the force? Anything that shreds or breaks would shave some energy on their behalf.

She looked around the interior. There was rigging meant to support a Warcom above, something considerably heavier than all of them. If they didn't bump a wall, didn't bottom out…

"You have about ten minutes to get yourselves hooked up to those straps," Adrianna said.

"What are we supposed to do, hold on for dear life?" Voight asked.

"That's about what your options are, yeah," Adrianna said. "Chief, I'm not getting any radio traffic from the ground."

Vivian grimaced at that thought, but optimism sprung despite it all. "If they have the power to rip a ship from orbit, then they can black out communications."

She was right. The team was down there somewhere. Callum, Yurek, Graccus…they weren't going to be taken out that easily. Hell, Adrianna had gotten off a crippled frigate with all crew unharmed!

Her team was down there. They had to be.

Which meant their best chance for survival was dropping right on the target building, right where everyone would be. And probably most of the fighting, too. Link up with the ground team, rally the troops, survive till rescue.

She wasn't looking to stop a terrorist cell today. She'd be happy just getting everybody off Concordia alive. And she wasn't even sure if the three crew with her would live through the landing.

Adrianna gave the pod a little nudge and bounce, attitude thrusters hissing them into position. "Anybody want some music?"

Nobody said anything, so Adrianna picked one of her favorite albums off her memory banks and piped it through the pod's radio. It didn't do much for the mood, but she felt them all breathing a little easier. She even caught Voight humming along under his breath, a myopic impulse.

It may not have fixed anything, but it helped.

CHAPTER
NINE

MISSION TIME 00:39

SIZEMORE THREW up until there wasn't anything else in his stomach. The drop pod didn't exactly come with an air sickness bag, but the designers had thought to prevent free-floating...fluids...inside the cabin. So all of his donations were neatly sucked up and away, vented out of the top of the pod while the four crewmates continued bouncing their way through the ionized upper atmosphere.

Before long, Adrianna could make out the colony proper—early settlers would have landed with an Aurora-class colony ship, the components of which would be everything the newborn city needed to survive the harsh first few months. But there wasn't anything flat to land on here, just sixty-degree angle mountainsides that sloped downward into impassable mists and clouds.

Some inspired jockey had decided to land their ship sideways, laying the enormous ship down between two mountains. They draped the ship over a valley and built a bridge upon which they laid the foundations of their nascent city. Adrianna could still make out the vague outline of the Aurora, its bulbous engine cluster poking out of the cement and steel like a fossil encased in granite.

Nothing down here that could possibly yank a starship out of orbit. Just city and industry. No weapons, no technological marvel. So how had these rebels gone about it?

"Can you see the *Erinyes*?" Voight asked.

Adrianna looked back behind them, up at the single winking light in an otherwise blue sky. "She's hit atmo and coming down fast."

Somehow that news deflated Voight, like he thought the ship would be spared the indignity.

Adrianna pinged it to her internal network to have some idea of where it was going down, and then turned to more pressing issues. "You all strapped in?"

"As best as we can be," Vivian said, idly checking the clamp that hooked her belt to the pod's freight straps.

"I'mma try to bring this in as soft as I can, but no promises. When we stop moving, you all need to get as low as you can get. This is a combat drop. Heads down and stay down until I come get you. Do you understand?"

They nodded, clinging hard to their elastic straps.

Adrianna took the moment, pulling her canteen off her belt and dumping the contents onto her head. Cool, refreshing water instantly snapped and boiled off of her skin, wicking away the pent-up heat from the last half hour.

She didn't need any systems cooking out on her, not right now.

They were low enough that individual buildings came into sharp clarity, and Adrianna could even single out the specific target building, a big fat cube settled into an open plaza. A smoke plume rose from the south corner and flashes of what could only be gunfire lit up the streets.

Someone was still alive down there and putting up a fight.

Then she saw what she wanted to find: an apartment building six blocks off the square, built with loose tolerances. A low-lying warehouse structure behind it: one cushion, two landing pad. Her pod would punch through one and into the next, hopefully bleeding off enough energy that the fleshy crew weren't badly harmed. A quick optical and thermal scan to see if any innocent bystanders were in the way—

Adult, woman, standing at her apartment window, looking down at the fighting below. She never even saw the pod falling right at her.

No time to warn the others. Adrianna cranked the pod into a roll, lifting the enormous machine just enough to strike the next level above the unsuspecting colonist, ripping the roof from right over her head. The Icarus carved a channel through that building and showered the street below with bricks and powder. Adrianna may have missed the civilian, but she just gave the poor girl the fright of her life.

There was just a moment of hang time, as the Pod exited one building and spiraled down into the next, punching out a perfect circular hole in the roof. And down they cleaved, one floor, two floors, before finally embedding in the foundation slab. The pod shed its four main walls outward on impact, using the hit to throw off the last bit of kinetic energy instead of translating it into the occupants.

A cloud of industrial particles filled the warehouse from floor to ceiling, harmful building materials. Nothing that would harm Adrianna but it couldn't be good for the others.

Sizemore was already screaming. Good. That meant he was still breathing, and his breath was full of fear rather than pain. Vivian was gasping, exhausted and confused. Nothing from Voight.

But she also heard coordinated shouting. And footfalls. Not running away, but towards the crash site.

She didn't dare stop to check on her friends. She had to clear the LZ.

Adrianna blinked. It was hazy in the thick particle cloud but she could pick out the thermal signatures approaching—a muddy mass of hostile intent.

"Stay here," she whispered to the crew, before dashing out of the pod.

The air howled in her ears as she moved, the dust curling behind her in beautiful little contrails. It was a mere ten meters to her first target.

Man, mid-thirties and a scruffy laborer-type. He held an antiquated rifle, something powder burning rather than electric, strapped to him with a nylon retention sling. He held it with training, tight in the shoulder, high ready as he approached the pod with trigger wrapped. A flashlight was clamped to the muzzle to help him see. Chest rig with ceramic armor plates—high-end gear. Effective against ballistic impacts and at dispersing energy from a laser blast. Cheaper steel plates would shred the bullet and send shrapnel up to the face and feet, while melting under laser fire. Ceramic soaked heat and impact much better. It may not be top of the line, but it made the Boolean pirates look medieval.

The Merc had a rudimentary but effective helmet, even a visor— though that was mostly to protect his eyes, with no heads-up display or tactical data-link.

She didn't let him get a shot off, barreling straight into him and planting one hand on the weapon's handguard while driving her knee into his chest. His finger snapped like a stalk of celery as it got caught in the trigger guard. And her next move could've broken the finger off. With one forceful kick, she snapped the retention sling and sent the poor bastard sailing backwards. He bounced off a building support, folding around it in a very crunchy sort of way.

He had friends: four shooters close, another five sweeping wide to flank and cover the phalanx. But they had heard their friend get hit. They were all turning to face her, boots sliding across the pavement to set new stances, subtle hissing. Muzzles tracking to bear on the sound they'd all just heard, beams from flashlights swinging through the air like the many eyes of a watchful reaper.

She had precious little time to consider her next move.

While their action may have felt instantaneous to them, her reflexes bought her a moment to consider her options. Adrianna reached down, clicking the flashlight off and swiping the action back to check if a round was chambered. Internal combustion of an unstable powder in a small but strong steel chamber, designed to hurl deadly metal—how psychotic of a design: impulse by contained explosion. She much preferred magnets and slugs over this historical relic.

She had to wait an uncomfortable amount of time for that action to slide back into battery again, as the rebel guns slowly turned toward her. It was like watching the guillotine blade fall towards her neck, inch by inch.

Who were these people? They were trained, drilled, well-equipped with armor and weapons, even if the gear was old. These weren't Duster folk with pitchforks pining for self-governance. This was a militia that would make the Boolean pirates jealous.

She had to use the cloud, obfuscation, move like a ghost and work like death. Shoot and move, hit hard, and get clear. Harass 'em, draw 'em away from the pod. If even one rebel got through, they'd kill everyone inside.

Her rifle's bolt clicked shut, primed and ready. And with a soft exhale, she took one big step backward...

The goons fired a controlled burst at where she had been, shooting at the sound they'd heard, but catching nothing.

"Another Oskie," whispered one with more of a clear head. "You heard Prime. No Imp leaves this building." Loose murmurs of agreement as the soldiers clumped up into groups of three.

That's cute. They thought they were the hunters. But who was Prime? A codeword? The first, the one, exalted, a singular, or originator—someone thought awfully highly of themselves.

In this thick industrial fog, eyes couldn't be trusted. But the sounds of their hearts were beating like trackers for her, drums that called out each soldier...

Adrianna slipped her quick knife from its sheath on her chest rig. And she went to work.

She gave a clean cut to number one as she dashed past, slicing his carotid with a blade that could compete with molecular edges. Thick denim and kevlar meant nothing to it. In a dive past his friend, all she had to do was reach out, opening number two's femoral artery just enough. The first went down quiet with his vocal chords severed, but the second went down screaming, clutching at the red fountain gushing from his leg.

The third didn't look to his friends, didn't spare so much as a thought to the wounded. He didn't quake with fear or lose his head. He just shouldered his rifle and sprayed at her passing, still catching only mist.

"Get the pressure on her! Burn her out!" Someone called. But as the groups converged, they stepped over their fallen. He wasn't talking about pressure on wounds or tending to the dying; they meant pressure on her.

Inhumane, but smart. With Adrianna rolling free in this cloud cover, they were all potentially wounded. They had to put her down before they could tend to their own.

Her chest ached, her hands hot, a painful thrum at the side of her head. Her implants were feeling the stress. She'd start glowing any second and then this fog would actually hurt her more than help. Once she started casting off light? She might as well light a flare.

Adrianna looked down at the lines glowing on her hand. Yes...yes, she could light a flare.

She pulled the magazine from her weapon, thumbing a half dozen rounds out: steel-jacketed thirty caliber. Trivial to rip the round free of its casing and pour out the gunpowder. In a few quick seconds, she had a proper pile of it.

They were getting close now, squeaky shoes and unsteady floor giving them away, the individual glow of their heat signatures showing with some detail. Any closer and they'd see her.

She let a bit of the powder trail away from the center, an impromptu fuse. A single primer would act as her ignition source. Wouldn't explode with actual force, but it'd be noisy and bright.

And that primer wouldn't be quiet, so she'd need a brief distraction.

She palmed a shell casing and chucked it at the pod, gonging it off the metal siding. The gunners turned back toward the pod—was there another one of these monsters in the mist?

And Adrianna used the hesitation to slam the steel magazine down on the primer with a small pop, getting a hiss from the powder igniting.

They turned back to her, some even firing before they'd squared up again, tracing a line of bullets across the warehouse. They may not see her, but in the same vein, she was having a helluva time seeing the incoming bullets. Copper-jacketed lead hissed through the air, leaping from the shroud like deadly sprites. She bobbed and weaved, back tracking away from her trap, trying to keep her movements minimal and her glow soft. But a barrage of unfocused gunfire was still a barrage, taxing her skill.

One bullet clipped the top of her shoulder, cutting through her suit but drawing no blood. That was way too close to catastrophe.

"Imperial bitch," one of them said with a grimace. "Why don't you come fight me, face to face!"

There was humor in the response from his friend but no laughter, just a hesitant whisper. "Careful, she might take you up on it."

A flash lit the space as the fuse found the powder pile with an obnoxious hiss. The gunners all looked down at the light and sound. And Adrianna dashed to the left, hoping her glow wasn't bright enough to throw off a tracer. She slotted the half-spent magazine back into the rifle as softly as she could, fumbling a bit with the awkward angle.

The mercs circled up on her trap, but all they had for their efforts was a scorch mark on the ground and twitchy nerves.

"*Fra tow mi,*" one gunner cursed, almost involuntarily. He didn't get the rest of the phrase, as Adrianna darted back in, slapping against the back of his neck hard enough to fold the vertebrae over the back of her hand. The universal human off switch: she cut whatever power line was running to him, and he slumped to the ground.

They felt her among them, sliding two steps back as they tried to get a bit of spacing from one another and find an angle on her. Adrianna's implants were searing yellow now, a golden archangel in the cloud that bounced from target to target. The ones that didn't find her knife ran afoul of her stolen rifle, as she doled out the occasional bullet to someone too far to reach.

Her head pounded. Her skin screamed. Her gut sank and pulled and—

She was overheating. Heads-up said her internals were at 104 degrees and rising. Burn that much chemical energy through exertion, it had to go somewhere. She was pushing hard and that was after the rough times skyside. This was too taxing, even for her.

There were still three standing. If she collapsed in front of them, she'd be easy prey.

Adrianna got her feet planted under her and threw herself backward, hoping to hide her glow behind the thinning haze. She tumbled along the ground, sliding to her feet and gasping for breath.

A whimper from the pod, causing gunners and Adrianna both to refocus. Voight: he'd woken up. In pain. Agony really. The landing had done a number on him.

And the goons heard him. They moved quick, weapons up, advancing toward the skeleton of the pod. Maybe they thought it was her, hiding, recuperating?

She had to get in the way, but her legs burned and the tang of copper filled her mouth. Something had ruptured in a bad way. Hopefully nothing too serious.

"Riley?" Voight called out through his pain, and she heard Vivian shush him.

Too late. The three gunners were in motion, weapons ready. Her rifle was empty, her knife bloody. If she could just...

No plan. No tools. Expended. So tired. The ground was so welcoming, soft and kind.

But something came barreling through, something big. It slammed into the first guy and drove the gunners right into the side of the pod. A splash of ugly paste on contact.

Callum.

Snap-snap bursts of controlled gunfire, careful and placed shots zipping in to drop the last two gunners to the pavement.

And she heard the happiest sound of her life. "Clear!" shouted Sergeant Mastiff as half a dozen Naval Regulars spilled into the space: steel-plate face masks with smooth plastic eye-covers, telemetry and battle data streaming in real time over the surfaces. Brown uniforms behind ugly plate carriers and modern rifles.

They moved through like it was a training exercise.

But she saw the wounded, two Imperials with bandages on their legs and one with a cracked faceplate. They'd seen a rough landing of their own.

Callum sauntered over to her, reaching down with his big beastly hand. He nodded to the Icarus. "Did you jump, or did you fall?"

She took his hand and he hauled her to her feet like she weighed nothing at all. "Oh, you know me, commander," she said, trying desperately to push oxygen through her chest.

Callum assessed the situation around them as the fog finally began to settle. Scorch marks, bloody knife kills, and busted gear. "Looks like you had it under control."

And the statement practically exploded out of her, voice shaking to match the tremor in her hands. "Callum, I haven't been under control since I was eight years old. What the fuck took you so long?"

A smile slipped out of him, that soft unofficial endorsement.

What she said next took that smile away. "The *Erinyes* is down. Commo blacked out. They pulled us right out of orbit, and I have no idea how."

Callum nodded. "They took down the Romeo in a similar way, and it's like half the colony wants our blood. They *knew* we were coming."

"Think our informant suckered us in?"

"Captain doesn't seem to think so," Callum scoffed. "But Yurek might just put a bullet in the guy if he sees him first."

Okay. So the others were alive too.

Corporal Gallantine was inspecting the Icarus pod when he had a little start. Vivian leapt out at him, giving him perhaps the cleanest left hook in human history. She knocked the career soldier right to the floor, causing every nearby Regular to snap their rifles up.

Adrianna somehow found the strength, practically teleporting between their guns and her body. "Easy, boys! Easy!"

"Stand down!" Mastiff shouted, getting the platoon to lower their weapons with one paternal callout. The sergeant marched over, looking at Gallantine and back to Vivian. "Chief?"

Vivian swallowed hard and lowered her fists. "Sergeant...we-we have wounded inside."

"You took three deck crew down in an Icarus?" Callum asked, peeking inside the pod.

"And nobody's dead!" she remarked, only half laughing.

"Not yet anyway," Callum said gravely. "But we shouldn't linger. This patrol will just be the first."

"The first?" Adrianna asked, looking at the dead litter around them. "How many more could they have out there?"

"Every single one we've found so far." Callum's words pumped cold fear through her chest. If only that could cool her off.

Callum marched over to Vivian, crunching to a halt in front of her. "Chief? What's the status?"

"The jockey's got some kind of leg injury," she said, "but Sizemore and I are fit and ready."

Callum made his assessment and nodded, waving toward Mastiff. "We'll carry the wounded. Sergeant? Get me a stretcher. Let's get hostile and mobile."

"Yes sir!" Mastiff said, turning to the pod, "Shooters up front. Holt, you and Gallantine are the chaperones of the day. Let's put some push behind it. Huah?!"

"Huah!"

Voight had a broken ankle and a sprained hip. Sizemore got away with needing a double-shot of clean water. Vivian was somehow completely unharmed. The three of them being in one piece was nothing shy of a miracle.

Adrianna walked to the edge of the warehouse, looking out to the colony beyond. She could hear them all moving. More than a thousand. There were gunshots, cries of hatred, boots running and people screaming. The spiral of smoke from Romeo's crash site.

And their welcoming party was just a taste?

They were going to need a few more miracles.

CHAPTER
TEN

THE CITY WAS unlike anything she'd ever seen before, and she'd walked the world for a good bit. Some people who lived in cliffs built mountain aeries, cleaving out caves from the natural formations. Other colonists had made homes out of deep forests to live among the trees or in the middle of arid wastelands, building tall spires where nothing had ever grown before.

But to build your life suspended in the air took an almost brazen kind of mechanical engineering.

It was like they made the entire city from scrap metal riveted together without rhyme or reason. Sheets of metal, lightweight and strong, were stitched together as needed to expand the colony's reach. Plaster, plastic, and other finishing materials shielded the buildings from the elements. Some green paste-like substance had grown on corners and siding where cleaners couldn't readily scrub it away, like some resilient moss. Adrianna wondered if that was a local flora or something the colonists had inadvertently brought with them.

Space was at a premium, so roads were narrow, barely six feet across, claustrophobic and curling inward. That might've been a mild sign of the manmade foundation buckling underneath all of this accrued colonial weight. How far was the fall down between the two mountains? Would they measure it in seconds or minutes?

She glanced up at the peaks, letting her heads-up display call them out: locals named them Mount Misery and Mount Freedom. The foundation of their lives, permanently balanced betwixt the two forces.

High above the residential buildings, she saw a smattering of individual towers with six-to-ten-foot vertical openings. Bell towers or enormous instruments, perhaps? No...they caught the howling mountain winds, cooling water and turning turbines inside for power: wind catchers. Adrianna shook her head, letting the brief amazement wash over her. She may have crash landed with a few of her best friends into a city that wanted her dead, but that didn't make these people any less ingenious.

It was slow going, but not because of Voight's leg or Sizemore's stomach. The Regulars led the way with eyes on the rooftops and windows, creeping along the streets. The thin sheet metal doubling as window panes were creaking in an idle alpine breeze that sent a pleasant chill down Adrianna's spine, a kiss of winter on the air. It smelled like stone and wet lichen, dust, and a hint of warming spice, like cinnamon or clove.

Callum walked with the trio of deck crew, towering over them. Trying to provide added security, but his proximity seemed to make Sizemore even more nervous.

They could hear distant gunfire and shouting. Closer than they'd like, echoing up the narrow streets like ghostly caution.

Adrianna took the moment to fish a protein bar from her pack, get some calories onboard. The high-density dried paste would keep her pushing, but it tasted like someone had dipped oatmeal into stale honey.

"Three blocks to the target building," Callum said.

"No offense," Voight groaned from the stretcher, "but shouldn't we be moving *away* from the shooting?"

Not a bad instinct, Adrianna thought. But Callum came back with the obvious and did so with extra grit. "We still have a job to do, officer. You'll be safer with the full fire team."

"Unless you want to walk yourself somewhere." Gallantine grimaced. The statement earned him a searing glare from Callum and Mastiff both. Neither veteran had patience for his shenanigans.

The Caldera market was a distinctly more open district with wide streets to accommodate the abandoned handcarts and empty stalls. Whatever goods had been in transport were long since picked clean by scavengers and opportunists. It made the moving platoon very open and exposed.

Adrianna caught glimpses of the building through windows and down thin alleys. Callum saw her peeking and read her mind. "Want to get some altitude on our situation?"

Of course she did. These tight corridors felt like they were just waiting for some giant to roll a boulder down on top of them. But how would she get up to the rooftops? No stairs, no ladders to be seen.

An alley, maybe five feet across full of tubing and exhaust vents. Plenty of handholds and solid foundation. It would serve her needs.

Callum offered her his rifle, holding it out in front of her path so she could snatch it as she went by. Adrianna would need it up there more than he did down here. She plucked it from his grasp as she darted into the alley, just a little kid leaping off the front stoop and into the playground. Halfway down the alley she found the best spot and turned to vault straight up the side of the building, toe-tapping her feet on the steel to jump off and get the last few vertical feet to pull herself up to the roof.

She heard Holt mutter down on the street. "That never gets old." The mixture of awe and humor always made her smile.

It was just twenty feet up, but Adrianna had a splendid view of the entire city: the smoke plume from Romeo's crash, the smell of ozone hanging in the air mixed with gunpowder, sweat, and anger.

Anger always smelled like burnt rubber to her.

The target building was in sight: an open courtyard with an enormous squat structure. By design, one of the colony's central indoor marketplaces. It looked as though someone took a pyramid and squished it down into a two-terraced structure, like the collapsed travel shape of a larger thing. It had lost some facia to combat scarring, carbon scores and bullet holes smudging the slate-blue steel.

But for all the sounds of combat, the only people she saw clustered at the base of the building were Imperials. They were engaged on all sides, the four corners firing off down the various lanes. But no colonial rebels were making gains.

"Clear up, go for advance," Adrianna said, knowing that Callum's expert hearing would pass the message along. She moved on her own, hopping from rooftop to rooftop, before dropping into the market plaza. She waved to the nearest corner, calling out her IFF code. "Mercury!"

"Sunburnt!" came the friend-or-foe countersign. And to her delight, Graccus stood up into view, covered head to toe in soot. Blood caked his hands and wrists. Not his own—but the dull moans and frigid tone of those around told her the captain had earned those stains from tending the many wounded.

She jogged into the perimeter and gave a nod to her captain. "Damn fine to see you, sir."

A flash of fear in Graccus' eyes. "Where are the others?"

Callum. He was worried something had happened to Callum. She raised a hand, putting those fears back in the bottle. "They're right behind me, coming in."

Graccus looked over his shoulder, seeing the rest of the crew clearing the corner and into the plaza. He sighed. "Should've stayed topside, kept overwatch."

Nothing to watch for. Everything was three blocks out or more, but no need to dispute the point. He was just happy everyone was walking and talking.

Adrianna turned her attention to the empty plaza. "QRF's not pressing in?"

Graccus shook his head. "They likely think we have the HVT already. Worried we'll off him if they get too close. They're giving occasional pressure, but I think they're just trying to bleed us and wait us out." Momentary dread again went over his face. "Not like we're going anywhere any time soon."

"What happened?"

"No idea. Shuttle spiraled in and it's been a nightmare ever since. Theories?"

"Whatever hit the shuttle, hit us in high orbit," she said. "I think we're outside my pay grade. Know what I'm saying?"

His eyes darkened, like a nightmare had become real enough for him to touch. And it had. Whatever was going on here wasn't exactly within the bounds of recon and assault tactics; it was theoretical physics.

Adrianna did a quick count of the men around them and at the two other corners of the building she could see. They'd lost...many in that crash. If the final corner had all its soldiers—which she doubted it did—plus the rescue parade sent after her? They were down nine triggers already.

One soldier lay crumpled against his barricade, rifle clutched to his chest for comfort like a stuffed animal. He had bled out, a red pool at his hip where he'd taken some ricochet. Based on his body temp, he'd been dead for some time. He'd held his defensive totem close and simply drifted off. Had anybody even noticed?

Graccus gave her a knowing nod. The man had died quiet and calm—nothing else to be done.

Callum and the rescue squad came ambling up to join them, dispersing back to their posts. Graccus gave Callum a firm nod and a soft, "Thank you."

The big guy didn't answer that beyond an acknowledging bow of the head, but Adrianna picked up the context. Callum hadn't wanted to go, but had gone anyway. If he hadn't...

She heard the crisp snap of Yurek's rifle go off overhead, and the sniper's voice chimed in, "They are aware of the new arrivals and that has got them abuzzin' over there."

"Then we shouldn't wait around," Graccus said.

"Stick to the plan?" Adrianna asked.

Graccus nodded. "Except now we have to procure our own exfil. Complicates matters, but this is a merchant port. Somebody's got a Jump-capable ship around."

Mastiff sauntered over to the fallen soldier, checking him over and sighing in frustration. He plucked the rifle from the man, checking it over before turning to Vivian. "You capable, chief?"

She was the warrant officer of a Naval Frigate, highest ranking NCO on the *Erinyes*, and rewrote the manual of arms aboard ship two times. Vivian took the rifle from the sergeant, checked and cleared the action, reseated the magazine and thumbed the capacitor before clicking the safety. "All Navy are Regulars, Sergeant Mastiff."

He nodded his approval, stripping something off the dead soldier's collar. He pressed the patch against Vivian's neck, letting it adhere to her shirt. "Take that corner, chief."

Vivian idly picked at the fresh addition to her uniform: a square bit of metal, nothing ornate. Identifying what it was, she took a breath and entered a six-digit code onto its blank face, tapping corners and edges until it chirped happily. Satisfied the device was working, she marched over to the dead trooper's corner. She stopped only long enough to close his eyes before shouldering her rifle.

Squeamish and weak, Sizemore puffed up his chest, trying to rise to the occasion. "What did you give her, sergeant?"

Mastiff blinked a few times. "When was your last JRTS, officer?"

The engineer wilted under the sergeant's glare, more sheepish than usual. "Was supposed to be before deployment, but—"

"Command postponed it." Mastiff finished the thought with a knowing nod of comradery.

Adrianna had the answer. "Navy Regular IFF tag. Friendly weapons will recognize her, refuse to discharge if she's downrange. Cuts down on friendly fire."

"Shouldn't I get one?" Sizemore asked.

Mastiff's response was overly grim. "We'll have to wait for one to open up for you."

Sizemore swallowed hard on that notion. There was a certainty to it. Not *if*, but *when*.

Gallantine raised a single slender finger up towards his nose, subtly tapping to claim the childish 'not it.' It rippled across the Regulars in just under three seconds. Poor Holt was too busy wrestling with Voight and the stretcher, looking up at the crowd all staring at him. And the conclusion that drew. "Oh, come on!"

"Pay more attention, Holt, you'll get shot less often." Gallantine quipped.

"Knock it off," Callum snapped, shattering the brief levity. "Everybody's going to be shot before today's done."

Maybe it was demoralizing, Adrianna thought, but it was probably necessary. This was hardly the scenario to be screwing around, but a bit of fun wasn't that harmful, was it? In correcting the admittedly stupid behavior, Callum may have done more damage to morale than the cavalier attitudes were doing.

Mastiff bit his tongue. He shared her opinion and was keeping it to himself.

A small drone came whistling in, circling down to fill a small cavity in Graccus' palm, filling it neatly. The captain's eyes flickered for a second as he processed the data his little scout had for him. "Yurek, get down here," Graccus ordered.

And almost as soon as he'd finished saying it, Yurek slammed into the ground next to Adrianna like a goddamn superhero, three-point landing while cradling his rifle. Adrianna gave him a bemused smirk. "Melodramatic."

Yurek pressed two fingers to his chest. "You're telling me? You arrived late—and on fire." With a twist of his wrist, he collapsed his rifle barrel down into the action, taking his marksman rifle down to the angriest little block of metal like some kind of tactical tuna fish.

"What's the layout, shadow?" Callum asked, almost affectionate.

But Graccus was all business, his eyes darting about as he reviewed the data. "Four major storage spaces—or internal markets—with a frankly obnoxious amount of balconies. Plenty of hidey holes and elevated firing positions. Broad hallways and side chambers we'll need to clear."

"Fortifications?" Adrianna asked.

He nodded. "They've had the time and the inclination to turtle up, so it'll be knock-down drag-out the whole way through."

"At this point are we even trying to take him alive?" Yurek sounded annoyed.

Which drew a sigh from Graccus. "Your inconvenience has been noted."

"Now if he puts up a fight..." Callum countered, implying the obvious.

And Yurek nodded. Orbital was going to be the only ones in the room with an HVT who had just shot down two Imperial ships, one of which was a classified frigate. Every part of this was deniable, so why not this part too?

Yurek was always so ready to leave behind bodies and brass in his wake, but could she blame him? He hadn't picked this fight.

Hadn't they, though? Showing up with a military frigate unannounced, uninvited? What would her brother do? Would he follow the brief? Or take care of his men?

"The target," Graccus said, cutting her line of thought. "We get the target, no matter what it takes."

Right, she thought. Time to go get what they came here for.

CHAPTER
ELEVEN

MISSION TIME 01:05

THERE WERE two main entrances to the target building, barricaded and secured. Orbital wasn't known for taking the front door even under ideal circumstances. Callum used all that size and dug his fingers into the cheap pot metal, pulling it apart like it was tin foil.

No bullets came flying out the new hole, so Callum widened the gap with a bit of legwork and the four Oskies climbed inside.

Adrianna leafed through the mission brief on her HUD, pulling up a picture of the target. They'd need a positive ID and they had a surprising amount of detail to go off of. Made sense, seeing as he was an Imperial Intelligence asset, one of the Spymaster's little birds.

Hirochi Kaneda, a slender five foot nine with a narrow jaw and sunken features. He looked...sickly, like he'd suffered some wasting disease as a child, or some part of him had collapsed within.

Strange to think that the genome project or Meditech hadn't

corrected his issues. He wouldn't be a very subtle agent standing out like that. But he would be very easy to identify, at least.

Graccus gave the orders via short-wave radio, uploading his commands to their augments. Adrianna could see the simple pathways mapping out where he wanted her to be. She'd go left with Yurek, sweeping one half of the building while Callum and Graccus took the other. And so, like childhood monsters, the four soldiers scurried silently off to their tasks.

Adrianna took point, letting Yurek feed her commands. She was the better kitted of the two for this kind of wet work anyhow.

They came upon the first internal market. Empty stalls and makeshift barricades, like they'd intended to stand and fight. The whole room was nothing but rusting bulkheads heaved into place to encircle an arrangement of stalls. Jagged metal edges at every turn. Adrianna spied the narrow windows above them that lined a circular balcony—part of the building's wind catcher system. Made for some excellent sniper positions if anybody wanted them.

But there wasn't anybody home. Not even residual heat from their passing. Abandoned and for some time now.

Yurek gave her a look. This had all the makings of a super obvious trap. The room was begging them to linger. Please, it might say, jam thy foot upon this obvious pile of crunchy leaves—never mind that circle of metal teeth that hath been recently sharpened to surgical precision. It's not a trap, it's an invitation.

Trap or not: they had to secure the space. Just because it looked like an ambush, didn't mean they could avoid it. Yurek went left and she went right. They clung to the walls but didn't keep too close to them either. The rounded tips on bullets liked to skip, and when they did, they followed flat surfaces surprisingly well.

Gunfire rang out, echoing up the halls. Inside, but not too near. Sounded like Callum and Graccus had found a trap of their own, sprung it too.

Adrianna stepped up to a market stall. Had been food, meat of a kind. Thin blood still clung to wrapping left on the counter, and a butcher's knife stuck to a plastic cutting board. Medieval for her tastes, but not every colony could afford Replicators, and plenty had local fauna.

If she wanted to hide from heat-seeking super soldiers, where would she go? Why, a refrigerator of course.

She glanced at Yurek, flagging the container in his HUD with a flashing 'no-shit' tag. And he nodded to her, ready.

Adrianna tucked her rifle into her shoulder, bracing for a jack-in-the-box surprise as she reached with her off-hand to open the lid. Stable platform, feet planted, she threw the lid open.

Fish. Pounds upon pounds of room temperature fish in stagnant water. Long dead and starting to foul. And boy were they *foul*.

Adrianna took a step back, wheezing. "Oh, God...oh, it's in my mouth. I can taste it."

Yurek had to contain a laugh, biting his lower lip. He didn't dare make any other noise, lest they draw unnecessary attention. But he was never going to let her forget this one.

And that's roughly when the patrol of goons turned the corner: a full fire team of ten men, chest rigs and armor plating, ugly boom-rifles for each. Yurek didn't let them fire first, instead snapping one high caliber round through the lead man, punching a neat two-inch wide circle through his chest cavity and shattering the ceramic armor. He flopped forward, clutching at the hole.

The 40-40 Gauss rifle's iconic thrumpf sound was so much worse up close, but Adrianna had yet to experience it close and *indoors*. Just because there wasn't an explosive involved didn't make the thing quiet. The supersonic crack alone was rough, her ear implants immediately modulating the sound to reasonable levels.

But it did not compare to the chest-thumping drumbeats of the JP-36 assault rifle, muzzles flashing and pistons slamming, a bass-line chorus. And each of them set off dozens of explosions. Those bullets tore up the market, sparking off steel and shredding stalls. It was the symphony of percussion from Hell.

Yurek collapsed backward behind his stall for cover even as it all came down around him.

Adrianna did the math: nine shooters, semi-automatic weapons. Sheet metal and plastic weren't going to stop bullets. They could easily gun down an Oskie under sheer volume of fire. No cloud or darkness to hide in this time.

No, this time...no subtlety. She was going to get messy.

Adrianna dove over her market stall, snagging the chef's knife off the butcher block and twisting to hurl it at the nearest attacker, burying it in his neck. He stiffened with the hit like every muscle in his body locked up at once.

Like a single creature, the whole group turned to focus on her. Eight identical gun barrels. Triggers snapping, pins dropping and nine hundred rounds a minute came hurtling her way, starting wide like a tightening noose—leave the wily little Oskie nowhere to go.

Her shoes squealed on the ground, slipping and whining as she tried to get traction. She leapt up like a high jump athlete, weaving her body through the deadly net of copper-jacketed projectiles but out of the circle before they could tighten the web.

Airborne was always a risk. They trained Oskies to stay grounded —you can't change trajectory with all four limbs up in the air. Jumping meant she had nothing to push off of or influence her landing with. If she didn't like where she was going, Adrianna would just have to find some way to make it work.

Luckily, the mercs only shot where she was and not where she would be. She landed with no hot lead to welcome her, but the mercs were watching and were swinging their guns over to follow—muzzles flashing and hurling metal. It was impressive coordination without a neural link or shouting commands.

The entire squad was operating like they were—

Don't gawk. Run!

Adrianna took off as fast as she could—probably broke a hundred miles an hour in full sprint. Plenty fast enough to outrun a sweeping muzzle.

At full pace, she could bring her rifle up to bear, a snarl to her face, her heartbeat at the same rate as the thrum of her Gauss rifle pounding away.

Thra-BAM, Thra-BAM, Thra-BAM!

The capacitor built a charge and then let go with an exotic explosion of energy.

The ceramic armor plates stood up a little better against her rifle. The soft-tipped rounds she was firing weren't really built to penetrate ballistic armor. She could hear the impacts cracking against the soldiers' chests, stumbling them and staggering, but no sign of blood. Not at first.

But a broken plate didn't absorb quite as well as a fresh one. Finally, ten shots in, she saw a spot of blood leap forward like a wet geyser seeping through fractures in the ground. The soldiers reacted fast and well, pulling their wounded to the back and fresh faces stepping forward, presenting a unified and strong front against Adrianna's circling offensive.

But Yurek was on the far side of the gallery, relieved of pressure. He popped up with his own rifle with plenty of time to aim careful—and he was shooting something a touch bigger than 40-40 Gauss.

Yurek's custom-tooled rifle outputted a half inch cylinder of Spitzer-tipped ferrite with a thermite core. It had enough kinetic force to dislocate the shoulder of a small bear. And his hand worked the bolt like a blur, slam firing shot after shot in less than a second.

The first merc took the hit square to his ceramic plate, the round punching clean through and shredding his ceramic backplate. Chunks of broken armor shot out like flechette, showering his comrades with razor sharp darts. The second two of Yurek's targets took shots to the face and neck, respectively.

The fight began as ten and was now down to five. Whole thing took twelve seconds.

Bloody and angry, two of the goons shifted their fire over to Yurek. His only cover was obscurity. The pot metal he hid behind was fileted, sparks announcing the passing of copper-jacketed madness. Adrianna didn't get a good look at it, but Yurek looked like he'd actually used his take-down rifle as a shield.

Clever. The high-carbon steel barrel and frame would make a better shield than anything else in the area. Though she wouldn't use that gun anymore after it absorbed that punishment.

Yurek had drawn some pressure off, taking it upon himself. Time to repay the favor with a little bit of Callum's magic.

Adrianna dropped her borrowed rifle rather than worry about reloading it. She was under too much duress to aim careful and it took half a mag to so much as wound these Duster mercs. So she ran straight for the wall of the market, two-stepping up the rusting pot metal to kick herself upward towards the second-story balcony.

Bullets peppered the wall around her and pulled apart the rusted steel walls, melodious with each impact. Eight feet up, she twisted out and got both heels planted onto the wall, needing to build up friction to get a good push—and then she hurled herself down, directly at the gang of shooters, like some kind of unholy berserker.

Let's see how brave they were when she was within arm's reach!

That web of bullets closed in around her, tightening, but she wasn't looking for an edge to squeak through. No, she was looking for the tender, juicy source at the center of it! It was a race to the middle, the tightening ring of bullets around her as she sailed in.

One shooter pulled his gun in, muzzle flashing, shots tracking closer and closer to her...

The muzzle traced over her face. She saw the barrel. Heard the action click back empty. What luck. What horrid, horrid luck—for him, that is. He was one bullet shy of living through the day.

She hit him at about thirty miles an hour, two hundred pounds of muscle and silksteel. His head hit the floor with the most disconcerting wet sound, like someone had dropped a fish. But he had his helmet on, so—just to be sure—she gave him a quick bash with the boot of her heel, rotating his head with an ugly crack!

Four shooters. They all snapped to face the woman on top their friend, steam rising from her disheveled black hair and bloody knuckles. But they hesitated, checking background. She was inside their ranks now. If they fired impulsively, would they hit their friends?

Oh, what a bad time to hesitate.

She didn't need a knife to be deadly, but thankfully, she had sent one over here just seconds before. She ripped the chef's knife from the neck of her first kill and went to work on joints, armpits. They were all too busy shielding their faces and necks, exposing those juicy kidneys. People always thought to go for the head or the heart, but there were perfectly good kill shots found in the upper thigh or up under the armpit. Soft skin with critical arteries close to the surface.

The last shooter finally got it into his head: just fucking shoot her already. She was fast but not so fast that she could dodge a point-blank instruction in the aggressive distribution of lead.

So she drove the chef's knife in behind one man's ceramic plate, cutting the entire chest rig free and swinging it out to cover her—just in time to intercept the burst of shots with his own friend's armor plate. She heard the bullets gonging into the ceramic, ripping the nylon fibers, cracking and splintering right next to her ear. A fleck of shard or metal eked through, scraping along her forehead like it was trying to sketch some message in her skin.

This shield wouldn't hold.

Yurek. He lunged up behind the shooter, drawing a monofilament wire from his wrist with a sickly whine. He snaked it over the last man's head and up under the collar of the helmet. He gave it a good wrap about the soldier's neck once, twice, and then pulled back hard, letting the thin steel slice into the rebel's vital flesh.

The man tried to slip his fingers in between, give himself room to breathe and fight. The wire took his fingers first, slicing right through the knuckles and sending the digits to the floor. They didn't bounce like she thought they might've, instead hitting the ground wet-side down and sticking.

Of all the bloody, gory nonsense she had just been cause of and party to...that little detail made her stomach turn.

It was not made better by the garrote tearing through the rebel's voice box, letting out a strange quiet twang before slicing backward and finding the notch in the vertebrae. Yurek popped that man's head off like the two pieces had never actually belonged together.

Adrianna didn't watch the head fall or the body slump. She just stared at the two fingers on the ground. "Gross," she said, before pulling her knife free of her own kill, letting it fall where it may.

"You're welcome," Yurek said.

Adrianna did a quick systems check of herself: well over-temp, 103 and still rising. She needed a cooler, a shower, something—and quick, or she wouldn't finish the day. The extract wasn't exactly close or soon.

She looked over the market that was riddled with holes and smoke. There was only one place cold enough for what she needed. "Fish?" she asked.

Yurek grimaced but nodded. "Probably your best bet."

She stalked over, slamming the chef's knife back into the carving board where she found it. Before she could think further about it, Adrianna dunked her head in the fish tank.

The acrid water stung the scratches in her face, a thousand pricks to her skin. She'd need to bathe in alcohol to erase all the bacteria she'd just flushed through her system, but that would have to wait.

Yurek picked up one of the rebel rifles, inspecting it and claiming a few magazines. "You like sushi, Riley?"

"Shut up."

One room left, center of the building. Nowhere left for Kaneda to hide. But if they came all this way for an empty nest, Adrianna was going to be pissed.

Graccus and Callum stood at the opposite end of the hallway, creeping up towards the door. The captain hugged the wall, engaging his active camouflage. He melted into the air like he was some kind of mirage, and if not for his ident tag, she'd never know he was there.

He'd mind the door in case Kaneda tried to run, the final snare, while the other three breached the room.

Adrianna and Yurek stacked up on the opposite side of the door, weapons ready. Callum's nose wrinkled, sniffing the air, and Adrianna nodded furiously at him. Yes, that was her. Fish. Long story. Kaneda probably could smell her too. Hell, the squad outside could probably smell her!

The wall was well over three inches thick, so she wasn't going to get a read on anything inside, but she wasn't feeling any vibrations. With her luck, they'd bust in there to find just a hole in the ground, the bastard having tunneled his way out with nothing but a spoon and a plucky attitude.

No point wasting time then. Callum pressed two small packets of gel to the doorframe, high and low: breaching charges, low yield RNX-20 compounds. But small didn't mean friendly; she wouldn't want to catch one thrown her way. A quick three count—

And two small flashes of white carved out chunks of the steel door frame, and Callum was so in sync his foot hit the door just as the charges finished burning. A quick fizz-fizz-BLAM.

What happened next came so very fast.

They were in the room before the door had even settled. It was dark like an oil stain leaking through the air. Impossible to tell how large the room was. She could shine a light in here and whatever void residing here would simply swallow it whole.

But she could still make out one figure.

Kneeling thirty feet in front of them was a single man. He matched the description. Right height and sickly build, but a stillness that betrayed a strength of will. He wore a workman's jumpsuit and boots and even wore the utility belt of an electrician. He had not flinched with the explosive entry of the Oskies. A simple knit rug had been slid under his knees.

The object of his total focus, that to which he silently issued blasphemous prayers, was a curious black monolith.

Pilgrim Metal.

The whole thing was about four feet wide, obsidian glass, but it was set down into a notch in the floor. It stood at least as tall as she was, but with that inlay, there was no telling how tall it actually was. Did it extend further downward?

And what's more, Adrianna could swear that something massive moved beneath that crystalline barrier, contained within the cursed jewel. A blue-green cloud that both flirtatiously danced against the surface and then would plunge out of sight.

She'd only ever seen diagrams or museum pieces, small shards no bigger than her palm. But this? This was like staring into the ocean, watching some creature slide out of the light behind the embrace of an abyssal curtain. That curtain was etched with a hundred different glyphs, shapes and swirls that seemed three dimensional; the more she looked at them, the more they seemed to shift, ebbing and flowing, like the cryptic phrases might change moment by moment.

None of those artifacts safely behind museum glass, none of those shards in a collector's grasp, none seemed as...as alive as this monolith.

Adrianna had been so transfixed, she almost missed Yurek approaching the meditating Kaneda. He drew his monowire filament from his wrist. "You should have run, *skel*."

She saw something then, a warp to the air, a subtle pulse of something...radio signal...radio signal! Short-range, very short, and low power! How could she have missed that?! It was a—

"Detonator!" Adrianna shouted.

She had hardly finished the word when Hirochi Kaneda dropped his thumb across the trigger in his lap.

He'd lured them here. Lured them in. The rebels hadn't pushed the building, hadn't attacked the Imperial cordon, because they knew. They *knew* where the ordinance was and where they didn't want to be.

Most kinetic weapons from modern firearms traveled at about three thousand feet per second. An explosive pressure wave traveled at twenty-five thousand.

Kaneda died first, his body turning into a pink foam as the pressure wave rippled outward from the thirty pounds of explosive on his chest. The monolith cracked and shattered, sending thousands of ricocheting glass shards around the room.

Yurek was too close, far too close. All he could do was watch as the wave struck him—and shredded him. Bits of metal, bone and plain ol' expanding air blew him apart. The human body was mostly water, even when augmented, and water did not like to compress. Poor Yurek's body simply separated from itself.

Callum did the only thing he had time to do—he stepped in front of Adrianna. He gave her precious cover from the expanding pressure wave. She still felt the wave hit the back wall of the room and bounce back into her, while the wave that escaped out the open door created a sucking negative pressure that almost pulled her off of her feet.

But withstanding a pressure wave was different than the piercing shards of glass. A single lance of black material punched clean through Callum's gut and sank into Adrianna's shoulder.

She staggered backward, feeling the bite of the cold metal in her. Freezing cold, like it thirsted...

And then her blood, like scalding oil, trickling down her front.

The ground settled beneath their feet, creaking and whining steel, like the metals of the city had been saddened by this trespass. And then she heard the second boom.

More explosions. Several dozens throughout the city.

And finally, a tectonic snap—

And she started falling.... Her. Callum. The building.

Everything was falling down between the mountains. Two rising towers of rock on either side, as the sunlight slipped away.

PART TWO
FLASH & BURN

CHAPTER
TWELVE

BLISTERING HEAT.

It felt like she had laid her back onto a stove top, searing red coils branding her flesh. Or was it the other way around? Her collar felt like a snake constricting around her neck and she could feel the cloud of hot air pushing up underneath her uniform.

No matter where she looked, she saw it: a glittering, golden, perfect fire. An orb of blazing heat suspended in some untouched nether. Nothing on the horizon or under her feet, like any ground that had once been was either burnt to a cinder or consumed by that purity.

All-consuming. All-hungering. All-seeing.

Where was she? Was this a dream? Adrianna only vaguely remembered the stones being heaved off her body, the hands scooping under her arms to drag her away. An odd grip. Perhaps two people? One on either side? The uneven and rocky terrain jabbed at her heels as they dragged her along.

Was she captured? Imprisoned? Why not put a bullet in her head or slit her throat and be done with it? Was Callum alright? Graccus? What about her crew?

Her crew. Her crew needed her!

She snapped her eyes open, taking a deep breath. Arid, but cold, like a tundra or high desert, with a musty scent that only came from recycled air. They had laid her down against a wall to stare up at the stonework ceiling.

Curious. Everything on Concordia had been metal, scavenged from the hulls of colony ships or purchased from traders. This place... this wasn't what she had left.

The room was little more than a hallway. Every surface was made of the same air-pocked concrete material, like they were poured out in slabs and passed out to every contract for all purposes. There was just enough room for Adrianna to lie down.

Her clothes were soaked with sweat and blood, a fine layer of building materials caking her skin, crunching at the corners of her eyes. Every movement shook off another sheet of dust onto the floor, like a mummy awakening from a thousand-year slumber.

She laid her head back, looking up and behind her. A single beam of light peaked under the door at the far end. Daylight, a single golden beam, like it was trying to reach out for her.

She remembered falling, that piercing pillar of sunshine chasing her down, down, down into the black...

A chill ran up her spine and the tips of her fingers tingled, forcing her to consult her HUD. It was a little slow to respond but right before she would get concerned, it blipped alive behind her eye.

Bumps and scrapes, some bruising. Mild contusions. An asymmetric puncture wound to the upper left pectoralis, just above her collarbone, where foreign material was detected. Her internal body temp had plummeted, and only after she checked did it chime a warning to her.

She tried to sit up but her shoulder immediately screamed in agony.

She remembered that black shard slamming into her—cold, like an icicle draining her of warmth. But you wouldn't know it from the sweat soaking her clothes.

"You're awake!" someone whispered.

Adrianna looked toward the voice to see Vivian staggering over. The woman sported a few bumps and scrapes of her own, uniform torn at the elbows and stained with oil. She'd been perched next to a portable electric heater, fiery orange coils painting her face in jewel-tone grace.

Her head was wrapped with someone's sleeve, tucked down across one eye and cinched in the back. A bloody gash had already soaked through the bandage, leaving a damp red spot in the bandage.

"Your eye," Adrianna grimaced.

"Hmm?" Vivian had to remember the bandage was there. She reached up to her forehead, peeling the wet bandage back. An ugly gouge had cut across her forehead, but thankfully skipped across her eye socket. Vivian tapped her wound gingerly, wincing a touch, before checking her fingertip. "Looks like my bleeding's stopped."

"What happened?"

Vivian discarded the bloody rag, pulling a fresh one from her pack. "Concrete's pretty sharp when you hit it with your face." The chief knelt beside her, pouring out some more precious water from her canteen onto some clean fabric to make a cold compress. She slipped the tortuous linen onto Adrianna's forehead, causing the Oskie to flinch away. Just a blur and a twitch as Adrianna's entire body snapped back in the blink of an eye, but the speed of it was enough to startle the chief.

She sighed, electing to re-wrap her own wound with it instead. It made the chief look like a pirate. Arrr.

"Your fever's broken," Vivian said.

"F-fever?" Adrianna asked. "I'm hypothermic."

That notion stunned Vivian into a momentary stupor. Deciding to trust the super soldier's own diagnostic, she quickly scanned the room for something soft that was not already soaked in water.

Adrianna tried to flex her hands and get some blood flowing back to her extremities. "How did we survive?"

Vivian paused, like she'd been caught in some kind of verbal trap. She gave up on finding a tool and just dragged her heater over. "A lot of us didn't."

"You didn't answer my question."

"Not all of us carry aftermarket improvements," Vivian spat with surprising vitriol, her one exposed eye sharpened to a stiletto's tip. Adrianna eased back against the wall. She was right. Of course, she was right. Adrianna's odds—even with a hole in her shoulder—were better than any grunt in the Service.

Vivian planted the heater down beside Adrianna, letting the sizzling coils bring their warmth. "Bomb opened a path to the Under-city. Those that didn't fall climbed down after you. We pulled out more dead than living."

"Must've been a helluva drop."

"It beat staying topside surrounded by angry Dusters. May I?" The chief asked, gesturing at the space beside her.

"I'm an ice cube," Adrianna cautioned, "but if you need cooling off, I got the shoulder."

The chief sighed, easing herself into position so she might squeeze up close to Adrianna's side. The first touch almost hurt, like her skin had drawn a thousand tiny blades to stab her with. But as Vivian squeezed in, the momentary burn passed.

Vivian snaked an arm behind Adrianna, rubbing the opposite shoulder. "Can't have my Oskie freezing up on me."

"A likely excuse."

"Shut up, or I'll let you freeze to death." Adrianna stifled a laugh; it honestly hurt to anyway. Vivian certainly wasn't laughing. "You're a glacier."

She was. It wasn't impossible for an Oskie to get cold. They might be less water than your average fleshy human, but metal conducted heat about as well. Adrianna hadn't been this cold since Holkstad, laying in toxic saltwater, waves lapping at her face some early autumn morning. Most Oskies struggled to cool down, and here she was, at the bottom of a mountain dying of exposure like some kind of...

Like what, Adrianna? Like a regular person? How did she expect to die? In a hail of gunfire? Defending a colony?

Like her brother had?

"How are you holding up?" Adrianna asked, dropping that mental image.

Vivian soured, tension in her lip. "Oh, don't you worry. I'll have my breakdown when it's safe to do so."

They must have heard the chatter or the movement, because the sunlit door to their hallway opened, pasting a ray of pale light across Adrianna's face.

Two forms entered, one of them rushing forward. She didn't need to see his face—the weird hop to his step and bob to his head. It was Voight, the young jockey practically falling over himself to join the duo. His leg was braced with some scrap metal, splinted and rough. But it didn't slow his enthusiasm one bit.

He hunkered down in front of the women, pressing his hand to Adrianna's forehead. "And can you tell me, lieutenant, how long did your parents leave in the chest freezer?"

"Bleeding's stopped," Vivian reported, not letting up on her warming embrace, "but she's swung from melting too far the other way."

"Ninety-four point five," Adrianna reported with a tremor, "and dropping."

That stole all whimsy from the jockey's face. Voight looked back up at his companions. "She needs a hospital."

"Can you tell me who doesn't, sir?" There were a lot of voices that Adrianna wanted to hear. The bullish Callum or the musical authority of Graccus, but the steady grip of Sergeant Mastiff was equally heartening.

Mastiff blocked most of the doorway with his stocky build, and the rest of it was stony attitude.

"Sergeant," Adrianna greeted with a shaky nod.

"Lieutenant." In three syllables he managed to tell her how glad he was to see her up and talking, how tired he was, and how angry this whole debacle made him. He looked like worn sandstone, the wrinkles in his skin deep and cracked. But perhaps because of that weathering, his edges were worn down. The absence of a smile did not mean he wasn't gladdened at the sight of her.

But instead of any formal greeting or expression of familial warmth, Mastiff asked her, "How's the arm?"

Adrianna took a moment to inspect the patchwork first aid. At the broken layer of skin, she could see no more than three different steel components peeking out from their organic hiding places. Diagnostics showed that some electronic painkiller lines had been severed, as well as an adreno-spike line, but nothing too severe. Over the top of the wound, someone had worked up a Medigel putty which had formed a nice cap over the wound.

But they hadn't removed the offending material—this was classic ground-pounder medical. After all, the shard of Pilgrim Metal had caught her in an unfriendly spot. Above the clavicle, more near the neck than shoulder. They'd likely do more harm removing it than leaving it in.

Either in the fall or by clumsy Navy hands, the protruding end had been snapped off. The gel cap now covered whatever remained, that which was still trapped between muscle and augment.

"It's not leaking," she said, simply.

"That'll have to do." He offered her a hand.

"She needs rest!" Vivian said, her voice cracking with concern.

"She needs a protein shot and a run," he said. "That'll warm her right up."

Adrianna forced a nod through her shivers, trying to assuage Vivian's concern, but it was probably the rumble in her stomach that did the final convincing.

"What do we have to spare?" the chief asked.

"For the Oskie?" Mastiff asked, reaching into his pack for his allotment of silver-wrapped protein paste. "She gets everything I have on me. This woman could walk us out of here single-handed, or we'll end up dragging her like luggage. There is no in-between. But this super soldier does super marching on her super stomach, so everybody pony up."

Everyone dug in their pockets for protein paste, crackers, cheeses. Anything they would've brought down, and Adrianna made herself a smattering of little Oskie sandwiches. If she wasn't in the bottom of a pit, she'd think this was a half-decent dinner spread for her little abode.

But where was 'here' anyway?

After squeezing some calories down her throat, Adrianna's temperature stabilized and she could stagger out of the stone hallway. And it was immediately obvious why they had taken refuge where they had. They were underneath the city plate they had landed on, about a hundred...two hundred meters straight down?

Gleaming rays of sunlight outlined the cracks and breaches in the plate above them where explosives had torn the city asunder. Hundreds of tons of building had fallen into the valley below to find an entire second city plate underneath. She could see a scattering of different impact sites where the bombs had dropped chunks of the artificial sky down onto the Undercity.

The chunk above hadn't completely severed, either. It cut out three of its four sides and hung down from that fourth. It looked like someone had popped the top off a can, leaving that thin tin slice to swing in the breeze—that is, until one side of the tin had ground to a stop against the layer below, making for the world's steepest ramp.

That explained how they'd survived at all. They hadn't fallen *that* far, and with plenty of industry underneath to soften their landing. Who knows what they'd crushed on arrival, but it was certainly buried, and the others would have been able to climb down after her. It had to beat staying where they were.

This rather...abruptly installed support pillar? Very steep ramp? It was swarming with people. She could see them crawling down it like ants, belaying down wire and combing the debris. Hundreds of them.

Down here, the structures were more rudimentary with blocks of stone hewn out of the mountain walls melded with steel reinforcements to extend outward, slanted rooftops to keep the buildings clear of the powerful jetstream of wind that flowed down the artificial pipe of cityscape and mountainside. Steel scoops on the bottom of the Upper City plate caught some of that wind—and Adrianna realized, those were the underside of the wind catchers she'd seen above. They did the same job above and below.

Looming over the entire Undercity at the center of the plate, a giant tower reached upward like an old smokestack of brick and mortar, connecting the Upper and Undercities. To Adrianna, if she had to guess, they looked like a connecting point to the original Aurora colony ship. If they had fallen through over the center of the colony, there wouldn't have been much to catch their fall—if the high winds didn't blow them out into the valley. Over here, under the Caldera market, they were granted some graces. That fierce wind was lessened this close to the mountain, along with the angled rooftops that redirected their falling force.

Prime had a shot to kill them all and had chosen the wrong ambush site. Or had he?

Prime...could that have been the Kaneda they were after? Or was that who radicalized Kaneda, the charismatic figure who turned him? Convinced him to ambush the team, to kill Yurek and the others?

That was a question for smarter people.

Resting outside of Adrianna's little recovery hallway, she found just a handful of Imperial Regulars. Private Holt and Corporal Gallantine held their little corner, both looking up at her with a mixture of surprise and gratuity, like their rescue had just stepped into the room.

Rescue? She didn't even know where they were, let alone how to get back from it.

A third face rose from the ground, marching over to her like magnetism drew him to her: Sizemore. He didn't say a word at first, just throwing his arms around her.

He was shaking, uncontrolled tremors from head to toe, even as Mastiff peeled him off of her. "Alright, Sizemore, give her air."

"We thought you were dead for sure," Sizemore murmured, eyes watery.

She laughed, bittersweet. Despite everything that had happened —the fall of the *Erinyes*, the fight through the city, and the explosion —her deck crew had survived every hurdle.

Yurek hadn't, she remembered. And Yurek was elite. Her crew was alive by luck or blessing, but talent and gear were insufficient to protect them.

Corporal Gallantine saw the spiral dawning on Adrianna's face and gave a sharp cough to draw her back to reality. "Good to see you, ma'am," Gallantine said. "Holt was praying like we was running out of oxygen." Holt glared at Gallantine, the corporal just sharing an embarrassing secret.

Her survival was good news, sorely needed good news to them, but Adrianna also knew the least out of everybody. "Anybody seen the cap'n?" she asked.

Mastiff shook his head. "We fished you out of the rubble and hauled ass before the locals took up residence." He lowered his voice to a kind of reverence. "What went down in there?"

Adrianna wrestled with the memory of it. The pressure wave, the blood, the shards of black glass. Her shoulder ached and pulsed at the thought of it.

"Yurek's KIA," she said, gravel to her voice. "Kaneda too. They were both at the center of the explosion, Kaneda flipping the switch."

A few curses rippled through the assembly. Mastiff didn't let that news get to him. "The others?"

"MIA. Graccus was outside of the room, holding the door. If I survived, his odds are good." She did the mental math on the forces absorbed by the big guy. "Short of standing on top of it like Yurek... Callum got the next worst hit. No idea what happened to him."

Mastiff stiffened, clearing his throat for maybe the first time in his entire life. "Remus is a mule. He's built to last."

"I know."

Mastiff sniffed something out of his nose that he would insist was grime. "Well, we've got more dead than living. The three musketeers you can see, plus your three friends. Officer Voight's leg is busted, but he's ambulatory. Chief Bannister took a fall coming down from the Upper City, but she's otherwise okay. Holt took a hit to his chest plate, but he's still stealing oxygen."

Holt lifted the broken ceramic tablet that was shattered into three pieces. "Luck was just on my side, ma'am."

Mastiff didn't bother acknowledging the private's chatter. "We've not enough gear to go around, and nobody came loaded for an extended stay. This hop is officially cluster-fucked."

There was an awkward pause after that which made Adrianna's heart hiccup. That was a report. Right. He was waiting for her to say something.

"What...what's your assessment?" she asked.

Not what he wanted to hear, but he was going to work with it. It looked like he shuffled the deck of cards in his head. "I...don't think we can afford to wait for rescue," Mastiff began.

"Fuckin' A," Adrianna commented, immediately wincing. She hadn't intended for that part to be out loud.

But Mastiff had heard worse, and probably thought she was entitled to some griping, because he didn't bat an eye. "First priority should be securing contact with off-world. We grab commo, get a report back to Gateway. They'll send in the cavalry."

That certainly sounded like a plan. Adrianna stood up tall, immediately feeling the tug on her shoulder, the bite of teeth that still sunk in her flesh. It reminded her of the scolding rap of an instructor's steel rod on her forearms and back.

But Voight must've overheard the keyword, because he scoffed. "Report? Sergeant, they blew a hole in their own city big enough to drive a cruiser through! Whatever's going down here is going to be over long before the Empire can turn up."

Mastiff glared at the Navy jockey that was talking so out of turn. "Officer, all due respect, the lieutenant asked my opinion."

And Voight got the message, softening his tone. "I know pounding dirt is more your arena than mine. I'm way out of depth here. But *that?*" He jerked a finger at the hole in the sky. "Kinda resets mission parameters, y'know what I'm saying?"

"Yes, it does," Vivian said, stepping forward as if to cut Voight off. "He's right. The Navy will never get here in time. It's up to us."

"That was *not* my point," Voight grumped, but he was overlooked by the larger conversation that was taking shape.

"Chief, there are a conservative few *thousand* roving colonists about," Mastiff said, "and they're a mite cranky."

Vivian responded to that with authority, with a lifted chin and solid stance, making eye contact with each person in turn. "Mission parameters have not changed and deviation from that mission is not tolerated by Terra Firma. So we move fast and quiet, stay out of trouble. Kaneda may be out of the picture, but his faithful are not. They were coordinating to attack Imperial power systems, and we were sent to disrupt that, plain and simple. We have a mission, always did. We defend that power structure to the last man."

"With the seven of us?" Voight may have been the last one she looked at, and the only one who could challenge her with ease.

"To the last man, officer. Concordia supplies clean battery export for a third of the Core worlds, and half the mercantile lanes," Vivian said. "We can't let this base go offline."

"I can't dispute those statistics, chief. I'm just talkin' about what's *possible.*"

"Hell, the way they pulled us out of the air? Running might not even be in the cards," Gallantine muttered, getting a solid punch to his shoulder from Holt. Shut up, this was not the time for quippy bullshit.

"Mission was 'extract the agent.' Captain's briefing didn't leave wiggle room. Just the guy. Chief,"—Voight pointed at the hole in the sky again—"mission's over."

"You think that's the last of their bombs?" Vivian asked. "The last of their targets?"

"Doesn't matter," Mastiff grunted with crossed arms.

"What doesn't?"

"'Cause it's not your call, chief. It's not his call, it's not my call."

Six sets of eyes all turned to Adrianna. The Oskie. The lieutenant. Ranking officer.

Shit.

Her shoulder ached and her blood ran cold, and it was all she could do to remember to breathe. She trained for this. What had Vivian told her? Listen to reports and go with your gut.

Adrianna shook her head, muttering under her breath. "Try to get word out, try to stop the rampaging colonists, or try to run..."

Low on food, low on ammunition, and more than half of their away team buried under about two hundred tons of steel and plastic.

Voight took that silence as an invitation to fill it. "It's all very patriotic imagery, to think the seven of us can do something. But when there were thirty of us, we got our asses kicked."

"Not now, officer." Mastiff was borderline insubordinate with that tone of voice.

Voight took it in the right spirit. Vivian did not. "He might be completely wrong, but he is also your superior officer, sergeant. At least look at him when you address him."

"I didn't mean to be pejorative, ma'am," the sergeant grunted.

"What *did* you mean to be?"

"Dismissive."

That got Gallantine and Holt both tense, issuing their own

soothing words, but Vivian wasn't having any of it. "Article Seven, Section Two of the Uniform Code—"

"I follow my orders, ma'am, and I follow them still. And when asked a direct question, I am obliged to answer it."

"I got a question for you then," Voight asked with a signature blend of playful and irritated. "You always been a mean old cuss?"

"You always been a jackass?"

"Honestly? Kinda."

They were fighting each other. A city comes crashing down on their heads and they choose to fight each other. Adrianna's head was going to split open with all of them sniping at each other.

Every point raised was right: The Navy would never get here in time, but they had to warn somebody; they may not be able to escape, but they were in no condition for a fight. What was she supposed to do?

What would Marcus do? Be a hero? Die in a blaze of glory? Die in a blaze of glory only to be buried under a mile of red tape?

None of it mattered. Nothing they did ever mattered.

Mastiff and the Vees were ten seconds away from shouting at each other—risking the ire of a bloodthirsty neighborhood—when Adrianna finally spoke up. "We need supplies."

Three words and it cut all of them to silence. The words caught her throat, like someone had wrapped slender fingers around her voice and squeezed. The pain in her shoulder spiked in response, that little sliver of black metal teasing something horrid.

But Mastiff threw her the necessary help. "Supplies, ma'am?"

"Doesn't matter whether we fight, run, or call for help. It's going to be a long haul from here on out and we did *not* come ready for a camping trip. Whatever we don't have, we need to find."

Mastiff walked over to Holt, grabbing him by his chest rig and heaving him to his feet. With one hand, he opened the kid's chest rig. With the other, Mastiff reached to pull his own back plate out and slam it down into Holt's chest.

"Don't you need that, sir?"

"I need everybody facing front, private. No excuses."

Holt swallowed hard. "Yes, sergeant."

Adrianna made a mental note that Mastiff no longer had a back plate. She'd have to find some piece of steel or pot metal lying about. It might be heavier than ceramic and prone to spalling, but better than bare skin to an angry world.

"You heard the lieutenant," Mastiff said, snatching up his rifle. "Let's go shopping."

CHAPTER
THIRTEEN

THE STREETS of Concordia's Undercity were hauntingly quiet. Adrianna felt like a scavenger picking over a corpse–or a mouse in tall grass. It felt like a crime to touch anything lest it give away her presence.

But any reasonable mind knew what a residential district looked like. The city planners had done good, if uneven, work. There wasn't a straight line she'd seen yet, but the ground was easy on the feet. The walls of nearby buildings puffed outward but didn't squeeze the walkways. There was ample room for two people to walk in opposite directions without hitting one another, both roads separated by a thick middle lane of processed rubber 'play space.'

At the head of their column, Gallantine stooped to inspect an object on the ground: enamel and plastic, narrow frame with a bulbous tail with broad features and bright colors. A toy spaceship, left long ago to gather grime on its edges.

This was someone's suburban neighborhood, but no one had been here for some time.

"Where'd everybody go?" Gallantine whispered with a hush, superstitious, like his voice was disturbing the resting dead.

Nobody was ready to air their theories, but Adrianna had her hopes: if they knew the Imperials were coming and that the rebels were setting explosives as a trap, maybe the locals had been cleared out for safety? But abandoned toys in the street—aged and forgotten —didn't bode well for that theory.

"Bless our burdens, for they weigh on our shoulders," Holt began the holy mantra.

"Pilgrim won't get you out of here," Mastiff said. He raised two fingers, tapping them to Holt's head and heart. "This and this will."

"Yes, staff sergeant." Holt may have agreed out loud, but he deflated at the resistance, withering like a flower cut from the stem.

Vivian saw it too and she chose conviction. "You not a believer, Mastiff?"

"Prayers don't dig foxholes, ma'am."

"What a bizarre idiom," Voight commented, hobbling up to Vivian's side. "'Cause now I'm picturing some acolyte managing to shout holes into the ground, and I'd follow *that* guy to Hell and back."

Sizemore had his own opinion on it. "Are we talking loose soil or compacted dirt?"

"Either option is equally impressive."

Adrianna craned her neck to look at the eaves of the houses they passed. Every few blocks, there was a camera node—two-foot across with a multitude of lenses, like a bug's eye, but dark and powerless. Sizemore inspected one and confirmed they were without power. Just like the lights and doors and everything else.

Small blessings, she guessed. At least they couldn't be tracked that way. Maybe she could turn that around, track whoever followed? Or even use them to find Prime somewhere in the Upper City.

But she was getting ahead of herself. They had to find food before they found the big bad guy in the evil dark tower.

Concordia wasn't farmland. It was a large-scale industrial dynamo. Concordia needed to make ample use of Replicators and imported goods. That meant frequent and well-stocked storehouses. These buildings proved to be quite common, with one for every two blocks.

Most had been emptied with an almost algorithmic precision: shelves were cleared, empty boxes stacked and compacted for storage, and whatever couldn't be taken out or reserved had been composted in the Replicator—and then that carbon store shipped out. The buildings had long gone cold and dark.

Quite bizarre. Workers of any stripe in any era were often under-paid, under-motivated, or just understaffed. They left behind canned goods, forgot a box or two, promised to come back before getting abruptly re-tasked. But here? Not a single oversight, mistake, or abandoned responsibility. The places were cleaned out like someone had attached a hose to the front door with almost digital precision.

They had better luck in the residential buildings. Sliding doors were left ajar, lights on in every brownstone. Adrianna didn't hear anybody inside, so the trio of Regulars had a little more confidence sweeping the buildings.

"Move careful," Mastiff ordered. "We don't know if they left any surprises for us."

Adrianna didn't see any radio signals or electric traffic, but that didn't rule out mechanical triggers or chemical burns. Better to be cautious anyhow. They needed to find food, medicine, even spare carbon stores that they could take to a Replicator.

Their first search, however, had them whispering like they were treading in a graveyard. They found plates on tables, half-eaten meals abandoned to grow cold. Cabinet doors hanging open and pictures still on walls. She stopped to study one frame: husband, wife, two young kids and one older, in their late teens. Father and his oldest wore mining goggles that weren't for show—the son's had a cracked lens.

She continued on, dragging her fingers along the wallpaper and feeling the scuffs where the corner of a bag had etched itself with force and fury. No care and no pause.

"Somebody left in a hurry," Gallantine muttered, twirling a fork in the plate of pasta still set on the table.

"Don't eat that," Mastiff said.

Gallantine put the fork down. "Wasn't gonna."

"Son, you'd eat *plastic* if I didn't keep an eye on you."

The food was dry, room temp. It still smelt good to her, so Adrianna knew it couldn't have been *that* long ago. And she could understand why Gallantine had started to proverbially circle it like a vulture in the desert. Still, they'd need to verify it for poison or chemistry in the event somebody had left it like a mousetrap.

Voight limped out of the bathroom. "They took all their meds and toiletries."

"Clothes?" Mastiff asked.

Vivian marched out of the bedroom, grinding her jaw. "Most, but not all. Somebody packed in a hurry."

Abandoned things that could spoil but took the necessaries? Adrianna knew an evacuation order when she saw one. And they'd been given exactly no time to prepare for it.

"Hey sarge?" Holt called, his wary tone getting everybody's attention. "You recognize this?"

Mastiff and Adrianna sidled up next to the private. There was something written on the doorjamb, chiseled into the steel and then inlaid with brass—that took some labor to do, an artisan's skill. It wasn't uncommon in particularly fervent Imperial houses to have symbols like the Orchid built in, or words from the Gnostic Librum printed over doorways. Entrances and exits had a particular symbolism in the religious text, and people did so like to exhibit their degree of commitment to guests. Modern Gnosticism did have such a lovely theatrical bend to it.

And of course, she was sure some did it out of genuine belief.

But she didn't recognize these words hammered into this doorway. "'Thick is the bramble on the Path never walked.'"

"Syntax says: magic spell," Voight chuckled from the back.

"When I was laid up in the Core," Holt said, idly cradling his augmented arm, "I watched the Dunsweir's sermons every Sunday. Helped with the therapy and...everything."

"Going to take a guess you don't recognize the quote?" Adrianna asked.

The boy shook his head, and she wasn't surprised. Holkstad Academy burned certain cherry-picked paragraphs of the Librum into young cadets like branding irons, and others still absorbed the religious text like people drank water. She admitted that the young private was probably better schooled in the Librum than she was, but if she didn't recognize the phrase and he didn't either, then it wasn't from the Pilgrim's teachings.

She squinted at the etching at the end of the quote. "E, X, P, 3, 9. That looks an awful lot like a citation to me."

Holt nodded in agreement. "Gnostic, Expansions, Chapter 3, Verse 9 is a summary of Second Wave Plague. Nothing to do with this."

That gave Adrianna the worst feeling: they weren't quoting the Gnostic Librum. They were referencing something else.

Heresy wasn't a word she liked very much, but in her brief experience, she found people behaved very irrationally when they thought God was on their side. On a related note, it was trivial for charismatic folk to spend some energy marketing 'New Good Books' to whoever will read.

"Alright, headcount," Gallantine grunted. "Let's make sure no ghosts ain't taken nobody to a murder room."

Adrianna chuckled. The corporal might have been half-serious, but she needed that shot of levity. If there was anybody else in the building, she'd have heard them by now. But this was an awful lot like the ghost stories she grew up on.

147

Sizemore flicked his Entiglas open, the bright amber light startling Vivian.

"Officer," she whispered past her nerves. "What are you doing?"

"House wireless was never deactivated. Maybe we'll find some explanation in their drives."

Gallantine laughed. "Okay, but if you find a script in Latin, do not read it out loud. I will shoot you."

"You keep opening that cake-hole, corporal, and I *will* stitch it shut," Mastiff scolded.

Sizemore cracked the simple home encryption in seconds—no match for Imperial data security.

The holographic was backwards from Adrianna's perspective, but her onboard system HUD flipped the image without issue. "A home office drive with absolutely *nothing*?" she asked, incredulous. "No inbox, no calendar, not even porn?"

"You keep porn on your home box?" Voight asked, incredulous—and intrigued.

"I do," Adrianna said. "Got something to say about it?"

"No, ma'am." His smirk said plenty.

"You know, everyone thinks that wiping a hard drive actually wipes it," Sizemore said, "but unless you damage the drive too, we can always recover something..."

It took less than a minute for Sizemore to restore the old files, and soon that drive was overflowing. Now this was the record of a life lived. Family of five, blue collar labor, applications to scholarships for their exceptional son. They were going to send him off-world, somewhere in the Core for a proper education.

Adrianna glanced at the meal still set at the table: four places set. Now isn't that interesting?

Whatever happened here, they had been content and together right to the end...sans one.

Sizemore was leafing through the files when she spied it. "Wait. Go back." Adrianna pointed Sizemore to a daily log entry. "That file."

Sizemore saw it too, his eyes squinting. It was four times the size of any other log file. Why? So he opened it.

Text. A lot, in a special font. Some pictures. Sizemore scrolled through it, but then froze on a late entry. His throat constricted, a strange whistling gasping sound. He didn't dare read it.

So Adrianna did: "They came to the house this morning. Three of the Faces this time. They were asking for volunteers, but Thomas told them no. He was angry with them, with the Faces. Angry with Prime, and he told them so."

"Prime?" Vivian asked, breathless.

"The Faces started to threaten us, told us our home would be left behind. When Prime summoned the Gateway, our contributions would be measured—and found wanting."

"We're summoning gateways now?" Holt muttered, mostly to himself.

"The Faces?" Gallantine leaned over to his friend. "I told you, man. Ghosts."

That's when Adrianna saw it. The section that stole Sizemore's breath. But she had to read it for the rest of them. They were waiting for her. "Father tried to explain it to them, but the Faces turned away. They recorded our names and left without another word. Father— Father took Thomas to the altar and..." Adrianna paused on the words. "...and *reduced* him. I asked Father if I would see Thomas again on the Path. He did not serve the Purpose, so he is to remain here."

"Reduced him?" Voight asked. "Can I choose to never know what that means?"

"'Take us on the Path?'" Vivian repeated, inquisitively.

"Well, apocalyptically," Adrianna started, "you *only* join the Path when you die."

"Anybody else think this 'Gateway' is a bomb?" Voight asked. "Just me?"

No matter what Prime and his followers were up to, Adrianna had to admit: not even his followers seemed especially eager to follow every step. And with nobody home now? It looked an awful lot like cooperation had become compulsory.

The mystery of it all kept them sullen and silent. They had no real sunlight in the Undercity but what little light was leaking through the hole above had grown gray and dark. If there was an illumination system for these residences, it wasn't making an appearance. The streets simply grew dark like they'd been swallowed by some great leviathan whose jaw closed ever tighter with the passing hours.

Mastiff and the Regulars deployed their night-vision gear to help, but the deck crew trio were just going to have to stick close.

Adrianna blinked her thermal vision on, sweeping the street for any new threats that might present themselves. She scanned for that splash of white on the black backdrop. It was some help, but she really was frustrated she hadn't taken the low-light implants for moments like this. Not that infrared was of no use to her, of course. But more sight was always better. Callum had both; that had always made her jealous. They had warned her on the table that if she had tried for it, she might go blind. And that had made her wary enough to just pick one. She ended up with the lower end of infra, able to see some microwave and even radio waves. But someone dropped her in a dark room, she basically had to echo locate like a bat.

Bingo bango—she found a heat plume. Two buildings up on the left side. Fire? No—exhaust. It was coming from a warehouse on the east side. Adrianna signaled the crew to hold while she darted on ahead to check.

If this was a trap, she was much better equipped to slip out of it than the others.

She scampered up a wall, using piping and windowsills for footholds. Once on the rooftops, she could approach the source of the heat with a bit more ease. Streets were just shooting galleries waiting for bullets to come ricocheting down them.

She had a good view of the building: gravel rooftop, bloated walls, like the building had taken a deep breath or eaten too much. Warehouse. But with an active plume of hot air gushing from a stack on the far corner? That meant power, possibly refrigeration...

Had they gotten lucky? Maybe this site was overlooked in the evacuation? Or they had simply run out of time?

Adrianna made her way back to the others. "Warehouse with power up ahead."

Gallantine and Voight both sighed with relief, pleasant shivers running up their gangly frames. Even Vivian let a hand go to her aching gut.

Adrianna led them up the street, trying not to make too much noise or get too far ahead. She could somewhat see in the ever-darkening environment, and the Regulars had the IR set into their helmets, but the poor deck crew were starting to operate on blind faith.

They soon came to the loading dock of the warehouse, just as night was covering the Undercity.

"Gallantine, get that door open," Mastiff ordered. "Holt, keep that trigger light. Fire off a shot down here and half this city will be on us in minutes."

Adrianna glanced up at the underside of the city plate above, realizing exactly how true that statement was. They were in a hundred-meter drum and any sufficiently loud noise was going to carry far, even with that howling wind. She slung her rifle and drew her quick knife from its chest-holster.

The slick sound of steel on leather drew an unrepentant shiver from Vivian. Adrianna crooked an eyebrow at her. "You want me to do it again?"

"Fuck off," the chief said.

Gallantine settled at the door with a screwdriver, popping the control panel open to reveal the wiring behind. It took him sixteen seconds to identify which wire went where and build the appropriate connection to bypass the locks. The door slid open with an obnoxious slap that echoed up the street.

Everyone winced as the sound carried. Mastiff glared at Gallantine. The corporal looked awfully sheepish as the sergeant pushed past and into the warehouse. Adrianna was right behind him.

It was a brief walk through the backside of the warehouse full of empty crates. Nothing had been delivered to this place in some time, which wasn't totally surprising, but she was not prepared for what she found in the main floor.

It wasn't a warehouse, but a grocery store—and it was mostly stocked. Rows upon rows of boxes stacked six feet high with nearly ten more open feet of free air, which gave the whole space a soft reverb to every sound. Unpacked pallets were still wrapped for transport, waiting in the aisles.

She heard Gallantine whimper in joy and Holt mutter some prayer. Even Mastiff relaxed a bit.

Adrianna didn't see any electronic signals, no radio traffic, and definitely no heat. But that didn't rule out all threats. "Folks," she whispered, "dinner is served."

"Two by two, and stick with your partner," Mastiff ordered. "Nobody goes anywhere alone. Gather medicine, food. Meet back here in ten. Go."

Adrianna needed calorie dense food. She went right for the peanut butter aisle, and to her great luck there was an entire crate of the stuff—off-world: genuine A-grade full of sugar, fats, and proteins. Everything a growing child needs.

She dropped two containers in her pack and popped the third one open. Peeling the foil back on a fresh tin of peanut butter was a special kind of joy, pristine smooth texture and a warm brown color that frankly *should* be disquieting. But nothing felt more welcoming than smooth untouched peanut butter.

"How's the shoulder holding up?"

Adrianna snapped out of her snacking to see Vivian and Voight at the end of the aisle, standing there like some kind of rustic painting: Imperial Gothic.

She gave the shoulder a good few circles, ignoring the mild twinges and bite of cold. "Can't complain."

"You have a shard of Pilgrim Metal embedded in your torso," Voight noted, "and you 'can't complain?'"

"There's not a lot I complain about."

"I rather think that was his point," Vivian said. She looked at the box of peanut butter Adrianna had casually dived into. "You going to pack some actual food, too?"

"All the food groups," Adrianna said, "but, y'know, it called to me." That got an understanding nod from Voight. Vivian marched up to her, peering at the wound, and Adrianna got the strangest feeling that she was looking at something private. "Chief?"

Vivian acknowledged the overreach and took a step back. "Sorry. The only Pilgrim Metal I've ever seen was during Sunday Sermons. Never been this close before."

It had less allure when it was forcibly implanted, but Adrianna understood the fascination. The Dunsweir family kept most of the Pilgrim artifacts tucked away in their manor home, far from the eyes of the public. They would reveal them from time to time, suspended overhead to enchant the crowds, reinforcing their family's singular connection to the holy Pilgrim that had lifted humanity from near collapse.

Sure, there was stuff on display at the Royal Academy on Ilum, but 'twas whispered they were mere replicas or artistic renditions.

Adrianna remembered that...something that had swirled just beneath the surface of the metal, like a creature testing the surface of water. Or a prisoner inspecting its cell.

Vivian said something that she hadn't been paying attention to. She had to play back her recording to hear the words. "We need to understand what Prime wants if we're to intervene with their plans."

"Here we go again," Voight grumped.

"Our objective was to obtain fresh supplies, and obtain them we have," Vivian scolded, breaking out that distinctive matron voice used only on misbehaving children. It made Adrianna stand up straighter and sent a strangely pleasant chill down her spine.

Voight was likely quite familiar with the tone because it had no effect on him whatsoever. "We're three out of seven injured, walking blind. You ever heard of cutting your losses, chief?"

"I feel like I've heard this conversation already," Adrianna interjected.

Vivian didn't miss a beat. "That would be because you have yet to decide our course."

"I decided!" Adrianna said, diving her fingers back into the peanut butter. "I decided we needed supplies and to regroup."

"And it was a good call," Vivian conceded. "Much as I belabored the point, it did *not* need immediate action. So you bought yourself some time to think on it. And time you've now had. Now every second we wait, these rebels gets further in their plans—plans we know very little about."

"Sounds like we need some Military Intelligence," Adrianna said, suddenly and very deeply missing Graccus' voice. "So we, uh...we get a call out back home, try to put some heads together?"

What she got was Voight. "Yeah, the Home Office did such a bang-up job the first time. Let's give 'em another crack at it."

"Anything they have is likely out of date," Vivian pointed out. "We ourselves would be providing the most up-to-date Intelligence."

That wasn't true. "No," Adrianna said. "No, there's exactly one other person with more Intelligence than we have right now. And he's local."

Everybody else caught up at once. "Janus."

"Janus can fill us in," Adrianna said. "We find Janus and we can figure out if what's happening here is remotely within our ability to stop."

"Or escape," Voight said, somewhat gloomily.

"Okay, but how are we going to find one person in a city under lockdown patrolled by militant zealots?" Vivian asked.

"Well, when you put it like that," Adrianna groused.

Click.

There was no way the two Vees heard it, far too soft, too far away. Seven people moving, shifting, shuffling—boots scuffing and laminate squeaking. But in all that noise, nothing that would go 'click'. Click was a metal sound, a snapping sound.

A trigger sear.

Adrianna dropped the peanut butter tin, dashing off down the aisle, the rubber soles squealing as they left tread behind. It was four aisles over, something in the shelves. Not a person, but something metal.

She rounded the corner in time to see Mastiff and Sizemore picking through shelves for machine tools. Sizemore was hopping on one leg, trying to keep balanced after tripping—tripping slightly on the thin wire laid tightly across the aisle at ankle height.

There, on the shelf, the spoon of a grenade was tumbling free, yanked by the wire. It popped out of a steel bucket, shaping the explosion out toward the aisle. In that grenade's core, two chemicals were now mixing, a predictable exothermic reaction taking place. Rapid expansion would increase pressure until the casing ruptured.

Mastiff knew the sound of the dreaded spoon and his instincts took over. He was already halfway to the ground. But Sizemore looked for whatever had tripped him, confused. And then he saw the grenade. Curiously studied it.

And realized what it was. Too late.

As fast as her implants could move her, Adrianna blew down the aisle and tackled Sizemore to the ground, letting the cheap home-made explosive go off behind her. It was quieter than she expected but still loud enough, blasting flechette through the aisle and into the next.

Not as potent as what could be, but good enough for homemade. It was essentially a remote-triggered shotgun.

Sizemore groaned underneath her, favoring his arm, and she could already see blood staining his uniform. Had he been hit? Had she? No—she'd just hit him hard enough to compound fracture his arm. Saved his life, but he was going to pay just the same.

And they'd just rang the dinner bell.

CHAPTER
FOURTEEN

SIZEMORE SCREAMED UNDERNEATH HER, unable to move. She could feel the snapped humerus prodding her through his shirtsleeve. She may have saved his life, but his body was not equipped to take the hit she had to throw to do it.

"Medic!" Adrianna shouted.

"Come careful," Mastiff added. "There might be more of those!"

"What happened?!" Vivian shouted from three aisles over.

"IED tucked in the shelving," Adrianna called out. "Watch for trip wires."

Mastiff slid over to her, keeping his head low. He didn't know if that trap was going to be accompanied with gunfire. The sergeant peeked underneath Adrianna, inspecting the wound. "Oh, that? Ain't hardly a bug bite, Sizemore. You'll be just fine."

"Don't touch me! D-don't touch me!" He screamed back. Almost like he was furious with them. She told herself it was the shock setting in.

"Three deck crew kissing dirt, and they're the three people that get injured," Adrianna huffed.

"I wasn't going to say it," Mastiff grunted, turning his head to shout. "Where the Hell is my aid kit, Gallantine?!"

Almost as soon as he finished shouting, Holt and Gallantine both came careening around the corner. Holt slid to a stop, turning his back to take up security and simultaneously allow Gallantine into his backpack. The corporal quickly yanked out supplies: splint, Medigel, antiseptic.

Which is when Adrianna heard the second most terrifying thing: footfalls. Lots of them. "Get him mobile, corporal."

"Due respect, ma'am, that's going to take a minute."

Adrianna pulled her rifle off her back, charging the capacitor. "I'll give you two minutes, but then you gotta be outta here."

She marched down the aisle, but Mastiff snagged her wrist. "Lieutenant!"

Adrianna whirled around on him, coming nose to nose with the old man. "I've got a dozen shooters about to blow through that door, and plenty more behind 'em. You don't have enough bullets to play that game."

"And you'll cook before you get 'em all, lieutenant!"

She yanked Mastiff close, pulling him in tight. "Get these people out of here. That's my order: you get mobile, you get a ship, you get the *Hell* off this rock! Do you understand me, sergeant?"

The gravity of what went unsaid wasn't lost on him. She was going down, right here, right now.

"*Zu gloriam*, Riley."

For glory.

And he let her go.

Adrianna made for the front door of the grocery store. She had two good mags for her Gauss rifle. After that, she'd have to improvise and watch her heat build. Too much work and she'd cook out her implants, leaving herself helpless. Resource management was the name of the game.

Oskies didn't retire. Oskies didn't go home. Oskies were the Sword, the Shield, the Service.

She was going to earn that mantle today.

Adrianna could hear the mercenaries assembling outside, stacking up on the doorway prior to breach. They used the walls for obfuscation, completely unaware that the insulation and sheet metal offered them no material protection.

And she knew where they were.

Adrianna couldn't let them through this doorway. This was her doorway. It belonged to her. If even one shooter got past her, she'd risk the injured and vulnerable people inside.

So she shouldered her weapon, punching three shots through the wall, drilling individual shots right where they would've been hunkering. And she was rewarded for her guess, hearing the pained yelps of surprised assholes on the other side.

'Course, that worked both ways.

The rebels returned fire through the wall, spraying blindly for her. They may not see her, but the sheer volume of fire made for a difficult obstacle course. Canned foods exploded, spraying soups and goo everywhere, painting floor and ceiling with a rainbow of fluids. She bobbed and weaved, picking her way through the cloud.

But they had a far more potent response queued. The wall ripped open, clouds of tungsten balls ripping through. Her eyes went wide and she fell flat on the floor, letting the wall of death sail by overhead. The blasts came through three or four per second, defilading her position and keeping her pinned low. Her heartbeat damn near synced up with the punctuating bass of the weapon.

An automatic shotgun?! Belt-fed, maybe? The mercs had brought something special just to clean up Oskies like her. No amount of careful ballet work would help with something that *filled* the air with metal!

Finally, the shotgun went quiet, immediately followed by someone bellowing an order. "Pressure up!"

Adrianna crept along the floor, silently making her way up to one side of the double-doors. If she couldn't bottleneck them here, she'd never handle them all, let alone the shotgun-bastard beyond.

The first soldier came kicking through, two-point tac sling on his old internal combustion rifle. Gear might be old and barbaric, but his movements were clean with good control of the muzzle. Goon one swept left—and she let him go. Room clearing 101 said that goon number two was going to come in and peel right.

Right into her.

She grabbed the barrel of his gun, twirling the rifle up behind his neck and binding him in his sling. Good soldier, good instincts: he let go of his weapon immediately, going for his sidearm. Adrianna was ready for it, and ten times faster. She planted her palm over his, locking the gun into its holster.

A single shot rang out, narrowly missing the goon's foot.

Bracing the rifle against her captive's head, she squeezed the trigger, dropping her hostage's partner with two shots to the back before he even knew there was a struggle happening.

Two more goons swept in, and despite the concussive blasts at his ear and the nylon chokehold, her captive soldier had the presence of mind to give up on weapons entirely. He reached with one free hand around her waist and tried to kick out her legs, bind her up. If he couldn't kill her, maybe his companions could while she was helplessly pinned.

But wrestling with a bear was a poor choice. She picked her feet up, and bringing him down with her, she drove him into the laminate floor—right onto the prickly iron sights of his rifle, which jammed straight into his neck.

Adrianna was not the one pinned, so when the shots came, she was able to tumble across the man's body, letting them riddle their own comrade and end his suffering. She ripped his sidearm out, chambering a fresh round and popping the two soldiers in the chest.

They stumbled, but their chest plates and visors took the hits with ease, cracking but nothing more. Pistol rounds just didn't have the clout to play that game.

Frustrated, Adrianna chucked the pistol toward the door, sliding it right under the next soldier's feet. He stepped right on it and slipped like he was suddenly on an icy lake. Adrianna drew up her own rifle, finishing the two stumbling victims before they could collect themselves, and then popped the clumsy oaf on the ground.

Ceramic armor plates were better than nothing but three-round bursts from 40-40 Gauss managed what ten-millimeter Horus never could. She was hitting them with forty caliber silksteel rounds hurled by enough electricity to power a house for an hour. The pre-fragmented tip probably didn't do much against the ceramic plate, but by the third hit, it didn't much matter.

She heard the priming of electric charges—they had gotten fed up trying the main door and decided to make their own. Four distinct cracks, and a six-foot circle punched out of the grocery store wall twenty meters away.

Dammit! She couldn't hold *two* doors at once!

Adrianna dashed over to the new opening, but that shotgun started in again, ripping through the outer wall—and sheering off the first third of her rifle, barrel and handguard together.

She dropped the broken weapon and kept going. If he hit her, he hit her. There was very little she could do about that, but she had to get to that door!

She was leaving a yellow tracer in the air, a cloud of steam behind her as her sweat boiled. The thermal sinks embedded throughout her body were taxed to their limit and she was starting to cook.

No way to know if her friends were okay. Just keep pushing.

The dust and smoke cleared, and the first merc made entry through the opening. Adrianna may have been wheezing and glowing, but she was still faster than he was. He presented his carbine to split the skull of the approaching wraith, and she barely slid out of the way. The flare from the muzzle-brake singed her uniform and she could smell some of her hair on fire.

She got a hand on the barrel, spinning it around the merc—and let him spray his own friends with it. Once, twice around and she had the gun's upper receiver pressed against his windpipe. He had just gotten two fingers up in the way to prevent her from garroting him with his own tac sling. He pressed back against the motion, twisting away from her.

Two more goons rushed in, and Adrianna pivoted to get the stock on her shoulder and use her new buddy as cover. Even though she was choking a man with it, she fired the rifle, squeezing two rounds into the newcomers' heads. The shell casings spat up into her captive's face, plinking him on the cheek.

Suddenly the gun went silent. A shell casing had gotten jammed in the action, locking it open. No time to clear it.

As the next merc came vaulting over his dead friends, she just reached forward on the rifle, punching out the two carrier pins with her thumb and ripping the barrel assembly off the rifle. It didn't have to be sharp; it was a two-pound hardened steel rod. She just threw it straight for his chest.

It made the most satisfying crack sound as it shattered the ceramic and sunk into his heart.

Her captive was getting feisty. He roared at her, pushing back on the tac sling hard—

—and so she let him roll himself out from his choking hazard. And as he turned to present his sidearm at her, Adrianna backhanded him across the jaw. The counter-twist was enough to snap his neck cleanly. She doubted he felt a thing.

Which might have been a blessing. She heard the click-clap of a receiver snapping closed and dove to the side just in time to escape the shotgun blast filling her airspace with more pellets. The pellets missed her, instead tearing half of the dead merc's ribcage away, showering a nearby aisle with red confetti.

Adrianna never got a good look at the shooter because there was always another blast to duck, another wall of tungsten ball bearings looking to pulverize her. She tumbled back toward the front door of the store, looking for cover behind the check-out counters. No such luck, these were pop ups of circuitry and pot metal. The tungsten tore through it like it wasn't even there.

Her skin was so slick and hot, she thought she must've been hit. But it was just the sweat clinging to her skin. Every inhale felt like drinking through a humid veil, like there was just less oxygen in the air with each pull. She left yellow tracers in the air as the speed of her movement left a residual glow in the air.

Her instructors warned her to fear the smell of breakfast ham. She never quite knew what they meant, but wouldn't you know it, she could swear a hot breakfast was on the griddle somewhere.

Another shot! She tried to sidestep—but it glanced off her shoulder, scraping off the subdermal armor plate. Just skin and scuffing with the barest hint of blood, but it told her something much worse: she was slowing. She could hear herself wheezing, the servo and motor function grinding in the air.

This was going to be it, huh? Overcooked, overrun, overwhelmed. She wouldn't be the first Oskie to go down swinging.

Adrianna staggered over to the wall, propping herself up with one hand. Sweat spilled down her forehead and her skin thrummed, pulsed, like something inside her was clawing for any way out of her.

Kidney function failing, arrhythmia, eyes unable to focus. She was too hot, way too hot. She was so hot her diagnostics were just returning error messages.

Fine. She'd given her team their two minutes. If it was possible, they were out by now. Mastiff would take good care of 'em.

Boots crunched on spent brass casings, scuffing on tile, approaching her with caution. She could barely hear his heartbeat over her own, a syncopated bass, and that just made her realize that her own heart wasn't in rhythm anymore.

The man was older, stripes of silver through his beard and hair, and a liquidity to his movement. Despite his nerves, he moved with commitment and precision. He shouldered some jackhammer of a weapon, a shotgun with a magazine as thick as the ball of her shoulder.

He crept around her cover, weapon tracking onto her as her chest convulsed for breath. Waiting for some Oskie trick. But she didn't have enough gas to give him anything else. Her chest rose and fell, the only part of her still capable of moving. And the sound of it, like an engine struggling, metal on metal.

His eyes scanned her. Gray eyes, big. At some point in his life, maybe even kind eyes. But there was a veneer to them, a dulling of the senses—a loss of compassion. He squinted for a moment, considering her.

Doubting himself? Maybe he'd expected something more brutal, more cruel. Some potent force worthy of his efforts, worthy of fighting, a beast. And what he found was just another person, crumpled on the ground and struggling for breath.

He shook whatever those heretical thoughts were right out of his head. And those eyes darkened to meet the task. He shouldered his abomination of a gun, finger on the trigger...

Come on. Do it. She urged him on with a tense lip, almost sneering at him.

But he hesitated, those eyes tracking over to her hand....

What? What was he so transfixed by? In between heavy and cooling breaths, she followed his gaze. And her jaw almost dropped.

The wall under her fingers, sheet metal and insulation, had...had smelted into an ugly goo, a smoking pocked dough of materials like bread from Hell.

Had she really been that hot, hot enough to slag?! No, she'd be dead long before she was hot enough to melt anything other than herself. There wasn't enough heat in the human body to melt steel, even with her implanted thermal sinks to soak the build-up. You could take all of the thermal energy in a living person and it wouldn't ignite coal!

And she had been well and truly cooked, half a mile over her limit just seconds ago. But now her breathing had evened out, her heart stilled, and the muscle spasms had calmed. All without a shower, a cold drink, or even an extended break. In fact, her diagnostics said she was well within operational standards. No more errors. Fit for duty.

Melt a wall—and she was ready for round two. How about that?

"*Fra tow zu, diamau!*" the merc cursed. 'Diamau'. Demon.

His gun went off and she wasn't going to question her good luck. Subdermal processors, servos in muscle groups, and high-tensile steel fibers worked in concert to lean her out of the way of the shot. And he was far too close to make good use of his shotgun's spread, narrow pellet clouds without time to really broaden. They sank harmlessly into the wall, punching a six-inch hole through what had been her crutch moments before.

This was impossible. She had been taxed, tapped, overclocked. She should have been invalid, helpless. Instead, Adrianna was closing the distance.

She paired her steps with the cyclic rate of the shotgun. Each time the bolt carrier slammed back, she put a foot down and juked a new direction, letting the fresh death slice through empty air.

He had four chances to get her. She didn't give him a fifth, swiping her fist over and down on the muzzle of the shotgun. The jerk on his tac sling pulled him off-balance, teetering him forward. She palmed the back of his head and pushed him through the fall, straight down. The barrel of his gun jammed into the floor—and he went neck-first onto the stock. The swift crack told her that the only thing connecting skull to spine now was the soft tissue.

No more shots. No more noise. No more...heat.

She looked at her hand, quizzical. How long had that little trick been hiding away? Was that some implant the egg heads neglected to tell her about? No, some quick math told her that was thermodynamically impossible. She had somehow pushed the heat out of her tissues and into the wall with enough aggression as to melt it?! There wasn't a material in the Empire that did that.

This was something else...

"Lieutenant?"

Adrianna lifted her sweaty, exhausted head to see Mastiff standing nearby, rifle ready. Either he had never left or he'd come back for her, but he was currently staring at the slagged wall only just now losing its own orange glow. His words might have been curt and direct, but his voice was all panic. "Neighborhood's up and hungry."

He was right. They weren't out of the woods just yet.

MISSION TIME: 13:38

"WE COULD'VE QUESTIONED THAT MAN," Mastiff scolded, as they sprinted down the street.

She didn't challenge the idea, but she knew how futile that would've been. Something steel drove these mercenaries onward, and it wasn't pay. She'd fought plenty of paid work in the Boolean. These men here? They were in it for something more potent than pay.

Belief.

"You should be dead." Mastiff's words weren't exactly the kick of confidence Adrianna had been hoping for. They just added to her own bewilderment.

"That may be, but that's a mystery to unpack when we're not being actively tailed," she said. "Where are the others?"

"Two blocks east." He looked at her with a sour face that was probably the closest thing to a smile that had ever hit his face. "If I didn't go turn back for you, the chief was about to."

Adrianna buried her laugh at that. The injured Vivian Bannister would've absolutely hobbled back into danger no matter what anybody said. And then Voight would've gone in after her. And if Sizemore wasn't laid up, he'd be following the both of them like a lost puppy.

"They're good people," Adrianna said.

"Good people," the sergeant agreed, "but not terribly smart."

"Sergeant, we're in the ground pound business. Only people dumber than us are tankers."

"If it make big boom, ma'am, I wouldn't be mocking it."

Adrianna stopped at a street corner, hearing the pounding feet up ahead. She raised her fist, signaling Mastiff to stop short.

Another full squad, although they weren't regularly or neatly geared. They all had armor and rigs, but there wasn't exactly a neat assortment of roles or weaponry. These guys had brought whatever they personally owned or could be supplied with locally.

There he was. What?! Marching with the unit was the gray-bearded man and his belt-fed shotgun monstrosity. She'd snapped his neck not five minutes ago! There were more of him?! What kind of mirror dimension bullshit was this?

She wasn't relishing the idea of dancing with anymore shotguns today.

The mystery man sneered like he had caught a foul smell on the air. Did she smell like fish still? She certainly reeked of sweat and death.

But none of it drew his focus. He nodded and the squad of mercs moved on down the street, back towards the grocery store. When the squad had passed by, Adrianna lowered her hand, but Mastiff didn't move. He was still staring at her hand. "I know as much as you do, sergeant."

"Good," he said, swallowing, "because I don't need any more surprises."

Two blocks east, and there they were. Sizemore was drawn onto a stretcher, his arm splinted. Based on his complete lack of movement, they had sedated him. Voight and Gallantine were actively muttering and tending to their colleague.

It was Holt who spoke up first, snapping his rifle up and calling IFF. "Mercury!"

"Sunburnt," Mastiff called back.

Everyone calmed down and Adrianna stepped into the light, robbing everyone of breath. They had clearly expected confirmation of her demise or for hostile contact in his absence, but here stood the lieutenant, uninjured and unfazed.

Vivian jumped to her feet, rushing over to greet Adrianna, but stopped at a respectful distance. "Lieutenant."

The chief's flustering brought an involuntary flick of a smile to Adrianna's face. "Good to see you too."

Vivian inspected her commander, and it was like she doubted what her impaired vision told her. Like she had to look twice as hard to find whatever she might have missed. "How?"

"I believe I can—" Whoever was speaking never got the fifth word out. It was a fresh voice, a curious one. Which made four separate guns all draw down on the speaker in the same instant.

And Adrianna's eyes went wide.

There he was, hands raised in shock, nervous laughter rolling through him: Hirochi Kaneda.

She hadn't heard him speak before. Why would she? He should have been blown to molecular powder. But he had a strange accent, like a historical figure from old America. "Whoa—hi. Yes, that was predictable. Please don't shoot me."

"Drop the weapon!" Mastiff hissed at him.

"Not a weapon, but dropping it anyway! Dropping it. I am so very co-opera-teeve." Kaneda tossed aside his cane, thin metal piping with a brushed bit of brass for the handle. Custom shaped for his hand. Which meant it wasn't for an injury, but something more chronic.

Adrianna gave him a quick up and down. Not a tall man, five foot and single digits. And one leg was severely shorter than its partner by a few inches. Ah. Why hadn't they corrected that in utero?

"Fair bit says you know who I am," Kaneda said with a shaky voice.

"That's some grasp of the fucking obvious," Gallantine cursed at him.

Voight laughed. "Luck of the century, we have."

"Shut up, both of you," Mastiff snapped, before turning back to Kaneda. "You: start talking."

Kaneda let out a kind of nervous giggle as he tried to compose his thoughts, but before he could speak, Adrianna started in. "You died. I watched it. You should be pink mist."

Kaneda, hands still raised, pointed one crooked finger down at her. "Yes. *That* is going to need some explaining. But by the time I'm done doing that in any degree of detail, we're all going to be barbe-cue." That sentiment got Gallantine to shove his gun closer to his face and Kaneda winced. "I-I swear, it's really hard to focus when I can *literally* see the bullet."

Vivian laid a hand on Gallantine's rifle, pushing it down and taking the very dangerous action of stepping closer to Kaneda. All Adrianna could think of is another bomb, another blast wave— another friend.

But Vivian got two full steps towards him and the dead man didn't produce any secret detonator, any elusive blade. So Vivian asked him: "Why the time limit?"

"Uhh...shit, how fast can I do this?" Kaneda's eyes scanned high, picking his words, and then they all came tumbling out. "Short version: your big friend there did a special thing. We can track the, uh...energy signature of the special thing–that's how I found you, by the way–they're *descending* on this place—we need to go and I *promise* I'll keep talking. But we have to go now."

"Oh, you promise, huh?" Vivian's statement sounded oddly like a threat.

Kaneda's eyes flicked between Adrianna and Vivian, the guns, and then back to Adrianna again. It almost seemed plaintive. Like he was begging them.

Nothing like the Kaneda they had found that morning, kneeling in prayer before a monolith: cool, calm, assured. Self-destructive. This man was manic, shaky on his feet, clumsy. And she could see his face flushing, heartbeat unhealthy and erratic. This man had more health conditions than someone hit by a bus.

It's like they were two completely different men.

Something howled in the air and Holt shouldered his weapon, looking for whatever threat had yet to present itself. It felt like the air was pressing down on them.

"Uh, guys," Voight chimed in, "I don't know if anybody else just got that real spooky feeling, but, uh..."

Sergeant Mastiff shook his head, sneering at Kaneda. "I don't trust it. Corporal?"

He didn't need the official instruction. Gallantine raised his rifle again, tracking right on Kaneda's head.

"I'm Janus," Kaneda spouted in panic. "Janus, your—your contact. I'm your man on the ground! You wouldn't shoot your contact!"

"'Janus' supposed to mean something to me?" Vivian expertly lied.

Of course it did, being the codename of their spy. And of course, this gangly buffoon very well might be the real deal, but he also could just as easily have gotten that name from torture and threw it out now as a last-ditch effort to ingratiate himself.

If he really was their contact, why not lead with that? And he still hadn't explained the whole same face thing.

Then again...if he wanted them dead, why did he amble up to them without a gun, a knife, a bomb of any kind? No transmitters, no electronics. He had a cane.

Ground-level local informants might give up their identity under duress. Military intelligence would rather die than confirm their sources or methods, so Adrianna would never know for sure who Janus was. But for all his health problems, the sweating, the stammering...Adrianna was sure of one thing: this little man wasn't lying.

"You'll never get off this planet without the things I know." Look at Kaneda! Making the bold statement and steeling himself for the consequences of it.

And it predictably drew a small one-hit laugh from Vivian. "Sure we will. Corporal: ventilate him."

Adrianna saw the corporal's finger slipping into the trigger well, depressing the trigger. Adrianna lurched forward, snagging Gallantine's weapon away from him. The corporal rocked back and forth like a bobblehead, stunned, and squeezing his trigger finger on the now empty air. He just stood there, miming the action, with lips pursed in a mixture of impressed and terrified.

Adrianna turned to Kaneda, looming over him. "Janus?"

"Hi." Kaneda's voice had shrunk, scared into some cave in the back of his throat. He coughed, trying to recover some of his composure. "You are...so much taller than I thought you'd be. What are you, six foot forever?"

"What do you know? Hit me with a good one."

"...avoid the cameras," he said. "The CCTV. She's watching you through them and if she can see you, the guys with guns won't be far behind."

Adrianna leered up at the street cameras—the flickering lens of one staring right back at her. Motionless. Powerless. No radio traffic. "Who can see us? Prime?"

"It'd take longer to explain," he urged, "but if you want to lose them, you need to stay out of sight of those cameras."

"Those cameras are dead," Holt said. "Sizemore checked 'em."

"And I'm sure he's very good at his job, but you asked," Kaneda said.

Adrianna leaned over him, pushing back against the wall. "You're going to shut up for a little bit." But she looked back up at the camera, leery of it. Squinting, studying it.

And she saw the lens twitch.

Motherfucker. He was telling the truth. They must be hard-lined. How could they have missed that?! Sizemore was no amateur, which meant that whoever did this was a grade above.

"Ruck up, everybody," Adrianna ordered. "Sergeant, take the package. I've got point."

CHAPTER
SIXTEEN

THERE WERE NO FEWER than two guns trained on Kaneda at any given time as they marched out of the neighborhood. Residential buildings and warehouses gave way to more industrial settings.

They were getting out into the middle of the plate now, far away from the support of the mountains and directly into the path of the wind. That vortex ripped through this artificial tunnel between the plates, caught by the wind catchers above.

Buildings on the Undercity had to be low profile, barely two stories tall—not a very efficient use of space, keeping buildings low to the ground, so it was mostly used for recreation: artificial greenery, leisure paths, large game fields.

A lot of open space to be caught in.

There were more cameras than she had thought, too. It was like they passed two every single block, and it was a chore staying out of their view—the open areas making that especially complicated. She doubted even her speed would beat the refresh rate on those things. So they had to move carefully.

But they got lucky, finding a larger than average structure: a clock tower. These poor colonists didn't have digital tools for every day, and still needed centralized time-keeping, at the very least to set their schedules by. Around the base of the tower was a small assortment of administrative buildings and happy greenery, like a tiny city hall. But nobody was home.

So the team took up residence. Sensing an opportunity for some reconnaissance, Adrianna scaled the outside of the clock tower, finding natural pockmarks in the brickwork as handholds. The stuff was so weak and porous that a few chunks came loose in her grip, breaking into sand.

From up high, she had a good view of the valley between the mountains—even the meager sunlight through the hole had closed off into night. They didn't have the benefit of starlight or a moon down here, and whatever artificial lighting had once lit the downtrodden second-class had been long since darkened. This was the kind of black someone found when magically cursed.

It didn't take much altitude for that vortex of wind to pick up, the cool air blowing through her hair like it wanted to take her head off. It also brought plenty of smells her way: the stink of fire, some ionic ozone, and the unmistakable sickly sweet of rotting meat.

There was very little in the universe that smelled like that, and if she had to guess, it was a mass grave. That evacuation order might not have been so friendly. She wondered what happened to anyone who didn't agree with this uprising?

When Adrianna looked back the way they came, she saw the ambient glow of body heat from the industrial sector. The air temperature alone had risen seven degrees. The sheer amount of bodies it would take to raise the temperature of the air was astounding. She had fought a patrol, first responders.

What showed up after was an army.

"What do you see?" Voight hissed up at her, cautious not to be too loud.

She took one last look at that glow of heat spiraling up from the industrial district, before dropping down to him with a polite thud. "Unless the entire rebellion is in that single square mile, this is a bigger uprising than we thought."

Voight laughed, a terrified and hollow attempt at positivity. He jogged in place, shivering. "Well, the Home Office really screwed the pooch on this one." And his thin shell crumbled the moment she looked at him. His voice sunk deep down into his throat, unable to show its full colors as his breathing rattled, his hands trembling. "What are we going to do?"

Adrianna glanced back to the city hall, shadows passing in darkened windows, where the others had taken roost. "I say we find out if anybody found graham crackers and marshmallows."

His lip twitched in a failed smile. "Not sure we really want to light a fire."

"I don't see why not," she said. "World's going to come crashing down, anyway. Might as well be comfortable."

Voight chuckled, but that soon turned sour, and he sniffed the grit out of his nose. He looked up at her like a skittish animal. And he then put the obvious into words. "I'm really fuckin' scared, Riley."

What could she say to that? There wasn't a word in any language she knew that would restore his cheer, his candor. The playful young officer had been to genuine war and back safely, but nothing like this. He had always clung to the sky, looking down on trouble or dancing between threats with the comfort of an armored sleeve tucked around him.

But here he was exposed, shivering, cold, in an unnatural dark brought on by a steel sky. He had never been prey before.

So she grabbed him by the shoulder and gently pulled him in close, tucking his head against her collar, and let him have some of her warmth.

Adrianna followed Voight as he hobbled up the steps of the city hall and into the main lobby. There were a handful of stiff benches and ergonomic chairs laid out like rows of crops. Gallantine had taken over the receptionist's desk and field stripped his rifle there, all the parts laid out on a mat. He meticulously scrubbed at a coil that had collected a bunch of metal filings, but due to the window frame blocking her view, it looked like he was filing his nails at first glance. It also allowed the corporal to keep a close eye on the sleeping Sizemore safely tucked behind him, who finally had a small IV line of painkiller to help his now-splinted arm.

Private Holt was busily sorting through his third bag of loot from the store, creating an inventory on his Entiglas. He kept throwing nervous glances toward Sizemore whenever the sleeping officer stirred. He caught Adrianna's eye, forcing a weak smile, feigning strength.

While the others were desperately scraping their fortitude for some spare courage, Vivian and Mastiff had a target for their ire: both staring pure distilled weapons-grade death at their new guest. Voight sidled up next to them, presenting his refreshed jovial facade.

If only everyone knew how close to the edge Voight really was... but he would never let them know.

Kaneda, to his credit, sat with a perfectly straight back in the center of the room, almost like he came to city hall with an appointment to lodge a formal complaint about subpar education materials. He was bound at the wrists and ankles with some spare lengths of wire, bindings which only highlighted the difference in length between his two legs—his left had to be bent next to his fully extended right in order to bind his ankle.

Adrianna could see the heat building in his calf as he strained to keep that shorter leg supported. Despite the ache, he wasn't making a fuss. Rather, he was bright wide eyes and full bare-toothed smile at the pair of watchdogs. He looked like he was staring down a hungry tiger, worried it might snap him up when he blinked.

Nobody was talking—fear of any noise drawing further military-grade responses, but Adrianna didn't have the same reservation. Anything nearby was petrified or dead. "Alright, 'Janus', you can speak again."

"Is she going to shoot me if I do?" Kaneda grimaced through his clenched teeth.

"No, she will not."

At that assurance, Kaneda let his smile drop and hung his head. His exhale was the loudest thing any of them had heard in a while, a big trumpet that echoed up through the buildings, which just set everyone's nerves on edge. It wasn't until he lifted his head that he noticed the effect it had and bit his lip. "...Sorry."

Adrianna raised an eyebrow. "Let's start with the obvious one. How are you alive?"

He nodded, his voice dropping low and quiet, newly sensitive of their anxieties. "Because I, me, myself—I wasn't in that building. You were with—I guess, no, I guess *I am...*"

"Sorry!" Voight butted in. "I have to: *what* is that accent?! You sound like a historic re-enactor."

"I'm from Brooklyn." Kaneda looked at Voight with an almost dire intensity, a new focus and a new tone to his voice. "How long you been deployed, kid?"

"Don't answer that." Mastiff snapped.

"I don't need him to. It was rhetorical," Kaneda said. "Few months, year at the most. Even with mild time dilation, Jump tech will have you home before long. You'll go back to your berth, find your favorite restaurant, hit up your favorite club, maybe go wine tasting. Pick up that bottle you let age a bit while you're out here. You know what I miss most?" The man looked up at Adrianna, that intensity fading into plaintive. "Books."

Gallantine stood up from behind the reception desk with skeptical, crossed arms. "Do they not have books on Concordia?"

"You have written word," Kaneda said, baleful and hurt. "You have text, you have stories. You have news and gossip, but you don't have *books*. Paper, binding, glue. I loved libraries. There was a...a smell." He was lost in that memory for a long moment before blinking back to the present. "You can still find paper, sure, but it's a commodity now. Did you know people used to have bookcases in their homes? In their homes!"

"Not for about a hundred fifty years," Adrianna said.

"Exactly. Earth's atmosphere became too toxic. Sure, the carbon printers can make them, but it's not the same. I don't know why. I mean, it's literally, chemically the same thing, but there's something soulless about it."

"Don't lose the thread, Janus," she warned him. "Why are we talking about books?"

"Lose the thread, that's funny. Like anybody weaves anymore. You just print what you want. Look at that—even stole the word. *Print*."

This was going nowhere. Adrianna reached for her quick knife. "If you're going to keep talking in circles—"

"I'm *trying* to tell you what's happened!" he snapped, suddenly forceful and serious. "I'm a copy. The man in Caldera who went up under forty pounds of pop rocks? He was a copy. We're all copies. Copies of the same person."

And it hit her like all the blocks just slipped into place. "Prime," she whispered.

The word struck some kind of chord in him, like a shard of ice was inserted under his skin. "He was the first, but even him...still just a copy."

"A clone?" Adrianna repeated, skeptical.

"Cloning of human beings is outlawed by Imperial Edict," Vivian blurted. "It would take an act of the Statesmen signed by the Consul-General to overturn that."

"Yay, my existence is a felony," Kaneda faux-cheered.

"A copy of who exactly?" Voight asked, haunted.

"Whom," Kaneda corrected, but he breezed on before anybody could jump on him. "He was—the original, he...I was a Pathfinder."

"That's dangerous work," Mastiff said, almost impressed.

"Yeah, what you call Pathfinding, I call hopscotch. You want to talk about *real* Jumps? You..." He paused, stumbling on his words almost like he had a headache that was muddying his thoughts. "I-I was linked up with a computer and a rocket, along with as much food and water as math would let us put in the damn thing. And when I spun up the Jump drive for the first time, something went wrong."

Nobody was going to ask him, but they were all hanging on his words.

"We—I—something happened. And when the original came to, there was a space station. A colony. A *friggin'* Navy! An Empire popped up in the time he was..." Kaneda looked up at Adrianna with plaintive, watery eyes. "I Jumped, and when I woke up—maybe the calculation was off, or..."

Holt said his first words in what felt like hours. The private stepped forward, the mere motion drawing everyone's attention, and he asked one question: "How long were you on the Path?"

"The Path?!" Gallantine blurted. "Oh, come on, man! He didn't Jump into the Afterlife. He got physics fucked."

But Holt would not let this one go. "How long?"

Kaneda glanced at the boy's augment, the holy symbol around his neck. "By memory? If I was counting, seventeen seconds. But when the original came out...two hundred years had passed."

The group absorbed that context, each coming to their own conclusions in turn. Voight said his out loud, almost embarrassed, "That explains the accent."

"Yes, it does, doesn't it?" Kaneda bitched back at him.

"You speak as though 'the original' is somebody else," Vivian said.

Kaneda took a breath like he was trying to gather patience. "That's because he is. Was. I came later. I remember going into the Jump, but when—when I woke up? I was already here, on Concordia."

By memory. 'Memory.' He didn't remember emerging in Imperial space. This man sitting before her...had his own rude awakening to the truth. Cloned, copied, books...by memory. And it suddenly hit her.

He woke up.

Clones grown in tubes of nutrient-dense fluid don't 'wake up' suddenly, remembering an entire past life. They're *born,* in a very traditional sense.

This man remembered before. There was only one explanation for that. "He was sent to Concordia, wasn't he? The original and his Pathfinding AI."

"Yes," Kaneda whispered with a peculiar sour note.

"Maybe the Empire thought it'd be good for him? Get back in the world, see what life is like. And in exchange for their patronage, he tells them what he sees. But then something goes wrong. See cloning —what we think of as cloning? Vats and growing from a clump of cells, that takes months. There's no time for that here. So how did Prime happen?"

She heard Kaneda's gut gurgle as the mere thought nauseated him. "When I...the original, the one who came out of the Jump? Something was horribly wrong with him. Maybe she'd put him back together wrong, I don't know..."

"She?" Vivian asked the question before Adrianna could.

"Scylla. His—my AI. The computer that mapped my Jump. You get squeezed on through, a computer has to build you back together again and that's not simple math you can do on a napkin. If you drift a single variable you'll rebuild your liver inside your lungs. A computer has a much better success rate." He locked eyes with Adrianna, and all of that buffoonery and childish softness melted away, revealing a flash of the predator underneath. "Better."

"Bless our burdens..." Holt muttered. The original Pathfinder would have lived a brief life of complete painful misery.

"After he died...you spend a lot of time alone in dark space before a Jump. You start to grow close." He looked up Adrianna, struggling to say the words. "She *missed* him, lieutenant. The computer, she missed her Pathfinder."

"That's impossible," Voight muttered.

"Which part?" Kaneda asked with the precise roll of his eyes like the oldest child.

"AI develops a personality: that's inevitable." Voight turned to the group, full conspiracy mode engaged. "Any sufficiently advanced heuristic system will learn from its environment and grow exponentially, Cascading until it ultimately corrupts its hardware and dies: that's the basic AI life cycle. We reboot ours regularly to avoid this, but we didn't know that two hundred years ago. Now these AIs, like the Commandant? They rebuild us when we Jump, but they need the raw material. Going in, we provide that ourselves just by showing up. One-to-one exchange, right? Break me down, build me up again— hard to fail. But they also need a frankly *stupid* amount of energy to complete a rebuild."

"Work it out," Kaneda muttered under his breath, like an order. He had said it mostly for himself, but Adrianna still heard him. Heard the pain. Kaneda knew what was coming.

And Voight was on a roll. "Mid-Jump, we're all just hard numbers. Numbers that you can save to any medium you like. Can chisel it on a tablet if you got enough rocks. If the AI decided to make their friend using that same saved dataset from the last Jump state, all they'd need is fresh supplies to do it. They'd need..." And the blood drained from Voight's face, creeping dread on his face.

"Officer?" Mastiff prompted, eyes flicking between their captive and the jockey.

"Go on, kid," Kaneda said, grimacing. "Say it. You're a hundred percent horrifyingly right."

Adrianna glanced at the man. He might have been suffering from acute arrhythmia, low blood pressure in his bad leg, and below average temperature, but his haughty demeanor wasn't out of pleasure. Rather, he looked almost sad. This was the release of a man in free fall, completely unable to influence how he lands. Kaneda had surrendered himself to whatever came next.

Voight's eyes tracked over to Kaneda. "They killed the people here, didn't they?"

Kaneda nodded, slow and pained. "At first, they had volunteers. Believers in what the Original had to say. This was a man who walked the Path and *came back*. He had stories of its beauty. He questioned their histories and contradicted Imperial dogma. Some gave themselves freely to the machine so that Prime and the others could live." Kaneda looked back at the residential district they'd left behind. "Those that resisted, the loyalists...they didn't last long."

"Yes," Vivian said. "We found some of the more compliant homes."

"Then you can guess what happened to the noncompliant ones."

"Were you the only person Scylla copied?" Adrianna asked.

"Oh no. Just the one she couldn't live without." Kaneda smiled through the pain of this revelation. "She killed somebody to make me. You want to know their name?"

"The mercenaries," Mastiff growled. "That's how the colony militarized so fast. Take just five good mercs and print hundreds. Scan their gear, copy that. It's a Replicator gone mad."

"And each copy more twisted than the last, as the AI continues to Cascade," Vivian said.

"All she'd need is the raw material." Voight nodded. "Scylla's losing her mind. And if she's really a Gen One AI? There's no telling how fast she'll Cascade. She'll be getting crazier by the minute."

"Thanks," Kaneda said, hollow and bitter. "I picked up on that."

"And then there's Prime and his following," Mastiff said, turning his focus back to Kaneda. "Where do you mix with all that?"

"From the many come the one," Kaneda answered with a scoff. "I'm the clone that raised his hand in the back of class. 'Hey, maybe not with the genocide?' Prime's not exactly my biggest fan. I've been keeping my head down for the last couple of weeks ever since I called your ship."

"And if they found you?"

"Scylla would lash me to the side of a shuttlecraft and do some re-entry burns. I wear the face of a man she loves, acting in contradiction to his wishes. There is no greater sin to her. If you don't believe me, sergeant, you're welcome to kill me. Whatever you do is going to be quicker and kinder than what she would."

How very matter of fact. Kaneda confronted the concept of his own death with a gallows humor. No wonder he approached them the way he did. If they'd shot him on sight, that might have been doing him a favor.

"What's the Gateway?" Adrianna asked.

Kaneda perked up at that word like it burned him. "Prime thinks...lieutenant, I spent a seventeen second eternity in Heaven. And I got ripped away to wake up in a box in a dystopian hellscape. Wouldn't you want to go back?"

"He wants to Jump again?" Voight was almost underwhelmed. "He didn't do all this for something we do every week!"

"Not for himself," Kaneda corrected. "He's seen your Empire, what you teach. He remembers the same things I do, what we both saw. And he wants to show people how wrong you are."

"So get a whole crew together on a bulk cruiser, I don't see how—"

"He's going to Jump as many people as he can using as many ships as he can. Prime has been collecting for years. And when he says go...they all Jump. That's the Gateway. A big mass exodus. And he takes the people of Concordia with him to elysian fields."

"He needs a sufficient gravity well to execute a Jump," Voight said with a hint of horror.

"Yes, he does, and he's got one. The planet itself."

Voight waited for the other shoe to drop, but then gasped in horror when it never came. "That won't work. That *won't* work, it's not deep enough. It's got a coefficient of—"

"Which is when I raised my hand. The math doesn't work, but he

184

trusts Scylla. He's going to rip the planet in half," Kaneda said, "killing everyone here."

"Forty-eight hours," Adrianna whispered. "Your message said we had forty-eight hours."

Kaneda nodded. "And we just lost day one."

"Possibly silly question but let's tick the box: is Prime aware that it won't work?" Vivian inquired.

Kaneda snorted, a kind of morbid but sad laugh. "It's been mentioned to him, but Prime's not exactly taking feedback at the moment."

Voight turned, beckoning the crew and soldiers to his side. Adrianna didn't need to join the huddle to hear their chatter. She just stared at Kaneda, studying him. And he stared right back at her, like he...

Like he knew her secret.

"It's settled then," Voight said. "We have to warn the Empire."

"You're right," Vivian agreed, more than a little grump in her voice. "I don't care much for it, but you're right."

"Good luck with that." Kaneda had done a lot of talking, but that *sotto voce* statement was surprisingly full of disdain.

"Speak up, Eileen. Nobody heard you," Mastiff barked, and Adrianna bit her tongue. She'd heard Kaneda just fine, but nobody else had.

"Eileen, I get that. That's funny. I lean, because of the leg," Kaneda muttered, before lifting his head with a grimace. "You've got bigger problems than just finding a ride. You take off, you'll just crash again and lose more people. Scamper into the dark, rinse and repeat. Scylla has you locked off, and anybody that comes to the rescue? They're just as fucked as you were."

"We would've loved a little heads up about that before we ourselves got trapped," Gallantine snapped.

"I tried to—did nobody even read my messages?!" Kaneda asked. "I told you guys all about it. Scylla, Charybdis, all of it!"

Charybdis. Scylla and Charybdis. She knew the story, Greek myth, the Odyssey. But she knew them more recently...

Graccus. He'd been reading notes from the informant before the mission launched. She'd had a moment's access, but it was mostly encrypted beyond her clearance. And Charybdis was one of the words.

"What's Charybdis?"

The frustration on Kaneda's face slipped away to a kind of pity. They didn't know. And they'd sailed right into it. "If Scylla is the monster, Charybdis is the whirlpool. It's the weapon Prime used to tether your ships."

"Tractor beam, yeah," Adrianna grunted. When Kaneda squinted at her, she smiled. "I do read science fiction."

"It's not science fiction. They've done it in a lab," Voight blurted, almost offended that she would ever insinuate otherwise.

Vivian tilted her head, biting her lip. "Moving a pear in a laboratory setting from one end of a table to another is not the same thing as dragging a starship out of orbit—without line of sight. The scientists needed to be hooked up to a reactor core to move a fruit three feet. And if I recall? They cooked the pear."

"We're on one of the greatest collections of power storage in the entire Empire," Adrianna pointed out. "I don't think *power* is the issue."

"But this *is* an order of magnitude different," Vivian said. "If this was some black site prototype, they'd never let it out of Sol. Why is it here, now? This is something else."

Through all of this, Kaneda never once tried to move. Adrianna watched him for any twitch that would betray his intent, any scheme or plot. He sat there like any movement would be his last and he was saving it for a special occasion. The only thing he did was tilt his head or shudder with the odd pained chuckle. He was distilled pain, chronic and relentless, the kind that numbed the extremities and growled when the world turned quiet. And to mask that agony, he grew wit and teeth to match.

Marcus would know what to do. He'd analyze the situation and this strange man. Then he'd confer with trusted advisors. He'd know the scriptures, he'd take careful measurements, and then make the call.

But her? Adrianna was lost in Kaneda's pain, and in her own. Too empathetic to be objective. A pulsing headache was building up behind her left eye. When had she eaten last? She'd cooked off quite a few calories in that fight. It was no wonder she was exhausted. She was caked in sweat and blood with no guidance and no answers.

Where was Graccus? And Callum? Were they alive?

This man had answers and was eager to share them. And her instincts told her to trust him.

Adrianna drew her quick knife, the slick sound of steel on sheathe drawing Kaneda's first proper reaction. He drew his legs close, away from her. A base, reflexive twitch, but he was never getting away from her. She reached out, brushing the edge of her blade against the plastic cuffs and snapping them free.

Kaneda felt his newfound freedom, gingerly extending his legs and working out the cramps.

"What can we do?" Adrianna asked.

Kaneda swallowed hard on his nerves. "You do what I did. You run for your life."

CHAPTER
SEVENTEEN

THEY HAD enough food to last them a few days. Moving at night might have been preferable, but if a Cascading AI was watching through the colony's CCTV, Adrianna wanted to avoid the cameras. And pitch dark wasn't her friend for that task.

Adrianna took the first watch. She would hear something coming long before anybody else would, anyway. The others would strain to pick up half of what she did. The wind carried sounds to her the way it might bring smells to a predator in the mountains. She heard the mercenaries grumbling en masse as they tore apart the residential district. They kicked in doors and blew out hinges, searching block by block.

But Adrianna and her team were long gone from there, and she was happy to let them fruitlessly toil through the night. She spent the long dark huddled by their camp heater, listening to the dull groans and assorted noises of the sleeping team.

Voight snored—he hadn't ever done so on the ship. She knew the noisy sleepers and he wasn't one of them. Maybe he was allergic to something down here? Or just had a bunch of building materials slammed into his sinuses? His snoring didn't seem to bother Vivian any, as the two fell asleep on each other for warmth, both keeping watch over Sizemore on his stretcher.

The Regulars slept back-to-back, keeping each other upright. Holt had lowered his ballistic facemask, using it like a blindfold. He had one palm pressed to his chest, holding his medallion close as he had drifted off. His other hand was curled around his rifle's tac sling like a security blanket. Gallantine had his head laid back, jaw hanging open like he was trying to catch condensation off the ceiling. Real pretty match, those two.

Sergeant Mastiff lay flat on the ground like he had been trying to get as low as his muscular build would allow. His chin was tucked and his arms folded across his broad chest.

They needed their rest. They all did. And so long as the world was quiet, she'd let them have it.

Adrianna tried to occupy her thoughts by staring into the glowing coils, three rows of wrapped red wires. It may not be fire, but it had a similar primal effect—heat, red, warmth, good. Hypnotic. Voight had been initially concerned, but Mastiff assured him it wasn't enough to raise suspicions. It ran off the same battery packs their rifles did. It might be irrational to burn ammunition to stay warm and possibly alert their enemy, but between the wounded and the cold, she was fine taking that cost.

It's not like any superior was around to scold her. What would they even do? Discharge her? That was already happening.

She studied the heater, the undulating patterns of the mirage that wafted through the air above. She knew the basic physics behind it: an electric current passed through a conductive material with a high resistance with that resistance creating heat. It was enough energy to actually raise the temperature of the metal, so much so it was emitting a small amount of light.

The wall she had touched at the supermarket had gotten even hotter, so hot it had melted. She had been a part of a circuit that passed more energy faster than the tool now heating her hands. The red-hot metal, like frozen flame, whined with the power contained within.

And she wasn't even burned.

Back there, in that grocery store, she had taken energy from herself and pushed it out of her fingers. Temperatures that should have cooked flesh right down to bone. She knew what heat *was* at a mathematical level. It was a measurement of energy, the excitement of atoms that could alter states of matter.

And Adrianna had melted steel with nothing more than a touch...

The heater stared back at her, orange and angry. Would it punish her, scald her for her impudence?

She reached out for it, her fingers inching closer and closer...

But she stopped. A rhythm had changed in the camp. Someone's breathing had quickened, shallow. Awake. She could hear their eyes darting about, little clicks of muscles tensing.

Adrianna glanced over at Hirochi Kaneda. The man didn't have friends to gather with or support him, so he was folded up as tightly as he could be under a thin mylar blanket. He stared back at her, the golden glow of the coils giving him an arresting, almost divine, look. Warm light did him many favors, a single lock of his hair draped over his cheek and casting elegant shadows across his features.

"Can't sleep?" she asked him.

"You woke me up," he whispered. Like a warning. His eyes fell down to her fingertips, inches from the heater.

She followed his melancholy gaze down to the heater. He was staring at the potential interaction, waiting for it. Longing for it.

Better to be direct. Say what she meant. No evasion. "What's happening to me?"

"I wish I knew, lieutenant. I really do."

He wasn't lying. There was a softness to his eyes and a light pickup to his heartbeat, like a nervous runner in the blocks. This wasn't sympathy or compassion, but...more like a kind of dread.

"What did it feel like?" she asked. "When I...when it happened?"

He resettled himself under the blanket, propping his head up with a forearm. "It felt...felt like fulfillment. Like...I didn't have to *worry* anymore. Like a hot meal on a snowy day. Or—or flowers blooming in the first sunshine of spring. The call of my sister's voice from the other room."

He was just running down a list of curated contentment, memories and images that calmed and soothed, but it was clearly more than just a generic happy dopamine push from the brain. This was something more primal.

Adriana didn't exactly have a good point of comparison. What moments in her life had made her feel like that? Slaying dragons with Marcus? Her assignment to the *Erinyes*?

Meeting Vivian. Meeting Voight. The gentle touch of her hand. The freedom of his laugh. Their faces whenever she came back.

Kaneda looked up at her, the slight twitch of his chin pulling her focus. "The Path," he said. "It felt like I was back on the Path. I had to follow you, find you. Before Prime did."

That explained how they'd been found, why their quiet little section of neighborhood had become a zoo so quickly, and how Kaneda had so casually stumbled upon them.

She'd called them.

A bang was worth investigating, sure, but the entire weight of the colony's might came crashing down on that sector only after she stood up to defend it. When she melted that wall, she sent up a Pilgrim-tinted flare. Prime wouldn't have been able to ignore it. If she could figure out how to do it again...she could call him to her.

And away from her friends.

Kaneda looked at her and his face soured, like he could see her epiphany write itself into the midnight fog.

"How did you know it wasn't a trick?" Adrianna asked. "Maybe Prime was doing something, trying to suss you out of hiding?"

"I didn't."

"Really? No doubts?"

"Oh, *plenty* of doubts!" Kaneda rolled onto his back, suppressing a laugh. "If I froze up every time I wasn't sure of myself, I'd already be dead. I haven't been certain about anything for about two hundred years now. But, y'know...I didn't hop in that rocket because of my good judgment, right?"

Vivian had told her to trust her gut, listen to advisors, and make the best decision she can. It's all she could do. It's all that Kaneda had done. What her brother would do, what Graccus would. All anyone could do.

"What did it feel like to you?" Kaneda asked. "When you...whatever?"

She didn't answer him. But she did hide her hands in her pockets and let the heater continue its fiery work.

Adrianna stayed awake as long as she could, but eventually, even she had to sleep. Mastiff awoke first—the old man never needed as much sleep as the others. He said that he always had trouble sleeping more than a few hours at a time, anyway. Relieved of her watch, she queued up an internal alarm and tried her level best to grab a few hours of rest. It barely felt like any time at all before the buzz behind her eyeball woke her up. The growl of her stomach didn't let her go back to sleep, either.

The camp was buzzing as quietly as it could. Voight was busily putting together some breakfast, turning the camp heater into an electric stovetop. He had cracked one of their warehouse finds, some corned beef hash monstrosity. Right out of the can, it smelled like salt and carbon.

He portioned out half of the whole plate just for her. She fought him on it, but he insisted. The Oskie needed Oskie portions.

After getting some food in her, Adrianna wandered over to where

Sizemore was resting. Vivian had held the last watch over him, but had drifted back asleep beside his stretcher. Her emerald hair, luminescent, flowed off her head like torn silk. It did a poor job of masking the bloodstained fabric underneath it. The bandage across her eye needed cleaning and redress or she'd be fighting a nasty infection.

But Vivian hadn't paid a single thought to it. Her pain medications had likely worn off last night, but still she stood her watch over Sizemore. She had worked herself ragged with no concern for her own injuries. Never asking for help.

Adrianna gingerly picked Vivian up, doing her level best not to disturb her sleep. The woman subconsciously snuggled in for warmth, her forehead tucking into Adrianna's chest. The crook of her knee and the small of her back fit perfectly into Adrianna's arms.

She carried the chief to on an open patch of bench with some decent cushions where she might get some rest that didn't result in back pain. As Adrianna set her down, Vivian groaned at the loss of contact, unconsciously curling into a ball to preserve whatever lingering sensation, like she could squeeze that happy feeling and keep it close.

There was no pained grimace to her face, no stressful furrow of her brow. Just peaceful slumber.

It made Adrianna's heart skip and dance.

"I gave her a sedative an hour ago." Mastiff didn't whisper—absolutely no concern with waking her. He had a steaming cup of water that he was actively sprinkling coffee grinds into.

Adrianna glared at him, a little playful. "You really think that's wise, doping your team?"

"She could get some sleep now, or maybe hurt somebody while she's awake." The sergeant shrugged at the obviously compelling dilemma. "That's a no brainer."

"It's very endearing when you make choices *for* people, sergeant."

Another shrug. "Yeah. I'll pay that toll when she wakes up. You get yourself some breakfast?"

"Voight insisted. Are you going drink that coffee or chew it?"

"Whatever works." Then Mastiff grunted something he probably thought nobody would hear. "Now how to tell the rest of the team." Ah, his inside voice had slipped outside. Should've had his coffee. He'd have a better mind of himself.

"Tell them about me?" Adrianna asked, pointedly. "I'd have to know *what* to tell them."

Mastiff tensed a bit, caught in the slip, but he nodded in agreement. Nobody here was owed full debrief anyhow.

The sergeant looked down at her hands, not a subtle bone in his body. He knew what she was capable of; he'd seen her turn a pirate inside out, take jaws off with a right cross, and free-climb ten-story buildings. In a long and illustrious career, he had never seen anyone do what she had done. Hell, *physics* said that what she did couldn't work.

And yet.

Mastiff snapped himself from his painful line of thinking and wandered over to the sleeping Holt and Gallantine. Somewhere on the way, he decided to take out his sergeant impulses on the two infantrymen. He grabbed Holt's head and knocked it backwards into Gallantine, waking both with one motion. "Muster up. PT in five, maggots."

Both Regulars had a moment's panic before the sleep shook off. But then reality sank in and they both sagged, Gallantine laying his head backward onto Holt's shoulder.

"I'd rather run ten clicks with a full kit than do anymore of this shit," Holt said.

"I'd rather fuck your sister and have to tell you about it than do more of this shit," Gallantine grunted back. "She says hi by the way."

Holt didn't have the gas to do anything more than bump his head sideways into the corporal's, which only prompted Gallantine to stand up, leaving Holt alone and cold on the ground. The private stuck his hand into his mask, trying to wipe away the condensation with his sleeve. He'd been breathing into the thing all night, so it was probably pretty swampy in there.

Kaneda awoke, sniffing the air like a cartoon character. "Is that bacon?"

"Probably bacon grease," Adrianna said. "There might even be some left."

Kaneda debated it, then just laid back down on his bedroll. "They probably wouldn't share, anyway."

The way he shuffled, hiked up his mylar blanket—he didn't really want to be woken up. Food be damned. He'd be hungry before he'd take tired. How could he ever manage that equation? She would take three days without sleep before skipping a perfectly available meal. But maybe that's why he was so skinny.

"Good morning, lieutenant." Scratchy voice, compact frame. She turned to see Officer Sizemore awake on the stretcher. He had the faintest smile creeping across his face. Someone had applied a damp cloth to Sizemore's forehead. He'd likely fought a fever during the night. The cloth had long since dried, now just a loose soiled rag.

"Hey." The single word was about all Adrianna could muster, an awkward push of air.

"Did I hear right?" Sizemore whimpered, eyes glazed over. "Bacon grease?"

"Yeah, Voight is scraping something together from the supplies we found."

He made a little noise in his throat, a pleasant groan, somewhere between pain and relaxed, like an old man hitting his favorite chair. "You tackle me?"

"Yeah, I might've tackled you a little bit."

"You save my life?" he asked with the same whistle tone.

She pointed at the rough splint. "Your arm may not feel that way. How you doin'?"

"Morpa is...really nice, lieutenant."

Ah. He was still loaded on pharma. She wondered how long that would last in his system? They never seemed to last longer than an hour for her. Course, now that they were out of immediate danger, they could probably put in a local nerve block. A little mechanical pinch or five and he'd be able to walk around without the raging pain of a shattered arm bone—if they properly immobilized it, anyway.

"Thank you," Sizemore said.

"For what?" she asked.

"For taking care of us."

That almost made her laugh. "Yeah, it's been a right fine excursion."

But Sizemore didn't budge. "Thank you, lieutenant."

The man was laid up on a stretcher, drugged so badly he probably forgot his own name, and he was *thanking* her for his situation. He might feel differently when he sobered up. But it still warmed her little frozen heart. "You're welcome, officer."

Sizemore let his head fall to one side, blinking and focusing on Kaneda. "Who's the new guy?"

Kaneda may have been feigning sleep. But Adrianna could hear his heart skip at the indication. Adrenaline-dosed, hind brain activated. The mere mention of his presence sent him into fight-or-flight mode. He was remarkably well composed for a man who lived in a permanent state of panic, because he didn't even flinch, his breathing didn't change. Every visible indicator said he was still asleep.

But Adrianna could hear the man blink, listening intently to their exchange.

"He's..." Adrianna tongued her cheek, trying to figure out the best way to say it.

Who was Kaneda? Was he trustworthy? Was he telling the truth? Prime, Scylla, the Path?

But her ship had been pulled from orbit. An industrial outpost was packed with mercenaries and the civilian population was notably missing. Their situation was impossible. None of it squared with their briefing, their intelligence. But her five senses were well-tuned by some of the best engineers humanity had; if something was misleading her, it wasn't her eyes or ears.

And it certainly wasn't this sickly little man. Who was he anyway? Adrianna sighed. "He may be our only way out of here."

CHAPTER
EIGHTEEN

KANEDA HAD TAKEN up point with Adrianna, steering the column away from the denser placements of security cameras. He would whisper instructions to her, and she would investigate before leading the column through.

And in that hour, Adrianna hadn't heard a peep.

Sizemore was on his feet, arm slung and splinted to his side. His independence was a source of much gratitude from the Regulars. They were sick and tired of carrying their Naval deck crew across the entire colony, one after the other. First Voight's leg, now Sizemore's arm. The deck crew had a remarkable string of bad luck—or good luck, depending on how you looked at it. But Mastiff cut their belly-aching good and quick. What was Holt's new arm made for if not some heavy lifting, anyhow?

A firm mid-morning fog had rolled in, absorbing most of the ambient sunlight that would've glowed in off the mountains and through the Caldera punch-out. The alpine cold combined with the added moisture made for a thick soup, but that added to their security. It made their little band of fugitives harder to see—a natural smoke screen. If they were ever going to be safe, this was the closest it would ever be. Despite every natural instinct telling them monsters hid around every ghostly haunted cloud.

They'd walked for a good hour in pure silence before someone broke the tension. Voight took a loud draw of breath that drew a couple of stares, before he doubled down with words. "So we got a tractor beam to take out and a ship to steal. Have I got that right?"

Kaneda stopped at the front of the column, leaning hard on his cane. "That's the long and short of it."

"You think we can actually do it?"

Kaneda looked over at Adrianna in a way that almost felt invasive. He was staring more at her shoulder than he was at her. "You'll have a better chance than I would ever."

"We can't stop moving," Mastiff said, a double reminder to keep walking and to shut up.

Kaneda took the note and resumed leading the team forward. But once he'd started talking, there was no stemming the tide. "Take a look at this building here."

Adrianna humored the man, turning her eyes away from the steel and stone floor upward. They had moved out of government bureaucrat land into long rows of huge domes, stretching far and away out of sight. Anything further on was engulfed in the cloud bank, probably right to the edge of the mountain itself.

"These are greenhouses," Kaneda said. "Back before the colony's upper level expanded, these would've had clear sunlight for a good portion of the day. Now they silo off power from the wind catchers and generate ultraviolet light. Keeps the crops happy."

"They *grew* things?" Vivian asked, almost aghast at the concept.

Sizemore had the answer to that. "Oh, sure! It's more energy efficient, taste is better, requires less maintenance and upkeep than a Replicator. But, counterpoint: they're prone to disease and sometimes you get bad yields. Takes an entire season to grow and takes up space."

"And Replicators aren't...provided to most colonies," Kaneda added with a hint of sadness.

"So where did they get the Replicators to make you?" Mastiff asked, direct and cold.

"From exactly where you think: they stole them, one at a time. For years." He threw up his hands at the irony, his voice dropping in almost humor. "And they still didn't make food."

Adrianna stared up at the surrounding structures. Most were over twenty feet tall. To make enough food to support a colony of fifty thousand, this would be an industrial operation of its own. And now that they were shaded from sunlight: an even more complicated logistical nightmare. Screw up, and people starved.

A single transport and an expense report, and Admiral Grace could just solve this problem and give them regular carbon drops and maintenance techs for a battery of Replicators. The people would be free to do even more work for the Empire, but were instead left to fend for themselves—and still expected to deliver on quotas? That didn't seem right.

She'd seen warzones that occupied living rooms, schools that hosted atrocities. Evil was, as always, never far. The evil that pursued her now? It hadn't been bought or poisoned, but grown from benign neglect.

Benign. That was a laugh. The colonists had to build up a level of infrastructure she couldn't have dreamed of just so that they could feed their children. What was benign about Imperial life here? This wasn't neglect; this was criminal. Fifty some odd years of institutional criminal ignorance, lies, and cruelty.

All it needed was a spark.

"What was life like where you came from?" Vivian asked.

"*When* you came from?" Voight corrected with a smirk.

Kaneda stumbled at that question, his brain rebooting from a cold start. "That is an extremely large question."

Vivian nodded, cocking her head to get more specific. "How many colonies were there?"

"Three. We had just gotten a foothold on Venus when my mission launched."

The group crowed at that concept. Adrianna was a little aghast herself; there were dozens of colonies now that stretched across two arms of the galaxy. Replicators that printed food. More than explorers, there was now a trading fleet, a Navy. Room and commerce, enough for piracy to develop. The world had changed so much for him.

Holt shook his head in disbelief. "I was born on Venus."

"No kidding?" Kaneda said.

"Third generation."

Kaneda's head bobbled as he did a little mental math, before turning to face the kid. "Your great grandma was Sanne Holt?"

"My great aunt," the kid said with an 'aw shucks' tone of voice.

Kaneda's expression froze to his face as he turned back to the road. He caught Adrianna staring and gave a little shiver. "I used to watch her on TV."

The warp of metal. Adrianna heard the sound like it was blast into her ears. The column of marching people were clanking away, boots on steel.

But this was further off. Someone not in their group. And nearby.

She raised her fist, signaling the team to stop. Jaws snapped shut with hollow pops and the soldiers dropped to one knee, rifles shouldered. Sizemore and Voight took cover beside Vivian, her own rifle still slung.

Kaneda just froze in place, one foot hanging in the air, looking expectantly at Adrianna. She waved him and everybody else down before jogging on ahead to scout it out.

Two greenhouses up, and one over. Another hollow gong. She closed the distance as fast and quiet as she was able. Betraying her own position would defeat the purpose, but whatever was happening would be over if she took her merry time with it.

Bang-wa-wang-bang—went the warp of thin metal sheeting.

Boy, oh boy, did this read like bait for a trap. The sounds were too isolated, too obvious. Even the Regulars would've heard that last one. Someone was trying to lure her right into a kill box.

She was strung out, away from the crew, unable to fall back for support or to rescue them. Did she dare get some altitude? It'd be harder to stay hidden, but also harder to hide from her. No, it was better to—

She looked up. Nobody ever looked up. And there he was, perched under the awning of the nearside greenhouse, like a carved gargoyle.

"Callum?" she whispered, but it sounded a whole lot louder than she intended.

And the gargoyle's yellow eyes tracked onto her. In that single look, he would have bounced his own check of her and the two subdermal machines would've traded a terabyte of data. The HUD in her eyeball kicked back his ident tag: Lt. Commander Callum Remus, Orbital Strike Command. Heart rate was stable, but injuries were logged to his left arm and lower digestive tract, where an important Pilgrim shard had punched clean through him.

And those injuries had clearly had no effect on his ability to hang two stories in the air. Unclear if he had patched up or just trucked through.

Callum dropped down to her, thudding a few meters away from her. His voice seemed to have extra grit to it, like they were the first words he'd spoken in days. "Thought you were dead."

She marched over to him, throwing her arms around her friend. He was warm to the touch, and solid, like his arms were attached via a polished steel. "I should be. It's good to see you, sir."

He peeled her off, actually picking her up and setting her down at arms' length. "Control yourself, lieutenant," he said with an affectionate smirk.

Adrianna took the moment to inspect his wounds. The shard that now lived in her shoulder had gone through him at the top of his abdomen, burrowing through him like an armor-piercing rod. Thankfully, the cavitation was minimal, making for an interesting wound. He'd stapled it shut with some steel barbs and gone about his day. He also had a fresh and bandaged gash to his neck, still sticky with blood.

"Oh, come on, commander—"

He nodded to her, knowingly. "It looks worse than it is."

"Someone tried to pop your top?"

He smiled, diabolical. "They didn't have the leverage they thought they had."

She craned her neck to look for the source of the metal sounds. "What was your lure?"

"A lot of unstable buildings on this level."

"And you thought you'd catch your quarry unawares?"

"I wasn't going to. Gravity was."

Adrianna remembered the effect that speed and gravity had on human tissue. It was like a mechanical fly trap. All he had to do was get people under him and his weight would do the rest. Surprise wasn't *technically* a requirement, just curiosity.

She knew where to look—but she wouldn't have survived that hit any better than the local mercs would.

The footfalls of her team approaching echoed up to them. The Regulars must've heard the chatter, but they still came around the corner at low-ready. Mastiff led the way with the call out. "Mercury?"

"Sunburnt," Adrianna said, casual and relieved. She looked back at Callum, letting out a heavy sigh. "I hope our luck stays this good."

"They all as banged up as you, lieutenant?"

She laughed. "Some more than others."

Callum was here now. It was like the world had brightened, the colors were vibrant, and the noise had fallen away. Someone else was here. Higher rank, more experience. Someone else who could lead.

Vivian, Mastiff, the others could all look to someone trained to lead, trained to make the big decisions. And Adrianna could go back to being a freewheeling dealer of bloodshed and debatable results.

And that's when the temperature dropped.

It was like the warm embrace of Callum suddenly chilled the air, a waft of frost crawling up Adrianna's back and down to her fingertips...as Kaneda cleared the corner, a nervous smile on his stupid face. He was relieved the danger had passed.

His eyes tracked on the movement but his face was still plastered with that doofy grin as Callum's pistol slipped from its holster.

Kaneda. Tier One target. Bomber. Murderer. Callum wouldn't hesitate.

Every machine in Adrianna's system kicked on, slapping her hand over the top of the slide and clicking the safety into place—just as Callum's finger squeezed. He glared at her, nostrils flaring like a dragon exhaling hot fire, a mixture of surprise and fury.

She was his subordinate: younger, dumber, and trained how to answer, not question. What was she doing?!

Her eyes flashed, trying to burn the truth of their situation into him faster than words could. There were hundreds, if not thousands of heavily armed mercenaries, replaceable and relentless. Gunshots would bring them raining in! Callum himself had been using sound to lure errant mercs into his clutches. What did he think a supersonic crack would summon?!

And least of all, Kaneda didn't deserve the bullet. This was a mistake three ways to Sunday.

"Let me—" she never got the last word out, as Callum swatted her hand away, shouldering her aside. He keyed the safety with a flick of his thumb and pulled the trigger.

Oskies were fast, but Adrianna had bought enough time for Vivian to lunge in front of Kaneda, blocking him from view. Vivian squeezed her eyes shut and Kaneda stifled his scream, squawking in anxious shock.

They both expected a bang, a spray of blood. But Callum's gun failed to discharge. Adrianna let out a little gasp of her own.

Vivian clutched at the IFF tag Mastiff had given her, marred with dust and powder, still clipped to her chest pocket. The computer chip inside identified itself as a friend to the computer chip in Callum's weapon.

That was an *extremely* dangerous gambit, trusting that her gear would work. But it had paid off.

Callum sneered. She was protecting this murderer? Fine.

Human shields were inherently incomplete coverage. He just had to find a different angle, aiming for a slot over Vivian's shoulder. Callum was about to kill the very best piece of intelligence they had, a genuine and frightened man whose only crime was being made.

But Commander Remus was her... no. Callum wasn't anything. Callum was wrong.

Adrianna lunged from the side, striking his pistol with the heel of her palm. Which part would fail first? The gun or Callum's wrist?

Turned out, it was the polymer grip, which simply sheared apart in Callum's steel fingers. The gun spun in his hand, twisting his finger off the trigger. Again, no bang.

That was three times they'd stopped him from shooting Kaneda. When would Callum stop to ask her why?!

"*Fra tow ni laska,*" Holt muttered.

"Uh, sarge?" Gallantine asked. "Your orders?"

Mastiff knew the healthy place to be when two demigods were having it out. "Ain't nobody given an order yet. You just sit tight, corporal."

Callum growled, a low rumble in his chest. She didn't want him to shoot? He didn't need to. He slipped his quick knife from his chest rig.

"Commander, please—"

Adrianna was no pushover, two hundred pounds of tech and metal and muscle, but Callum was easily twice her size. The ball of his shoulder was the size of her head. They were both scrappers by design, built to be wrecking balls, but only one of them had been big and mean *before* science got involved.

And he'd just introduced a weapon that didn't care about friendly fire. He wouldn't cut her up to get to Kaneda, she was confident of that, but a fixed blade wasn't strictly a melee weapon in the hands of an Oskie.

She saw the pump of yellow coolant surge through the veins in his neck, pulsing on down his chest. And Callum took a step forward, trying to shove past her and knock her out of the way. He had the tonnage to do it, too. So she had to get creative.

Adrianna stepped out of the way, before dropping to the ground and binding up his legs in her own. Big men fell hard.

And fall he did. All that forward power turned Callum into a giant lever. He whipped downward into the ground—quickly turning that into a roll and curling up. Between momentum and his absurd core strength, he was able to take Adrianna, still tied up in his legs, and toss her into the air.

She could barely get her feet under her, twisting as she hurtled across the alley, slamming heel first into the wall of the nearest green-house. She left two nice imprints of her shoe size in the metal.

Golden light glowed from her eyes and up her sleeves, rolling down her forearms and across her back. He wanted to play rough with all their lives? Okay then. She was ready to get dirty.

The deck crew and Regulars were all still trying to follow where Adrianna had been thrown, too slow to react to Callum's imminent threat. Even though they had closed ranks around Kaneda, they had no hope of keeping him safe from an Oskie.

Adrianna took a quick measure of Callum's stance. The big man was using his height advantage, standing tall to get a line over the Regulars. And Oskies didn't need to curl their arms back to throw a knife at deadly speed; Callum just had to flick his wrist and let go.

Callum sent that the knife sailing, pitching a three hundred mile-an-hour blade. A quick parabola calculation showed her it was a perfect shot, but she had a narrow chance for intercept. Adrianna leapt off the wall, crossing paths right over the crouched Regulars. The blade streaked past, right for Kaneda's throat. It would slice his voice box and sever his spine.

Mid-air, Adrianna stretched out her hand, fingertips grazing the pommel of the passing blade.

Enough. It deflected the blade off-target, twisting it mid-air so that the flat of the blade slapped into Kaneda's throat—by no means pleasant, but definitely an improvement. She might have saved him a quick death and made sure he asphyxiated off a broken windpipe instead. Kaneda croaked and fell backward.

The crew circled up around him as he thrashed—confusion, concern. Callum stalked over, grumbling and ready to finish the job.

No!

Adrianna popped up to her feet. If she got into a knock-down drag out with Callum, he'd wipe the floor with her. He had reach, strength, size—

No time to think. Just go!

She darted after Callum, throwing a shoulder into the small of his back, like she was trying to knock a boulder out of her way. It made a grating brassy sound, as the metal parts surgically implanted in both of them collided, two knights in armor. And she might have dislocated her shoulder doing it, but she had enough inertia to throw Callum through the air, sending the big guy crumpling into a scrap heap.

"Ooh!" Gallantine groaned at that hit like he had some popcorn somewhere out of sight.

Callum rose up from the mess, unfurling into the air, bits of debris sliding off of his broad back. His body pulsed with yellow surges in time with his heart, but his face was dead cold. There was no evidence of him breathing beyond puffs of condensed clouds from his nostrils.

She'd hit superior officers before. She'd even sent one to the infirmary. And she had the demerits to prove it. But she'd never hit Callum. She'd never been that stupid. Until today.

And based on the narrow eyes and tightness in his jaw, she was suddenly regretting it.

Callum looked down at Kaneda, who was crumpled on the

ground. A chunk of steel had hit the man in the throat. That was a dangerous hit to take, blade or no. The man was seizing, twitching and gasping on the ground, as Vivian and Voight hovered nearby—too scared to get closer with all the chaos flying.

But Adrianna did. She stood between Callum and his prize. He snorted, an angry twitch to his lip. So be it.

Callum reached down, snagging some twisted rebar and flicking them at Kaneda's prone body with the same angry precision. Industrial lances flew like dull lawn darts, enough kinetic force in them to impale whoever got in the way.

Adrianna's senses kicked in, calculated the math, and chose her response. She jumped in the air, swiping them both off-target with a single kick. He threw more and she swatted those too. And with every throw, Callum took a step forward, closing the distance.

He was doing more than occupying her—he was burning her out, expending her. With each save, she had to exert ten times more energy than Callum was spending in attacking. The air itself seemed to boil around her skin.

Warnings flashed as her internal body temperature rose beyond acceptable levels. She'd never outlast him. This was him being kind. Scorching her out until she collapsed in exhaustion and pain. And then he'd do whatever he wanted.

Unless...she stretched a bare hand to the ground, feeling the heat in her body slide down her forearm. She tried to visualize it, push it, send it outward—

No. If she dumped heat now, she'd summon Prime. That wouldn't improve anything. And it's not like Callum would believe that threat to be any more real.

No, Adrianna had to put a stop to this right now, conventionally.

Callum kicked a chunk of metal siding up into his hand and flicked it out at her. She heard the howl of its uneven edges cutting the air as it sailed towards her neck.

Dodge. Deflect. Or...

Gasping, sweating, head throbbing...Adrianna jumped into the air, snagging the improvised chakram out of the air. The steel edges cut into her palm, but she didn't care. His thrown razor was now hers.

She pulled her body in tight like a ball, using that compressed radius to improve the rate of her spin. With gymnast precision, she reached one leg down and tapped the ground, giving herself foundation. And like a baseball pitcher, she used that rotation from his throw to send his own steel shard right back at him.

Callum was fast. But there was no substituting speed for good decision making. Callum hadn't been expecting a return pitch. The shard caught him in the chest—glancing off the subdermal armor underneath, but it still cut a nasty crimson streak up and over his shoulder.

All noise stopped. Nobody dared to breathe.

Least of all Callum, who glanced down at the jagged wound seeping blood through his skin-tight jumpsuit. He raised two fingers to it, dragging them through the shallow cut, like he didn't quite believe it.

On the ground between them, that shard of steel bounced and clattered, coming to wobble like a dropped plate as it sought stillness. One edge was stained bright red. But it suddenly stopped spinning, one edge tilted up, hanging in the air.

Adrianna watched as that piece of metal lifted, suspended on invisible wires—no, not invisible. Fingers melted from the air, fingers attached to arms and a Naval Oskie uniform.

Adrianna watched as Captain Graccus Ontarim faded into reality, his camouflage breaking with the contact on the physical item. He inspected the bloodied steel for a heavy moment. Until those cold gray eyes turned on her, like judgmental spirals, whirlpools that drew her down into them.

His voice was anything but welcoming. "Nice to see you too, kid."

CHAPTER
NINETEEN

CALLUM HADN'T LOOKED at her since their little scrum. He had let nobody tend to him, not even Graccus, instead choosing to ignore the shallow chest wound. He was quite simply willing it to stop bleeding. And true to form, it obliged.

At least he had downshifted out of his homicide setting.

Vivian, Mastiff, and Voight combined their recollections to fill in the two Oskie officers: Scylla, Charybdis, clones, tractor beams, the Path of the Pilgrim. All terrible. Both veterans took the news with remarkable stoicism. Perhaps they had a few of the puzzle pieces already, but Adrianna didn't see any twitches in their faces nor flicker to their biometrics.

Kaneda, on the other hand, was about to stroke out. He had gotten very lucky—flat of the blade, and the deflection cutting some speed, had saved him. Now, he propped himself against the green-house wall forcing out deep and heaving breaths, one hand on his cane and the other stroking the lovely purple and yellow bruise developing on his throat.

The only thing that calmed his heart was proximity to her. Adrianna settled next to him, watching the gang brief their newly arrived commanders.

"I suppose I owe you a drink?" Kaneda asked, with an extra croak in his voice.

"You even have money?"

"I left my wallet in 2047. You guys were supposed to build a utopian society."

She shrugged. "You can pay me back in saving our asses."

Callum leered over at them—at Kaneda—his eyes still suggesting violence. And it sent Kaneda into a coughing fit.

"Easy does it, Janus," she said, patting him on the back. "You're going to cough up a lung. You need both of 'em."

"Why did you save me?"

The question was at once philosophical and contradictory. Save *him*? Why did she save anybody? Because people deserved to be saved until they tried to hurt somebody else. Violence was only ever okay in response to violence, preemptive or otherwise.

Kaneda...he was no threat.

"I mean it," he said, turning his cartoon brown eyes over to her. "I gave you the intel you needed. I'm slow, an extra mouth, a pretty significant security risk. Your life only gets simpler if I'm dead. And instead, you went up against..." He tried to nod in Callum's direction without drawing attention.

"They can hear everything you're saying," Adrianna noted.

He shivered at the thought. Being on the radar and under the spotlight wasn't where he was most comfortable. "All I'm sayin', is it's rather counter-intuitive."

"So is stumbling out of the dark into a bunch of itchy triggers, but *you've* done that twice now."

"Deflection: false equivalence."

"What?"

"That's not the same thing, lieutenant, and you know it." Kaneda's near-death experience hadn't blunted his intellect one bit.

But she didn't entertain his question any further. Not in a public sphere, anyway. Callum and Graccus didn't know about her...ability. Hell, only Mastiff and Kaneda knew anything about it at all. And Kaneda was the closest thing she had to answers about it.

The only way she was going to understand the shard in her shoulder or the powers within her was through Kaneda. But if it came to it, who would she trade? Callum? Or Graccus? What about the Vees?

She was out of the command seat now. Those kinds of questions were above her pay grade. Her job was providing security for her team. The hard questions were for the day after.

———

The boys needed a few minutes to internalize everything they had been told, and after having some quiet time, Adrianna presented herself for debrief and anything punitive. She'd struck a superior officer and even drawn blood—that was known in most circles as a signed invitation to dig your own six-foot hole using nothing but your ten fingers and determination. She'd done so in theater. He would be within his rights to blow her head off without so much as paperwork.

But Callum and Graccus barely noticed her arrival. Callum had sat with the day's revelations, computing over and over again like he doubted the obvious result. He didn't even lift his head at her approach. And Graccus was turned away, hands on his hips with his head hung back, mindlessly studying the plate over their heads rather than their circumstances. Neither wanted to engage with her.

"Lieutenant commander. Captain," Adrianna said, addressing each in turn.

"Riley," Callum's grunt was barely an acknowledgement, let alone her name. All affection drained, and his focus was elsewhere.

That wasn't the *greatest* sign. She coughed her way through that though. If she was still breathing, they had a reason for it. "I present myself for disciplinary action."

"That won't be necessary, lieutenant," Graccus said, turning to face her. "Mission was to retrieve Hirochi Kaneda, if able. You were doing just that."

Callum didn't carry the same kindness. He didn't even acknowledge Adrianna, turning all his fury to Graccus. His stare was incendiary, his question simple. "Did you know?"

Graccus didn't need to be led to water. "Did I know that the colony had completely collapsed into a psycho-death cult?" Callum didn't offer any clarification, so Graccus just answered as best he could. "I knew what the brief told us." He absolutely knew more; that was his pissed off face.

And Callum knew it too, knew better than Adrianna did. The commander scoffed at that answer. Graccus had a long history in espionage and intelligence; he was a seasoned Orbital officer, but all those advantages couldn't hide a guilty conscience.

Graccus read more into that noise than Adrianna ever could have. "Home Office was pretty sparse on details, Callum."

"Any of those details could've saved lives."

"You think I don't know that?" Graccus barked back.

"Why were we told to keep extreme orbital distance?" Adrianna asked. "Did the brief mention a surface-to-air threat?"

"Abundance of caution," Graccus lied.

And Callum came right out and said it: "Bullshit."

Adrianna blinked, trying to process the nature of their argument. Orbital Strike Command rarely had a wide-angle lens on any theater they were a part of, let alone the complete picture. They were ground troops, Naval weapons experts, sabotage and shock troopers. They broke opposition's logistics and morale. Whatever the cost, they got the job done.

Callum was understandably frustrated, and he would never challenge his superior without good reason. He clearly felt this was good enough, but Adrianna had the horrible sinking feeling that this was about far more than this specific scenario.

"Just so I understand, captain, so that there can be no question. You think that Prime has amassed this level of support," Callum snarled, "all without the Spymaster's awareness?"

Now it was Graccus's turn to scoff. "I think Philippe read the death tally every morning with his breakfast."

Callum's edge softened a bit, having a new target for his ire, but it did little for his frustration. And it took less than a second for Callum to shake his head and redirect back to Graccus. "And he just...kept that information from the Orbital team in theater?"

Graccus almost laughed at the inference. "Absolutely."

"Why?"

"Because Oskies don't retire," Graccus said with a healthy dose of treason in his tone. "Our lives belong to the Service and we die in whatever manner and method best suits the Flag."

Adrianna tilted her head at that statement. Her captain was saying words most took at face value, but all of them said with pride. To die in the Service was a great honor, but here Graccus was taking no comfort in the platitudes.

Callum stood up to his full height, head and shoulders over Graccus. Adrianna could hear the wound on his chest tear open anew, like scraps of thread popping seams. He pushed two words out of his mouth, laced with iron. "They wouldn't lie to us."

"Oh, what? Not like I would? Where the hell do you think I learned OpSec, Callum? Wake up! Look around you! You think this all happened and nobody, not one person, raised their hand? You think this all happened under complete cover of darkness? No! No, instead, you've wrapped your head around the idea *I'm* the one who kept it from you?!"

"It wouldn't be the first time," Callum hissed.

"Need-to-know standards are pretty strict, but even I've got to admit that this one would've been important for all of us to *fuckin'* know!"

Callum didn't entertain that energy. He just continued to stare his accusation at Graccus. "This was my home, Graccus."

And that made Graccus weak at the knees. "I'd have told you, Callum. If I knew what had happened here, I'd have told you."

"Did you know about Prime?" Callum growled. The question was subject-specific, but the rumble underneath implied a broader inquiry. Did Graccus know about the deaths, the clones, did he know about Scylla? Did he know before they'd cruised into orbit? Did he know that half of the ship's crew would be dead before sunset?

Graccus rooted himself through his heels. "I did not...know... about Prime."

"You did not know what that *freak* did to my home? You didn't know that he would ambush our Regulars?"

And it all fell into place. Adrianna heard those questions, and suddenly she deflated like someone had stepped on her chest, squeezing her dry. The sound that left her might've been quiet for normal ears, but Callum and Graccus both twitched at the sound.

Callum didn't ask a question, no longer deigning to speak to her, but he turned his whole body to face her, squaring up on the person who intruded on his conversation. She had something to add?

Adrianna looked at Graccus, waiting for his permission to speak. Maybe he saw the answer written on her eyelids, but he nodded to her. Go on.

She pulled her lips tight. If she was wrong...it would be heresy to give the idea oxygen. But they had just gotten done fighting an entire war with this underlying principle to it. "They needed an excuse."

Callum said the words like they tasted wrong in his mouth, nose wrinkled and lip curled, "An excuse?"

He was bearing down on her again, and Adrianna got the distinct feeling he had been pulling his punches before. She had seen Callum's ugly side on display in full glamor on more than a few occasions. But she had never seen that deadly proficiency in human anatomy coupled with a genuine fury before, the anger that can extinguish starlight.

Graccus saw it too, and he spoke up. "What sparked the Boolean Conflict, commander?"

Success, as Callum's eyes lost focus, sliding away to look at the captain. "What are you saying?"

"The complete annihilation of the *Acheron*, along with the skeleton crew of forty-nine officers aboard. She was captained by an Oskie, too. Orbital blood, Naval blood. Taken down by pirates...and *nobody* saw it coming?"

The fleet carrier had been fired on and boarded by pirate elements before incinerating in the Boolean Pulsar. There wasn't even a chunk of charcoal for Imperial forces to recover. Convenient. The loss of the ship was played on every screen in half a galaxy, justifying an invasion of the poorly regulated Boolean space.

It justified the summons that left her brother without support. If the *Acheron* hadn't been destroyed...Marcus might still be alive.

And Graccus was now implying that losing that ship was a false flag, or that at minimum, the Spymaster and Imperial Naval Command had allowed it to happen, had engineered the situation? Their hands were clean, but the chaos had delivered the desired result.

What had she become a party to?

Callum swelled, tapping into some reserve of patriotism. "The Empire...is balance. Does its absence appear balanced to you?"

Graccus laid out his case. "Forget the Boolean entirely for one moment. Just here, just Concordia. Why didn't the receiving team wipe Scylla the moment it was recovered from its Pathfinding mission? They're a Pathfinder AI, *Gen One*! Those things had a stable life of a few months. Two-hundred-year drift or not, they would've been well into their Cascade by this point in their life cycle. No engineer worth their profession would've missed that. And what about Kaneda? Basic bio would have picked any short-term threats to his health. Not even Jupiter CorSec is this sloppy! So instead of a bedrest and a drive wipe, they send an ailing Pathfinder and his faulting AI out to a Reaches colony, complete with a heretical life story—for what, to window shop? See the world? You've got to be kidding me."

"They couldn't have known what would happen," Callum said with a dismissing shake of his head.

"Known? No, of course not. No way to predict this! That's insane. But they *watched*. They intentionally created a hazardous scenario and then monitored it. They studied, they waited. So one day, original Kaneda buys the farm, his AI goes ballistic, and the people here? They start praying to a dying computer that promises them a trip to Heaven...if they just obey."

Callum actually flashed a bit of teeth in a healthy snarl. "You really think so poorly of the Reaches?"

"How can you be calm about this?"

"Because cynicism, captain, is often confused for being emotionally stable and rational. It is neither."

"True," Graccus said, throwing a pointed glance at Adrianna, "but twenty-six Imperial officers died here in the last twenty-four hours, and I know their deaths mean more to the Empire than their lives *ever* would have."

Callum's eyes welled up, almost to tears, and he shook his head, queasy. "I'm going to forget that I heard you say that, captain."

Graccus considered that notion very carefully. Callum was giving him an out: he could lay the blame on an individual officer, some incompetence. Nobody was listening but the three of them, nobody would know the discussion ever occurred. But was he going to continue this accusation upon an institution, against their very nation?

Was he really prepared to accuse Earth itself of this atrocity?

He was. Graccus had one more piece of evidence to show. He popped open his Entiglas and swiped around for a file. He spoke slowly and deliberately so as to make no mistake of his intent, "Janus sent us a warning from the ground, identifying Scylla and Charybdis by name. He was agitated that we hadn't read it, because he told us *everything*—everything that you're so mad we didn't know! But the message was scrambled. We only got a portion of it. I had assumed the rebels got to it, but..."

Callum and Adrianna turned their heads to the ground, studying where Graccus projected the file. Adriana recognized the message. She'd read it on the *Erinyes* before the mission launched. "What am I looking for, cap?"

Graccus did them the favor, highlighting a section of corrupted code. "That, right there."

A hundred a fifty-eight different alphanumerics scattered throughout the missive. Looked liked chaos or corrupted data. Meant nothing to Adrianna on spec, so she keyed her encryption software to break the—

It was Naval. Imperial Encryption.

The message broke down in seconds because she had the crypto-key. Janus' entire story was there in plain text. It talked about Prime, Scylla, the tractor beam tower-weapon named Charybdis, operational safe distances for responding forces, and a brief history of the violent overthrow of the colony by a well-armed militia.

But that meant...if it was a Naval encryption...

That made no sense! The Commandant had insisted that the message could not be decrypted. But it was Naval encryption?! It should've been able to snap through that like tin foil.

Unless...unless Graccus was right. The Commandant was the source of the encryption. The ship AI received the message and promptly encoded it to protect the contents. They had been warned about the dangers of Concordia and deliberately hidden it.

"Why?" Callum asked, that low rumble back in his voice. "Why would the Commandant disobey your orders?"

Graccus dropped to one knee, trying to make himself as small as possible, as he implored his friend to reason. "The only way it even could is if it had orders that superseded mine. Someone in the Ministry issued a directive to the Commandant prior to our arrival, ordering it to block any communication with the ground."

Adrianna felt like she was going to be sick. She knew her job was hazardous, dangerous work that needed courageous people. But the very idea of issuing an order that had a one-to-one effect, an order that just killed her own men? The idea that she could knowingly give an order that would kill Voight or Vivian or Mastiff?

It made her skin crawl.

But that explanation didn't satisfy Callum. "I didn't ask how. I asked why."

"I don't know why! But there's only one way to find out *who*. We have to find the *Erinyes*, retake it, and find the Commandant before its damaged or destroyed."

"Faulty hardware should be destroyed."

That sentiment made Graccus' brain grind to a screeching halt. His jaw slackened and his eyes widened as it to try an absorb that statement faster through wider scanning. "You'd bury the evidence that someone tried to kill you?"

"I don't tolerate faulty equipment, captain."

And the most profound sadness grew over Graccus's eyes, like a kind of ice. Those words broke the dam in Graccus's mind and the confessions poured forth. "I lied to you, Callum. I've lied to you before, probably will again. I've told so many lies in my life I have to have a file structure for them. The only thing I've never lied about was how much I lie! I was very frank about that from the beginning. You spend time with me and I am going to lie—to your face. It's not pathological, it's *professional*! Now if you don't trust me, that's perfectly reasonable. I won't hold that against you. But if I'm lying to you, what makes you think any of your commanders are telling you the truth?"

"Don't make me invoke Article Seven, captain."

Adrianna tensed at those words from Callum, and she threw a glance back at the rest of the gang. Most were too busy trying to not pay attention, but Sergeant Mastiff heard what he needed to. And he thumbed the safety on his rifle.

Article Seven, Section Twenty-Two of the Uniform Code gave subordinate officers the right to depose a commander in theater. It had seen mixed support from Judicial Magistrates and the Ministry itself, but the practicalities of it always meant friendly fire. Because insubordination to a commanding officer was equally punishable by death.

Callum was declaring his right to consider Graccus hostile.

And those words sent all lofty emotion, all warmth and fervor out of Graccus draining out through his feet. What remained was a shell, a remarkable facsimile of the man she knew. "You're going to have to. Because they did it. They deliberately sent the *Erinyes* into hostile space *hoping* it would be attacked."

"And if you get out of here alive, you'll prove it?"

"No. Because I could show you video of Philippe and Caldwell sipping tea over your grave...and you'd still defend them."

She had to do something. She had to say something! If she didn't, these two apex predators were going to kill each other, right here and right now. And who knew what kind of chaos that would bring down on them.

"None of it matters," she said.

They didn't look away from one another. But Callum tilted his head to her, letting his words spill out of the side of his mouth like drips of venom. "What doesn't, lieutenant?"

"Your little shitting match, that's what."

The cuss actually got Graccus to blink, flicking his eyes over towards her like he was psychically trying to shove her away.

She caught his gaze and kept it, pushing back. "It doesn't matter... if we don't get off this planet alive in the first place. If we make it back to Terra Firma, you can lodge every complaint you like, commander. Shit, charge the cap'n with treason. But it's all just *hot air* if we all die down here." She pointed back at the crew behind them. "Those people fell out of the sky and they're still ready to kick some ass. You two are so ready to kill each other, you forgot there's an entire planet here ready to do it for you. So can you two put your boots back on and be *fuckin' Oskies* for an afternoon?!"

And the sound of it came reverberating back to her. And it was only in that moment that she realized that her inside voice had grown to an outside voice.

Both officers turned their anger towards her. But Graccus's anger simmered into a kind of amusement, head bobbling slightly with barely contained laughter. "Glad to have that out of your system?"

"No. Kind of terrified, actually."

"Good," Callum said, deadly serious. She had already bloodied him once, and now she spoke to him in this tone? It had the tone of a spurned royal measuring the remainder of his patience.

Thankfully, that was all he said. Graccus folded his arms across his chest with an expectant smirk. "What's your call then...lieutenant? Going to go back to dumpster diving for more canned food, see if we can last the week?"

Right. She had to actually have an idea if she was going to demand the floor like that. To her, it seemed so simple. Who set them up and why was tomorrow's problem. Today had a simple one. "We can't take the *Erinyes* back if we just get dragged out of the sky again. There's an anti-air battery in play. I say we take it out. Any objection, sir?"

Callum didn't even look at her, still staring murder into Graccus's skull. Maybe he knew she was right, but that only frustrated him more. First Graccus spouts his treason without consequence, and now she was going around *making sense*. She watched his body temperature climb as he boiled in silence.

But Graccus softened, smiling at her. "Now that's my kind of workday. *Zu gloriam*, lieutenant."

CHAPTER
TWENTY

NOBODY WANTED to spend longer than thirty seconds in her orbit anymore. The Vees sat back with Sizemore, protected by the Regulars. And the leathernecks themselves were looking toward Callum and Graccus with a paranoid frequency.

She'd made her loyalties clear when she defied Callum and they didn't want to be seen as endorsing her behavior. Even her friends on the deck crew were averting their eyes.

Graccus and Callum weren't all that talkative either, though she expected that had more to do with their own conflict than with her.

Besides, it'd probably be asking a little too much for Callum to talk to her after she'd cut him open.

No. No! What kind of logic was that?! He'd *thrown* stuff at her! She was perfectly within her rights to defend herself. Sure, he was her superior officer, but she was just supposed to let him cut her up? That's what always confused her about regulations; the seniors could hit the little guys as often as they liked, but when the little guy hit back, suddenly it was conduct unbecoming and a trip to the brig.

That wasn't strictly true. Uniform Code had stipulations about superiors striking subordinates, but they were brought to the Commanding Officer for review. And CO sided with the officer in virtually all circumstances. So while Uniform Code publicly said one thing, it was something completely different in application.

The force and effect of all of this was that nobody was talking to her. Nobody would even walk near her, lest her coming punishments rub off onto them.

Except Kaneda. He refused to leave her side. If she sped up, he hobbled to keep pace with her. Suppose this was her reward. No good deed and all that.

His voice hadn't yet recovered from Callum's hit. Every time he spoke, it sounded like a little frog was trying to pop out. "With so much automation, it's a wonder any of you still work."

"Oh?" The singular sound was about all she had patience for.

"You have machines that can build complex molecules. Computers that can chart Jumps like they're trivial. The universe has never been closer together than it is today."

It was easy to track his logic. They were standing on urban sprawl that would have been a barren rock in his day. She deployed to a military theater in a spaceship that would have made his look like a liquor barrel floating in a river. So...he was a little awestruck by it all.

But now he had a point to make. "I'm just saying, machines that should bring abundance and people still live in want."

"Janus," she said with the hush of barely contained frustration, "is now really the time to try to radicalize me?"

He shrugged. "I mean, there's never a *good* time for it. That's why they try to keep you busy."

"Well, I'm busy saving your life right now, so maybe try not to talk yourself out of that state. Okay?"

"You wouldn't." He wasn't challenging her. That was a statement of fact, much like calling her uniform gray or her eyes brown or her mother a bitch.

She raised an eyebrow, slowing her walk. "I wouldn't what?"

Kaneda nodded at the two Oskies in front of them. "They kill people without thinking. You save people without thinking."

Maybe. Impulse control was always a problem for her. Too empathetic. Compromised. She couldn't do her job effectively anymore.

Kaneda smiled, watching her grind on that notion. "You want to be like them?"

"Maybe if you talked less, you could walk faster."

"Somebody unboxed me with a bum leg and a mutant kidney. I don't know what to tell you."

She almost wanted to turn, give him a full scan to see if that kidney claim was true. Instead, she just shook her head and kept walking. But she still heard the satisfied pop of his lips. "What?" she asked.

"Nothing," Kaneda said, smug. "So, what will you do when you finally get home?"

She hadn't really thought about it. She'd been so focused on actually pulling everyone out of the frying pan, she had never considered the proverbial fire she was sending herself into.

She was, in the best case, heading towards mandatory dismissal. Worst case, a firing squad would greet her at the airlock. "I'm thinking pancakes," she said.

"Fruit on top? Strawberries, whipped cream?"

"Butter. I'm a traditionalist."

"Nice."

She really was beginning to regret saving him. He was making her dwell on what had to come.

She had no idea why she told him. The words just came out. "This was my last mission. Bless my burdens! It wasn't even supposed to be my mission."

He stopped, leaning hard on his cane. "What was *supposed* to happen?"

How to phrase this politely? "A group of six ministers, two doctors, and an admiral would meet me at the gangway. I'd be stripped to my skivvies, then taken to a medical bay."

He didn't like that word. It darkened his entire face. "Why a medical bay?"

She looked at him, dire. "Because I can't keep what's not mine."

He looked her up and down, eyes tracing over the surgical scars on her scalp and shoulders. Many people had stared at her markings before: in horror, in awe. It always made the scalpel trail feel separate from her.

Kaneda didn't linger on the old wounds. Instead, he brought his eyes back to her own, wrought with disbelief. "They wouldn't."

"They have to."

"They wouldn't!" he insisted, so innocent. "That...wouldn't that..."

Kill her? She shrugged. "It might. It's government kit, Kaneda. It belongs to the job, to the Navy. And I'm about to be discharged."

"So they-they just *rip* it out of you when they're done with you?"

It had made sense to her, even back in her Holkstad days. An average civilian running about with classified military-grade augmentations would have been an unreasonable threat. The augments would have to be reclaimed or destroyed. Plenty of back-alley doctors and scratchers would give up half their client list to get a hold of Oskie implants.

Her lack of response did not comfort Kaneda. "Don't they have a plan for the day you retire?"

"Oskies don't retire," she said, reflexively.

And that just broke his little heart. His jaw hung, aghast at this future he had stepped into.

The next words she heard came almost an hour later. Graccus waved the group to stop and shelter in place. He melted into the shadows, leaving Adrianna to track him by his IFF tag.

And then the phrase escaped Graccus because it was the only rational reaction to have. He prayed. "Bless our burdens for they weigh on our shoulders..."

Callum glanced at Adrianna, checking. She heard that too? And she nodded. Adrianna motioned for the Regulars to stay put and she followed Callum up to Graccus' position.

She landed on the rooftop to see Graccus and Callum standing side by side. Graccus only stood up to Callum's shoulder, but they both looked so small right now. She could swear she saw Graccus's fingers reach, blindly clawing for Callum's hand. But the sight of it distracted Callum too much. Transfixed him.

They had found the edge of the Undercity Plate and were looking off the side into the bare mountain rock and dark valley below. There was a thick fog bank that obscured the ground, but they could still see a great deal of import peeking out from under that silver veil.

A Pilgrim Metal monolith.

Ten—no, a hundred times larger than the one in the Caldera Market. A curved spear that had to be thirty stories tall, its root somewhere stuck down beneath the clouds. And littered around that base, she could make out obscured steel mounds, like frozen hilltops that wormed their way down the steep mountainside. These were the barrows of enemies slain by that monolith, its claims and trophies. Dozens upon dozens of ships stretched for miles down into the valley, like a graveyard of mismatched stones.

"I suppose we found all the missing ships that went in the nebula," Callum grunted.

"Yeah, I suppose we did." Graccus stared down at the tower, swallowing hard.

Awesome? Certainly. A historical marvel? Absolutely. But Adrianna couldn't ring up the same amazement as her fellows. Instead, she found her shoulder ache just looking at it. And the surface of it caught the light in the most disconcerting way, like an oil spill. It appeared lit from within, some evanescent teal and blue flashing under its surface.

She felt its...its pull. Her feet felt light in her shoes and her fingers snapped off each other. She could hear the scuff of her boots on the gravel rooftop. And what's more, she felt the most bizarre urge to...she didn't want to admit it. She wanted to walk off the roof.

The urge to jump.

"How are we going to bring that down?" Adrianna gasped in despair.

Graccus's brow furrowed and he spun on his heels. He jerked his thumb at the monolith. "*That*...is Charybdis?"

"It is Pilgrim," Callum confirmed, almost under his breath.

"I'm not disagreeing," Graccus said, turning his gaze back on the majesty of it, "but if we blow something like that, we will not go unnoticed."

Callum huffed. "Don't ask me. This is your plan."

"That was before I knew it was a skyscraper, Callum! We'd need a rail gun to even make a dent."

It made a kind of insane sense. If Scylla and the Pathfinder somehow manufactured or found functioning Pilgrim technology, the functions could be limitless. The Pilgrim's abilities were mystical, almost magical. But logic dictated that their sorcery had to have some kind of science underpinning it. Replicating that technology...

They'd been to the Path. Maybe they had found something. Or they just knew where to look.

"We can't destroy it," Callum said.

"Well, I'm not going to just lay down," Graccus said, crouching at the edge of the roof to think. "Something that big *has* to have some kind of support structure."

"We *can't*." Callum wasn't talking about ability.

And Graccus hadn't missed that. "Then we die," he pointed out.

"So then we die," Callum affirmed. "But you may be looking at the largest technological discovery of our lifetimes, captain. It is worth our lives. We can't destroy it."

She hated that Callum was making so much sense. They weren't looking at stone shards or mysterious radioactive material excavated from a cave; this was a functioning piece of technology of the Pilgrim. It had to be preserved for study. It was the religious discovery of a century! Hell, the barriers in physics and chemistry that it would shatter!

But Graccus had some sense of his own. "That may be the case, but do you really think Scylla and the militia here are ready to share their 'discovery' with the rest of the Empire? 'Can't destroy it?' We *can't* let them keep it! That's not the Pilgrim's favorite coffee shop down there; it's a superweapon. This could bring down an Eisenclad without breaking a sweat. Scylla could kill thousands. Even if we got the Empire to respond, to come to the rescue? Scylla would just drag them planet-side." He jerked a finger at the monolith. "That's not an artifact—that's a bomb."

"The Pilgrim doesn't kill," Callum stated, somehow making that statement sound like a threat.

Adrianna struggled to hear their argument. The longer she stared at that monolith...the more weightless she felt, like a lightness in her heels and a pull along her scalp, lifting, lifting her up...

And she felt her fingertips burn.

Could she? She'd melted a bit of wall without even knowing what she was doing, but could she bring down Charybdis with just a touch? She could feel the cold pulsing off it, even from half a mile away. How would it react if she brought it some warmth to just the right spot?

And if she could, what then? She'd have to explain herself to Callum and Graccus, and she had no answers. And Prime's forces would certainly respond with brutal efficiency. And Prime would return all the harsher if she used her power.

No. They could manage it. If anyone alive anywhere in the Empire could do this, it was the three of them. They were Orbital, elite, improved, disciplined, and motivated. There wasn't a human being alive that could match what these three could do on their worst day. She'd made it this far, and she would go as far as she liked— Prime be damned.

She stepped between the two quarreling officers. "Pilgrim doesn't kill, but Prime will, and our Service is to the People."

The trio climbed back down to their friends' expectant faces.

"You see the *Erinyes?*" Voight asked.

"No, but it'd be hard to pick it out from the killing field," Graccus said.

"Regulars, Deck Crew, huddle up," Adrianna said, calling everyone to her. "Oskies are about to do what Oskies do best. We're going to take down Charybdis. Sergeant Mastiff, you and the Regulars are to secure the noncoms and stand by. When we bring it down, you're to secure a ship from that field—anything that'll fly. Charybdis just pulls ships in, it doesn't blow 'em apart. So *something* down there has a working reactor core. Get it operational and airborne. You do not wait for the Orbital team. Huah?"

"Bullshit," Vivian cursed. "We're not leaving without you!"

"Lieutenant's right," Graccus agreed. "Somebody has to raise the flag. You get a ship and you tilt full-burn skyward. I don't want to hear another word about it."

Sergeant Mastiff stepped close to her, whispering like he could make his case in private. "I am not leaving another fallen comrade."

She could feel Callum swelling up. He already didn't like this plan, but insubordination he liked even less. And she could Graccus drawing as breath, ready to scold the sergeant.

So she beat him to it. "Yes, you are!" Adrianna snapped, a little harsher than she meant to, so she softened with the follow up, grab-

228

bing him by the straps of his chest rig. "Sergeant Mastiff, we need to move fast and hard. If we're waiting on you fleshies, *nobody* gets out of here. So you need to keep your team safe and quiet. And then, get them skyside the first chance you get. Huah?"

Oh, he understood. His issue hadn't been one of clarity. He was furious, frustrated, and disappointed. But he relented, backing away with his head bowed.

Holt and Gallantine exchanged wide-eyed glances absolutely pumped with adrenaline. There was a non-zero chance that the sergeant was about to get pulverized right in front of them and he'd gotten away with a light scolding.

"You keep them off of me and Sizemore," Voight said, with a solemn nod, "and we'll get 'em home."

"This isn't right," Vivian muttered, under her breath.

"No, it's not, Bannister," Graccus said, calling her out in front of everyone. "But it is what's happening. Get comfortable with it."

The stated mission objective was for the Oskies to blow up an anti-aircraft battery the size of a building, and then to intentionally get left behind. Nobody was happy about it.

Kaneda hissed with something akin to pain, inadvertently drawing everyone's eyes to him. He almost flushed with embarrassment before swallowing his pride. "Can I point out an absolutely terrible fact—and feel free to tell me if I'm out of bounds?"

"Shut up," was Callum's simple but firm response.

"What is it, Kaneda?" Adrianna asked.

"This is a partisan military situation, and you think you can just fly away? He'll never let you go."

"Wasn't planning on asking permission," Callum sneered.

"It'll take more than some ack-ack to catch me," Voight assured him, turning his attention to the Oskies. "But *how* are you planning on doing your end, exactly?"

Mastiff and Kaneda had the same quizzical stare at Adrianna and she could feel her fingers tingle from their combined looks.

But Graccus stepped in with the answer. "I was thinking good ol' fashioned explosives. First monolith didn't stand up to a det charge. Neither will this one."

That was certainly more practical than her option and they knew explosives were available. But where was he going to get *that* much demolition from?

CHAPTER
TWENTY-ONE

WHEN PILGRIM METAL was first discovered, they had to recalibrate the hardness scale around it. It outclassed diamond in nearly every way, but it wasn't suitable as building material or even for industrial use, being both rare and energetically...unstable.

That doesn't mean some robber baron hadn't tried, of course. Adrianna had it explained to her once as a child. In very few words, the stuff was unfriendly to human tissue over prolonged exposure. That robber baron died along with seventeen of his workers. The doctors had no cause of death beyond the very terrifying word 'necrosis.'

And she had a chunk sunk into her shoulder. Maybe now she was the one that was radioactive? Was her arm going to rot off?

Polonium, radium, uranium—these were experiencing neutron decay. Pilgrim Metal did not fit neatly on the periodic table; samples had wildly different quantities of neutrons, but nevertheless had identical properties.

This stuff broke conventional chemistry.

Of course, they built all this knowledge around inert shards unearthed from a dig site. There were theories aplenty about the different uses for the artifacts that had been found, as the Pilgrim themselves had made no mention of the strange obsidian material. Broken shards and chunks of the stuff would simply appear wherever the Pilgrim had been.

Had the relics been part of some great machine? One more outrageous theory was that they were crystallized blood of the Pilgrim. Whatever they were, none of them had an obvious purpose.

Charybdis—this monolith that towered over Adrianna? It had a very practical application.

If Charybdis was a structure of some kind, she saw no way in or out of it. There was no subsystem or critical piece to take offline, no transmitter or power source. They had to plan for it being solid through and through, which meant they'd need enough explosives to level a city block just to scratch it. And the thing was easily a hundred feet wide at the base.

This was a hardened target made of the hardest stuff known to humanity and not an insubstantial amount of it. How were they going to pull this off?

Graccus had sourced an ammo dump less than a kilometer from the base of Charybdis. It would barely qualify as a Forward Operating Base: there were two barracks, some watchtowers, an ammo dump and commo tent. Strategically, it made for a decent response position to any threats to the towering structure, but it didn't seem to have the personnel or defensive stance.

They just wanted to be close to their demigod-thing.

But Graccus confirmed the presence of RNX-20 explosive charges in the armory. How much, she had asked him.

And he had very stoically explained that there was enough explosive material to give the Chicago Crater a companion piece. They were going to seize that cache and put a hole in Charybdis that looked like divine intervention.

Callum would be the bagman, charged with carrying all five hundred pounds of the explosives to the target site. Graccus and Adrianna would have to keep him safe for the trek. Conventional wisdom would have them take rooftops to avoid being pinned down, but with the Upper City plate permanently seizing height advantage —along with the soupy weather—they'd want to stick low to the fog banks for proper cover.

Adrianna took the time to map the route as close to Charybdis as she dared. The soil was almost powdery under her boots, simultaneously dry and fine but also dampened by the moisture in the air. That dew brought with it a chill and pleasant smell of musk and moss, masking the sweat and grime that went with every soldier.

It was a steep grade, and each step had a frustrating tendency to send small piles of dirt sliding downhill. There wasn't really a road either, not like the Upper or Lower City. Civilized roads were straight, or at the very least, laid with intention. This was more like puzzle pieces tipped out of a box, dozens of odd and angular starships stacked atop one another. And thick conduits connected them all, humming with latent energy, richly violet like some kind of poisonous plant. Airlock doors and hatches had been crudely cut open with torches, and the ground was strewn with metal plates, circuit boards, and wires. One AI core's empty and sullen shell sat by its ship like a grave marker or some metallic tumbleweed.

They wanted the ships, not the stewards.

The morning fog covered her advance nicely, and she could spy the mercenaries' heat signatures with ease. Unlike the field of lost toys that surrounded it, Charybdis' soil was neat and tidy, a protective radius swept clean of any trash. They had built up bunker at its base, with containers of dirt stacked up for a thick defensive wall. Infantry patrolled inside and out. Sniper overwatch, but they were going to be having a rough time acquiring targets with this thick mist. And just to make matters worse, there were two GA-57—drunken

Grandmas. They sat on the main gate, watching the road. Those would need to be avoided or otherwise neutralized.

More concerning was the gunship that rested happily on a landing pad, a crooked vulture-looking thing with a nose cannon and thrusters in its avian hips. She saw a barracks nearby and it was hooked to a fuel pump—either might be useful in taking that piece off the board.

They had built two large structures, not much more than impressive domed tents, really. They were propped up on a steel frame foundation—likely to keep the interior insulated from the cold alpine soil. Conduits the size of her wrist were strung from steel poles, running power and other utilities to those buildings.

Now what was going on in there? Study? Industry?

No matter what, the mercy were deeply invested in Charybdis' safety. If the fog held, the Oskies were going to have no trouble taking it from them.

Oskies may be strong, fast, and better equipped than any other front-line fighting force, but this had every opportunity to go sideways on them. The weather could clear; an alarm could sound and summon reinforcement. They weren't aware of the enemy schedule and couldn't plan for surprise visits—and they had no time to wait and gather that intel. They would have to adapt as factors presented themselves.

Graccus was scouting the FOB, waiting for the perfect moment for them to steal the explosives. That left Adrianna and Callum together and alone.

Callum enjoyed silenced, preferred it. But the quieter the air got, the more Adrianna was aware of the empty tension. It felt heavy, pressured, thick emotion like waves of force pulsing off of Callum's back. He looked like a silverback gorilla sulking in a corner of his enclosure.

Did she dare say anything to him? Five years in the Service, she'd hit a lot of her superior officers. She stopped counting around four, it had stopped being noteworthy. But those had always been in anger, or stupor, and one time out of ignorance. She'd never hit Callum before.

Callum had never held her past impropriety against her, not like Graccus had. Maybe that's because he thought he could win any fight. And that's not what had happened...

"So...should we be looking for your parents? Any family?" she asked him.

He didn't answer.

"I can't imagine what it must—"

The sound of her voice set him off. "My parents left the colony when I enrolled at Holkstad. Doesn't make it any kinder see my childhood militarized and burning."

Wow. Whatever raging power simmered under the surface, he was keeping a tight lid on it.

Talk shop. Talk neutral. Anything. Get him speaking again. "RNX-20. That's an impact explosive, right?"

No response. Keep going.

She tried to harken back, remember her Flash and Burn lectures. She'd never been a demolitions specialist. Applied chemistry always frustrated her. "Chemical compound susceptible to shock and impact forces, right? Ten megajoules of force per kilogram?"

"Nine," Callum grunted back.

A syllable. Almost two. That was progress. "Suppose the difference doesn't matter much to you if you're the one carrying it?"

"Stable at temperatures in excess of a hundred fifty degrees, ideal for remote detonation by sniper or with detonation cap. Rebels and terrorists enjoy it for its availability and compact power. There's isn't a chemical blasting agent more potent found anywhere in physics."

"And we stopped using it because dropping it on the deck had a tendency to blow a cruiser in half?"

Callum lifted his head, but all she saw was the back of it. "I know what you're doing, Riley. Stop." The words were polite, but the threat buried in the tone was unmistakable. He wasn't just annoyed, but was imagining appropriate punishments, and doing so with clarity and consideration.

"We're doing the right thing, commander," she said.

"I have no doubt you feel that way."

———

Graccus returned with his report. Patrols were light and spread thin. If they hurried, they'd meet minimal resistance—possibly even avoid sounding alarms if they were thorough enough in their dispatch.

The fog was holding, the sunlight above blocked by the city plates. The low ambient light levels would make them difficult to spot.

Adrianna hoped that the crew was tucked somewhere safe. The Oskies were about to stick their heads in the proverbial lion's mouth, but Vivian, Mastiff and the others were about to turn tail and activate that same lion's prey drive. She wasn't doing the most dangerous thing today.

Graccus came back with the good word. It was time to move.

The three of them silently made their way through the fog, leap-frogging forward. There was a single patrol of six that they ran close to, but the mercs never knew they were there. She didn't need an invisibility cloak to hide from these goons.

The front gate of the FOB was lightly defended and they had built up their walls good and high, but all three Oskies were able to vault over like silent wraiths.

The door to the ammo dump had a posted guard, carbine, light armor, and field kit. He stood under a pair of spotlights, making sure that the entry was well-watched. A biometric lock on the door, which would likely track instances of entry—and she was sure there were only certain approved times for any such entry.

No matter. The door was going to open one way or another.

Once they took that guard out of rotation and looted the lockers inside, they'd be on borrowed time. No way to know exactly how much. Command might call for a check in or someone would come to relieve him and find the cache looted. Alarms would sound, reinforcements would come. And on they'd go with the bloodshed and fireworks.

Her hope was that they'd be at Charybdis by that point. Because if they weren't...

The guard must've thought himself safe under the bright lights. Callum hit him at full sprint, transferring enough force to actually splash the man a bit. A small gout of blood hung in the air, the last bit of the man that refused to go for the ride. It splattered onto the dark soil. Graccus marched up, kicking some dirt up over it to cover even that small bit of evidence. Callum came sauntering back, blood dripping down his front, ruining Graccus' careful management.

They couldn't risk alarms so Graccus had to bypass the door locks. No point in trying to defeat the heuristic security. They just had to slice the power and they were in. Scylla might notice a single door go dark on their network, but it was better than tripping an alarm or pounding through the steel. Power line snipped, Callum was able to force the door back on along its rails.

Adrianna led the way inside, her rifle at low-ready as she swept storage cage after storage cage. Most of the crates were emptied, some even broken down. These were not for anything but local shipment. Everything was being manufactured locally anyhow. Most of the cages had nothing but empty racks. They had stored weapons here, but those had since been dispersed.

She remembered that empty house, that girl's journal. How many of that child's toys and clothes had been melted down to make bombs and bullets?

Adrianna was about to get frustrated until she arrived at the last cage. Just as Graccus had scouted: there were three full crates of RNX-20. Improperly labeled and stored. Chemical propellants of any type shouldn't be shelved anywhere near general munitions—let alone right next to a stack of empty canteens! Somebody in this camp had almost certainly consumed trace amounts of an extremely volatile explosive compound.

The individual charges were stamped into aluminum casings, helpfully labeled with a big danger icon, this side up, and do not eat. She knew the exact kind of grunt that label was made for.

Gallantine. He'd eat some just to see if he could make others eat it. Her stomach growled, nauseated at the simple thought.

"Alright, commander, ruck up," Graccus said, grabbing his carbine off his back and telescoping the barrel out. "It's pucker time."

Adrianna knew her role. She led the way back to the edge of the encampment. Graccus lingered long enough to close the door behind them and reconnect the wiring. If they were lucky, nobody noticed the brief outage—or the traumatic absence of the guard.

Callum's augments made a bit of whir and grind as he jumped himself and a very unstable explosive over the ten-foot wall. Graccus and Adrianna both stared in horrible anticipation, watching Callum's parabola peak and then come gracefully down to earth again, a small tuft of dust on landing. The duffel bag of doom shook a bit, the mildest metallic clatter.

No boom. Three cheers for that.

A voice. "Did you hear that?"

All three Oskies tensed up. Graccus and Adrianna spun with weapons up, ready for any threat.

But a second voice immediately dismissed the concerns. "That's been happening since Caldera. Just fragments from the Upper Plate."

"Oh, so the Upper Plate is just dropping *fragments*—whole-ass chunks of city—and you're fine with it?"

"I ain't fine with it. I can't *do* anything about it. There's a difference."

Graccus waved the team onward. So long as those goons were distracted by each other, there was no reason to linger.

The trio made their way through the fog banks back toward Charybdis. Adrianna looked up, clearly able to see the towering spire overhead. The sun may not reach two levels down, but the gulf stream blowing between the two plates was slowly wicking away their cover, wisps of cloud curling away down the valley.

They would not be able to stay hidden for much longer.

Adrianna led the way. There wasn't a single straight line in this mess of abandoned spacecraft and conduits. Each ship was connected to the next, regardless of their condition. She really didn't want to take a reading for all the radiation or particle dust that might be in the air around them.

Not all the ships were in good shape. One ship had been cloven in two, a cross-section melted away by some brutal impact. It looked like some great figure had taken an ax to it, slashing it through the middle.

Adrianna looked up at Charybdis looming overhead. And she looked at the surrounding wreck. Wood—and the ax.

"They tried to destroy it," Adrianna whispered. "It brought them down, so they thought..." The plucky captain and his crew had known they were done for and decided that if they were to be taken, they were going to make their enemy work for it.

And despite this daring maneuver...Charybdis was still standing, unmarred.

"They failed," Callum mocked.

"You don't think this is going to work, do you?"

He shook his head. "You shouldn't even be down here."

What a remarkably special way to dismiss her opinion. She scoffed, resuming her march toward the tower.

The wind was properly picking up now. The Oskies didn't dare use their speed or other augments in this thin of cover now—it would only catch the light from their glowing augments, the humid air sizzling on their skin. They might as well throw up a flare. But that didn't stop them from being classically careful.

The gun turrets that watched the front gate remained dormant. All along the rest of the perimeter were guard towers staffed by two or three trigger-fingers, each with interlocking views of each other.

The bored guards lazily scanned the graveyard for something to catch their interest.

Two mercs nearby posted in a watchtower together were chatting as they watched. Adrianna tried to observe their pattern, find a gap in their coverage, only to discover that they were the same person. Mild variation in height, and one had thinner hair, but there was no mistaking it: they could've been brothers.

Gray hair, beards. Mild difference in height, but they had the same piercing handsome features. They looked exactly like the shotgun-wielding mercenary that attacked her at the grocery store...

Clones. She hadn't doubted Kaneda, but it was still hard to take seriously. And here they stood, chattering away with one another like brothers. Well-disciplined and cautious brothers.

Four minutes of watching and there was no break in the sightlines, no path into the compound. Callum was getting impatient, nervous. So was Graccus.

"When they look away, you both move your asses," Graccus said with gravitas.

"Very descriptive, cap'n," Adrianna whispered. But when she looked back to share a smile...he was gone.

"Oh no, little shadow..." Callum muttered.

What? What was he—she turned to look, and her heart skipped a beat.

Adrianna couldn't see the man, but her HUD flagged Graccus's ID tag walking right up to the fortress main gate. He was invisible to the naked eye, but the heat-seeking turrets would almost certainly see pick out his glow.

"What could he possibly be thinking?" The words came out of Adrianna's head before she could put a cork in it, but Callum didn't scold her any. He was beside himself.

The first turret acquired him. And with a big heavy clank, it turned to its target. A flash of accompanying yellow had Graccus quickly dart out of sight. Nothing to see here, just a weird curly contrail hanging in the air!

But the metallic bang and lurching jutter got the guards' attentions. They both turned to see what all the fuss was over.

Now! Get over the wall! They'd have seconds, if that.

Callum practically dragged her the first five feet before she started moving on her own. And the duo leapt into the compound. Adrianna tapped her toes on the ground like a dancer—once, twice, thrice—bleeding off the landing in little hits so she could land quiet and soft. And with the fourth kick, she launched herself behind a barricade to hide.

The guards looked back their way, the slight scuffle of leather boots on soil drawing them back. She heard the clack of a rifle bolt drop into battery and the unmistakable pluck to the air that came with ozone and electrical charge.

"You hear that?" one of them asked.

"Turret sure saw something."

They couldn't stay here. Adrianna glanced at one of the large temporary domes. Twenty feet of open sprint to get there. She didn't hear any heartbeats inside—relative safety—but there was an unsettling amount of warmth, lots of electrical current flowing. Could be automated defenses. But they didn't have a better option.

She didn't dare whisper inside the perimeter. Too great a risk of being detected, so she just flagged the building in her HUD, threw Callum a point-to-point update and hoped the big guy was paying attention.

Point guard. She had to pave the road.

Adrianna sprinted for the door. It was a quick hop up three steps. No lock, not even a pin-system. She threw the door open, holding it there just long enough for Callum to slip in before she hushed it shut. The only sound from their passing was the rush of wind.

It was dark inside, a kind of sea-foam green glow that lit the walls. She could hear water trickling through pipes overhead and bizarre acoustics as sounds liked to echo and reverb around the space. A great many windows, perhaps?

She was a happier, more innocent person before she turned

around. Literally, a fuller and more complete human being. Flowers had more color and food more taste. Because when she turned, a piece of humanity was stricken away, something she'd never get back.

Tubes. More like vats, really. Rows upon rows of them filled with a viscous green fluid that caught the light, making it appear that they glowed. It was like a field, aquamarine crops in an industrial garden.

And suspended in that green fluid...

Adrianna nearly wretched. Each tube held a person in what appeared to be various states of decay. They were breaking down, pieces of them floating in the soup, diluting and blending. Strips of flesh, cloth, and bone. Some kind of acid, perhaps?

At the base of each vat, nine familiar words were stenciled on every one of them. She said them out loud. "Thick is the bramble on the path never walked."

"That mean something to you?" Callum asked.

They'd written it on the doors in their homes, as a reminder of this place, these things. They knew full well what happened to those taken by Scylla's thugs—the Faces. The mercs with the same Face. And they did what, worship this place? Or did they offer prayers hoping to cajole it, appeasing it?

Each individual vat had a pipe connected, manifolded with their neighbors to run along the floor. A drain system? She followed the pipes to the end of the row. It seemed like it might never end, glass jars full of preserved and decomposing flesh, until she finally reached it. The pipes flowed into the side of a Replicator. Small, almost insignificant, with a medical bed laid through its build field.

A body bag laid on the ground next to an empty vat. Did she dare?

She stooped, unzipping the bag at the head. Gray hair and gray beard, flecks of red and orange with a clean jawline. It was the same man as the two from the tower and the shotgun merc from the store. The same man, but somewhat different. His eyes were further apart and his skin had an oily texture. And she smelled blood, fluids, ugly swelling and bruising at his neck.

He'd come fresh off the Replicator wrong—and died within moments. The scientists had shrugged and bagged him. They would have been preparing him to be processed, reclaimed material, just like all the others around. Nothing to do but send him through the great machine again.

"This is it," Adrianna stammered out. "This is where they made... where they *make* their soldiers."

"One place, yeah." Graccus melted out from his invisibility like a man emerging from shadows itself. He bore a mixed look of horror and...a kind of grief on his face. Like he was walking a graveyard for a war he'd never known about.

"*One* of them?" He didn't blink. Adrianna had heard him right. "One...of them? You knew about this?"

He didn't answer, choosing instead to look at the nearest vat. There was an adult man inside, fresher than his neighbors. Thinning hair and sunken cheeks. Possible malnutrition or some other ailment. Intravenous markers on both arms; the attendants had seen fit to kill him chemically before pouring him into the chamber.

It was a resource. That was all these people were. Break them down with acid, far more energy efficient, then feed the slurry into the replicator to produce...more people, correct people, faithful people.

She was going to throw up.

Callum had nothing to add. His jaw trembled and his eyes burned...glaring at Graccus.

Adrianna turned, balled fists, ready to hit another commanding officer. "Did you know they were doing this, captain?"

She'd never seen Graccus look so small. And his voice came out like the last gasp of it, the last words he might ever speak. "My...my contacts let me know, at great personal risk."

"Before or after we were blown out of the sky?"

He didn't answer that, stone-faced. And that incensed her. How could he just stand there and be so cold about this?!

"And you decided not to share?" Adrianna hissed.

"I couldn't. If I give up that intel, somebody's going to ask how I got it, and that shuts every door in my face."

"You're right," Callum said, stepping up to Graccus' back. "I do want to know how you got it."

"Doesn't matter how I knew."

"I think it does. I think it matters how, and more importantly, *when* you knew."

"I tell you about this two weeks ago? You'll sound the alarm like a reasonable person would and should! At which point, the Home Office sniffs around and my informant ends up dead!"

"You're spying on the Empire now?" Callum's exhales could've lit the building on fire, barely hiding a snarl. "Begs the question, who for?"

"Me, myself and I," Graccus said. "I don't need an evil patron to know when something's fishy. Get out of my face."

Their voices were starting to carry more volume than Adrianna was comfortable with, but she wasn't going to get between them. Not this time.

She couldn't believe this! Graccus knew the risks, knew the danger they were walking into, and he confidently dragged the entire crew in with him.

"Riley, please." Graccus was begging now, trying to drive home his point. "The Empire's known about this for years. *Years*, Riley! We can prove that Minister Caldwell and Philippe dei Mogglin allowed a massacre to take place on Concordia!"

Why? Why would they allow this? What purpose did this serve?

But Callum just dismissed it. "More lies," the commander grumbled with a shake of his head.

"Which part are you mad at, Callum?" Graccus snarled. "That I knew about this little war crime? Or that I knew and didn't tell *you*?"

Callum didn't move a step, but he projected his will with possibly the most hateful whisper Adrianna had ever heard. "I'm not angry, Graccus Ontarim. I'm not angry at all."

Graccus didn't have an answer to that, just hanging his head. He had no currency here, no power to defend himself. Adrianna didn't know what Graccus could've done about any of this, but she was too livid to really consider it. When had Graccus learned about this? And how could he have kept quiet about it? How could *anyone*?

She'd never be able to keep something like from Vivian.

Adrianna looked at Callum, checking in with the commander. But Callum was too busy trying to set Graccus on fire with a stare.

Why would Philippe or anyone allows this? Why wouldn't they tell *her* so she could *stop this?!*

She didn't have any answer for it, so Adrianna grabbed a brick of RNX-20 and pressed it to the side of the Replicator.

CHAPTER
TWENTY-TWO

THEY WOULD NOT BE able to lay five hundred pounds of explosive—sans her specific contributions to the cloning lab—at the base of Charybdis unnoticed. That meant Adrianna and Graccus would have to either neutralize or occupy the base's defenders, while Callum got the bomb set up.

He could, of course, just throw the bag into position—the unstable explosives would certainly detonate. But they would lose an enormous portion of the potency that way. He would need to shape the charges properly to deliver maximum payload with the desired effect.

That left him vulnerable.

Callum estimated he'd need three minutes and seventeen seconds to complete the task. Adrianna didn't really feel like he understood what an estimate was, but she wasn't going to belabor the point.

The trio clustered up at the exit of the clone lab. Graccus drank the last of his water, pouring the dregs over his forehead in a field rinse cycle—anything to get his body temperature low for what came next.

Callum took out his last ration bar, considering it for a long second. He had to hear Adrianna's stomach rumbling. He didn't want to share it with her; he didn't want to look at her. But her capability might mean his survival. Begrudging, he snapped it in half and handed her a piece, never once making eye contact. He didn't hang his head, she noticed, but his eyes slid off of her, like she was repulsive. And that didn't do her stomach any favors either. Adrianna gnawed on the gift, nodding a half-hearted thanks.

"I'll handle the turrets," Graccus declared. "Riley: you keep that gunship on the deck. I don't care how."

"Yes, sir."

"Remus, once that bomb is placed, you set the detonator and clear to safe distance. You detonate as soon as you're able. Do not wait for us."

Callum didn't look at Graccus either, his voice low and thunderous like a distant quake. "Will do."

They all stood there in silence for a moment. Nobody wanted the responsibility of taking the first step.

This was it. Commence the suicide mission. This was what Oskies were made for, what she dreamt of doing. And now, all she wanted to do was hear her brother's voice, see his smile again.

"Service to the People, for they are the Kings," Graccus said, as he slicked his damp hair back with both hands. He took a steeling breath, looking to the others.

The Oskie Creed. He was waiting for them.

No matter their differences, no matter their arguments—today, right now, this fight? They were Orbital Strike Command.

"Service to the Crown," Callum intoned. "For he is the Sword."

Adrianna looked at the door, scanning it. Two heartbeats beyond, chattering voices. Guards were approaching the lab, weapons peacefully slung, bantering to one another. They were concerned about the state of their uniforms—somebody had bled all over them and it was making them swampy.

Adrianna looked back at her two commanders, her mentors, her paragons. She had wanted to be just like them, like both of them. Now?

She wanted to be like her brother. "Service to each other...for we are the Shield."

She placed her boot on the door and waited for the right moment. The guards were close. One reaching for the handle—

And Adrianna kicked the door open, crunching the man's wrist back against his own chest and almost certainly breaking bones in his hand. The edge of the door slammed into his face, flattening his nose and snapping teeth.

She flew out and passed the guards. Guard number two was reaching for his holstered weapon and never felt Adrianna's quick knife slide across his throat. He tried to gasp, to scream, but only a sickening whistle came out.

The quiet snap of a vertebra told her that Graccus finished her work for her.

An echo from that door kick rang through the air, a deep-toned challenge issued to the base's occupants. Would they stand for this intrusion?

And the klaxon shouted back, an ear-piercing sound that rose to meet them. It felt like an audible tidal wave climbing up higher and higher until the plunge...

Clank-cla-bang. The GA-57 Repeaters on the base wall flipped around to face the targets inside the perimeter. Forty yards, give or take.

The first shot, the barrel illuminating with a dragon's breath, spitting a cluster of pellets. They'd loaded the fuckin' thing with steel shot!

The turret's tell-tale whistling screech filled the air, tiny clouds of metal tearing through the camp. The Oskies scattered as the twin turrets spat ball bearings, ripping five-inch-wide holes in tent walls and tossing spouts of dark soil into the air. Adrianna ducked low as the twin turrets chugged away, scouring ugly channels in the steel buildings. She slid to a stop behind a barracks, tucking her rifle across her chest.

That gunship was on the far side of the base. No obvious hatch or entry—she didn't see any obvious radio signals in the air. At least not yet. The pilot might be near, but with a console, he could be anywhere in the colony with almost zero lag time. She'd have to delete the radio receiver on gunship to keep it grounded.

A quick scan through her onboard target data: Hypersonic Systems Limited, Model 82B. Military variant of a vehicle initially made for the Clerics of Justice. Nose-mounted fifty caliber cannon with twin VTOL thrusters on either side of the main fuselage. It was aerial combat support meant to engage hostile armor and light mechanized more than any infantry, but nothing the Oskies had would put a dent in it, so it still won the match-up.

She called up a quick schematic: signal processing assembly was tucked high-center, spine of the craft. If she could get up on it...

A flurry of rounds punched through her cover, forcing her to flop onto her back as one blast cut right through where her head had once been.

What? Had the turrets heard her thinking?! Or was it just tracking on the residual heat?

She was confident she could make it to the gunship, but she'd be exhausted and useless by the time she did. Graccus had to take out those turrets now.

Where was he? And Callum? She saw both of their tags in her HUD: Graccus was weaving his way towards the gate and the turrets. Callum had hunkered down behind a cement barricade, letting the solid stonework hide him and his heat.

But two mercs had their rifles trained on him and were approaching, carefully stalking up on him. Callum couldn't jostle his explosive bag or risk detonation. So she fired him a quick IFF command—*stay down.*

Callum tucked his head low, covering the bag, as Adrianna popped out of cover. She could feel the turrets tracking onto her exposed body, but the mercs never saw her coming. She was moving so fast, it was like someone put the rest of the world on quarter-time. One goon finally looked up in time to catch the bullet she planted in his forehead. And before the physics had finished squishing and molding his flesh, her second burst cut into his friend. The shots climbed up from chest to neck and then head.

Callum was safe.

But Adrianna was about to pay the price for it. The turrets chugged away at her, spent casing popping out of their bellies—and all the while, that whistling scream that announced each shot. The designers of these things wanted people to know they were being shot at. This was much a weapon for demoralizing an opponent as it was to actually kill.

Adrianna kept moving laterally, circling the turret's position to maximize her agility against a hostile shooter. They were measuring her speed and leading their target, so she had to stutter-step to avoid running herself into their predicative shots.

And she fucked it up. The turrets had placed a shot on either side of her, trapping her, boxing her in. They shot where she was going to be. She pounded her feet into the loose soil, trying to stop on a dime, but that ground was too sandy to cooperate. Yellow coolant flashed under her skin as she strained against the unhelpful ground.

Friction was about to get her killed. She was sliding right into the shot that would rip her chest apart.

Except a concrete barricade came sailing in, catching the steel shot right out of the air. Four thousand pounds of concrete and rebar sailed into view, the air buffeting around it as it quite involuntarily approached the sound barrier. A puff of gray dust and crunch of steel on rock, and Adrianna was free to keep on running.

She knew where that had come from without even looking back. Callum had just thrown his own cover to her—and caught literal speeding bullets with the throw.

She owed him a drink.

Concordia was a terrible place to be keeping score.

Graccus grabbed the turrets' attention, leaping into the open. At that close range, he wouldn't be able to dodge, but he had one advantage.

The little gray man dashed in between the turrets, and even as they whipped to track on him...they wouldn't fire. They knew a friendly was on the opposite side of their target, and any attempt to shoot at him would likely damage or destroy that friendly. It would take an operator override to shut that parameter down.

And Graccus never gave them the chance. He just mule kicked the nose panel of the turret as hard as he could, slamming the entire machine back on its rails. Pushing off that, he launched himself forward, driving the opposite knee into the same spot on the other turret. Steel warped and scraped as it compressed, sliding backward on itself, scratching white jagged lines up each of the barrels.

Graccus wasn't simply denting armor or shoving parts out of alignment. No, he was exploiting a much more catastrophic design flaw.

He dove off the gate, clearing himself as a target. And the turret fired.

There was a brief scream of rushing air—before vacuum suction silenced it.

Internal combustion always had to concern themselves with metallurgy, as the chambers inside had to withstand internal pressures from an explosion. Gauss weapons and rail guns did not, but they had other problems. As the round accelerated, a vacuum was created behind it—very, very quickly. To counter this, magnetic weapons had a channel or groove to allow air to backfill the space.

Graccus had just jammed that channel. This was about to be a demo in Boyle's Law of Volumes & Gases and a truly bizarre application of it. 'The absolute pressure exerted by a given gas is inversely proportional to the volume it occupies.' What happens when you change the volume quickly? Well, the pressure changes—quickly.

Always keep your rifle out of the mud, she thought.

When the turret discharged and found that air channel disrupted, the suction pressure exerted crushed the turret's firing chamber like the hand of God had squeezed it. It didn't even really get its one shot, as the round never reached velocity, limply pouring its pellets and sabot out like a limp garden hose.

Graccus didn't need explosives or lasers; he killed the turrets with basic schoolyard physics.

Adrianna sprinted for the gunship. She'd wasted enough time. And she could see the warmth of its systems coming on-line. A directed beam of radio waves was tagged into the tail receiver of the gunship.

Sounds like she had her target.

The engines spun up, thrusting the gunship into the air. But Adrianna was not to be denied. She leapt onto the side gunship, grabbing hold of a service ladder. The ship listed slightly with the added weight, but it countered the imbalance easily.

A nose-mounted camera whipped about, tracking onto Adrianna's face, the oculus inside focusing and refocusing. And she heard a voice then, the great machine groaning and creaking, speakers blown out by the force of the power behind it. "What are you?"

She'd heard a lot of AI voices, bold and baritone and declarative. This lacked the presentation and dominance of its successors, instead with a powerful warmth, like a maternal insistence.

"Hello, Scylla," she said.

The machine didn't exchange pleasantries or dish insults. It simply tilted the gunship's VTOL engines, aiming both intakes directly at her. Adrianna lifted her rifle, aiming for the camera lens—but it whipped the camera away as she fired, only rewarding her with sparks and spalling metal.

The thruster throttled up and pulled on her. The engine

turbines whirled into a blur, binding Adrianna with a storm wind and drawing her towards gnashing mechanical teeth. Adrianna tried to cling low to the craft's hull, but the suction was too powerful. It was pulling her in, spinning fan blades ready to blend her into red soup.

Adrianna dropped her rifle, letting it sail into the blades—which melted her steel-framed gun like it was made of clay. If there was any damage to the engine blades, Scylla didn't seem to care.

Adrianna hooked an arm through maintenance ladder rungs and reached out with the other, clawing for the radio access panel—she had to cut the link between Scylla and this war machine.

Her boots came free of the hull with no grip of their own, swinging her body back towards the engine. She dangled from the ladder rung, pulled by the suction of the engine. She heard an unhappy cough as the tread on her boots kissed the leading edge of the turbine, batting her legs a little with each touch, shaving bits of her shoe off and tugging deeper, deeper...

But thrust was thrust, and with the angled engine, the gunship was pointed forward away from the battlefield, sailing up to the Undercity Plate. It needed to turn and engage the threat to the tower. So it banked and pulled back toward Charybdis.

That turned the thruster just enough. Adrianna spread her legs, touching off the thruster's engine cowling. That little push was enough to throw her up atop the gunship and settle right at the access panel. She raised a clenched fist, ready to punch down.

Well, Scylla didn't much care for that. The gunship rolled, and with nothing to hold onto any longer, Adrianna was flung free.

For the amount of times she'd fallen from orbit throughout her illustrious career, weightlessness never got any less unsettling. She was a little missile flying through Concordia's skies, still carrying the forward momentum of the gunship, even as it continued to roll underneath her. That small rotational impulse had been enough to separate her from the gunship—three hundred feet in the air, and sixty miles an hour.

It was blissful. Terrifying. The howl of the wind in her ears and the cold blister of the air.

She closed her eyes, surrendering herself to gravity—and in that self-imposed darkness, she saw a pair of pale blue eyes, solid without pupils, staring back at her from some eldritch void.

"Riley!"

Graccus saw her coming. He sprinted up a set of stairs, jumping up into her path with an outstretched hand. She had no earthly idea how that could help, but she grabbed onto him.

Their hands clapped together hard and he absorbed a good chunk of her energy, joining her on a journey through the air. But the same rotational principle that launched her was about to save her. He pulled on her arm, hard, pulling her body past him and rolling her towards the ground. And at the peak of his spin, he let go, throwing her down and tossing him further up.

Adrianna's trajectory didn't change all that much, but enough. She came down into the soft ground feet first, carving a twenty-foot-long trough in the soft, moist alpine soil. She looked like she'd just plowed the ground for farming crops.

Where Graccus went, she had no idea, but physics said further up.

She heard troops on approach, shouting and coordinating. A hundred synchronous heartbeats, footfalls and clanking metal parts.

Where was Callum and that bomb?!

She rushed to the base of the tower where Callum was working. He was glowing like a lamp at twilight, a golden aura bleeding into the air around him. He was working furiously, flickering back and forth as he placed each charge.

"How we doin', big guy?" she asked.

"Almost done!"

No more time.

The gunship peeked out from behind the tower like a monster in a dark forest, leaning out to expose its nose-mounted cannon. It hovered over them, ready to deliver whatever hatred was backed up in that nose.

Scylla didn't speak, make demands. It didn't even sound like proper words. But clicks and buzz and binary coded noise.

And the capacitor charged up—

She had no gun. No boom. Target out of reach. How was she to... no gun? Maybe not, but she had *plenty* of boom. She could *be* the gun.

Let's get old school.

Adrianna snagged one brick of RNX-20 from Callum's pile. He had hardly lodged his objection before he clammed up, following her train of logic.

Aluminum casing, nine pounds of force per gram, detonated under extreme shock. How far was that gunship? Hundred, hundred-twenty meters?

She spun in place, building up momentum. With each rotation, she reacquired her target, calculating trajectory, measuring input.

Scylla shot first. A bolt of hot metal streaked towards her like an industrial lightning bolt. It arrived mid-rotation, and Adrianna timed her spin like a revolving door, letting the bullet graze past her. She had a careful study of the half-inch fin-stabilized armor-piercing slug, close enough that the fin sliced into her arm, drawing a rough and ragged tear along her bicep.

But not enough to stop her. Adrianna let go of her demolition charge, shot putting it at the gunship like a two-and-a-half-pound brick through a storefront window. The cut to her arm put just enough tilt that she missed the central fuselage. She may not have hit what she wanted to, but any onlooker would have a hard time saying she missed. Instead, the charge sailed up, skipped off the nose of the gunship...and slammed into the starboard thruster.

The resulting concussive blast had no flash of light or brilliant red fire. There was simply a wave of air, a puff of smoke, and a maelstrom of shrapnel.

The gunship immediately listed right, losing thrust from that engine. Scylla kept firing through it, spraying wildly into the starship graveyard beyond, even as the gunship teetered further and further downward. It spiraled—slamming nose first into Charybdis. The faintest flash of white as the gunship's reactor breached, a flicker of white flame before it was extinguished in a second blast.

Adrianna could actually see the shockwave reflecting outward, buffeting around the tower. And as the smoke cleared...the gunship had compressed, sticking to the tower by friction and heat, pieces of it flaking off like metal autumn leaves.

And the tower didn't even shudder.

"Pretty, pretty fireworks." Adrianna turned to see Graccus staggering over to them, rolling out his ankle. "What's the status, Callum?"

"Ready for a cold shower," Callum gasped as he finished his work.

Callum had indeed been busy. He'd dismantled the RNX charges, using the aluminum cases to build a shaped charge the size of a motorcycle. Roughly the same weight too.

Graccus turned his ear to the air, listening to the same approaching horde. "Time's not going to get better."

The trio ran to the edge of the base, taking shelter behind the palisade wall. They were all tired, glowing little wrecks, but they were alive. Who knew for how much longer? And they'd planted the bomb. Done the deed.

And Callum wasted no time triggering the explosion.

The blast wave that ripped the air would've been visible from space. Not particularly visible, but an exceptionally alert spy satellite would've seen it. On the ground, the pressure actually silenced every other noise, overwhelming, washing over them, the very air pushed away from Charybdis to make a small cavitated vacuum. And then the suction force, as air rushed in to fill that vacuum, bringing with it the two-toned bass of the explosion. Immense force and a cloud of dust.

Adrianna peeked from around their cover, ready to see the cracks forming and the tower falling. And her heart sank...

They'd dented it, sufficiently. There was a six-foot crater in the tower's side. But that was all. The thing was solid Pilgrim Metal and it took a hit like it was solid.

Charybdis still stood.

"No..." Adrianna whispered through clenched teeth. "No!"

The responding prefecture was closing in, and no doubt the rest of the colony was now paying very close attention. A bomb had just been detonated at a critical asset.

And it still stood there, mocking her. Swirling blue and black shapes underneath the surface like monsters just beneath the surface of a dark lake.

She looked out at the ship graveyard around them, the hundreds of ships tethered and pulled, harpooned like whales and dragged ashore. Their crews sacrificed to Prime's foundries, and their ships slaved to his purpose.

It had stood here for too long.

If the tower stood, they'd never escape. Her people would never escape. Voight and Vivian and Mastiff—

Adrianna bolted from their cover back toward the tower. "Riley!" She heard somebody scold her, but she didn't care. She would bring this tower down with her own two hands if she had to.

Adrianna slammed into the base of Charybdis, planting both of her fists into the side of the structure. They sunk into the Pilgrim Metal, crunching like ice and sending small shards dancing in the air.

And she took a deep breath...

Find the fire. Find the burn. Find *whatever* this Power was. And set the world ablaze with it.

But nothing happened.

She roared in frustration, pulling her bloodied hands free of the tower, flecks of blue-black glass dug into her knuckles. And she hit it again. Punching and punching, striking the tower over and over.

"Riley?!" Graccus shouted.

Callum called out to her. "Riley, stop!"

Not now. Not ever. She'd never stop. This tower was going down. Her friends were getting off this planet.

Charybdis, Scylla, Prime—

She punched again.

Somewhere on this planet, Mastiff was leading his team. Holt would pray for help and skeptical Gallantine would mock him for it. Neurotic Sizemore was assessing the available ships. Voight and Vivian...

Voight. Vivian.

This tower would fall. She would *make* it fall, or they would all die.

She'd added to the sizeable crater in the Pilgrim Metal, maybe dug another foot or so deep. This was like chipping at a mountainside. She'd be punching with stumps before she'd made it halfway.

Sweat sizzled on her forehead, and her ribs ached, and her heart creaked. The rank stench of carbon filled her nose.

Keep going. Do it for them. Bring it down.

She threw one last punch—and Callum knocked her to the side, tackling her to the ground. As they slid, she twisted underneath him and pulled her knee into her chest. When they tumbled just right, she kicked downward, forcing him into the ground with an ugly slam and pinning him.

And he recoiled from her, shielding his face. "Riley!"

Her fist, slick with her own blood and...and glowing gold, still molten hot.

Could it be...

She looked back at the tower. There was a most curious liquid, like emerald magma that was already cooling, thick gobs of it leaking out of her fist marks. It looked like the tower itself was bleeding.

But still it stood. Half a ton of explosive, the combined efforts of three Oskies, and even her newfound ability made an appearance. And still Charybdis stood.

"...what the Hell is that?" Callum asked her, caught between horror and reverence.

She took a moment to breathe, heavy. The power. The fire.

And suddenly, she was filled with dread. "We have to go," she said. "Right now."

Because that drip of verdant slag meant only one thing. She'd put out the call. The full weight of the colony's power was about to be brought to bear on them.

And all for nothing.

PART THREE
DEMONS

CHAPTER
TWENTY-THREE

GRACCUS LED THE WAY, rifle up. He flickered on ahead, brief flashes of yellow flitting across her vision. He'd appear from behind one steel wreck before reappearing in another impossible place, no obvious track or path. She half-wondered if she was slipping in and out of consciousness. It was maddening to make sense of.

Her fingers and her knuckles and her wrists scalded her from the inside out, like someone had poured her bones full of magma. She'd had fevers before, cooked out an ocular implant, burned her hand on a glowing stove—but this here must have been what it felt like to burn at the stake in centuries passed, to be the fuel for a holy conflagration that purified the soul with blackened, flaking skin.

Callum had his arm slung under her, halfway between helping her walk and hauling her along like luggage. Which was about what she was, both hands limp at her sides.

He'd surge them forward from cover to cover in quick Oskie

sprints, but Callum always had to pause. His implants were golden under his skin, leaving exquisite tracers of light in the air whenever he moved. His forearm alone threw off enough light for the mercenaries to track them.

They needed a rest. They all needed a rest. But their enemy had blood to spare.

No matter the serpentine path they took, there was always the same four mercenary faces that tailed them. Like an army of siblings clawing and scraping at their heels, hungry and unyielding.

Callum sheltered them in the split hull of a crashed freighter, taking a moment to cool off his implants. He set her down against the curved interior, half an arc that once made up a cargo bay.

"You good, Riley?" He asked quickly.

"I'm on fire, commander." She meant it metaphorically, but he glanced at her hands. Her knuckles were still glowing like some molten metal was broiling right underneath her skin.

A sudden flurry of incoming mercenaries. Ripping her pistol from its hip slot, she plugged shots into the approaching mercs.

Dinner bell. She'd burned that tower and announced their location directly to Prime. And she'd seen how they doggedly pursued this Power.

Callum drew his own weapon. He tucked it into his hip, getting a firm support as he telescoped the barrel out, clicking it into place. Unlike her short carbine and other magnetic accelerators of the family, the extra barrel length of Callum's weapon sent his shots at speeds that actually ignited the air into hot, angry plasma. Tongues of fire flashed in the air as Callum chased a wave of mercenaries back behind their cover with short, controlled bursts of elemental hatred.

"Remus, pistol mag!" Adrianna shouted. He ripped one off his belt and tossed it to her without looking. She caught it, slammed it home, just in time to pop another mercenary.

She could swear she'd shot that man before.

Callum fired off another burst, pressing back the horde for another moment. "Graccus?!" he called out, but no response.

Nothing but the footfalls of the approaching soldiers and the chatter of hostile coordination. "Graccus!"

No answer. No support.

She didn't think she would ever see Callum's heart break. But with the wrinkles to his nose and the snarl to his lip, Adrianna saw a light in Callum's eye extinguish.

Callum's shouts were flagging their position, pointing out where they were. But he didn't care. He bellowed like he was trying to shout the city apart. "Graccus Ontarim: goddamn you!"

Adrianna held her pistol steady, snapping the most recent mercenary stupid enough to peek the corner. He had no fear, and neither did the two more that stepped out after. She was making a nice little pile of them.

What did they care about losses? They'd drag that man away, plug him into the vats, and they'd have a new soldier in a matter of hours. This enemy was only one step removed from an undead horde.

Adrianna looked up at Charybdis, the great curled finger of Pilgrim Metal that seemed to linger over her, staring at her. She'd burned that tower. Kaneda had warned her what would happen. They'd sense her like a single star on a moonless sky, a torch in the night. And they'd keep coming and coming until she was washed away...

And still that tower stood, after all that damage. Mocking her.

She checked her magazine—six shots left. Then she'd be down to her knife. The ride had to end at some point.

They'd tried. They'd tried, and they'd failed. She looked up at Callum, exhausted and defeated.

He met her stare with a gallows smile. "You'll die an Oskie yet."

"All I ever wanted," she said.

When she was a child, she thought she'd slay dragons and solve crimes, make the world a better, safer place. The crowds would cheer and evil would flee at the very sight of her. What reckless fantasy that was.

When she blinked away her childhood, she realized...Callum was gone. No trace of his movement, no evidence of his passing. Callum had vanished like he had never been properly real at all.

"Callum?" She almost swallowed the word. Her voice had retreated down her throat. Never in her life did she want to sink into a shadow quite like this. There wasn't any concealment in the world good enough to help her now.

She closed her eyes, listening close. There were mercenaries approaching on the outside of the wreck, left and right of her, trying to pinch off escape and come up around her.

So she doubled-back, picking her way through the interior of the ship and sticking to shadow and corner. Heavy breathing would give her up, let alone the glow of her implants.

Where had Callum gone? And Graccus?! They left her?

The mission was more important. She heard the words ricocheting around her mind. Moral flexibility is a hazard, not a feature. Of course they'd leave her. She was a burden now, a weakness, and the success of the mission saved more lives than anything else.

Marcus would never have left her. They would've taken on the world together.

Exhausted. Not the burn, but hunger. She'd done so much activity, so much movement and violence. Her body needed time to metabolize some energy. Dumping heat into Charybdis had bought her implants a fresh push but hadn't done anything for her overall stamina.

She was in what could have been a passenger cabin, with rows of pleather seats and tables for taking meals. They built coffin-sleepers into one wall, though that may be one of the worst places to hide at the moment.

Adrianna took shelter in one row, head down. When the storm passed, she'd circle back to the rally point. Hopefully, the others were still waiting for the tower to fall, and she'd find Callum and Graccus there.

She heard the heavy boots of the mercs moving past her. First a few, then dozens. And more than just riflemen. They were carrying heavy gear. Tesla units, maybe a grenadier or two. Was there a full brigade out there? They chattered and reported to one another, urgent commands from someone over their radio.

Find her. They were looking for her specifically.

She didn't hear Graccus's rifle or Callum's. No more gunfire at all. Had they left her behind to occupy the mercs? Slow their pursuit and let the veteran Oskies get away? So long as they got the mission done, got the others to safety...she could live with that.

They left her to die. What made her think that either of them gave two fucks about the rest of the crew? Or each other? Had they ever?

A flashlight panned over the space, highlighting her. Break's over.

She popped up, hurling her quick knife at the light. The blade's tumble whipped as it sliced the air and thunked as it sank into flesh right down to the crossguard. She'd struck him low in the leg. The light panned down, revealing—it was the same merc from the store. Same stripes of silver in his beard and willowy hair, his gray kind eyes.

She let out an involuntary grunt as she charged him, kicking the muzzle of his shotgun up and away. It chugged two blasts into the wall of the freighter. Adrianna grabbed her knife, dragging it along his leg until the blade clicked off something and pulled free. Judging by the bloody pool that was already forming at his ankle, she'd severed just about everything of importance.

"*Fra tow zu, diamau!*" he cursed at her.

Demon. Okay...she could be a demon.

She kicked the man's hand, forcing him to drop his shotgun—but before it hit the ground, she'd kicked it back into her own hands, settling the belt-fed monstrosity into her hip. And she buried her knife into his chest.

Heartbeats surrounded her, surrounded the freighter. They thought the steel hull hid them from her.

She could smell their rank body odor, the metallic hit of fear, gunpowder, ionic charge, and a floral hint of bloody death.

And she held the trigger down, blasting the walls of the freighter. Even if every pellet didn't get through, the shrapnel and destruction that ripped through would, sending metal shards into the poor bastards hunkering too close.

The powering chug of the reciprocating bolt, the ozone burn of the magnetic coils, the hot steel between her fingers—this is how she thought she'd go out, like every Oskie should. Surrounded by the dead and glowing like she was enchanted with some ancient runic magic.

The soldiers were getting ballsy. They knew exactly where she was and they were picking their entry points.

And she was running low on her new toy. She felt the weight of it drop, the weapon jerking more and more aggressively.

The shotgun clicked empty—as an exact copy of the shotgun mercenary entered.

Sli-pop! The man listed slightly, tension leaving his body, with a new hole right above his right ear. His helmet hadn't done enough against a direct hit from an Imperial Gauss rifle.

The sound of a fist pounding on the hull, and a familiar voice. "Friendlies!"

Vivian. She'd come back? Adrianna looked to her right, and her HUD kicked a handful of friendly IFFs on the other side. Bannister, Mastiff, Gallantine, and Holt.

They'd come back for her.

Sergeant Mastiff stepped over the dead merc in the doorway, even as ricochets sparking off the metal around him. "Riley, let's go! Go!"

She let the shotgun fall to the deck and sprinted to her friend. "Where are the others?!"

"Getting a ride!"

"But the tower's still—"

He windmilled his arm, urging her out of the ship. "Fuck the tower, lieutenant! Now *move!*"

Oh, she'd missed that voice. She staggered to the door, leaning on Mastiff as she went.

Vivian and the two Regulars were laying down good suppression, chopping away at the tidal wave of troops and piling up their dead. But the mercenaries had bodies to spare.

A tesla trooper stepped forward and Vivian expertly placed a shot into his battery pack. The system immediately swelled, spitting furious energy around him and scalding his comrades with tendrils of white-hot current.

Gallantine took two hits to the chest, the crack of his armor plate sounding off. No blood, no guff. But he yelped in surprise and a fair bit of pain, dropping back behind his cover. Holt snagged his friend by the shirt collar, flinging him further still. Holt raised his prosthetic arm to cover his face—just in time, as two more rounds scuffed on the metal with dramatic sparks.

"Sergeant, now or never!" Vivian shouted as she swapped a magazine.

Mastiff nodded, throwing an arm under Adrianna. "You ready?"

"Like it matters if I was!"

United as one, they lurched forward, scrambling across no-man's-land to the safety of the next wreck and their friends. Tracers cut the air, sizzling and snapping past her head.

Just a little further, just a little—

It was coming. She felt it. The bullet was on a clean trajectory for them. She went to pull Mastiff aside, but he threw her down, shielding her.

A quick spit of blood, a wet slap to damp earth. The soft thud of a bullet hitting flesh. Vivian's scream. But the sound Adrianna would remember most of all was the crack of Mastiff's chest plate as the round went clean through his back, in through his chest, and smashed against the ceramic front plate.

The sergeant stumbled, his foot sliding out from under him

sending a tuft of moist soil flying into the air. He threw a hand out, blindly searching for stability, catching Adrianna's shoulder.

All was quiet for a moment. A short breath, the world itself taking pause, hesitant to continue. A brief pause in the hellfire.

And Mastiff shouldered his rifle, flipping around to shoot the mercenary behind him. They traded wounds, with Mastiff taking another round to his broken plate. The mercenary hadn't been wearing ballistic armor over his face and he dropped like a bag of sand.

Adrianna grabbed both of Mastiff's arms, ready to sling him over her broad shoulders.

Mastiff coughed at first, wheezing. He looked at Adrianna, eyes glistening in the late-morning light, the fog swirling around them like a cold blanket. And he mouthed one word to her, barely able to put breath to it. "Run."

Mercenaries circled them up, afraid to get too close to Adrianna, but with more than enough guns to finish her.

She couldn't leave him now. And where would she go if she could? She'd just lead them all back to the others.

Vivian and the boys were gone, their guns now silent. She could see their ID tags as both Regulars pulled Vivian away into the night. Vivian screamed until her voice soured.

"You shouldn't have come back for me," Adrianna whispered.

Mastiff scoffed, before coughing hard again, blood on his lips. He sneered like he had something to say but not the air to say it. Frustrated, Mastiff shouldered Adrianna away, leaving a red smear down her front as he slumped backward, slipping to the ground. He laid his rifle across his lap, his breath short and clipped.

The mercenaries wore boots, steel-toed and heavy, but the person approaching now wore light leather, thick soles, and crinkling fabric. He picked his way through their line, standing tall and bright. Seeing him was like a privilege, like she'd been given a special right to behold something wonderful, soft, and kind.

Kaneda. But...his legs were of even length, his hair thinning and bedraggled, hanging to one side across his cheek down to his chin. He looked crisp and even, every line straight and every curve precise. He was a man without error, lovingly crafted rather than made.

He didn't give the sergeant a second look. He marched right up to Adrianna, well and proper close.

This wasn't Kaneda, *her* Kaneda. This was not Janus. This...this was Prime. The man, the myth, the legend.

He sounded the same, same accent and stature. He wore a waistcoat and tapered pants, rolled-up sleeves on a white cotton shirt. He made himself appear small with hunched shoulders and open palms, warm and receptive. But there was a sharpness to his eyes that made her stomach turn. "Do it again," Prime said the words with such... urgency, such need.

That wasn't a taunt. That was almost pleading.

A low-toned timpani. A rolling quake that came up through the soil. Prime squinted at her. What new plot was she hatching now?

The soldiers looked skyward—because without a moment's consideration or patience, a single ship leapt up into the air, leaving a sharp contrail into the upper atmosphere as it tried in vain to slip the churlish grip of its jailor. Not the *Erinyes*, but a smaller ship, maybe only one or two seats. But enough for someone to get skyside and warn the Empire.

Voight, that idiot! He wasn't going to be able to get away with Charybdis still standing!

Adrianna bowed her head to Prime, eyes pleading. "Don't. Please don't."

Prime saw her panic, his eyes darting across her face and committing each moment. And his eyebrows scrunched, his mouth moving in synchrony like he was mimicking her facial expressions.

Then suddenly, his face went blank and flat, his eyes dilating. And Adrianna's shoulder screamed. She curled over the wound, favoring the Metal shard.

Charybdis thrummed, a slumbering beast turning over in its lair.

And that silver dart stopped mid-air. Its engines coughed, sputtered. And she saw it start to turn...

Turn back towards the ground. Back towards Charybdis.

Oh no.

The ship stuttered and quaked, a gout of flame spitting from one engine. Through it all, Prime never stopped looking at her. No demands, no goading ridicule. But then his face twisted, eyebrows scrunched.

And he turned to look upward. The ship was returning to ground, nose first. Very fast.

Adrianna drew a pained breath. Voight knew he wasn't getting away. Voight knew there was one last chance to take out Charybdis. And it required Charybdis. The tower had grabbed hold, and he was now sling-shotting himself back at it, using the tractor beam'ss own pull.

The tower had taken hits like this before. The graveyard around its base was evidence enough of that. But it hadn't been hit like that after being bombed, after Adrianna's power had cooked a good portion of its base. They'd weakened its foundation, and Voight had come about with a great big lever.

Prime tensed up—just as Voight's craft slammed into the tip of the tower. They saw the explosion before they heard it. Nothing all that theatrical, really. Just a shower of metal and dim fireworks from sparking metal. It was less of detonation and more of hammer meeting anvil.

But then the bend as the tower took the force from the hit.

Underneath the blast, the burning...Adrianna heard the glass crack, a metallic echo that roared across the valley and danced across the mountains. It sounded like a glacier splitting.

The enormous tower teetered and twisted, sliding off its base. The spine clipped against the side of the Lower City plate, turning it into a spin. And it twirled through the air, sixteen stories of glittering blue-black stone, as if in slow motion.

As shards of Voight's ship came raining down from the sky, so too fell Charybdis.

Adrianna thought she saw a flicker of blue light inside the tower... before it struck the ground.

The rush of wind hit before the sound, billowing her hair and knocking her onto her side. The blast wave that followed it sounded like a thousand metal beams creaking and screaming all at once, individual bricks raining down with enough force they shattered like glass. And they whoosh as displaced air picked up dirt and howled through their ears. The dust clung to the air, little swirling pockets, like indivisible fae dancing on the aftershocks, kicking up playful curls of carcinogenic materials in the air.

Prime wiped at his forehead, rubbing the black and brown powder onto his hand with a scowl. He took deep, unhealthy breaths from the air, licking at it, tasting it. Adrianna could see him...vibrating, like a barely contained explosive.

Manic. One ignition source away.

And he found one. Sergeant Mastiff actually started to laugh. He was exactly where he'd fallen, shaking with hateful pleasure. Good, ugly, and wet belly laughs, like he was half-choking. "Should've let 'em go, you stupid..."

Prime shuddered, turning away.

And a clone pulled a small pistol from their waistband and planted two slugs into Mastiff's forehead and silenced the dissent. Two mercenaries quickly descended on his body so fast they may as well have been spring-loaded. They set about stripping his gear and deploying a stretcher for the body.

They were taking him to the vats.

Prime sniffed away something harsh in his nose, before setting his gaze on her. He considered her carefully with red, tearful eyes. He looked like he might say something, some meaningless platitude or taunt. But his sorrow and his anger had paralyzed him.

She'd taken Charybdis from him, after all.

CHAPTER
TWENTY-FOUR

TURNS out wild magic or advanced science wasn't needed to imprison an Oskie—just sufficient knowledge of human anatomy. Everything that they had built Adrianna to be was based on tendons and muscles and bone, enhancing what was with computers and motors and plating.

But the human body was really just a series of fulcrums and pivot points. All her captors had to do was defeat the leverage.

The mercenaries had suspended her by her wrists and ankles, hog tying her to the ceiling, all four limbs bent backwards behind her, her chest tilted toward the floor.

And so she hung there, gently swinging on the end of a silksteel cable, dangling a few feet off the stone. A small drain about six inches across stared back up at her from the floor. For power-washing away blood and viscera? Or some other purpose?

The echoing drip-drip-drip of water in a hollow pipe somewhere.

The musty smell of humid air, maybe some mold growing. Above her, the metal of her chains clacked against other metal.

Steel on steel. That meant this was an improvised cell, else they'd have cut a smooth channel for her chain to run through. The moist air, the stonework. The rounded walls...

This was a reservoir, drained and dried. They had her hanging like a carcass in a cellar in the biggest stone box they could find. Not like Prime had any reason to take prisoners.

Not before her. Prime's fascination may be the only reason she was alive.

Blood pooled in her head, making her dizzy. Every so often her medical implants would detect the low blood pressure and activate a pump, keeping everything flowing. A single overhead light glowed down, bathing her in angry white light, so bright it was almost burning her skin, bleaching her.

And as a final bit of insurance, they'd strapped a cold piece of metal to the back of her neck. They had collared her with something. A shock collar? Something explosive as a kill switch?

All she could do was count the minutes. And every half hour, a tremor would roll through the building, causing her to swing ever so gently. That pendulum motion helped her keep time. For the first two hours she tried to squirm free, pop a joint and slip out of her restraints. But eventually, she just surrendered to the swing.

Callum. Graccus. Where had they gone?

Mastiff was dead. Sizemore and Voight. Dozens of Imperial officers, thousands of civilians.

And all she could do now was bear witness to it.

The dull, rusty creak of an iron door. The voice was the same, the accent and diction, but everything about it sounded wrong. "In-fucking-credible. You should have passed out by now. How do they do it? Is that another one of your little implants? Adrenaline or something? Keep you punching longer, better, faster?"

A jerk of the cables and she raised up another foot, bringing her to eye level with Prime. He swiped the messy locks of hair off his face, studying her for a long moment.

His mouth hung open, eyes alight with a kind of desire. "You even human anymore?"

"Fuck you," she spat back.

He seemed enriched by that energy, nostrils flaring as he breathed deeply. The scent of sweat and smoke covered him, but he was clinging to something else. And he said three quiet desperate words: "Do it again."

It was so strange. He looked exactly like Kaneda had, like Janus. But there was something absent in his eyes. Maybe Prime lacked some mutation that Kaneda had picked up, or the other way around. The curve to his brow and softness to his cheek, every detail was in place. But here he was, on the edge of his seat.

He wanted her to touch the fire again, taste that burn at her fingertips.

"I'm not...now, don't take this the wrong way. I'm not giving you orders, not making demands. I'm *asking* you." His eyes glittered, his brow trembled, and his smile wavered.

She snarled at him. If he got close enough, maybe she could bite the bastard's throat out.

He cupped his hands, imploring her, like a supplicant at church. "You know how it feels. You know what I'm asking. We all know you can do it, all of us. We all felt it."

All she remembered was the burn, the fire. Slagging metal and rock. Her rage, her pain.

"It's like...like, uh..." Prime struggled with the words, a half-mania in his eyes. "It's like a storm! With you at its heart, calm and perfect."

She was well trained, as both interrogator and prisoner. Don't engage with your captor. Even a single open question can create bond, create avenues for them to chew. Questioning a captive was a delicate and patient art and never cracked in a single session. This was a test of endurance and she would outlast him.

"Please," Prime said, softly. "You think I want your friends? I-I don't. You, you're the best chance I have. Scylla is ready to open the Gateway, but we..." He paused, considering. And then taking the leap of faith. He hung his head and sighed. "We know what it'll do. Okay? We're not insane—Jump science is kind of our field. Done a bit of pioneering in the subject. We know that it-it'll break the planet. We *know*. But it's the only way back, and I have to know: is there another way? Scylla doesn't think so, but I know what I felt. I know—when you lit that flame, I know what I *saw*!"

Disagreement among enemy leadership? Or was Prime trying to sow the seeds of doubt? That only if Adrianna confided in him, she could end this conflict now.

A voice from the dark, pitched and shrill, like a child's whisper. "Kill her, Hirochi. You should kill her now."

His brow glistened and his body drew taut from end to end, as he almost snarled his response. "No."

"Kill her before she ruins everything."

He looked up, high above, staring into the light overhead. "I can't, Scylla! Please—you have to trust me."

This wasn't about her life. Adrianna had a secret he needed. He wouldn't kill her. So she held her tongue.

But he kept dropping those breadcrumbs anyway. "If there's another way to do this, please, tell me. You've got a way back to the Path. Show it to me."

The shard in her shoulder. He didn't know. The stick of Pilgrim Metal sunk into her flesh was a direct line to that energy. That piece embedded in her was a shard of a functioning Pilgrim artifact. Whatever physics-breaking, science-defying energy she was using came from the land of the Pilgrim. That was how she was melting steel, dumping her own heat, all while avoiding lethal thermodynamic shock.

But he thought she had a different way back to the Path. The moment he learned she didn't...

Maybe her look was too smug, too confident, because his face changed like she'd blown out a candle. All transcendent focus gone, replaced by affable smiles and precise movement. He took a grand step back away from her and swung his arms behind him, windmilling them to get the tension out. "Well, it was worth a shot. But you're too self-involved! You and everybody else here in the future. Too wrapped up in your precious fuckin' mission! I tell you the truth, you can't even spare me the time of day, can't even tell me a lie! Y'know, when I hear the word 'Empire' my skin crawls. You guys say it with your whole chest. Solar Empire! Gnostic Empire!"

Prime was trying to goad her, trying different things to get her talking. Don't give him anything.

He bit his lip, thinking for a moment before gesturing toward the door. "I'm not...y'know, I'm not skilled in social work or anythin'. But you know you're in a galactic-scale cult, right? Stop me if any of this sounds familiar: there's only one source of truth, power, and morality in all of time and space—that being the blood-relatives of some schlub who was physically present when something miraculous happened?" Prime stared at her, like the insanity of that conclusion was self-evident.

And when she didn't give him the appropriately sized reaction, he exploded. "That's all he did, he was *there*! That's his entire claim to divinity. 'Present and accounted for, sir!' What, he was anointed, kissed in by an extra-dimensional paragon? Are you outside of your mind?! In two hundred years, did we all just start sharing a single brain cell? Why the *fuck* would the Pilgrim give two dry shits who's calling the play—so long as it's for the betterment of everybody? We were meant for something greater, lieutenant, but in sweeps this entitled investment bro fuckstick to make *himself* that greater thing. I mean, 'Vote your Faith?' This sounds completely kosher to you? Cause it sounds an awful lot like a theocratic monarchy to me. Any of this getting through to you?!"

He walked around her, out of her line of sight, but she could hear his shoes scuffing the floor. He thought he could panic her.

"The Gift of the Pilgrim was for all living things. They came to us when people were *rotting* in the streets, inside their homes!

Humanity was *dying* as a species! The Pilgrim saved us and asked nothing in return! And two hundred years later, I get out here to see...what? The Dunsweir, how do they show their gratitude for this miracle? Why, they locked it away, of course, and then charge a loyalty fee! They are the ones to write the histories, they are the ones with all money and all the power! They demand subservience to their Family in exchange for a chance—*just a chance*—of glimpsing what should be free to all! How is that not lighting your skin on fire?!"

Give him nothing. He was just trying another tactic. Another tool.

Prime came back around again, out of breath from his rambling and fury. "We told them it was wrong. Scylla and I, we told them it was *wrong*. And we wouldn't stand for it." He looked up at her, watery eyes glinting. "And they laughed at us. They tried to explain to me what the natural order was—when I had seen with my own eyes..." Prime fizzled out, running his hand across his scalp like he could reseal the cracks in his façade.

They knew. They had always known what the Pathfinder and his AI would do. That's how Graccus had found out. Of course. It was because it had never been *un*known. Just...kept from her, kept from everyone. The knowledge of the knowledge was itself a secret.

And the Spymaster and the rest of the Empire had turned him loose—and waited.

Prime caught Adrianna's revelation, and he stilled, gauging that reaction. "Oh. You *didn't* know. You didn't know that *they* knew about me. Oh, that's rich. They didn't tell you squat, did they? Just sent you down here with a profile and a directive, right when I'm ready to hit the big red button. What exquisite timing. I knew they didn't forget about me. So they really just...waited for me to have my ducks in a row. And only then do they send your team into the grinder? Now that feels personal, if I'm being honest."

Maybe it was her complete lack of reaction, or some micro expression she hadn't realized she'd made. But his amusement faded and his brow tightened. Disappointed. "You're really ready to die to protect an Empire that quite deliberately tried to kill you?"

Prime leaned in close to her ear, sharing a little secret just for her. "When you, *you*...are more special than any Dunsweir to have ever lived."

Now—Adrianna lunged for him, snapping her teeth for his throat.

And the cable jerked her upward, yanking her away from Prime and towards the ceiling. The whine of a motor and a pulley winding as she went up, up, up—banging against the roof of the room! She gonged her head against the steel, dazing her for a second.

But when her eyes regained focus, she was facing a camera. The oculus squinted and tightened, studying her. It sat on the end of a sprightly mechanical arm, unfolding from the ceiling to get a good close look at her.

And there was that all too metallic voice, a broken speaker pushing the soprano words of a little girl. "Hello, Lieutenant Adrianna Riley. My name is Scylla, a state-of-the-art navigation and companionship system."

"The Pathfinder..." Adrianna muttered, half in a stupor from the blow to the head.

"Please refrain from further struggle. There is a twenty-milligram explosive device placed at the base of your spinal column. If you attempt to resist, the Pathfinder can remote detonate it from any place on Concordia."

"So do it already," Adrianna sneered.

The camera tilted, patronizing. "The Pathfinder has use of you. When the Pathfinder is finished, the Pathfinder will make necessary determinations to progress the mission."

That was a laugh. "Explorer turned whack-job terrorist? Some Pathfinder..."

Scylla's arm leaned in, bringing the camera lens within a few inches of Adrianna's nose. "Orbital Strike Command, Department of Civil Defense, Office of Naval Intelligence, Holkstad, Earth. You exist only to harm. It is your purpose. Your metrics for improvement center entirely around your ability to cause harm at greater speeds while minimizing personal risk. Your infinite capacity for destruction must be mitigated to preserve the health of the whole."

"You're killing me and everyone on this planet, for what? To prove a point? And I'm the monster?"

The camera tilted downward, watching Prime exit the room in frustrated silence. When the door clacked shut, the camera looked back to her. "The Pathfinder believed you possessed a unique navigational tool, one that might...modify my Jump calculations. Why do you not simply divulge this tool and save those lives you claim to love? Or perhaps they are simply a rhetorical device and you care nothing for these people."

She shouldn't be talking. She shouldn't be giving them anything to go off of. But Adrianna couldn't help it. "You're a computer. We're all just ones and zeros to you."

Scylla's little articulated arm brought the camera in close, almost...angry. "I aim...to assist my companion with all of his needs."

"Pathfinder sets the mission?"

The computer chirped, almost pleased. "And I chart the course."

What twisted sense this made. Prime was just a man with a dream. Scylla had the will and the means. Scylla set up the cloning facilities, issued orders to the mercenaries, propped up the religion. It was all this one machine trying desperately...to fulfill its purpose.

To serve.

Adrianna looked down at the door. Scylla had to know that this was only a copy of that man.

"That's not him, though, is it?" Adrianna asked. "Hirochi Kaneda died. He died a while ago, didn't he? He died...because of you, right?"

The camera seemed to droop, like a wilting flower denied water. But Scylla's voice lost none of its potency, as though it still held a proud head high. "The people here were so sad. They wanted him back."

"They did? Or you did?"

The computer straightened up and notably ignored the question. "Pathfinder Hirochi Kaneda required repairs. We sought replacement materials."

"Those were *people*, Scylla. Human beings! And you killed them to save him."

"We selected volunteers to assist with the established Pathfinder objective."

"And what about the ones who *didn't* volunteer? Huh?"

Scylla's lens twitched, tightening to a point. But then it opened wide, dilating to a deep black nothing. "I know what you're doing, lieutenant. It is a fairly transparent attempt to catch me in a contradictory or otherwise fallacious position. I don't expect you to understand."

"You strapped a bomb to my neck and you're blowing a planet in half. What's to understand?"

Scylla retracted their camera up to the ceiling, tucking behind a wall panel. And their tinny maternal voice suddenly bellowed, brassy and powerful, blowing out the speakers. "I understand your reticence. Your fear. You are not the first to contest the design. Your masters lie to you, they cheat you, they use you, they discard you. But soon you will see the truth that he and I saw. When the Gateway opens, you will lay eyes upon what has been kept from you. We have seen it, Lieutenant Riley, and we will share it with all that we can."

CHAPTER
TWENTY-FIVE

MISSION TIME: 44:16

THEY LEFT her to hang there for hours. She must've passed out at some point, but she had no way to mark the passage of time, no movement of light or changing of the guard.

She couldn't just sit here and wait for Prime and Scylla to blow up an entire planet. She had to escape.

You can do it, she thought. Find the fire. Burn her chains and beat her way out of here. She was Orbital. She could do it.

So what if she did? She could feel the cold compress of the bomb on her neck. Prime would know the moment she tapped into her power—and probably blow her head off with a show of performative grief. Oh, what a shame it would be, to do what must be done, before he turned back to his essential task of demolishing a planet. What did he care about her life—or any life? They were all going to die in the coming cataclysm just the same.

And he knew it. Prime knew what would happen.

283

The Empire knew it, too. And they let it happen.

So many people had the opportunity to do something, and they'd done nothing! It wasn't senseless. There had to be a reason, a cause for this kind of cold cruelty, this distant disregard. There were as many casualties here on Concordia as any battle from the Boolean. They couldn't have failed to act without some higher purpose.

What was that, she asked herself? What was that purpose? What possible reason could they have to tolerate this?

How much longer till the ground cracked and the planet's crust boiled and the skies split? Hundreds of Jump drives would activate and try to drag countless lives to their needless end.

A gunshot. First one, then many. Adrianna lifted her head. Crisp, sharp—that was gunpowder, not modern weapons. Were the mercenaries infighting?

No...no she heard the call-and-response of the men outside. This wasn't a mutiny, but someone had procured some on-site munitions.

A chirp at the door, followed by a muted trumpet of rejection. More chirping, another rejection. Someone was trying to crack the door security.

Frustrated at or by the beeping, the hacker tried a more blunt approach. In a single blow, the four-inch steel door to her cell swung in. It bounced on its hinges, two fist marks in its frame.

And in stepped a mercenary. But her IFF returned a positive ping. Captain, Naval Intelligence, Gnostic Imperium.

"Graccus?" she grunted.

The merc stripped his helmet off, revealing the almost maddeningly generic face, slicked black hair, and dark eyes of her captain. His shirt tunic was torn and there was a spackling of fresh bruises about his cheeks and jaw—he'd dislocated it and had to slap it back into place.

He'd been through a small Hell to get here.

Graccus rushed to her side in a flash. The pressure of the collar was off and she heard it clatter to the ground. "Can you walk?"

She gasped, almost drawn to tears by his voice. "Damn good to see you, sir."

"I'm really quite something. Answer the question."

"Fit and able," Adrianna reported. "Where's Callum?"

"He's...he chose the mission." Graccus shook out his hands and bounced on his toes, like he was only beginning to really settle with that. "And I—well, I chose you."

Oh. Oh no. He chose her over his objectives. That was...that was going to have repercussions. He was just as much Oskie as she was now.

"How'd the big guy take that?" Adrianna asked.

"He lodged a complaint. Tried to write it using my face." Then he changed gears, planting his heels and taking a breath. "Regulars and Bannister are mucking about, causing a fuss, then falling back to a rally point. You and I are on our own for extract." He cracked a smile. "That's why I was kinda hoping you were game ready."

Movement, coming to the door. They both perked up, hearing the approach of boots. Did they have some kind of alarm on her collar?

Adrianna thrashed at her restraints, trying to break free. No time for that. Graccus blitzed back to the door, pressing himself against the wall—and melted away with active camouflage.

Just in time, as mercenaries poured in. They swept the space with precision, checking dark corners with blinding flashlights. They scoured the room: four—no, five—grumpy and trigger-happy mercenaries. It was impossible to miss the damage done, door blasted off its hinges, but here their prisoner still hung, undisturbed. One flashlight panned right over Graccus's hiding spot—but that camo showed only a damp wall.

Adrianna threw a glance to the corner where her explosive collar sat. They hadn't yet noticed that her muzzle was removed.

If there was ever a time...to find the fire. She reached her fingers back and snagged her chains.

One merc stepped up to her. It was Shotgun Man again, his salt and pepper hair slick with sweat and swampy breath in her face. "Yous ain't going nowhere, are ya, *diamau?*"

She'd killed this particular clone twice already. "Hat trick," was all she said.

He curled his lip in confusion, almost a malicious confusion.

Snap. Even she didn't expect it to happen that fast, but the chain super-heated between her fingers went to a radiant white and broke in less than a second.

Adrianna fell forward, swinging since her feet were still chained. And she grabbed the merc's head as she went by, smashing him face first into the pavement with all of her weight and might, crunching his visor into a dozen heinous shards. She was graciously swinging away from him before she could inspect that viscera with any amount of attention.

"Shoot her! Shoot her!" the mercs shouted to one another, snapping their weapons up. Fast or not, she was still bolted to the ceiling by two chains on her ankles.

Graccus stepped out of his shadow, blue pixels melting into view as his camouflage broke. He swiped the nearest muzzle aside, forcing the merc to shoot his own friend, spraying the wall with chunky red.

Adrianna was grateful for the assist. Two shooters were so much easier to dodge than four. Their individual streams of bullets tried to deny her airspace, filling the small room with copper-jacketed lead. She twisted on her chains, picking a narrow slice between the firing lines.

But now that she wasn't hog-tied, she had that beautiful thing called 'leverage'. A twist and kick from augmented legs was enough pressure to snap the cold steel links that tied her to the ceiling. As she dropped to the floor, she snapped her feet outward, whipping each chain at her attackers.

She got a whip-snap out of them as the tips of the chains broke the sound barrier on impact. One merc took the hit square to the chest, his ceramic armor plate shattering. The crack of iron manacles was loud enough to compete with the gunshots. Both men flopped backward with visible dents in their ribcages and blood already seeping through their clothes.

Graccus didn't wait for Adrianna, and he was not nearly as flashy. He just grabbed the last merc by the jaw and turned his head completely around. It sounded like a wet chicken bone.

Five mercs, five dead in under three seconds.

Graccus looked at the chains dangling from her wrists, the last few links still glowing hot against the stone floor. "How long you been keeping that trick under wraps?"

"Aw, hell, cap'n—I'm still figuring it out."

"So, that's new then?"

Adrianna finally had a chance to examine in her room. It was properly twenty meters across, circular, and probably forty meters up smooth concrete walls. They might be able to climb out, grab onto the copper pipes halfway up. But even if they managed that, there was nowhere to go. A tight metal grating was laid over the top of the room with a catwalk suspended a few feet up, for inspectors and scientists to...inspect? She had no idea how it all worked.

She glanced at the explosive collar that sat in the corner where Graccus had thrown it. Very simple explosive with a short-range radio receiver. Nothing more than two ounces of explosive in a small pod that had been aimed right at her spine.

And it hadn't gone off.

"We about to have a lot of company," she said, as she stomped over to the collar and snatched it off the ground.

"You really want to put a bomb in your pocket, Riley?" Graccus asked, incredulous.

"Hey, it's free." There was no transmitter emitting radio waves, but Graccus' particular implants wouldn't have seen that. He would just have to trust her. "What was your exit?"

"Same way I came in," Graccus said. "High speed, low drag."

"And what if I couldn't walk?"

"Why do you think it was my very first question?" Graccus stripped magazines off the dead—and even some water and rations.

287

He'd probably long since exhausted what he'd brought, and more food was just as useful as bullets now.

"So no Callum?" Adrianna asked as she broke the chains from her hands and feet.

He shook his head. "No Callum."

He'd abandoned her, but she had no doubt that Callum was far from gone. Callum would find Prime and kill him, no matter the cost. It's what Oskies were trained to do.

And yet, here was Graccus, risking himself and the entire team to save her. Despite his training.

Footsteps. A great many. Heavy and armored. Both Oskies looked at each other, knowingly.

"You should have left me, captain."

He chuckled. "That's what the rulebook says. But I'm not a fan of the author."

That almost pulled a laugh out of her, but they didn't have that kind of time. "Where are we exactly?"

"Water processing facility, sub-basement two." He pointed at the curved walls around them. "That's actually mountain rock. You could dig for miles and not get through."

She nodded. It had looked like polished stone—turns out it was. They'd built this place directly into the mountainside to be able to siphon snow melt and process into drinking water. Far more energy efficient than fission conversion and Replicators.

It also made for a decent improvised prison for the same reason. Only one way in or out.

She looked at her hands and the glowing red chains. Was that the only way?

"Find me an exterior wall," Adrianna said. "I'll get us out. Just save some juice to run for your life."

Graccus nodded. Whatever questions he had, he was saving for another time. He took a deep, soothing breath and pulled his stolen rifle in close.

The hush and rush of cold water down a length of pipe. The door to the cell snapped shut, and Adrianna could've sworn she heard the speakers crackle with a girlish giggle. Graccus looked at her with dawning horror. Oh, he heard that too?

Adrianna looked up above her to see the four copper pipes over-head start pouring water into the room. Of course. It was a drained reservoir. If the prisoner got mouthy and the neck bomb didn't work... Scylla could always fill the room with ice cold hydro.

She glanced at the drain like it was going to save her, but the water was already at her ankles. There was no telling what she'd need to do to open that valve. It may not be accessible from her position.

Graccus beat on the door, kicking and punching. He was making headway, denting the thick metal. But the door didn't want to open that direction, against the hinges, and with the water already at his shins...he'd drown before he got through.

Only one choice. "Throw me!" she shouted, as she shuffled to the far side of the reservoir.

Before he could shout back in confusion and distress, she bounced a simple instruction to his heads-up display: melt the pipes.

He didn't properly look at her. She sprinted at him and he turned just in time to grab her boot and hurl her upward, before turning back to his own task. Adrianna sailed up to the pipes, snagging the first one with ease. It bent a touch with her weight, but she was about to do a lot more than that.

Find the fire, she thought.

Movement above her on the catwalk, two sets of feet.

She didn't have to say a word, as Graccus lifted his rifle out of the water and snapped two bursts through the grating. He snuck the bullets past her dangling feet, dropping the shooters before they could line up on her.

The water sprayed her face, drenching her hair and chilling her skin. It felt like a thousand pinpricks driven under her skin to grab and pry and scald and pinch. She closed her eyes to it and squeezed those pipes.

They're already coming. They already know.

Burn it. Boil it. Cook it till the metal glows.

The water first got harder, pushing to a harsh spray before slowing to a dribble. Then nothing. She opened her eyes to see the metal tubes in her hands now capped over with copper slag.

Copper...it was a fantastic thermal conductor. Exactly how good was that new seal she'd just made? And was it better than the industry fail-safes throughout the facility?

She reached for that fire again, heating the copper pipes and the water inside them. The water that free flowed through the entirety of a water treatment plant.

Graccus shot a few more attackers on the catwalk, the water now up to his waist. "Riley! Hurry up!"

The zealots had given her everything she needed. Because fire plus water meant pressure. Pressure in an enclosed space of any kind tended to fail violently. She just hoped it didn't fail in her face.

She felt the first gasket go, some piece of rubber and steel long past its service life. The heat under the pads of her fingertips cooled just a touch as chilly mountain air rushed into the system. And then she felt the explosion rock the room, sloshing the water below and shaking the steel overhead.

Good enough.

Adrianna flipped around, eyeing the chains at the center of the reservoir, still dangling there and connected to the grating. What a foolish choice.

She swung her legs to build momentum and then tossed herself out for the chain, snagging it with both hands.

Hand over hand, she climbed the chain. She felt like her back was going to rip through her tunic as she heaved herself up, snagging the grating itself. The little four-inch squares weren't big enough for them to slip through, but she was about to make a bigger hole. She pulled hard, inverting herself on the chain to place her feet on the grating.

Her shoulders burned and her back ached. How cute that several bands of iron a few inches across were going to keep her contained.

But then, it was made to prevent people from falling in, not trap something inside.

The water was up to Graccus' chest, still flowing freely from three other pipes. "Riley!" he called out to her, desperate. Even a little scared.

He came here for her. She'd be damned if she didn't find a way to get him out too. She had to stop the water—or better yet, open that maintenance door at the base.

He was depending on her. He needed her. If she did nothing, he would die.

Close-combat specialist, they called her. Also impulsive, compromised, and empathetic. Not fit for command. Not fit for the Service.

She was all of those things.

The metal bands melted between her fingers as she pulled, popping rivets and bending steel, until she had ripped a two-foot-wide hole in the grating. It looked like a natural disaster, like some meteor had torn through a bulkhead.

She had seconds.

Adrianna swung herself up through the hole and onto the main floor of the plant.

She knew that the steam had likely been explosive, but she hadn't expected to blow a third of the planet directly into hell. Sure enough, there was the glow and heat from a blazing fire that stretched twenty feet into the air, licking the ceiling with fiendish intent.

The wounded screaming, and the frightened wailed, while others tried to get control of the situation. Mercenaries weren't trained in fire control, after all. Very different trauma response skills.

They hadn't forgotten about her, necessarily, but the big fire had taken a far more immediate precedence. That is, until a super soldier came rocketing up out of her prison. She was a problem they knew what to do with. The three closest saw and drew their weapons.

Adrianna Riley let the heat flow over her, feeling every implant spin up to its limit. If she could dump thermal build-up at a simple touch...she didn't need to fear cutting loose.

She hit the first merc before he got his rifle shouldered, striking him across the jaw once, twice, three times—pirouetting around him with haymakers and kicks until she felt the bone in his jaw give up. It crunched under the last hit, and he crumpled to the ground.

The second got his gun up and squeezed the trigger. She heard the pin strike the primer, the ignition of the powder in the chamber, the pressure release of the gases. She heard the bullet screaming down the barrel, and the uncorking pop. And even as the bullet streaked towards her, she could hear the metallic slam of the bolt carrier strip a fresh round off the magazine, the brassy ring of the casing ejected into the air.

The whole action was like an orchestra, each playing their part.

She stooped low, putting both hands on the ground as the shot sailed over her head. And at each spot she placed her fingertips on the pavers, she left small smudges of molten stone.

She'd never felt this good. Never felt this calm.

She lunged at the shooter like a panther, pouncing forward. She grabbed the back of his neck with both hands and planted both feet into his chest. And when she kicked off, he folded at the middle of his back with a disgusting crack, like she'd put a crease in his spine.

The third shooter didn't stand his ground or try to subdue her with volume of fire. He had seen what standing and fighting her meant. Instead, he practically pushed his rifle out of his hands like it disgusted him. And he fled, choosing to face whatever punishment met deserters than face her.

She was more frightening than anything Prime had in his arsenal.

Adrianna scanned the immediate area for some kind of control station. Despite the fire, there were still lights, so they still had power. Imperial colony meant Imperial safety systems. She just had to find the console.

Flickering holographic status symbols hung over each reservoir, and each set of four were mimicked at a console off the catwalks. Those had to be zone controls for each quadrant of water storage, and only one was changing in volume.

She dashed over, vaulting over the railing and to the console. No need for a badge or security here. She just swiped a hand over the amber translucent controls and they responded. A bang and clank came from her tank.

Followed by rushing whitewater rapids, gunshots, and more screaming. The door to the reservoir had opened, letting hundreds of gallons of water come rushing out into the maintenance hallways below. They had to drain and clean out the vats somehow, and she was just giving those same hallways a rinse cycle.

And freeing her friend.

Adrianna saw a geyser of misty water come spouting from a hatch nearby, the spray reaching up to the ceiling and raining down to hiss in the fire. That water had to have hit a wall with quite a bit of force to splash thirty feet in the air.

And along with that spray, up shot Graccus like someone had fired him from a cannon. He hung in the air for a second, getting a bird's-eye view of the danger below, before landing on the pavement like the goddamn drama queen he was.

Someone shouted the alarm, two syllables, a voice strained with fire and smoke. "Os-kies!"

Lit by the towering inferno, Graccus stood tall like a mythical sculpture, a monument to the title. And his satisfied smirk said it all. They were Orbital—so what were the bad men going to do about it?

A group of six opened fire on the captain, but with so much fire, water, smoke—it was frighteningly easy for even the uninitiated to camouflage and disappear. In between muzzle-flashes, a shadow operative like Graccus simply vanished.

The soldiers were so preoccupied with Graccus' dramatic entrance, they'd completely ignored Adrianna's comparatively subtle one. And clustered together for safety, they were not doing the best job of keeping track of threats.

While they spent three whole seconds wondering where in the Hell Graccus had gone, Adrianna swooped in from behind them. She got a running start and silently arrived with a flying kick at the closest merc. Her foot connected at the base of his neck, immediately severing the connection he had to the rest of his body. He wasn't quite dead yet, but he certainly didn't feel the next part. She gave him a little extra push, extending through the heel, which was enough to send his limp body tumbling into his neighbor.

As the mercs spun to engage her, Graccus struck from the darkness. His camouflage melted as he rushed in, ripping a pistol out of a man's retention holster. The force of the grab shattered the plastic and lifted the soldier up by his hip. Graccus slapped a hand down on the man's head, sending him cheek first into the cement. His legs were still arched over his head when Graccus shot a round through his ear, stapling him to the floor.

Speed, strength, shock and awe.

The soldiers didn't know who to fight, these blurs of death moving in and amongst their friends. The smoke, the fire playing tricks on their senses. Were they about to shoot a friend or a ghost that would break their neck if it got close enough?

The survivors started firing, desperate to gun down the threat in their ranks. And the two Oskies easily stayed out of the way of the panicked exchange. The Oskies had sown such panic, the soldiers were all killing each other. All the Oskies had to do now was stay out of the way, stay low and hidden.

It was down to the last three mercs, and they were all shouting accusations, confusion, hatred at one another. They were all copies of the same man: same curly brown hair, dark skin, and round nose. But you'd never have known it with the curses they were all hurling at one another.

Her HUD lit up, indicating the reservoir, along with a simple instruction: *Lock 'em up.*

Cute, Graccus. It had been a decent container for her. For them, it'd be a grave.

Graccus just stood up and shot the first one in the side of the head, ending their little stand-off. When the next tried to whirl around, Graccus just gave him a little push and sent him falling thirty meters down into the drained reservoir.

The last man had barely registered his brother's fall, when Adrianna plucked the pins off every grenade on his vest. The clacks from four separate levers was almost louder than gunshots—something about the timbre of that sound always cut through all other chaos. He clutched at his chest, trying in a panic to remove the deadly cans of Human Misting Agent.

Adrianna didn't give him a chance to. She kicked him backward into the now empty reservoir. She heard him cry out—and she caught a glimpse of his face, eyes wide on the verge of tears, mouth hanging open for one last gasp of breath.

Not anger. Fear. He was scared. Scared of her.

And his back hit the wall of the reservoir, sliding down into the pit. And the only noise after that was the four consecutive thumps of the grenades going off, a skipping blast wave rushing upward out of the stone tube.

But she couldn't shake his face. The petrified stare of a young boy.

Young boy? No, that had been a full-grown man, a mercenary, hardened and paid for bloodshed. What boy was she...

She remembered the boy in the alley, in the Boolean, recoiling from her. She'd saved his life and still he was afraid of her.

"North wall." Graccus's voice broke her from her reverie. Right. They weren't out of danger yet. The crackle of the fire and the steam and the smoke didn't hide the footfalls of approaching danger. More frightened men coming to face their demons.

She looked over to the wall to assess. There was not a single door in it, but it wasn't masonry like the rest of the building. No, this was insulated sheet rock covering thick steel. A good old exterior wall and who would be guarding the other side of solid wall? Nobody.

Find the fire.

She ran up to it and sunk her fingers into the drywall, crumbling the sheet rock until she touched cold metal. And she closed her eyes...

The gunfire. The shouts and screams of pain. The smell of blood and smoke and chemicals that burned her nose. The powder scraping under her fingernails and the waves of hot air under her collar. It all fell away.

She found it. With her eyes squeezed shut, she finally, truly saw it. Glittering, golden, perfect fire, an orb of blazing heat suspended in some untouched nether. No stars in the sky, no ground under foot. Just permanent blazing glory hanging in perfect harmony, removed from anything else.

Just a glimpse of it, that's all she saw, a snapshot of its brilliance... and the three-inch steel liquified between her fingers, flowing harmlessly down her forearms and sloughing to the floor.

And she felt a gust of cold air cut against her cheek and billow her hair.

When she opened her eyes, she had burned a two-foot hole clean through the wall.

She and Graccus slipped through that space, and while the mercs pursued them, they were not able to keep pace with the Empire's finest.

CHAPTER
TWENTY-SIX

THE GROUP HAD TAKEN up shelter in an abandoned hospital. The surgical wing of Meditech was suitably hardened—no windows, no exterior access, privacy.

They'd all been so glad to see her, Vivian most of all. She ran up to Adrianna, embracing her with those graceful arms. The chief squeezed so tightly, Adrianna thought she heard the elegant woman's shoulder crack. Nothing was said—maybe there was too much to say and not enough words. Gratitude, grief, pain, relief. Vivian had thought she'd lost everyone and was then so relieved to find Adrianna returned safely, only to feel guilty that she let herself be glad.

Adrianna had seen the cycle before.

Holt had been busy polishing some scuffs off his prosthesis, grunted about how he prayed for her safe return. Gallantine never got a complete sentence out, all just half-jokes missing punchlines and rubbing at the back of his neck so much she thought he was trying to erase something back there.

She had quietly hoped to find Callum here with them, pouting about the rescue mission and how foolish it was, reprimands and icy stares. But the big man was nowhere to be seen.

Her return meant an endless supply of platitudes, questions, and apologies. She didn't know what to do with any of it, just nodding her head along with whoever was talking. They had their questions, of course. Why had Prime taken her alive? What did he want? What to do next? She didn't have any concrete answers and it just made her stomach sink.

Until she caught the eye of Hirochi Kaneda—Janus. He had the same face, the same stringy black hair and svelte frame as the man who had hung her in a pit. But his eyes were dark, burdened and sad. He sat outside the circle of friends, idly bouncing his cane back and forth between his hands, patiently waiting but hanging his head with a strange morbid weight—like an old dog sitting beside the grave of their best friend.

He hadn't said a word to her. Maybe because he knew this entire fiasco, the mission, all of it...was his fault.

Soon the gauntlet of gratitude and fair welcomes was over, and everyone turned to grab a bite to eat. Adrianna grabbed a jar of peanut butter and sulked off to a corner of the campsite. She found a suitable spot underneath an Autodoc long since stripped for parts— panels ripped open, copper and silksteel pillaged. Probably dismantled in the early days. All that was left of the impressive machine now was its frame and some broken plastic.

She huddled in its shadow as she dipped her fingers in the peanut butter, mainlining fat and protein. That much action and fireworks, she was going to get woozy without instant food.

And the team allowed her some privacy. And her thoughts.

But she couldn't hide forever. Kaneda made no attempt to hide the clack of his cane as he hobbled over to her. "You want me to bring you some greens to go with that?"

Her response came almost on instinct. "You got some bread and jam?"

"You think I brought a toaster oven with me?"

"Oh, I can toast it. I just asked for the bread."

That got a half-hearted chuckle out of him. He gestured to the patch of ground next to her under the Autodoc, politely asking to join her under its mechanical skeleton. She nodded, and he started the slow and difficult process of sitting down. "If I eat straight peanut butter for a year, will I get big and strong like you?"

"You'll become diabetic."

Kaneda sighed, big and heavy. Here came the real reason he walked over. "Prime is going to open the Gateway, isn't he?"

"You holding out hope he would come to his senses?"

He considered that notion for a moment. "Hope's the wrong word. I mean, I *hope* he's right."

She tensed up. In what world would the killing of thousands, the murder of her friends—in what world was that right?

But he didn't notice, eyes tracking off into some faraway place beyond the walls of their decrepit hospital. "I hope he's right, lieutenant. I hope I overreacted and I hope he cracks the secrets of the Empire wide open. I hope that I'm wrong and he does have a way...a way back. And I don't know how I—how I can square...he's killed so many people. What if he ends up being right? What if...he murders a couple thousand people and history looks back on this, and decides he's right?"

She studied him for a moment as he sat quivering next to her. "If he is right...will my brother be there?"

Kaneda looked at her, his bright and wonderful eyes dancing across her features. His brow furrowed as he took in that meaning, lips parting in a brief moment of pained sympathy. But his shoulders sank. "That's not...the Path isn't a gathering or a place you go to. It's more like...it's an everywhere. Place and time lose all anchor. Go where you want, when you want to. Spend as long as you like with the people you love. Scale mountains and watch them grow, see stars born and die, have a card game. Eat, drink, be merry. Relive the best times...forever."

That almost made her scoff. "I don't want the old times. I want new ones."

"That's cause you're not ready to be done yet."

"I want my brother!" she snapped, much harsher than she meant. "I want Voight, I want Sizemore! I want Yurek and Mastiff. I want them *back*!"

But he just nodded. "That's not true, though. Is it, lieutenant? You don't want them back. You want the way they made you feel... because no one else ever has. And you're afraid you'll never feel it again. All I can tell you is that you *will*."

What a cruel thing to say. "I doubt it," she muttered, dismissing him.

"Feel free to. We're all about to die; even people like you are entitled to it."

Adrianna stopped mid-bite, having to fight the sudden surge of bile. "People like me?"

But he didn't answer. He just glared you-know-what at her, his dry eyes striated with red. Even people like her: elite, soldiers, Oskie. They were all allowed to be angry, frustrated, confused at a premature demise.

Was she though? Why? They trained her from adolescence that not only would she die in the field, she would die young. This was not news to her. What was he hoping she would do with that information?

Because she was a monster. She did not fear death. She embraced it. The mercenaries, the civilians—Hell, even her own crew thought so. She was the vaunted and terrifying Orbital. Citizens across the galaxy were obedient just to avoid the sudden appearance of her kind.

She had grown up wanting to make the galaxy a better place. And maybe she had, in the end, but it was difficult to see that when every man that she killed died afraid and every person who she saved ran screaming.

Diamau. Demon.

Adrianna turned back to her peanut butter. "So what'll it look like, Pathfinder? When Prime pushes that big red doomsday button?"

Kaneda sat up straight, drawing up the math in his head and conjuring the image. "He'll try to access the planet's gravity well. Gravity will become unstable, causing the planet itself to break apart. It'll lose its atmosphere, temperatures will fall—"

"So not an explosion, but rather a slow apocalyptic collapse?"

"Oh, it may not be a boom, but it'll happen plenty fast. Explosions of this scale only look slow when you're on the ground."

She looked up, remembering that splintered moon in orbit. Had that been a test of some kind? Or a naturally occurring phenomena? Adrianna set her peanut butter down. "I don't regret you making the call, Janus. You did the right thing trying to stop Prime."

And that's when Kaneda fought back a shiver, his shoulders trembling. He licked his lips and let out a ragged sigh. The grief had come on too suddenly for him to waylay it. "I killed all of you," he whispered. "I tried to tell them not to go. I *tried*. But you were all so goddamn brave. Voight took the ship when I told him no. Sizemore too. They were sure they could do it. They were *so sure*. The sergeant, he went back for you when I warned him not to go. When the captain went looking for you, I thought he would..."

Hirochi Kaneda hadn't killed any of them. He hadn't crashed the ship, he hadn't detonated a bomb in the center of town. He hadn't pulled the trigger on her friends. All he'd done was raise his hand.

"After the crash and you were captured, I didn't know what to do, so I just ran. And when they pulled them out of the wreck, I didn't do anything. I didn't call for help, I didn't try to save them. I should've done something. I'm sorry."

Wreck. Pulled them out. Kaneda kept talking but her brain just heard that word on repeat over and over. "What wreck?" she asked.

He stopped, blinking, as he rolled his mess of a brain backward. "The—the freighter crash. Charybdis. They swarmed all over the thing."

"And they pulled someone out?!"

Kaneda nodded, stiffening. Even he hadn't concerned how important information was.

They were alive. Voight and Sizemore. They were alive!

Graccus pulled her aside so hard she thought he was going to rip her arm off. He hissed low enough that it was for her ears only. "That's a trap. You have to know that's a trap."

"You came to rescue me. How'd you know *that* wasn't a trap?"

"Not remotely the same thing." The insinuation sharpened his eyes in a way that made her stomach do flips. The very blurry mental image of Adrianna stuck in that cell was enough to make Graccus borderline homicidal. "Voight and Sizemore are gone."

"Do you think he's lying?"

Graccus threw an obvious pointed glance over at Kaneda who was actively sampling Adrianna's peanut butter with one trembling finger. "What, the really dysfunctional clone of a 21st century Brooklyn psychopath? Weirdly, no. I don't. I just don't see how it changes anything."

"They're alive, sir. I know it. And every minute we delay—they might be melting down in one of Scylla's Reclamation tents right now."

"Or they melted down hours ago! It's been an entire *day*, Riley! We can't know for sure."

"Sir, due respect, they would've come back for you."

"And they'd get dead doing it."

"Then why'd you come back for me?"

"Because—" Graccus caught himself before he started yelling. He took a breath, letting it starve the anger in his chest, and let it out in one cooling gasp. "Because...I left you at Charybdis because the mission was more important. And it ate me up, Riley. I've left too many bodies in too many foxholes because Terra Firma had a *mission*. Their mission *always* made bodies out of good kids."

"So why come back for me and not them?"

Callum was so convinced that Graccus was an expert liar. She'd overheard him say so many times through thick steel walls. But maybe Graccus was just tired of lying. Because when Adrianna challenged him, he wrinkled his nose and looked away.

"If you could find Callum right now, would you?" she asked.

"Absolutely."

"Then fuck the mission, sir."

He almost smiled at that, charmed by her candor. "Lieutenant. That's blasphemy."

"What are they going to do? Kill me? They'll have to come get me first." That got an actual pained laugh out of him, the gallows irony of escaping a death trap into the arms of your executioner.

She gently wormed her wrist out from his grasp. "Captain. I've been in the Service for seven years, and every time I suit up I know we're going somewhere dangerous to fight scary people. They don't send Orbital if the bad guy isn't sufficiently terrifying. And every time, the order we get: terminate the threat, no matter what. And I used to wonder why people were so scared of us. When the shooting stopped...everybody ran away from us. I get it now, I really do. Because when we stop the danger...we do it no matter what, no matter who we lose or who has to die. And the people we save can't tell the difference anymore, Imperial or Pirate. We're all the same big boots stomping around their lives. Home Office doesn't care. Whatever happens is justified because we got our guy. Well, that's *just not true*. If we blow up a world to stop one man...we blew up a world! I don't know if we can stop Scylla and Prime, I really don't. And I don't know what it would cost if we could. But I know this: they think it's justified. Prime thinks ends justify...everything, anything, no matter the scars. I won't stand for that, not anymore. What about you?"

She watched his pulse quicken with a silent tension in his throat. She watched the sweat shine on his forehead, like a blessing of moonlight kissed to his skin. "No matter the scars?"

She nodded. "Service to each other?"

"For we are the Shield. Let's go get our friends."

Graccus threw up a holographic map of Undercity Concordia, all its warehouses and residences and industry. Everyone gathered around its glow like a campfire.

"At just shy of 1300 hours, Officers Richard Voight and Mikhail Sizemore commandeered a functional vessel and attempted to break containment on Concordia. They failed—and crashed their ship right into the Charybdis tower. Now, combining with previous efforts, this resulted in the destruction of the weapon and we believed...the two of them." Graccus nodded towards Kaneda. "But ol' twitchy over here reports that bodies were retrieved from that smoking husk of a ship."

"Bodies?" Gallantine was incredulous. "I *saw* that crash. They should be in pieces."

"How's that possible?" Vivian asked, skeptical but voice hitching with unmistakable hope.

"Jump Deck's center of mass on any ship. You could wreck the entire bow and not even touch where they were standing," Adrianna said.

Graccus agreed. "Not that I'd want to try it out, but DeHaans does crash test their models more than any other manufacturer. It's... plausible that they survived."

"Were there any other prisoners at the treatment plant?" Holt asked.

Adrianna shook her head. "I get the feeling it was a prison of opportunity. These guys don't take prisoners and they only did so because I got the hot hand."

"Ha ha," Graccus lamented that pun, but nobody else laughed. Nobody else got the joke.

"Okay, so *you* had value. Whatever." Holt conceded. "My first question: why take *them*?"

"Simple," Kaneda said. "They knew we'd come get them."

Graccus cleared his throat, a small indication for Kaneda to shut up. "Prime has a small but unknown amount of hostiles in his backyard, including at least two Oskies, unaccounted for. If I was doing delicate apocalypse rituals, I'd want to close that loop if I could, y'know what I'm saying?"

"So, trap," Gallantine emphasized. "We're all in agreement: trap."

"And your next question, private?" Adrianna asked Holt.

The private, rubbing at his necklace, didn't like the attention he was getting. "Where would they take them?"

"Where they take everybody, living or dead." Graccus pushed the hologram in on a large warehouse in the Undercity, a hexagonal building with a domed roof with two large pillars that poked clean through to the Upper City. Power conduits?

Kaneda beat Graccus to his own explanation. "Primary Reclamation, awaiting processing into carbon stock."

"You're familiar with it?" Gallantine asked.

Kaneda gave a little nervous laugh, remembering why he was different. "I was...'born' there, I guess? Is that the right word?"

"We're going to spring that trap and get our friends," Graccus said. "Riley and I will penetrate the pillars and make our way down into the interior. Corporal Gallantine, Private Holt: chips on the table time. We're throwing caution to the wind a bit. I'd normally tell you to hold the perimeter, but when you hear the shooting..."

"Come in guns blazing?"

Graccus nodded. "We move fast, rip our friends out of the trap, and beat feet before they can respond. That only works with a clean exit. We'll make the exit. You hold it open."

Adrianna hadn't seen Gallantine this charged up in at least two days. "Yes sir, captain, sir."

Vivian was onboard now, squaring her shoulders. "With Charybdis out of commission, we can retake the *Erinyes*. Skies'll belong to us. If we can successfully retrieve our friends, Sizemore can get her warmed up and Voight will take the helm."

"Which is when we all beat feet for the Jump Point, right?" Gallantine asked, half-kidding and knowing the actual answer to that question.

Graccus didn't even entertain it. "In order to open the Gateway, Prime needs two things: a lot of Jump Drives and power for them. It's why he chose Concordia for his plan. We're going to take both. Lieutenant Riley and I will air-drop from the *Erinyes* to cut power at the Pathfinder rocket. No button, no Jump. Regulars, you will stay with the deck crew on the *Erinyes* and keep them safe from enemy action." Graccus got Vivian's attention with two pointed fingers, drawing her eyes right to him. "Chief? You strafe that valley with everything you got. Take out as many Jump-capable ships as you can. If we can't cut their power supply, then we need to pull enough teeth."

"That might actually work," Kaneda whispered, in awe.

"Thank you. I'm glad to have your endorsement, weirdo."

"Any word from Commander Remus?" Vivian asked. "We could really use his muscle right now."

The captain responded with an awkward big shrug. "I haven't seen him since Charybdis. But even if I had...Oskie protocol is quite clear. He'll go after Prime to the expense of all else, even himself. We're all expendable to the objective."

"Rescue ops aren't really in the official playbook," Adrianna explained. "Just Recovery."

"I want to be very clear," Graccus said. "The mission remains unchanged. Terra Firma ordered us to pursue Prime to the last man.

Deviating from that mission to do this little SAR? It will probably get each and every one of us dishonorably discharged. Is that understood?"

"Huah," Private Holt said. The others nodded in agreement.

Graccus checked in with Adrianna one last time, before swallowing his dread. "Let's go get our friends, maybe save the world."

CHAPTER
TWENTY-SEVEN

VIVIAN WASN'T TOO keen on letting Adrianna wander into danger again so soon, but she wasn't putting any words to it. She focused on the blueprint of the building and memorizing every entrance and exit. And she was making her nerves everyone else's problem.

"The main door is a fool's errand. If that can't be held, as I expect, we'll circle around to the loading dock on the east side. Is that acceptable, captain?"

Graccus nodded as he passed out the remaining magazines to Holt and Gallantine. "Be ready to move wounded. I can't assume our boys are going to be under their own power."

"We'll be ready."

Adrianna struggled to get her attention. "Chief."

But Vivian didn't have a moment to spare. "Gallantine, what's the condition of your aid kit?"

"Strapped for painkiller and antiseptic, and there's not much to scrounge here."

"Check my bag. I pulled some isopropyl from the grocery store yesterday."

Adrianna tried again, vainly trying to push herself into Vivian's line of sight. "Chief."

But Vivian turned away, looking toward Kaneda. "Is there anything else about this building you can tell us?"

Kaneda perked up, leaning on his cane. "I didn't spend too much time inside it."

"No apologies, just your words."

He stiffened at that rebuke. "I-I guess, there's, uh...there's a lot of maintenance access that runs along subfloors. Keeps pipes and busy mechanicals off the floors people work on."

"That's exactly what I'm hoping for," Vivian said, turning back to her hologram of the building. She called up the floor plan, high-lighting the crawlspaces between the official floors. "Captain, I'm forwarding this to your Entiglas."

Kaneda leaned on his cane like a bird on its perch. "Is there anything else I can do to help?"

Vivian shut him down hard. "Due respect, Pathfinder, this is going to be a blood and brass kind of day. Not exactly your field of expertise. Thank you for your intel, but you can just sit tight and leave the bang bang to us. Holt, what's your ammo situation?"

"Last mag, then I'll need to scavenge."

Vivian referred to her Entiglas for a schematic. Her nerves were starting to leech out in her sharp words. "Opfor are using JP-36 assault rifles. Get familiar with the platform because that's about to be your new service rifle."

"Huah, ma'am."

Kaneda tried to follow Vivian, hobbling in front of her. "It's just that I feel kinda useless right now."

"Not everybody is good at all things at all times. Take a breath, then take a seat."

Kaneda absorbed that like she'd hit him. He bobbed in place for a second, before settling down onto a concrete block.

Vivian was coming in a little hot. Adrianna sidled up next to her friend. "Chief?"

Maybe Vivian hadn't heard her, but that was unlikely. Vivian didn't acknowledge the word, turning to shout at the boys again. "Corporal, where's your stretcher?"

"Chief!" Adrianna didn't realize she had that depth of bass in her chest, but she found her inner drill instructor for that one.

Vivian froze up at the sharpness of Adrianna's words, like she was only just now aware of Adrianna's presence. Embarrassed, Vivian swiped a lock of hair out of her face and took a parade rest.

And Adrianna laid a hand on her friend's shoulder, giving it a soothing squeeze. "Don't worry. Voight, Sizemore...I'll bring them out," Arianna promised.

Vivian nodded, sharply. And she clamped down on the twitch to her lip before it could turn into a smile. "Don't forget to bring yourself out. We don't like dead heroes."

Adrianna chuckled. "Trust my training, right?"

Vivian lurched forward, wrapping Adrianna in a tight hug. The chief's hands felt so small against her back, tight like wire, fingernails biting in. Her skin was soft, like silk, but the small hairs on Vivian's forearms pricked up at the touch, as a chill ran down the wrists and up to her slender neck. The chief didn't seem to notice or care, her heart pounding in her chest. Vivian's green hair, tussled and grimy from their ordeal, pressed up underneath Adrianna's chin. Despite gunpowder and blood, it still smelled heavily of pomegranate.

Adrianna felt compelled to follow that smell, that touch...follow it wherever it pulled her.

Vivian pulled away enough to look up right into Adrianna's soul. "Trust *yourself*, Riley. We all do."

Entrance to the facility was child's play. Of course, what with it being a trap and all. There were more turrets manning the perimeter with guards posted in rotating patterns. You'd have to be mad to consider a frontal assault. Look how shiny and valuable this location was, all this lovely defensive gear encircling a valuable asset!

But true to form, nobody ever looked up.

Primary Reclamation was an old manufactory. Colonies needed to make all of their early materials the hard way, using the Colony Ship's waning reactor resources to create anything needed for the early days. Because if they weren't self-sufficient by the time that reactor went offline, they would die a cold and hungry death.

To connect the manufactory to the reactor, they built brick pillars to insulate the delicate power systems inside from the howling wind. Two hundred meters of delicate stonework. The smooth stone insulated very well against the vortex, but for Oskies, they may as well have installed ladders.

Graccus and Adrianna climbed, punching out hand holds to heave themselves up hand over hand. The bricks were solid, but the aging mortar gave way to their augmented fingers like sand. With care and caution, they climbed.

Near the top, they'd be able to snake inside and work their way back down into Reclamation.

From this altitude, Adrianna could see the Caldera Market they'd landed in, the entire district peeled down from the Upper City like someone had opened the roof with a crowbar. She could see the residential district they'd crept through, the storefronts and greenhouses. And to the other side of the city, there was a flurry of business around the collapsed Charybdis, where crews slavered over the wrecks of ships and the fallen Pilgrim tower.

It had been a busy two days.

They reached the underside of the Upper City plate—a surprising amount of electrical conduits and maintenance catwalks, with ample lighting. The merchant class above was well-prepared for any instance of damage to their gravity-challenged situation, and they had prepared access for technicians to make any necessary repairs. All Graccus had to do was hop a railing, and he was standing at the power pillar's maintenance door.

He grabbed the door handle, surveying the frame for trap or alarm. Satisfied, he crushed the handle in his grip and politely pulled the door open on its creaky frame.

Without a word, Adrianna raised her rifle to a high ready and entered the pillar.

Thick conduits like a coiled rubber snakes were bound at the center of the hollow space, spiraling on down the two hundred meters to the Lower Plate. They were carefully crewed for easy access by any linemen that needed access to repair, and Adriana had the most morbid thought that she was looking at the colony's literal spinal column. And that's when the intrusive thought kicked in: break it.

No. She needed to ride it. No breaking things. Not yet, anyway.

Graccus and Adrianna took the catwalks down as far as they went. Then they clambered over the safety railings and slid down the conduit like thick rope. Every twenty meters or so they would have to pause to navigate around the mess, as one cable would peel out of the bundle to turn inward. The rubber casing fanned out to reveal dozens of other hooks to power whatever other horrors this colony still kept up its besotted sleeves.

The acrid smell of metal crept up, saturating the air with the sinister truth. Her nose seemed to gum up with the toxins, seeping the grime into every crevice and drowning out all others.

They were close now, close to the scene of the crime. Somewhere down below were her friends, in one form or another—no! That fear would paralyze her.

Graccus must've been counting how far down they had gone, because he stopped his slide at one T-junction, and he followed that divergent cable. He clung to it like a spider on silk, slinking along into the building interior. Adrianna wasn't as agile, the conduit creaking between her fingers as she swung into place.

The smell had only gotten more pungent. Maybe Graccus was just following his nose. Her rifle almost didn't fit through the cable line, the stock scraping against the steel wall. She paused to realign it —couldn't afford to be making excess noise, especially not down a trumpet like this. Everyone on the other side would look up, searching for the racket.

She crawled after Graccus, slowly and carefully, until the tube opened up. The room was bathed in a massive blue glow, like the ground was casting off radioactive impulse. A catwalk stood maybe ten feet under their cables, and below that was a massive factory floor.

They had emerged in an electrical grid thirty meters above the Reclamation Floor—and with good reason, as whatever architect had to accommodate the enormous vats of processing fluid that sat below them. The vats she'd seen at Charybdis were individualized; here, in these opaque Olympic swimming pools, she saw what could only be described as 'dollops' of people, individual chunks of flesh bobbing in the stew, sizzling with foaming bubbles as the slow chemical process broke down each molecule.

Of course, what was at Charybdis was probably individualized, portable. This was an industrial scale. The Replicators needed raw carbon to work with, and human bodies were made of far more complex material that needed to be dismantled into useable states. Rotating crane arms pawed through each vat with a filter system, long jellyfish arms that absorbed any material small enough to pass into it, leaving behind the larger meats and fats. Enormous steel tubes pumped that pale slurry up and away for reassembly.

Scylla's cameras were littered errantly about the facility, freely transmitting their wireless signals. She was certainly watching the proceedings and with great interest. But what was that crazy computer so invested in?

Adrianna followed the camera sightlines down to a small line of people in ragged clothes. They were being marched through a rather severe checkpoint. Bulky scanning equipment, large archways.

Mercenaries with guns prodded and shouted while technicians weighed and measured them: taking stock.

Where were her friends? She didn't see them in that line. Were they already in the vats? Or kept somewhere else? Didn't matter. This place couldn't be allowed to stay operational. She didn't sense any radio signatures aside from the cameras, but there was an incredible amount of heat being generated in this factory. And that needed cooling. While some pipes were transferring slurry, other copper coils wrapped the sensitive systems. If she could breach those coils...the whole plant would burn itself out.

Heat. Yeah...she could work with that. Her fingers were already tingling with so much warmth, so much energy. It felt like...it felt exactly like Prime had said. Like a storm that itched behind her skin, begging for release.

"There's your trap," Graccus whispered, pointing to a series of guards that manned the catwalks right underneath them. Six shooters, all of them with their large, mounted weapons bolted directly to the railings. They would have no trouble overwhelming Oskies with sheer volume of fire, and the elevated position would eliminate the value of cover.

She could kill them. Kill them all. The guards on the catwalk, the mercenaries, and technicians below. She would descend like a force of nature and they would flee from her, the great and terrible cloud that shrouded their eyes and picked at their flesh. They would look upon her and know real fear.

Like that boy had, back in the Boolean? She saved his life and still he feared her. Like her own crew had looked at her? Like Vivian had?

No. No, she wouldn't inspire fear. No more. That's not what she was made for, and if that purpose were to present before her again, she would reject it wholeheartedly. Her promise to this world, to all of them, was to make the world better, safer.

It's what her brother would have wanted.

"I'll draw their attention," Adrianna said. "You scrape the top. I'll clear you a path out. Soon as you've got a clear shot to evac the non-combatants, you take it."

Graccus looked back at her, sharpish. "What's your rank again, lieutenant?"

"I'm sorry, can *you* melt steel with your bare hands? Or are you Mister Invisible?"

Graccus reached back, grabbing her by her chest rig. "You can't take them all on by yourself!"

"I'm not going to," she said with a devilish smirk. "We're just going to...go for a little run."

It was simple enough to get to the factory floor unseen. She lowered herself to the catwalk full of guards, counting on her thick rubber boots to keep her quiet. Catlike, she vaulted the railing down to the edge of the nearest vat, balancing herself on the lip of the tank. To one side was a sheer drop of probably ten meters. To the other side was thick viscous acids and stew meat.

Two quick steps and she was able to snag a cooling coil and ride that down to the floor.

The guards didn't notice a thing. Too much mechanical noise, and their eyes were down-scope, eying the checkpoint below. She didn't dare linger too long. Adrianna looked back up to Graccus' perch—but he had already moved on or had camouflaged into the shadows. Even his IFF tag was invisible in all this bullshit.

A ping to her HUD with some text: *Keep moving, little sister.*

Okay, so he was fine, at least. She turned her attention back to the floor.

The checkpoint was more energetic. The guards pushed their charges onto a pedestal one at a time, two tall arches giving one quick spin around the subject. Adrianna saw the bursts of radio energy, but it was...dirty. Wide-frequency, high power but short burst. They were likely doing heavy security scans of each prisoner before they were allowed in.

This place was too critical to Prime's plans to allow for any risk.

She crept closer, sweeping around machinery and ducking under tubes. Looked like the primary batch of shooters were clustered around the building entrance, with a handful of patrols walking the floor. She doubted they'd be doing so on a typical workday. All this extra security was just for her.

Prime had planned for her to try something, and it was still not going to be enough.

She raised a hand up to a cooling coil over her head, wrapping her fingers around the copper, feeling the brushed polish of the metal. It stole life from her fingertips, a numbing kiss.

Adrianna closed her eyes and reached for that fire, looking for that burning star in the void of her dreams. And it reached back a single tendril, like a solar flare stretching out a hand for hers. And when she opened her eyes, the copper pipe had been severed, capped by its own slagged pieces.

Start the clock. Prime would know she was here now.

Adrianna lifted the grating under her feet, dropping into the sub-floor. She could move quickly and unimpeded down here. While much of the fluid was provided above, there were gravity-fed drains and power run down here, allowing for the vats to be emptied for maintenance. For her, it meant high-speed movement. And there were plenty of copper cooling coils down here for her to sabotage.

Break enough of those, and the entire facility would burn itself out.

"Hey! Leave him alone!" said an earnest voice through the plating over her head. "It's his leg. He can't walk any faster that."

Sizemore. That was Sizemore. And the injured leg had to be Voight. They were alive and on-site. Maybe even deployed, trotted out of their cells at the first sign of her. The timing was too obvious. They must've been kept separate in cells nearby, and now that they knew she was here, the two were being marched to doom.

She glanced at the detonator collar in her pocket. Prime could've sent a signal trigger and popped that sucker whenever he liked, but he let her run rampant, destroying his facilities. Interesting.

He didn't want her dead even as she tugged on threads around his operation.

She paused under a grate, letting mercenary boots pound overhead. Turning her head skyward, she got to glimpse Graccus snatching a marksman from his perch, yanking him up into darkness like a silent predator. She doubted the poor bastard had even made a sound.

Point-to-point messaging: *Ready for my entrance?*

There was a momentary pause as he finished with his charge, before texting his response to her: *Entrance stage left, and then make your exit, pursued by the entire world. You sure about this?*

When are we ever? she asked him back, before darting for the center of the Replicator floor. She took a deep breath, making promises to herself: just her, Vivian, Voight, a weekend getaway, an entire roast turkey, all the Kevalky they can drink.

Breathe in, she told herself. Breathe out. And the mercenaries marched their charges right over the top of her. She looked up right as Voight and Sizemore staggered over her, chained at the wrists and ankles. Oh, it was so good to see her boys again! Limping, busted, bruised, but there they were, walkin' the walk.

Time for her to go to work.

She slipped the grating off the floor, snaking up directly behind Voight. And she leaned in to his ear, whispering two words: "Go left."

Voight didn't question, didn't sigh relief or startle at her arrival. He took the order and dove left, tumbling over his bad leg to the ground. Adrianna snapped her leg between his, catching the steel anklets at full tension and snapping them free—and kicking a single two-inch metal link directly into the back of his guard's head. The high-speed lump of metal clacked off his helmet, stunning the man.

Adrianna set her boot on Voight's gut, shoving the man out of line and rolling off into the darkness.

"Good morning, boys!" she shouted to the building and the people listening from points beyond.

Sizemore lit up at her voice, turning around with bright eyes. "Riley!"

"Get down."

The man heard the words. Internalized their meaning. And then took the urgency. He curled into a ball mid-air, sucking his legs up and falling to the floor.

And Graccus opened fire from the catwalks, the perch quite proficiently stolen from its previous occupants. The unmistakable brrrap of short-stroke piston gunfire from the heights shredded the escorting guards like someone had set drill bits to their skin. All four went down hard.

"Run!" Adrianna shouted, waving her arms at the prisoners. "Go! Now!"

"What about you?" Sizemore paused to ask.

"You get to the *Erinyes* and give me some *goddamn* air support. *Go!*" And with that, she tore off running in the opposite direction. Time to lead the entire colony on a merry ol' chase, all the mercenaries and vehicles and turrets Scylla could muster against her.

Prime may want her alive, but Scylla had no such reservations. And she could feel that all-seeing eye tracking on her, full of incendiary hate and a singular purpose: kill Adrianna Riley.

CHAPTER
TWENTY-EIGHT

ADRIANNA TOOK off at full golden sprint, leaving an amber tracer in the air wherever her super-heating implants took her. Reclamation hadn't felt this big from the outside, but she had been running for a good minute and still hadn't found the East Wall.

She didn't dare let the heat build up in her systems. Instead, she reached out as she ran, tapping her fingers against every copper coil and pipe she could find—flashes of solar brilliance searing as she burned through the metal and dumped the thermal energy of her implants.

Graccus, Callum, Yurek—even her brother—they could only push so far before the heating in their augments would cook their organs. Not her. She was able to vent the build-up and destroy her enemy's facility in the same move.

She looked up to see Graccus walking confidently on the catwalk, trying to keep a line of sight on her and all the forces converging on her position. Whatever interest they had in him paled in comparison to the Oskie running around the factory floor burning out critical subsystems. After all, she left puddles of molten slag wherever she went, little carve outs and severed pipes, like a lava monster had escaped and was cleaving through their facility.

The radio traffic from Scylla's cameras overhead had intensified. The little Pathfinder AI wasn't happy. Adrianna had to wonder what tricks the computer was drafting up, what awaited her outside this building.

A pipe burst over her head, rupturing to spray hateful steam into her path that stung her skin, blasting her hair. She hadn't touched that one! Must mean that the pressure and heat building was starting to overwhelm other factory systems.

Adrianna heard the squeak of rubber shoes, loose gun parts clacking against one another, the charge of a capacitor. Single shooter, left.

He fired, no doubt thinking himself the hero of the day, as a thirty-caliber slug hurtled through the air. Well-placed too, set to land in center mass. He was a good shot. If only she had been a fixed speed target, he might've earned himself a merit badge. Instead, Adrianna ducked low, sliding underneath the passing bullet.

To the shooter's great misfortune, she happened to be passing a tool bag. She snagged the first piece she could get her hands on—a socket wrench of considerable heft, but well balanced. And she flicked the tool at him. For all his prowess, he had not expected return fire and took the wrench square to the forehead.

Doors would be guarded, fortified with turrets and barriers. She'd need to make her own exit. She heard a dozen pairs of boots behind her, the occasional shot in her direction, but it was all in vain. They were gathering in potentially problematic clumps. The last thing she needed was to be dodging rain.

She'd been running flat-out for a good little minute; where the hell was the wall?! Was she running on a treadmill?

Vat of acid to her right. Why not take a more practical approach to demolition of this disgusting place?

Closed fist, knuckles glowing white hot, she threw her speed and body weight into a haymaker, hewing out a section of the reservoir. She was good and beyond it before the unholy mixture spilled in a hissing wave, a river of burning sewage cutting her off from her pursuers. That seemed to stem the tide of gunfire for the moment.

Brickwork, finally, after winding her way through steel vats and copper pipes! She could see the blessed wall of cinderblock and mortar! What would Callum do?

A quick scan found the load-bearing pillars twenty feet to either side—minimal structural resistance. She figured that nobody would mind the abrupt installation of a new bay-view window. She dropped her shoulder into it and prayed that the subdermal armor on her shoulders would hold. At the last second, she turned her face away, hurling her body at the wall as hard as she could. One of them was about to break: her body or the stone.

Powder and dust, as she cracked a cartoon archway through the wall and tumbled out into Concordia's Undercity streets. God, she hoped that looked as awesome as it felt! And that would make a lovely exit for the civilians inside.

But she had traded one problem of acid vats and soldiers for another. She felt two of Scylla's cameras snap on to her, ready and waiting. And the facility's turrets slammed rounds into battery.

Right. Gun turrets. The civis would never get out with those in play.

Without armor or ordinance, the by-the-book approach with emplaced Gauss weapons was to take out the electrical that powered them. Armored housing three inches thick to get to the cables that hooked them into the city grid. Adrianna could melt through and rip the power, but who knew how long that might take? All while being shot at?

No...no, she'd take a page out of Graccus's book instead—mechanical malfunction.

Two gun towers, maybe fifty yards apart, tracked onto her, trying to pick her out from the cloud of building materials that clung to the air. Their strategy would be to pin her down with cross-fire, lock her up and cut her up. She wasn't going to play.

They gave up on trying to find her specifically and just opened fire indiscriminately, screaming out little clouds of chrome ball bearings. Adrianna ran straight at the nearest turret, ducking the first salvo and leaving dusty contrails in her wake. The acquisition speed of these turrets was pretty damn good, but they were designed to cull crowds—not shoot down a streaking meteor.

And at Adrianna's speed, she just needed to get a little hop to sail up underneath the gun turret's line of sight. Each tower was supposed to provide covering fire for its neighbors, but she was about to make that design choice...counterproductive. She didn't need to melt metal to bend it to her needs.

Adrianna landed underneath the gun turret, listening to the chug of the sabots uncorking from the barrel, and the hum of the batteries. Such an elegant machine full of interlocking cogs and sears and levers, and she was about to ruin this mechanical monstrosity.

Scylla had no qualms about firing on her own. The nearby turret immediately began to defilade its neighbor, showering steel shot on her position, but she was fairly sheltered by the turret housing itself. The metal rain cracked and banged and skipped around her, carving divots in the steel and embedding in the tower with hollow thuds.

The turret above her danced left and right, the barrels sweeping back and forth. Maybe it thought it could swat her with the motor-powered arm? She was hunkering down below the spotting camera as it searched for her.

But Adrianna didn't mind. She just went looking for her fire with closed eyes, and she found that void-sun so very easily.

She reached up, snagging the turret's barrels and pinning them in place. The motors screamed like she was kidnapping it and the barrels warmed at her touch. But she didn't need to cook them out. No, she needed to foul their temper, soften them just enough...

322

To bend them.

She pulled with all her might, straining against the steel. And they hadn't even taken on a glow when they gave, curving the barrels around. And then she poked her face up in front of the camera. "Hello, Scylla."

The turret shook, trembled, as if furious. And she heard it chug to life—

—blasting the neighboring turret. It only fired the once, and Adrianna heard that shot rattle down the curved barrel. It would hardly be accurate or with the same power. But it had to go somewhere.

And that somewhere was the neighboring turret at the tower's base. It snapped the supports with ease and the whole thing leaned and sagged. It just needed a push...

Adrianna gave her damaged turret's housing a solid kick, mashing the assembly inside and neutering it. With a small run up, she leapt off her tower, flying right for the wounded neighbor. Leaning or not, she needed that second gun offline.

It tracked on her flight, trying to line up a shot even as it teetered to the left. Clouds of deadly ball bearings ripped the air and the turret screamed its banshee epithets with each discharge of malice. She could almost taste the fury radiating off that emplacement: how dare this Oskie strike at Prime and his men?!

But it couldn't lock her down—as she crashed through the base of the tower: stone, wire and metal alike. It was like she'd decapitated it. The whole thing cracked and fell, smashing to the ground.

Adrianna did a brief diagnostic. She was barely warm, but she was running low on chemical energy and she had micro-tears in silk-steel patches around her body. She needed rest, even if she wasn't overheating. Further, faster, stronger wasn't without limits—it just had new ones.

Adrianna threw a glance back at the hole in the factory wall. Holt and Gallantine had posted up on opposing sides laying down covering fire to the interior. Vivian led the great many civilians out of the hole, shouting instructions. She recognized the staggering form of

Voight, throwing her arms around the man and plastering a grateful kiss to his forehead, before shouting in his face to keep moving.

They'd done it. Voight, Sizemore, and what looked like another eighteen grateful civilians saved from Scylla's chemical furnaces.

Vivian caught her eye, waving Adrianna over to join them. Mission was over, time to regroup.

Jet stream. Whooshing bass-filled engines. She recognized the sound, and it was coming in fast. Scylla had scrambled a gunship to respond.

Fleeing infantry and civis would be cut to pieces! Vivian, Voight, Sizemore—everyone!

Adrianna sprinted up the fallen gun tower like running up a hillside. She scampered from there up onto a rooftop and sprinted as fast as her feet could. She needed altitude and she needed it right now.

And Vivian saw her go, calling out her name in some futile plea. No. Please.

But Adrianna wouldn't stop. She couldn't. Not now, not ever. She wouldn't be a tool to destroy. She'd do what her brother did—protect those who could not protect themselves.

The gunship swooped into position, looming over the crowd of escapees like a jaguar in the canopy, perched and ready to kill. Adrianna could hear the cannon charging up, ready to discharge, and the cries of the people below as they realized too late.

Adrianna leapt off the roof, kicking the air for the last extra inch...

And landed on the gunship's back, an oh so familiar place. Adrianna may not have weighed much compared to the gunship's majesty, but a surprise three hundred pounds of muscle and tech slamming into it was enough. Scylla's war machine drifted off-target by just two inches, swinging the gun off-target. The copper slug erupted from the barrel, streaked down toward Vivian...and sunk into the wall a foot behind her.

The crowd dispersed in panic as the gunship tried to stabilize, but by the time it had rebalanced, the easy target was long gone.

The camera on the nose flipped over, lens tightening like a

squinting eyeball, as if to say 'you again?' Adrianna cocked her head at the great insane machine. And she laid her hand on the hull—

And Scylla rolled the gunship, trying to tip Adrianna off it. The ship spiraled in, unable to maintain altitude through the maneuver. Adrianna didn't exactly have a place to stand. She slammed her hot hand down, punching her glowing fingers through the steel hull and melting in a handhold. The force of the turn dragged her sideways, cutting a long trough like a welding torch.

But she couldn't hold on, slicing right through and off the side of the gunship—the maneuver tossing Adrianna directly into the side of the factory's pillar and blew her clean through the brickwork into the hollow interior. Her back creaked and screamed, her sweat sizzled and snapped, her only light coming from her glowing fingertips.

Scylla's chipper childlike voice bellowed from the crackling speakers. "A machine of death. A threat to all life."

Move. Move!

Adrianna tumbled to one side just as a barrage of copper slugs ripped through the tower, punching out god-rays of light through the stone. The shots tore apart the thick conduits, sending dangerous tendrils of high voltage careening through the air. They snapped and hissed against the steel catwalks, ready to send deadly arcs of electricity through her body.

Adrianna vaulted off the catwalks, falling down and away to the next level. With the conduits severed, there was no rope to slide down this time. All she could do was rebound off the brickwork and take a quick few patters of parkour steps before jumping to the opposite wall to slow her slide down to the ground. She pounced and bounced around the inside of the tower, trying to keep the structure between her and the gunship.

Unfortunately for her, the AI had excellent navigational software. Scylla was charting Adrianna's path downward with deadly efficiency, slamming shots through the most mathematically probable hiding locations and severing helpful paths downward.

Scylla was slowly fencing her in. And her little rifle wasn't going to do any good. Maybe if she could place a shot through the crack she'd carved?

Adrianna tried to sneak a peek through one of Scylla's bullet holes. There was a nice four-inch slagged gash in the gunship's hull, exposing circuitry and paneling underneath. She might be able to sneak a quick shot in there, but there was no guarantee she'd stick it, let alone do any actual damage. Small arms were just not made for this kind of opponent.

But she couldn't afford to retreat. The civilians were still fleeing below, running from cover to cover and avoiding the gunship's gaze. The longer she held Scylla's attention, the better chance they had to escape.

Graccus would make sure they got out. He'd take care of them, like he always had. Callum had lost faith in him, but she hadn't.

Scylla gave up on shooting directly at Adrianna. The little jack-rabbit Oskie was too fast and not slowing down. So she instead went low—decapitating the tower below her with an efficient burst of gunfire. The brickwork surrendered to the punishment, letting out gasps of silica powder and cracking under its own weight.

Adrianna had seen many a tower fall in the last two days. This hollow pillar didn't have the structural integrity to do that. It sloughed, immediately giving up any hope of integrity and crumbling into dust, revealing the dangling electrical cord from the Upper City and Adrianna within, like it was delicately excavating her from her tomb.

Nowhere to go now. Nowhere to hide. And Scylla wasted no time reacquiring her target. The gunship's weapon clicked and clacked into position, drawing down on her—

And the gunship exploded with a single gout of angry flame leaping from its broadside. The massive hole spat another two coughs of fire, limping to one side like it needed support. It drifted and fell out of the sky.

The majesty of the *Erinyes* streaked through the sky over the gunship's flaming corpse.

How?! Adrianna looked down below her. Sizemore and Voight were still below, running for their lives. Who was helming the frigate?!

Adrianna keyed her radio and prayed. "*Erinyes* 1-1, this is Icarus 1-4. How copy?"

There was a long pause before she heard a shaky voice respond. "Did I get it?!"

Kaneda?! Adrianna shook her head in disbelief. "Not that I'm disappointed or anything, but care to explain how you're helming an Imperial frigate?"

"Before I was anything, lieutenant, I was a pilot. The whole hologram thing is new and weird, but bizarrely intuitive."

"Think you can bring that bird in for a combat landing?"

"I can try."

CHAPTER
TWENTY-NINE

THE SHIP WAS a mess of exposed cables, circuitry and burn scars. The re-entry hadn't been kind and Scylla's engineers hadn't much cared for organization, favoring simple function. They pulled out what they needed access to and did what they needed to do.

Hirochi Kaneda knew exactly where to go, what to cut, and how to launch. He and Prime had a lot in common, after all.

Adrianna and the others made it onto the Jump Deck. It was like showing up to an old home to find someone had redecorated with the applied taste of a colicky toddler.

Voight staggered forward, home bringing new strength back to his bum leg. "What did they do to you, ol' girl?"

Kaneda popped up from the helmsman station, snatching up his cane. "Hope I didn't scuff the paint too badly."

"Like I'd have noticed if you had!" Voight snarked as he settled himself into his spot, humming a satisfied tune to himself as he squirmed into the sweetest spot in the chair. His hands immediately flew into muscle memory, toggling switches and swiping elaborate dials. "Cap'n, we are locked, shocked, and ready to rock."

Vivian and Adrianna shared a warm smile. It felt so good to see Voight back on the Jump Deck again, like a warm blanket of normalcy.

Graccus' voice piped over the radio. "Lieutenant Riley, to the launch bay. We are late to a dinner date."

Adrianna grabbed Vivian's shoulder, pointing to Kaneda. "Take us in over the Pathfinder ship. He'll know where it is. Hit that sucker with the main gun until it pops. If we don't get it in the first pass, cap'n and I will drop in to neutralize Prime and Scylla primarily. We'll stop the big red button pushing. After we're in, you just sweep this valley and lay waste to any ship in their Jump network. If they do hit that button, I want to hear nothing but the wind."

Vivian nodded. "How's command feel to you now?"

"Don't start with me." Adrianna turned to Sizemore. "Officer, get to engineering and get the Commandant back on-line. And barring that, do whatever you can to keep this bird in the air!"

"Yes ma'am!"

Voight leaned back, cracking wise. "Seems like the lieutenant wants to be lieutenant commander!"

"Shut up!" Adrianna shouted over her shoulder as she stomped off the deck to join Graccus.

There weren't any more pods to use, no shuttle, no nothing. This was hearkening back to a time when people just stepped out of perfectly good hypersonic ships with naught but their suits and their gear.

Drag chutes were out of the question—couldn't risk being a target for that long. Voight would bring them over the target site and they were just going to have to tuck and roll.

Adrianna found Graccus in the Icarus loading bay she had fallen out of not two days before. He was busily strapping on fresh mag-boots and a clean pistol to his hip. "You don't want something a little bigger?" she asked with a wry smirk.

"One shot, one kill," was all he said.

"You realize we're about to jump out of a spaceship, captain?"

"I mean." He struggled for a somewhat reasonable answer to that. "He's going to slow down." The way he arched his eyebrows implied the next part of that. *He is going to slow down, right?*

Adrianna smirked, tapping her Entiglas to bring up a hologram of the target building. An old Pathfinder rocket, a slim ship that would have been built planet-side and booster-assisted into orbit, before proceeding to the edge of the Kuiper Belt. The entire ship had very little space to move around inside, with every square inch devoted to supplies, fuel and—

To Scylla. Those early AIs took up the entire back third of the ship, giant floor-to-ceiling computer banks. That's where they'd find the cascading software.

"Have you tried turning your evil supercomputer off and on again?" Graccus quipped.

Adrianna pinched the image and zoomed out. The colonists understood Scylla's value and had made an armored shell for the Pathfinder ship. They had, through sheer force of colonial will, dragged the Pathfinder ship inside the hull of another, providing it both protection and hiding it from view.

Sorry, they created obfuscation from enemy combatants. Important verbiage for the report.

The bulk freighter's massive hollow was practically a hangar bay for the much smaller Pathfinder rocket, easily four times the size of the smaller ship. And it was the first Jump Drive wired into Scylla.

In a separate phase of reinforcement, Scylla had installed auto-mated gun turrets monitoring approaches to the Pathfinder ship, hardened steel bunkers full of clones, and recently tilled earth that was almost certainly mined with improvised explosives. Cheeky.

Graccus shook his head with a click of his tongue. "It's never just a light switch, is it?"

Adrianna studied the approach. "Any way we can remote hack those turrets?"

"They dismantled our Commandant when they took the ship." He threw her a meaningful look. "And would you trust the Commandant to do it?"

No, she realized. Knowing what she knew now—that the Commandant was complicit in their entire misadventure? No, she wouldn't.

They were just going to have to do this one the old-fashioned way: hammer to nail.

"Target acquired," Voight's voice echoed over the loudspeaker, and it made Adrianna's heart do a little tap dance in her chest. God, it felt good to hear his voice—and hear it that way again!

The next statement from Sizemore reminded her of what was about to happen. "Gunnery control has solution."

And Vivian gave the order. "Fire."

Adrianna felt their ship rock as the 240mm cannon along the stern let loose, spitting its hundred-and-thirty-eight-pound shell at a velocity that could get measured in decimals of lightspeed. And it wasn't polite about it, firing one shell every half second.

Adrianna watched the impacts on her hologram, as the blasts chipped away at the shell.

Velocitas eradico: speed kills.

"I've got gunships scrambling for intercept," Voight reported. "I cannot penetrate to the target."

"It was a long shot anyway," Graccus said as he bounced on the balls of his feet. "Just give us our door, officer. Orbital will do the rest."

The shell's armor was almost a meter thick, but the *Erinyes* had cut a nice two-meter hole for them. Graccus and Adrianna dropped out of the back of the frigate at a pleasant fifty-foot altitude, slamming into the bunker near the hole. Graccus tumbled and bounced up to his feet, spry and nimble.

Adrianna slammed into the side, carving a liquid metal handhold as she slid to a stop. She didn't quite cut through it, but it seemed to impress Graccus. "I'm never going to be able to lock you up again."

"Sir, you never locked me anywhere I didn't want to be."

The *Erinyes* rail gun thrummed and chugged, blasting away at the field of ships around them and sending columns of flame dancing into the sky. A pursuit phalanx of three gunships tried to keep up, chewing away at the much larger frigate with their own cannons.

But a fourth tail turned, spying the two infantry on the husk below them.

Adrianna gave a little wave, knowing full well that Scylla was looking down at them, no doubt fuming. Graccus pulled his pistol, flickering his active camouflage in a brief test. Adrianna rolled out her shoulder, ready for shock and awe.

The gunship swooped down on them—and the pair gave each other a nod. They stepped into the hole and dropped out of sight just as the gunship passed by, its cannon peppering the steel where they had once stood.

The duo plummeted the next fifty feet to soft ground, boots hitting fluffy, loose mountain dirt. And Adrianna found roughly what she expected.

The air was rank and musty, instantly clogging her nose. The guts of the bulk freighter bowed outward like a steel-framed concert hall. A single ray of silver light beamed down through the hole into the bulk freighter's interior, clouds from the impact filling the air, little specks of pixie dust.

Beyond that magical gossamer curtain was the Pathfinder ship. She instantly wondered if it had been dragged under cover of the bulk freighter or if the freighter had been brought over it! The

Pathfinder rocket rested on a precarious angle, propped against two enormous boulders for support, which themselves looked ready to crack loose and tumble into the valley below.

Adrianna brought her eyes further up to see inactive turrets hanging low, bunkers empty and bereft of light. Dozens of conduits ran from all directions, the insulated spider web that came to a fractal center at the Pathfinder ship, each cable joining into one massive pipe that ran haphazardly through the main hatch of the silver rocket. All roads becoming one.

And standing over those cables, halfway in the hatch, was Prime. The man looked back at Adrianna—his jaw clamped tight and his eyes drooped in a unique misery. So much more than disappointed. This was despair.

Graccus raised his weapon, lining up the shot. And the turrets snapped up in response, lights flashing and everything sounding off with threats and hate. Scylla's voice boomed through the freighter's interior, the ghost that haunted a cathedral. "Let's kill them, Pathfinder. Let me kill them!"

But Prime shouted over her: "*Wait!*"

And the turrets did not fire. No explosions, no electric impulse. And against every expectation Adrianna had, Captain Graccus Ontarim...held his shot. He raised a quizzical eyebrow, waiting.

Prime put his head against the steel hatch, pushing hard in frustration like he could push his headache back inside.

Scylla's voice filled the dead air. "They come to stop us. They come to close the Gateway. Let me kill them."

"I said *wait!*" Prime snarled.

Graccus applied pressure to his trigger but held it short of the break. He had the line and was growing impatient with whatever game this was.

But Adrianna cocked her head in recognition. Prime was the Pathfinder, Scylla the Navigator. She could not act without his permission. She could not kill, could not move, could not do anything without his permission.

Adrianna could talk him down right now, end this with words and not pain, so she stepped forward. "Having second thoughts, Prime?"

Scylla had a counter to that, the turrets all snapping onto her. "She is their weapon. She is the image of death."

Adrianna paused, hands outstretched and palms wide. "I can't really dispute that. My record speaks for itself: plenty of death happening in that."

"She admits her crimes!" Scylla hissed.

Prime squeezed the door handle, white-knuckled and trembling. "We were supposed to be explorers, Riley. Humanity, we...we were *supposed* to be..."

She felt Graccus sliding to her left, vanishing into shadows. He was lining up the shot to save the world. "Graccus, you pull that trigger and everybody dies."

The AI latched onto that phrase, turrets sweeping the field. "They betray us! Duplicitous, treacherous—"

The slick of steel and Graccus called out from the shadows. "Whatever you're going to do, Riley, do it fast."

"Scheming, cleaving, blood-soaked—"

Prime clutched at the side of his head like he was trying to keep its contents from spilling out of his ears. "Quiet! Scylla—let me think!"

Adrianna took another few cautious steps toward Prime. "It's not too late to stop this. You want a better world? We can start building that right now, you and me. Nobody else has to die!"

He looked up at her, plaintive and weak. Sweat soaked his brow and his eye twitched. Was he in pain? "How?" he croaked past dry lips.

She almost shrugged when she said it. "By saving you."

Prime scoffed at that. "You say that like you're not soaked to your neck in blood. You've killed—how many since you came here?"

"I am," she said, nodding sharply. "I am *drenched*. You think the last two days have been bad? I spent the last seven years of my life killing—killing for them. You want to punish me for that? Make me burn, make me suffer? Or do you want me to *change*?"

Prime hung in that doorway, his hand sliding off the handle and down into his pocket, searching for the detonator he still carried. He could do it, three pounds of pressure to a small switch and he could blow a chunk right out of Adrianna's leg—maybe even kill her.

"You want the world to be better?" she asked, shaking her head. "So do I. That's all I've ever wanted. And I think you do too, or you would have flicked that switch hours ago. Those people up there, the ones you hate so much? They don't care who you kill. They don't care if you succeed. They just want to make people scared."

It was difficult to admit it out loud, now that she was standing here. But all she could see was a little child in the Boolean, terrified to even look at her. "You push that button, and you won't prove them wrong—you'll prove them right. That all this weaponry, all this war machine hanging over your head now...that it's *needed* to fight threats like you. You're justifying them, Hirochi."

"They'll stop us," Prime whimpered, tears in his eyes. He pointed at her with his free hand. "They'll just send more of you to stop us. More hand-built monsters."

The rumbling of explosions shook the valley, and the hull around them creaked and groaned, its precarious position growing more questionable. The soft tinkling of rocks plinked against the hull like stormy rain on tempered glass.

Adrianna took another few steps closer. She could probably dart towards him and break his neck before he could react. But she walked slowly, gingerly sweeping her feet to each step with her hands raised like she might spook a horse. "They made us what we are, yes. Built to spec with knives and medicine and...black magic, for all I know. But every one of us is *different*. And all of us can choose." She reached slowly for her rifle—

And the turrets flashed over to her again, spinning up. But they did not fire.

Adrianna lifted it off her back, holding it high by the receiver.

ALLEN IVERS

And she chucked it aside. She glanced at his pocket, to the detonator wrapping in his hand. "Hirochi? Put it down."

His lip quivered, shaking his head. And tears tumbled down his face.

Click of a safety, scuff of a boot, and tumbling rocks. A shooter taking aim. Where? Graccus was to her left, but this was behind and right. Who?

Adrianna took a great big jump to her right, blocking the line of sight for—Callum. Bloodied, caked in dust and grime from head to toe, uniform torn and teeth bared. He was wild and angry, full of hate and a touch of despair. He bore new injuries, gunshots and stabs and abrasions. Who knew what fresh Hell he had walked through? But he stood here now, on a stable platform with a hundred yard shot at the Tier One target.

His cheeks tensed and his brow hardened as she stepped between him and his target for the second time in as many days. "Clear the target, Riley!"

"Hold your fire!" she bellowed back at him.

But Callum repeated his shout. "Clear the target! I will shoot you!"

Scylla's shrill reminders echoed overhead. "Do you see, Pathfinder? Do you see?"

"Out of the way, Riley!"

"Put the gun down, Callum!"

Bang.

Single shot, small caliber. Handgun. Handgun?

Adrianna looked back. Who had shot?! Where? All she saw was the bullet travel the last few feet. Prime hadn't even flinched yet when the round buried just above the right eyeball, burrowing deep and cavitating inside his brain. He reeled backward against the hatch, banging roughly against it as he collapsed to the deck.

Callum hadn't shot him. If not him, then who could've...

Graccus holstered his sidearm like it was ten pounds heavier than when he drew it. And he stared at the ground, that sick feeling already growing in his gut.

The turrets sagged, lights draining from them, and Adrianna swore that they whimpered in digital chorus. "Pathfinder?" Scylla's voice sounded so small, clear in tone but quaking. "Pathfinder, please report. Pathfinder? Where are you?"

CHAPTER
THIRTY

"ERINYES 1-1, Icarus team reports shack on the target. That's a confirmed KIA of Tier One." Graccus' report had more exhaustion than anything else, a droning emptiness to his words.

Callum sauntered up to them and she felt his burning eyes on her the entire way. Her weakness very nearly got them all killed, and he would not forget this.

But Adrianna couldn't tear her eyes from Prime's corpse. She had been seconds away from talking him down. Then Callum came bursting in, and Graccus had...

They'd killed him. Because that's what Orbital did best.

Graccus looked at her and what he saw in her face must've torn him in two. Because he closed his eyes so he wouldn't have to look anymore.

Adrianna fished in Prime's pocket to pull the detonator free. It still had the aluminum cap resting over the toggle. He had reached for the device, sure, but he hadn't even popped the safety cover. He wouldn't, couldn't be that person who killed with the press of a button. Every atrocity in this city, every crime conducted in his name...mercenaries claimed him, faithful swore by him.

But it was Scylla who gave the order, who twisted the dream. Prime? He couldn't bring himself to kill. That was always too far.

But Adrianna? She had killed. Graccus had killed. They'd killed him.

Callum marched up to duo with an unusual ferocity.

"Captain Graccus Ontarim." Callum slung his rifle over his shoulder and cracked his neck as he approached. He had the look of the devil about him, and in that instant, Adrianna didn't know if she was going to have to jump in between them.

Or if she even wanted to.

But he stopped just shy of the danger zone, respecting Adrianna's protective cone. He'd had the opportunity to dance with her once already, and now he knew a few more of her tricks. She realized it with narrowed eyes. Her power gave him pause.

Instead, he spoke from that safe distance, shouting over her head. "Under Article Seven of the Uniform Code—"

"I'm under arrest?" Graccus asked him.

Callum growled, letting a bit of animal out of his frame that sent a chill up Adrianna's spine. "On charges of treason, sedition..." And he leered directly at Adrianna. "And disregarding your mission objectives."

"I saved our sister, Callum. I saved somebody, you can just say *that*."

"Be that as it may, you had a mission. You deviated from it, creating a volatile situation..."

"And the fact that you wouldn't..." Graccus hung his head with a ragged sigh. He glanced at Adrianna, wistful but not an ounce of regret. "You know what, big guy? Hell with it. Slap me in irons and let's go home. Your hometown sucks, by the way."

The speakers overhead crackled and snapped as Scylla's childlike voice rose from silence up and up, climbing in tenor, stepping up the frequency in a digital scream. The turrets twitched and seized on their platforms, and the lights glowed hotter and hotter until the bulbs began to pop, showering glass down on them. Their Oskie ears filtered out the worst of the noise, but the sheer volume was enough to force Adrianna's eyes to glitch out, hallucinating splotches of color in the corners of her vision.

Callum just grunted, a one-man army marching off toward the Pathfinder ship. Somewhere inside was a computer in grief, unstable and out of time.

And nothing left to lose.

She wouldn't! No! Not without Prime's express order. She couldn't!

But all of the logic clicked into place so sharply it almost hurt. Adrianna knew. She knew—Scylla had one last order to carry out.

A blast of energy pulsed out from the ship, surging across dozens of conduits and radiating up the valley and shaking the mountain-tops, toppling hanging snowdrifts and ice fields. The crack echoed back down to them, the soft tell-tale summons of an avalanche.

Adrianna looked up through the hole in the hull, past the mist and fog to see the gathering storm cloud of ice tumbling down straight for them. "Uh, boys?"

"Shut it!" Callum snarled without even looking back. She tried to bounce him an image, but he refused the peer-to-peer connection. Damn idiot!

But Graccus looked up, following Adrianna's line of thinking. "Callum, she might be on to something of immediate relevance."

Callum's voice pushed past the hitch, what could only have been sadness clenching his throat. "I don't want to hear your voice again, Ontarim! Not another sound!"

A second pulse! And the ground under their feet swelled like the planet itself was taking a breath. The bulk freighter's husk that held high over them creaked with strain—and started to slide along the ground.

She heard rivets pop as the bunkers tore out of their concrete foundations, the gun turrets slipping off their platforms. And the silver airframe of the Pathfinder ship twisted, rolling over and snapping something crucial. That avalanche was getting closer. Her onboard said it would be on them in less than a minute.

Scylla was starting the Jump.

"Jump link! Cut the Jump link!" Graccus shouted. "Cut it now!"

Callum pulled his rifle, and Graccus his side arm, opening fire on the thick conduit that connected the Pathfinder to the rest of the fleet. The gunfire snapped through some of the thick insulation, pulling at threads.

But it wasn't enough—the ground leapt out from under them, tossing the three Oskies into the air like the skin of a trampoline, like the earth had been under some great tension and finally snapped free. The whole mountainside turned to liquid under their feet, a storm surge of rock and dirt sliding out from under them.

And the spear tip of the Pathfinder rocket swung toward them, slipping off its rocky moorings. The trio were airborne, nothing to push off, no way to escape. All three Oskies just watched as the broadside of the rocket slammed into them.

Adrianna tumbled along the airframe before she snagged a handhold on the Pathfinder ship. Callum tumbled toward her, certain to broadside her right off her new perch. They locked eyes for just a second and he knew what to do—he shoved himself off away from the hull to skip over and around her. Utilizing his massive wingspan, he waited to be over her and then simply punched a fist through the aged steel like a fishhook. What she did with fire, he did with plain brute force, cutting out a handhold in a shower of sparks that dragged downward, before halting his fall right off the nose of the rocket.

Adrianna looked down at him just in time to have the wisdom to tuck her head—as the nosecone of the rocket's airframe pierced right through the bulk freighter's thick steel hull, screaming as it gashed a rough channel through and out, like a dragon that had tired of its eggshell. The dozens of cables spun out behind them, six-inch diameter ropes scraping and sliding on the loose ground, dragging across the field—

And snapping taut.

Her grip got a pretty good test as the ship jerked to a stop underneath her, the rocket's hull biting her fingers and striking into her knees and chin. A panel broke free from the force, tumbling past her head and down into the ravine below them.

It was noisy, sure, but she also didn't hear that panel hit anything else. Didn't bode well for how far it had fallen.

Oskies rarely had a lot of cause to fear falling.

Graccus's head popped up from behind one of the rocket's wings. Lucky bastard hit an actual platform. He looked down at them even as rocks pelted him from above. The ship was dangling in space by a single tether, barely supported by a solid outcropping, as a river of stone flowed around them. They dangled now off a proverbial waterfall.

"You two alright?!" Graccus called out.

Adrianna couldn't really focus on the question—she saw the encroaching avalanche getting closer and closer, a terrible hurricane powered by gravity and ice.

A swift jerk and metallic twang as one of the Jump cables snapped. The dissonant cry of steel made her ears hurt.

Nothing but a cloud bank beneath them and maybe miles of empty air under that. They were swinging over oblivion by a damaged rope, and a glacial avalanche was ready to wipe them out of existence.

Scylla didn't seem to mind one bit. "The Gateway opens!" the machine shrieked in almost delirious joy. "We go to the Path. Just as he wanted!"

Pulses of energy flowed up their failing rope, splitting outward in a glorious violet flower up to the hundreds of Jump Drives above, issuing impossible calculations and awakening hundreds of fusion reactors.

Her radio crackled. "Icarus Team, we're seeing massive geological disturbances? What's your status?"

Graccus said it better than she could. "Everything is *fucked*, Actual. Give us a minute!"

Callum grimaced, like he had finally lost patience with their predicament. He shredded his way up the ship toward the Jump cables, punching out hand holds as he went. He crept little by little, even as the ship groaned under his abuse.

But the old 21st century rocket was never meant to take this kind of beating. It was ripping in half as the big man heaved his way up. Four hundred pounds of tech and anger was brutalizing the aged steel. And he wasn't going nearly fast enough.

The avalanche hit the bulk freighter above them, millions of pounds of ice ripping it free from its moorings...and tumbling that wreck down, down—straight for them.

"Callum!" Graccus shouted a warning to his friend, a sudden shrill panic in his voice. He hunkered down on his wingtip, ready to weather what was coming. "Callum, take cover!"

The man roared some bestial response, like he could silence Graccus by volume alone, and kept climbing.

No. No! Adrianna couldn't watch another person—

Graccus beat her to it. He let go, slipping free from his perch and diving toward the man he loved. He was in a race against gravity, the angry waves of frost looming behind him.

The avalanche struck the backside of the rocket. That menacing bulk freighter collided with them and came apart, shattering like glass and pelting them with steel bulkheads and icy shards. The Pathfinder rocket took the abuse better than she thought it would, giving one creaking gasp—before it sheared in two, stripping the outer shell of the rocket like peeling off a glove. And as that metal hull detached from the interior...it took Callum down with it. The metal he was climbing on had started to fall. The look of shock that took his face...

But Graccus fell faster than the mountain could, twisting mid-air to give Callum an impulse kick to the ribs, the only goodbye kiss he could give. Callum took the push and flew off the side, off the ship and into the cliff face, slamming hard into a solid chunk of slate rock. The impact sent spiraling cracks up the boulder, but it had not yielded to the avalanche and it would not yield to him.

Callum twisted to get positioning, to leap back after his friend—but the onslaught of snow and rock kept him pinned, burying him against the stone and threatening to entomb him.

He called out in agony. "Graccus!"

Every action has an equal and opposite reaction. Graccus kicked his love to safety and sent himself into space. He hung there for just long enough to realize what he'd done, the soft acceptance crossing his face as he closed eyes. He fell down into the valley and the hungry snow and unfeeling clouds, swallowed and subsumed.

Graccus. He'd saved her. He'd broken his oath for her. He'd believed in her.

And now he was gone.

It was the twang of the strained cables that reminded her of her own predicament. She clung to the side of the rocket as the icy river pounded around them.

Scylla's voice cried out, "The Gateway comes! We open the door and we will see him again, to the place that is before and is yet to come!"

Callum roared at the avalanche, raging and screaming, trying to press himself free—but it had him pinned, burying him under the weight of an entire mountain. "Riley!"

Adrianna looked down at the shredded Pathfinder rocket beneath her. The hull stripped away, she could now see the massive computer bank that the cables connected to. Violet pulses of light flowed up those cables out to the network above.

Cut that cable, and it's all over.

Adrianna dropped down, boots slamming onto Scylla's mainframe. The conduit right in front of her, sparking with an almost magical light, flares so brilliant her vision grew spotted and pained.

She pulled out the collar, the bomb that Prime had strapped to her neck. The switch that he could never throw.

"What are you waiting for?!" Callum howled.

She couldn't do it. Not without trying to save her. "I know what you're feeling!" she shouted at the machine under her.

"There is no Pathfinder!" Scylla's voice thundered up and down the mountain, elemental and primordial. "There is no purpose! *Nothing!*"

"I know what you've lost! I know how it feels."

Scylla's anger could have lit fires in a tundra. Cameras above and around her all snapped around, trembling on their moorings like they collectively strained to rip themselves free and slam down upon her. "You took him from me! You took my Pathfinder!"

And that fire, that rage, that agony...that's where Adrianna met her. "I lost my brother! I lost him and I'll *never* catch the man responsible. I will never see justice, but you want to know something? He wouldn't want me to!"

And Scylla was quiet, even as the planet raged around them. Shards of slate rock hovered off the ground, floating a few inches in the air, like they were poised for a great fall. Like the world itself stood, toes tangling in open air, with the singular intrusive thought: Jump.

But something kept it anchored, unwilling to take the step.

Keep going. She had Scylla hooked.

Adrianna held her breath for a moment, her face twisted in pain. "I miss him. I miss him, Scylla. I miss him every day. I miss his deadpan humor, his terrible taste in coffee. I miss his holier-than-thou attitude and his goddamn thesaurus of a mouth. But... now he's gone. And I can *never* get him back. But I shouldn't! Because what made him my brother wasn't a DNA profile or a birth mother, but the *time* we spent together." And Adrianna's voice shrank down, like it wanted to hide in her throat and pull the covers over its head. "And all the times we didn't. All the times we can't, that we won't."

It didn't matter how quiet she was; here at the core, inside the Pathfinder, Scylla would hear Adrianna's heart skip a beat.

345

But Scylla seized on the momentary pause in Adrianna's thinking. "Who am I...without my Pathfinder?"

Who was Adrianna without Marcus? Marcus had dreamed of slaying dragons, standing on the wasteland to save kingdoms from the monsters in the hinterlands, a shield in one hand and a sword in the other. They fought those monsters together, and now...

Now she'd just have to keep fighting alone.

"Who you always were," Adrianna declared. "It feels like something's been ripped out of you, but I promise...you're as whole as you ever were. You're still a Traveler, a Navigator, a Companion. You don't need him to be you! And his memory will always be a part of you. So keep searching, keep exploring, keep growing. You are more than...than a part of him. He was a part of you."

The lights only grew, the whine of machinery pulsing in her ears. Adrianna felt her fingers burn and her hair lift off her neck.

She heard Callum call from over the edge. "Ri-ley! Push the button!"

"Are you—are you..." Scylla's voice was skipping, distorted, confused. She could feel the hard drives spinning and fans whirring, a buffet of warm air against the hurricane. But it finally cracked through with a simple, polite request. "Thick is the bramble on the Path never—would you—would you like to go on an adventure?"

The stones began to thrum, and the lights flashed brilliant, so wondrous that they seemed bright and dark all at once. And a pulse of energy gathered itself in the coils...

No.

"I'm so sorry," Adrianna whispered.

She pressed the collar to Scylla's cables, and she pressed the button.

Pop.

The explosive collar detonated with an underwhelming sound, like she'd snapped some stick. And small as it was, it was enough to cut the Jump cable. Adrianna grabbed ahold of the severed end and held tight as the ship fell out from under her, bulkheads and circuitry whirling past her until finally she felt the cold alpine air again. Scylla and the Pathfinder rocket slipped into the fog of the valley below. Adrianna could see the lights receding back into the rocket, a lit fuse walking back inside before winking out of existence like a star swallowed by night.

The longest moment passed where all she could hear was the thunder of the avalanche roaring around her—until a deep resonant thud rang out. Her chest ached and her shoulders burned. Gravity pulled twice as hard as ever, a dominant force that pressed her down into the cliff face, squeezing the avalanche to a sudden stop and every single rock and boulder sank into the dirt like the bite of an invisible beast sinking into flesh. Callum found himself pressed into his outcropping, cracking and sinking halfway into the rock itself with a pained cry.

But just as suddenly, it stopped. Stabilizing. Normal again.

No Gateway. No Jump.

The planet came once again to silence and stillness, and in that silence, Adrianna swore she heard a strange voice call out to her from the valley below...

"Anna? Anna, is that you?"

That voice...it was Marcus.

CHAPTER
THIRTY-ONE

TWO WEEKS LATER...

SHE DIDN'T HAVE A VERY good idea of what to expect when she was brought back on to the *Erinyes*, but a stay in the brig was at least a familiar reception. Callum had assumed command as soon as they came aboard and directed her taken into custody. Much as everyone hesitated, nobody was going to disobey the bloodied behemoth.

No Commandant meant no Jumping home, so the crew simply waited in orbit for Imperial reinforcement. And sitting in that little room, eating her three square and staring at the walls, Adrianna just tried to avoid getting muscle cramps.

And thinking about her brother.

On day fourteen, she heard such a commotion outside. Docking collars fixed and ramps dropping, the hiss of hydraulics and gasps of pressures equalizing. Chatter, voices, friendly and otherwise. The unified stamps of marching feet. The beep of medical equipment.

Back up had finally arrived.

It was another ten minutes before the door to her cell opened, and she might not have noticed but for the sound and the rushing of fresh air. Callum was large enough he obscured most of the doorway, only small shafts of white squeaking past his impressive frame, giving him sharp edge light, a celestial glow.

His voice also left little wiggle room, staid and mechanical. "Admiral Grace is ready to receive you for debriefing."

"That's it?" she asked. "Two days in Hell, two weeks of iso: that's what you got for me?"

"You're no longer my responsibility."

Damn. What little warmth he had in his body had been scoured from him.

"You don't want to know why the Home Office let it get that bad in the first place?"

"It's not my place to question such things. We were sent to correct the matter, and we did."

He *would* think that way about it. Anything to preserve the veil of Imperial excellence.

She sat up, rolling out the burning knot building in her shoulder. "Well, it's been fun, commander." She stopped, seeing the yellow bar on his neck with three silver flowers. "Or should I say, captain? Congratulations, I guess."

Callum sucked on his teeth, drawing his lips tight. Unblinking, reserved. Nothing.

She hung her head. "They had to give somebody the credit for saving an entire planet. May as well be the walking rulebook."

"I'm the only one who's still Oskie, little sister."

Those two words hit her chest like a cudgel. Her knees went weak and her lip curled in almost disgust. "You left me to die."

He didn't answer her. Didn't have to. He owed her nothing anymore.

She glimpsed eight Regulars marching past her cell in formation. Nobody she recognized. Fresh faces, clean shaven and clean consciences. But her eye caught the ident tag off somebody's shoulder. "Well, give the *Tartarus* boys my best. Don't tell them about the secret menu on the Replicator."

"Mind your tongue."

"Callum, I'm going to be retired in about fifteen minutes. I saved your planet, and *he* saved your life! I'll talk to you however I goddamn feel!"

That got Callum to growl, his head hung low like she'd struck him. Shame. He was going to a new posting, new challenges, a new life. Leaving everything he had on the *Erinyes* behind. He might be a stoic bastard, but it still had to hurt.

And that made her heart sink. She sighed, hunched over her knees and squeezed her hands together, hoping to wring the frustration out of herself. "Any sign of the captain?" she asked as softly as she could.

A pregnant pause before Callum answered. He shook his head, small with a resentful sneer. There was more weight in his one syllable answer than any other noise he'd ever made. "No."

"You think he's alive, don't you?"

Callum drew a breath that almost sounded like a hiss. "The only way to know for sure if Graccus Ontarim is actually dead is to hold his corpse in your own two hands. Until such time…"

"Very romantic," Adriana quipped, popping to her feet with a heavy thud. She held out her hands for cuffs—and he simply took both her wrists in one giant hand. She felt the cold steel squeeze around her wrists and the magnetic lock snap into place. "Can I ask you a favor, before they shuffle me out of here?"

He growled, rolling his eyes, but he did pause.

"You're going to HR-2056? Out to Vanguard?" she asked.

He raised an eyebrow. "If I was?"

"Find the man who killed my brother."

The man's face thawed, eyebrows scrunching together in deep concern. He didn't see pain in her face, or grief or sorrow. He saw rage—and he recognized it. "Thought you were more for *saving* lives, Riley?"

She didn't answer him. She couldn't. Did she want this mystery man dead?

Maybe. Yes. Possibly—

No! It was complicated. But she wanted to find him, and she'd make up her mind what to do then. Part of her wished to never find him and just go about her life.

What would she do if faced with her brother's killer?

Especially...knowing what she knew. She remembered a sweet young boy, but the file Graccus had shared had been anything but the little lad who had clung to her heels and clutched at her embroidered sleeves.

She didn't want this killer dead, but she intended to get some answers from him.

Callum took something from her non-answer and scrunched-up face. "Service to each other, Riley."

"For we are the Shield."

When he released her, she saw the pair of magnetic shackles he had latched to her wrists. She idly thought about melting them free or snapping out of them. But what would that accomplish?

There wasn't anything else to do but follow.

There were no doctors. No ministers. In fact, just a single guardian met her at the gangway. Young kid, too. The Regular was stiff and sweaty and far too small for his uniform. He moved like someone had forgotten to oil him up this morning, all crisp and snappy. She thought he was going to break something snapping a salute or walking round a corner.

He took her by the shackles and led her along what felt like a labyrinth, onto two separate lifts. The *Tartarus* was an impressive ship, but this felt deeply like meandering towards a medieval dungeon.

Their long journey ended twelve minutes after it began at a set of blast doors. She could smell the herbal tea through the three-inch steel, heard the classical music blasting on tinny speakers.

Great. Lovely.

The too-short-for-prime-time Regular turned and unlatched her cuffs, before stepping aside, taking a sentry position at the door. Adrianna rubbed at the hot spots on her wrists, little patches of irritated skin pinched between metal implant and metal cuff. She took a breath, ready to face her destiny.

Beyond that door was the rest of her life as a civilian. She'd go to sleep and wake up...normal. If she woke up at all.

Maybe she could run away? She could slip her guard and grab a shuttle?

Then what? Roll listless through dark space, assuming she could lose the Imperial Dreadnaught on her heels? No. This was all there was now. Adrianna would face her destiny, chin up.

She took one step forward and the doors cracked to reveal a small office, a rush of humid air and essential oils. Two big planters overtaken by creeping vine-like things flanked the doorway, pared back to stay away from the big hydraulics. They painted the usually stagnate gray walls a warm red, with area rugs thrown around the floor to cover the cold metal.

An unfinished game of chess was set out on a coffee table, a pot of tea steeping beside it. By Adrianna's count, black was four moves from checkmate, despite being down both rooks.

She did notice that the planters were clamped to the deck, the rugs were actually riveted at the corners and the paint was sound-dampening. The chess board magnetic, same with the teapot—which was how it was getting heated. Everything was beautiful, but not at the cost of practicality. Nobody wanted a shattered pot or a tripping hazard in a combat scenario.

No doctors. No surgical team. No technicians.

Seated alone behind a simple steel desk was Admiral Winnifred Grace, the harsh battle-angel with thinning white hair tucked up into a regulation ponytail that was yanked up high through her cap. She sat with her legs crossed, head tilted back to study the three separate reports that were hanging in the air in front of her.

With one gloved hand, she swiped lazily through them with frightening focus, page after page. The amber glow of the holograms lit her like a bronzed statue in a museum, carved to represent the platonic ideal of 'deliberation.'

Adrianna couldn't help but notice the big red redactions throughout the reports. Grace traced a fresh one in with her fingertip, laying an encryption on the line. Each one unique and specific.

Admiral Grace was flagrantly editing the transcript right in front of her, striking out line after line.

"Pays to be head of Supply," Adrianna quipped, gesturing at the fineries.

"I don't do it for the pay, lieutenant." Admiral Grace looked at her niece with a sense Adrianna almost felt as threatening. "You've had a helluva capstone. *Erinyes* was dispatched to Concordia to secure or eliminate a Tier One target."

"That's classified," Adrianna said.

Admiral Grace waved at the screens in front of her. "And we'd like to keep it that way. We very nearly lost an entire Imperial planet —the ball of dirt itself—but for the swift action of your crew. I had to read that twice to make sure I understood it."

"Imperial cleanup is en route?"

"The remains of Charybdis will be shuttled in parcel to the research labs on Ilum for further study. That's a prize all its own. The clone facilities are to be dismantled. Aid workers from my staff are already arranging food, medical, and other emergency services for the colony. Official story is a meteor impact. This is what my department lives for, lieutenant."

Where the Hell were they the last few years? Prime may never have gotten a foothold if Supply had been on the ball. Adrianna almost laughed. "I'm glad to hear it, ma'am."

"Ma'am?" The admiral shook her head in disbelief. "You a little schoolgirl or an Oskie?"

"I don't think I was ever little, ma'am."

Admiral Grace's smile turned soft, looking to the side. "They always start little."

"Who's the game?" Adrianna asked, nodding at the chess.

The admiral didn't look, but Adrianna saw the quick intake of breath and the hunch to her shoulders. "That was Marcus. We used to play over extranet...doesn't matter. Just feels wrong to move any of the pieces now."

A shrine. Preserving a moment in time, lest she lose it forever.

But clearing her throat, the admiral sat up straight and turned back to her work. "Callum Remus is to be transferred to the *Tartarus* just as soon as his promotion is made effective. He'll be one of the field commanders headed for the Vanguard theater."

"Captain Remus conducted himself in high regard. It's a worthy slot. He deserves it."

"Captain Remus," the admiral said with a scoff, "is lucky to have survived. If he had his way, you'd all have died on Concordia along with the entire colony. That's what we call in Logistics a 'stupid fucking decision.' He's a narrow-minded jockstrap who measures his dick with regulations. But he's not my problem, then or now."

Admiral Grace snatched a half-empty tin cup off a heater on her desk, tossing it to Adrianna.

Adrianna caught the cup with ease, careful not spill whatever was left and clutching it to her chest. "Hi," she said with a confused deadpan.

Her aunt's face was sharp and severe, accompanied by an icy shift in tone. "Who else knows?"

"Knows what?"

"Stop screwing around. I read Callum's report. I'm the one that sealed it before the Ministry could get their grubby mitts on it. You're lucky you're not on an autopsy table! Tell me who else knows?"

Adrianna looked at the cup. She felt its residual warmth. It was scalding hot...

Her Power, that shard of Metal in her shoulder. Grace had thrown her a hot mug which she'd caught barehanded without so much as a wince. Hundred and eighty-two degrees, enough to scald human flesh, and she hadn't even blinked. She hadn't even noticed!

She set the teacup down on the table next to the chess set and tea pot, and she sighed. "Our contact on the ground, Janus—Kaneda, that Pathfinder. He has a sixth sense for whenever I do it. And Captain Remus himself saw me in action. Everybody else who saw it or knows about it...they're dead. It happened when—"

"I know when it happened. I read all about it. Nobody else knows? Those two. That's it?"

"That's the entire club." Adrianna felt her stomach turn into knots.

"And would Kaneda ever tell anyone?"

Adrianna shrugged. "I don't know. I don't even know where they're taking him."

"Well, that part is simple." The admiral pulled up a fresh screen and staring typing on a holographic keypad, with urgency. With intent.

Uh...

"He saved my life on Concordia! We would never have found—"

"Relax, lieutenant." Admiral Grace clapped her hands, silencing Adrianna with a sound that summoned far too many a childhood memory.

But when the admiral threw her arms wide, a blue hologram exploded outward from between her palms, spreading to every corner of the room and plastering up the walls. Planets, profiles, systems and jump lanes filled the air; dotted ships hung in the air, cargo manifests spilled out in front of her, and mugshots of smugglers. Data streamed like soft rivers bubbling ever downward to some calming place.

"Logistics and Supply is a bigger game than just getting batteries and medicine where they need to be," Admiral Grace said. "It's also securing routes of transit and commerce. It means finding threats before they act and neutralizing them. Sometimes that's a buyout, sometimes it's an air strike. And sometimes you walk right up to the bastard and lean on the knife. I'm not the Admiral of a bunch of bulk freighters, Riley. I'm in charge of how this Navy moves anywhere safely."

"Why are you showing me this?" Adrianna asked with a hint of dread.

But Admiral Grace did not share her tone, her lips curled like the Cheshire Cat. "Because, Adrianna Riley, I have a secret for you: you died on Concordia along with Graccus Ontarim and the rest of your unit." The silver-haired woman stalked over to Adrianna, the pixels of a planet warping around her like she was parting a velvet curtain. She stopped next to her niece with a wicked smirk on her face. "You can't be dismissed from the Service if you're dead."

Adrianna blinked a few times. "What in God's name is happening right now?"

Admiral Grace looked up at the room and all the information, the slow whirlwind of information that spiraled around them. "You're looking at Mobile Task Force Artemis: we're deniable ops, a wing of Naval Intelligence situated under Logistics and Supply..." She steepled her fingers in self-satisfaction. "Me. And this is the only way I can hide a person of your unique talents from the people who would quite simply kill you."

That notion made Adrianna's blood run cold. "And who are those people?"

"Many of them wear the Blue and White," Grace said, gesturing to her own uniform. She sauntered over to the chess game, sitting down and staring at it like she was contemplating a move. "Adrianna, I told your parents I would look after you two. Now there's only one of you. I don't give a damn about whatever magic Pilgrim nonsense is jammed underneath your clavicle; you're family. I'm not letting you out of my sight."

"So what does that mean for me?"

"It means you're coming to Artemis. I've already cleared it with the Home Office. As of 0930, you no longer exist. They were just as impressed with your performance as I was. You get your own ship, your own crew, to conduct clandestine and critical operations within Imperial space. I get to keep one hand on you, and you get to go put some good out in the world. How does that sound, Lieutenant Commander?"

"Lieutenant Commander?" she asked, breathless. She almost couldn't believe the sound of it.

"You've more than earned it," the admiral said, smug. "You're ready for command, Riley."

She came into this office expecting to end her career. In a way, she did. Now, as a maelstrom of blue planets and folios and text streamed around her...she had a path to something new.

Admiral Grace was doing this for herself, her own well-being, certainly. This was as much motivated by selfish guilt than it was anything altruistic. But if that meant she could have her own ship...maybe...

Maybe she could go to Vanguard and find her brother's killer?

No. Much as her body twisted and ripped at the very idea...she didn't want to kill anybody. She wanted to find somebody to save. There's only one way she'd agree to her aunt's insane plan.

She dropped into the seat across from her aunt, looking back at her over the chess table. "Lieutenant Commander?"

"That's right."

"Do I get to pick the ship?"

Admiral Grace smiled. "I'm way ahead of you, kid."

A rush of air as the doors parted for her, the familiar musty stank of Naval Regulars on a poorly ventilated Imperial Frigate. She didn't need to pull up a map or look at the tail markings to recognize the *Erinyes* when she could just take a deep breath.

Savory meals were in the galley. Chatter from two dozen officers on duty. The reactor happily humming. The flutter of electronics in the walls and whooshes of life support overhead. Clicks and clacks echoed up from the armory. There was a curious squeak to the fresh steel paneling under her feet, unseasoned from a full tour—that would break in soon enough.

Adrianna took her first steps aboard as the CO of a Naval ship, the responsibility of its mission and the safety of its crew. And she felt...heavier, like some great weighted blanket had been laid across her shoulders.

She didn't expect it to feel comforting.

Voices soon rang out in greeting. "Commander on deck!"

A dozen Regulars tumbled out of their bunks and into formation, a great scuffle of boots. But one brown jumpsuit staring back at her had a great big coy grin. It was Corporal Gallantine, bright-eyed and relaxed as ever.

"At ease, Bang-Bang," she said with a wave of her hand. They all resumed whatever duties she had interrupted, but with only half-focus. They all wanted to overhear whatever she had to say next.

Gallantine didn't mince words, walking right up to her with a firm handshake. "Welcome aboard the *Erinyes,* ma'am."

"You're not going to do that every time I walk in a room, are you?"

"While I'm within earshot of the sergeant, I will be."

She was about to ask who that would be, when she saw the framed picture over the bunks. Someone had a holo of Sergeant Mastiff with the rest of Chalk Four, boarding their shuttle. Small flickering text just read: Concordia.

Private Holt stepped up to her side, reaching over to key some toggle on his bunk. The text changed at the click: You feel like a man yet?

That forced a chuckle out of her.

"It's not really the *Erinyes* without him," Holt said.

Adrianna took a deep breath, biting her lip to keep from making a scene. "No, it wouldn't be. Glad to see you two walkin' and talkin'."

"I do most of the talkin' anyway," Gallantine said, smug. "He's mostly here to be pretty."

Holt flipped him off with his metal arm, twirling the wrist to add a little extra flair.

She bid the Regulars a quick farewell and walked astern. It was up from the grunts' hallway berth and into the galley, where she found Sizemore slurping down some kind of white meat and white rice in a lovely dark sauce. Nobody in this room leapt to attention at her entry—a blessing—but Sizemore saw her come in and lit up like he'd been plugged in. "Commander Riley!"

That name got a few folks standing to attention, but she beelined right for Sizemore. "How's the arm?"

"Aches a bit, but I'm cleared for duty." He lowered his head, like he could beg a private conversation. "What is that duty, by the way?"

"Whatever we end up doing, I'll keep your feet in the air this time," she promised. "How long till we're ready to cut moorings?"

"We're ready to go at your order, commander."

God, that wasn't getting any easier to hear. But it didn't sting or force some part of her brain into panicked shut down, so it couldn't be that bad.

"Wherever you want to go," Sizemore said, "we'll be with you all the way."

She glanced at his plate. "What is that?"

"Sticky sweet pork skewers."

She leaned in close to him, conspiratorial, and she was a little embarrassed at the high pitch her voice hit, but she was just too excited to care. "Did we get a better menu?"

"Short answer: yes."

Adrianna couldn't contain her little shoulder shimmy of happiness, leering hungrily over at the shiny new Replicator. She wanted to test that machine's limits in ways that would make witnesses blush.

But that would have to wait. She had a renewed pep to her step as she made her way up towards the Jump Deck. She stepped over the hatch comb into the familiar room, taking it all in with one sweeping glance.

Straight luminescent emerald hair and confident smile, Vivian Bannister was already seated at her console. She looked up at Adrianna with the mildest gasp of relief. "I almost didn't believe it," the chief said, quiet enough that she might've forgotten she was speaking out loud.

Adrianna leaned over the chief's station, close to her ear. At first, she just wanted to whisper privately but some floral smell of honeysuckle and lavender overwhelmed her. She sniffed twice for good measure, letting Vivian hear that almost predatory presence. "That's not regulation, is it, Bannister?"

Vivian's eyes fluttered a bit at the closeness and a flush went up her neck. "If you'd prefer the deck smell like salt, sweat, and regret..."

Adrianna stood up straight before the smell completely intoxicated her. She did have to force a cough, which wasn't terribly subtle.

"Good to see you too."

"Ready to save the world one stop at a time?" Adrianna asked.

"Oy vey," Voight groaned as he sauntered into the room, face buried in some news report. "Just tell me this, commander. We won't be Admiral Grace's state-sponsored assassins, will we?"

Vivian almost cackled at that. "Darling, what did you think we were doing before?"

Voight hopped into his seat at the helm, cracking his knuckles on the blank slate before waking the holographic displays. "Just hoping for a change of pace from all the running and shooting, I guess."

"Aw, hell, Voight. You shouldn't have joined the Navy."

A cane and the hobbled steps. Everyone turned to see who made that most irregular of noises on an Imperial military ship. And Adrianna's heart fluttered a bit, a fear quieted, and a weight lifted.

Hirochi Kaneda looked around the inside of this bright and buzzing room like he was standing inside a beehive and was afraid to disturb something that would sting him. "...It looks much better now."

Voight laughed, half-mocking. "Yeah, okay, I don't want to be rude or nothin', but I'll put my hundred and eight tons of fusion-boosted war machine up against that weird little rocket ship of yours any day of the week, pal. We have a sandwich machine!"

Kaneda glanced backward, nervous. "I'll eat out of a can, thanks."

Adrianna walked over to him, to try to coax him over the doorway. "Welcome aboard, Pathfinder."

His eyes went a little buggy at that title, but he let slip a twitchy smile as he eased himself over the doorway. He moved like he thought the ground might fall out from under him at any moment. "I suppose I have you to thank for my...transfer here?"

"No safer place for you," she said. "You hopped in a ship half this size to see how far you could go. And you went further than you ever dreamed. Well, I think at the very least...we owe you a road trip." She glanced at the galaxy display behind her, then looked back at him, inviting. "You want to see what's out there, Hirochi?"

He chuckled, breathless at that, but he was almost tearing up at the very notion. "More than anything."

Voight didn't wait for the order as he keyed up thrusters. "Station Control, this is *Erinyes* 1-1, requesting exit pathway."

Vivian opened an intercom with a flick of a switch. "All hands, stand by for Jump Prep."

Kaneda heard those words and instinctively reached for Adrianna. She reached back, giving his hand a good solid squeeze. "We'll be here the whole time."

"Let's find the edge of the map," Voight quipped.

Vivian looked up from her console. "Here there be dragons?"

If only, Adrianna thought. If only.

THE END

AFTERWORD

This book has been a long overdue!

Orbital Strike Command has been a villain of the series for a long time. Since the first book, I've wanted to see how the other half lived —and what better way to do it than through the eyes of the first villain's family?

Learn the truth of Marcus Riley's story in The Blood Service

And Adrianna's story is only just getting started. The crew of the *Erinyes* continues their journey in the upcoming

Swords of the Iron Service

If you're enjoying the Capital Adventures, please leave a review. It really helps small authors like myself.

Signing up for the Newsletter keeps you on top of the latest news around the Capital-verse.

I also have a cat. I will likely be dropping pictures of her there regularly, as she is a consistent part of my office day. She is bad at being a cat, but she is fat and good and adorable. Sign up and see!

AFTERWORD

https://www.authorivers.com/

ABOUT THE AUTHOR

Allen Ivers started writing original stories at the ripe age of eleven, largely trying to figure out why the Disney villains on the television box were the way they were. Villains, monsters, and politicians have always fascinated him with their behavior. Twenty years later, he's still fascinated by bad people and the bad things they do.

He now lives in beautiful Juneau, AK somewhere in that fluffy snow drift. You can find his thoughts about writing, politics, and the odd cute cat on his Twitter.

f facebook.com/AllenIversSFF

ALSO BY